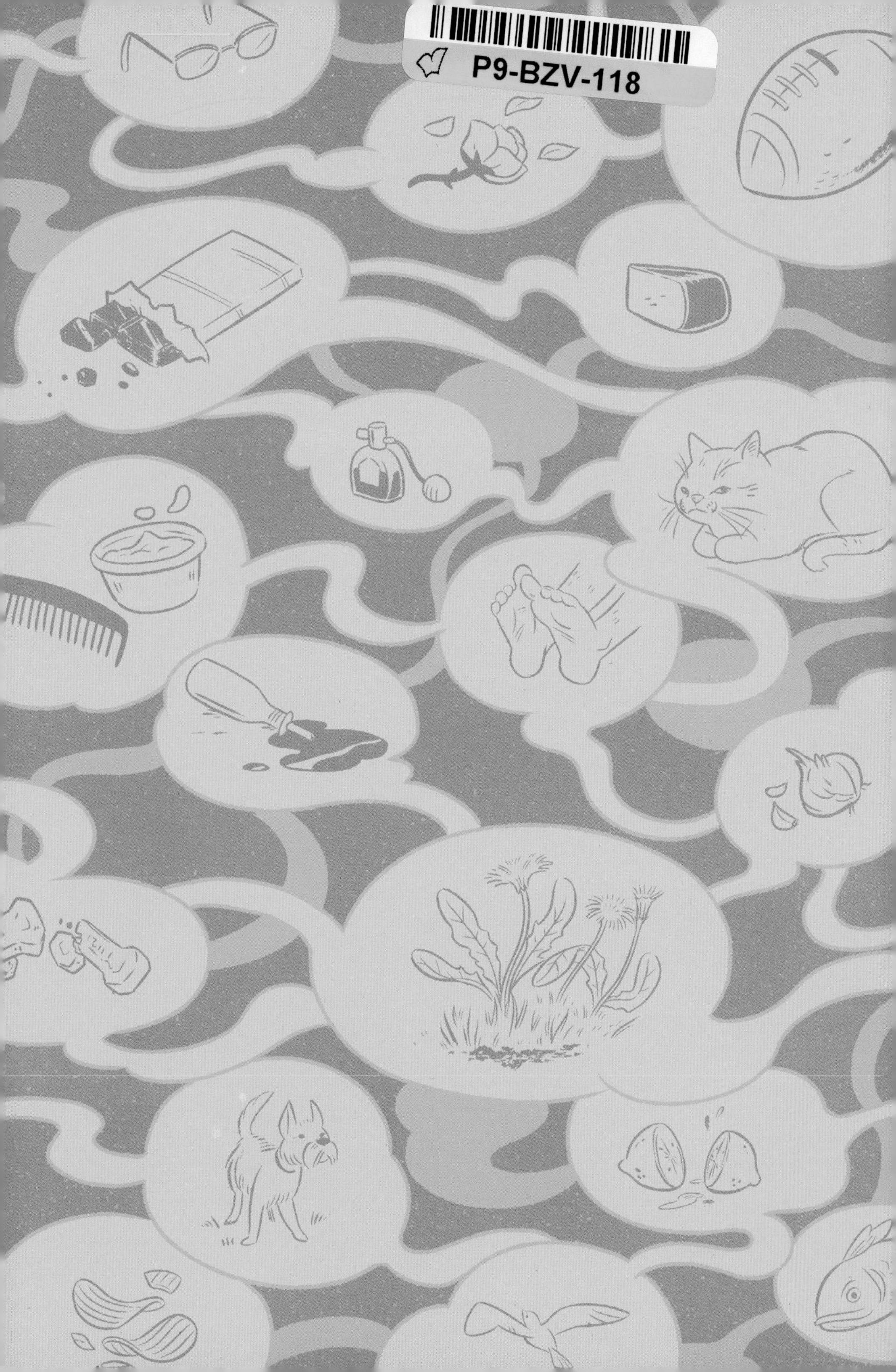

Making Scents

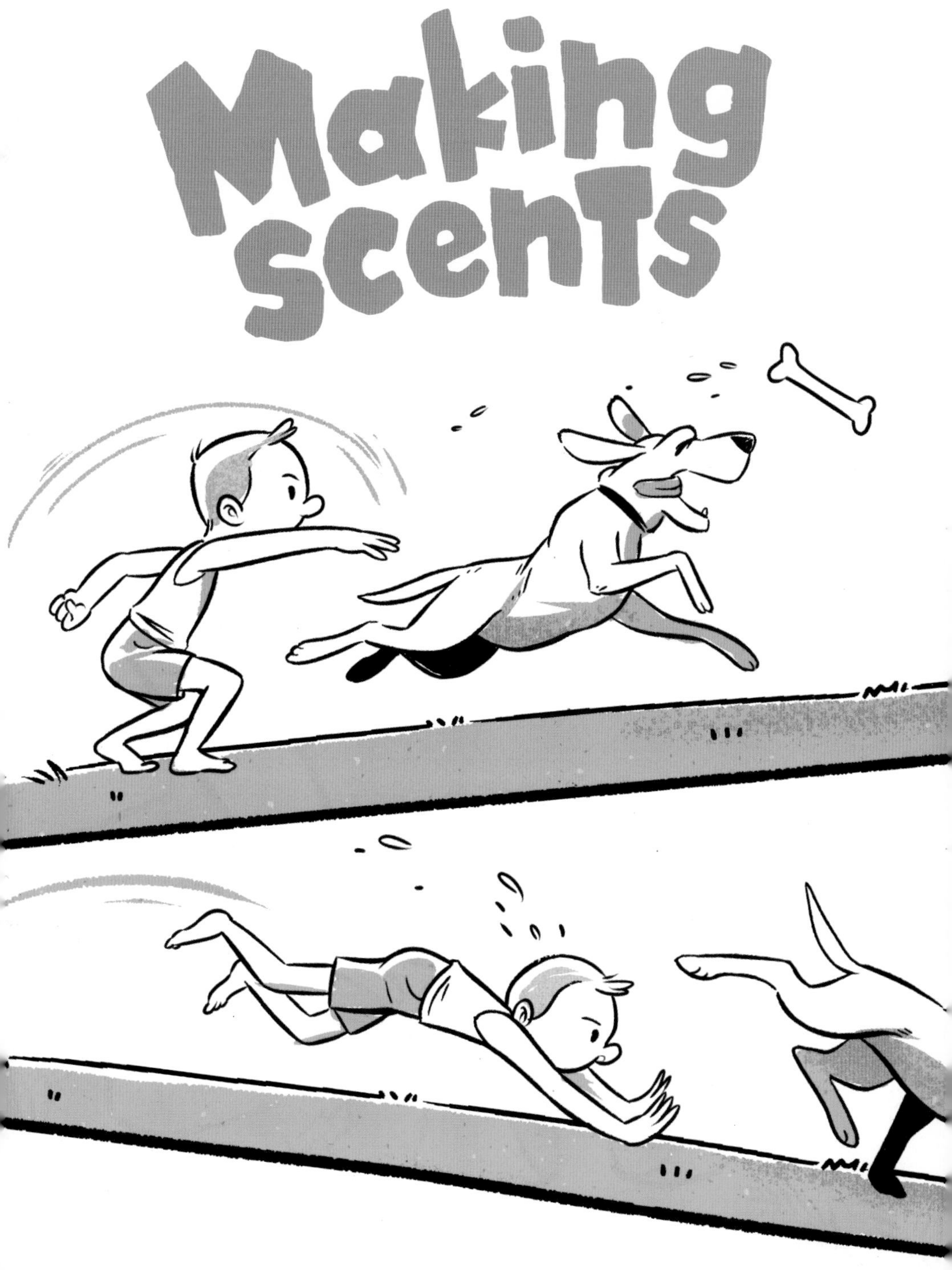

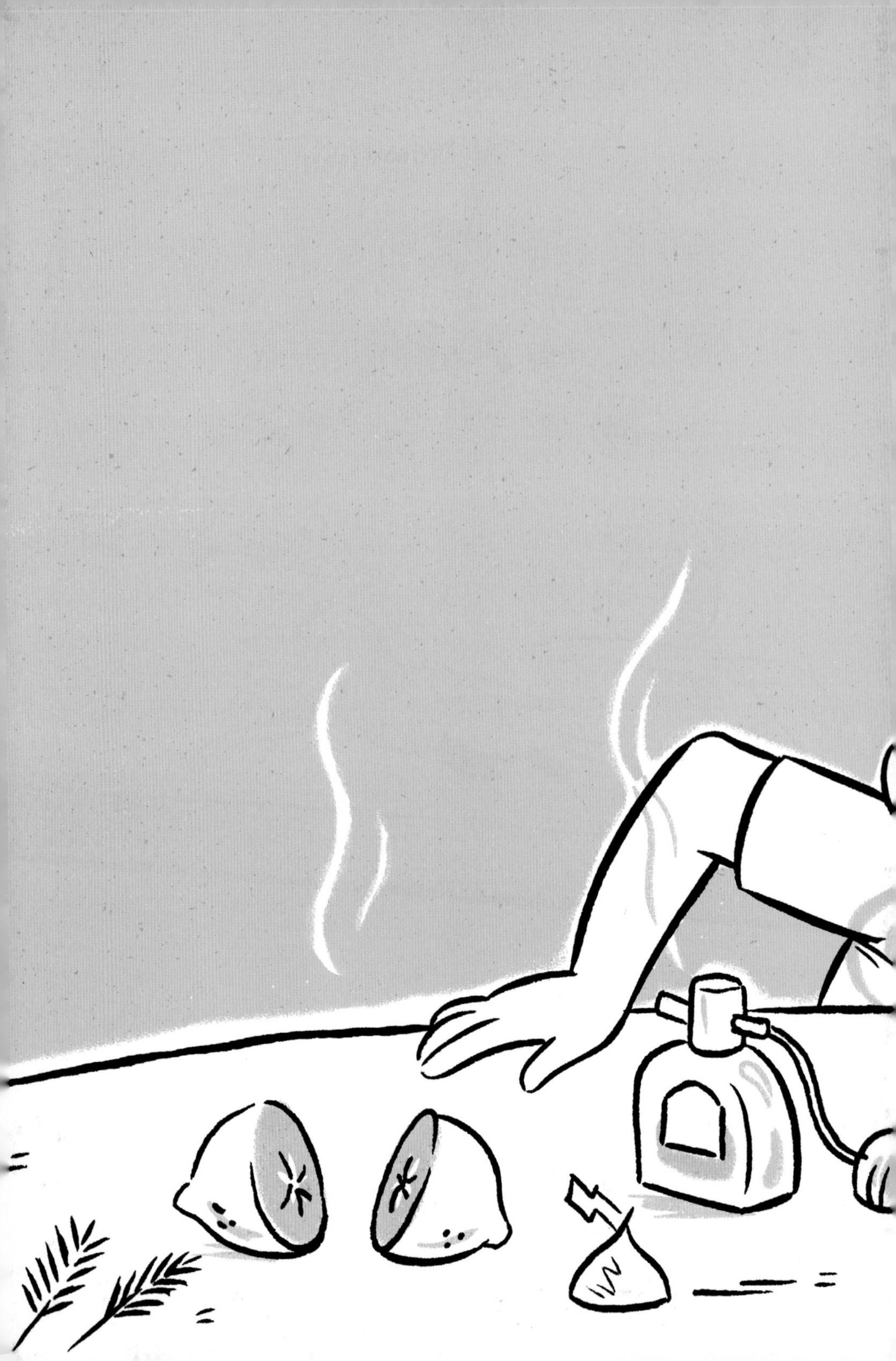

Making Scents

Arthur Yorinks

ART BY Braden Lamb & Shelli Paroline

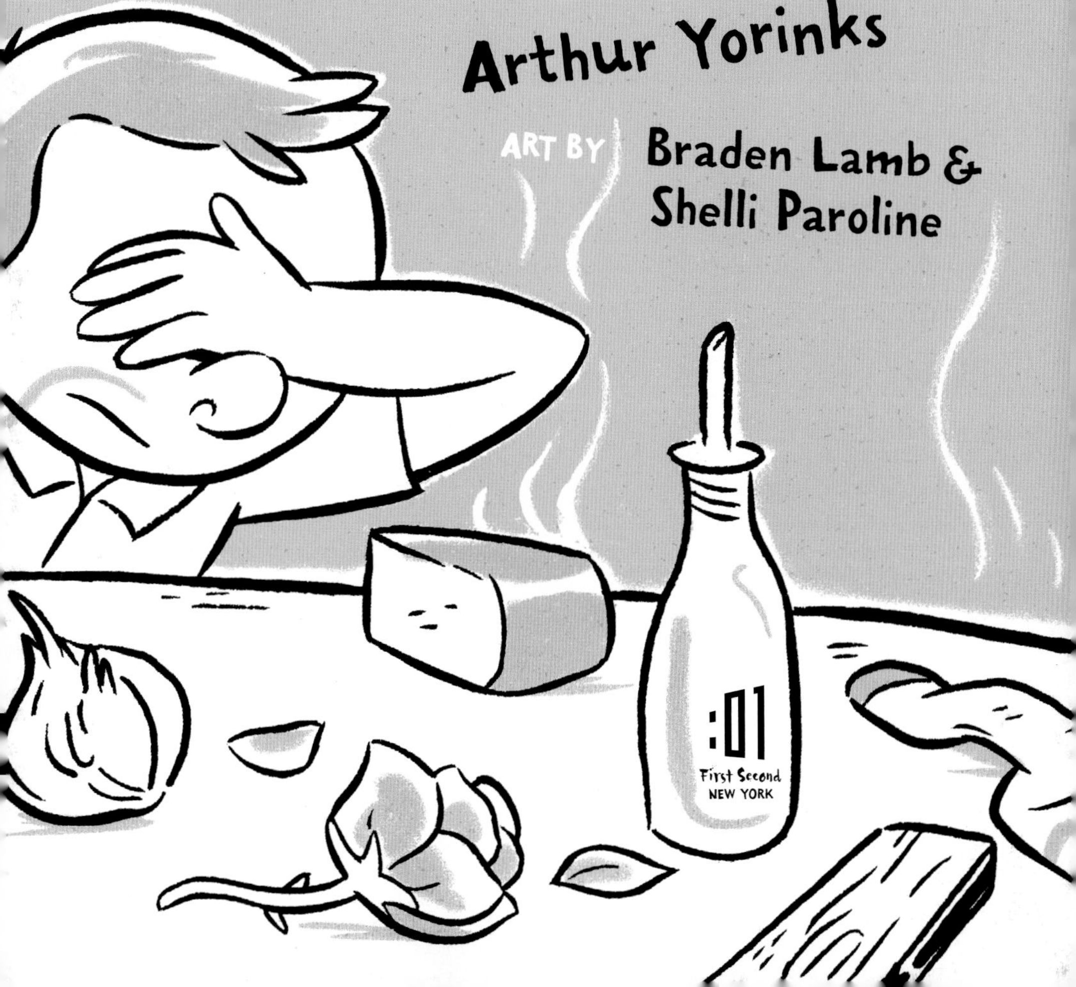

:01 First Second
NEW YORK

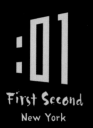

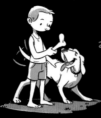

First Second
New York

For Ania, Lego & Elka
and in memory of Nettie, Ruggles,
and all the NZ border collies
—ARTHUR YORINKS

Published by First Second
First Second is an imprint of Roaring Brook Press, a division of Holtzbrinck Publishing Holdings Limited Partnership
175 Fifth Avenue, New York, New York 10010

Library of Congress Control Number: 2016945550

ISBN: 978-1-59643-452-3

First edition 2017
Book design by Danielle Ceccolini
Printed in China by Toppan Leefung Printing Ltd., Dongguan City, Guangdong Province

Penciled in Manga Studio. Inked with a Kolinsky Sable #2 brush on bristol and in Manga Studio.
Colored digitally in Photoshop.

10 9 8 7 6 5 4 3 2 1

BY ART WE LIVE

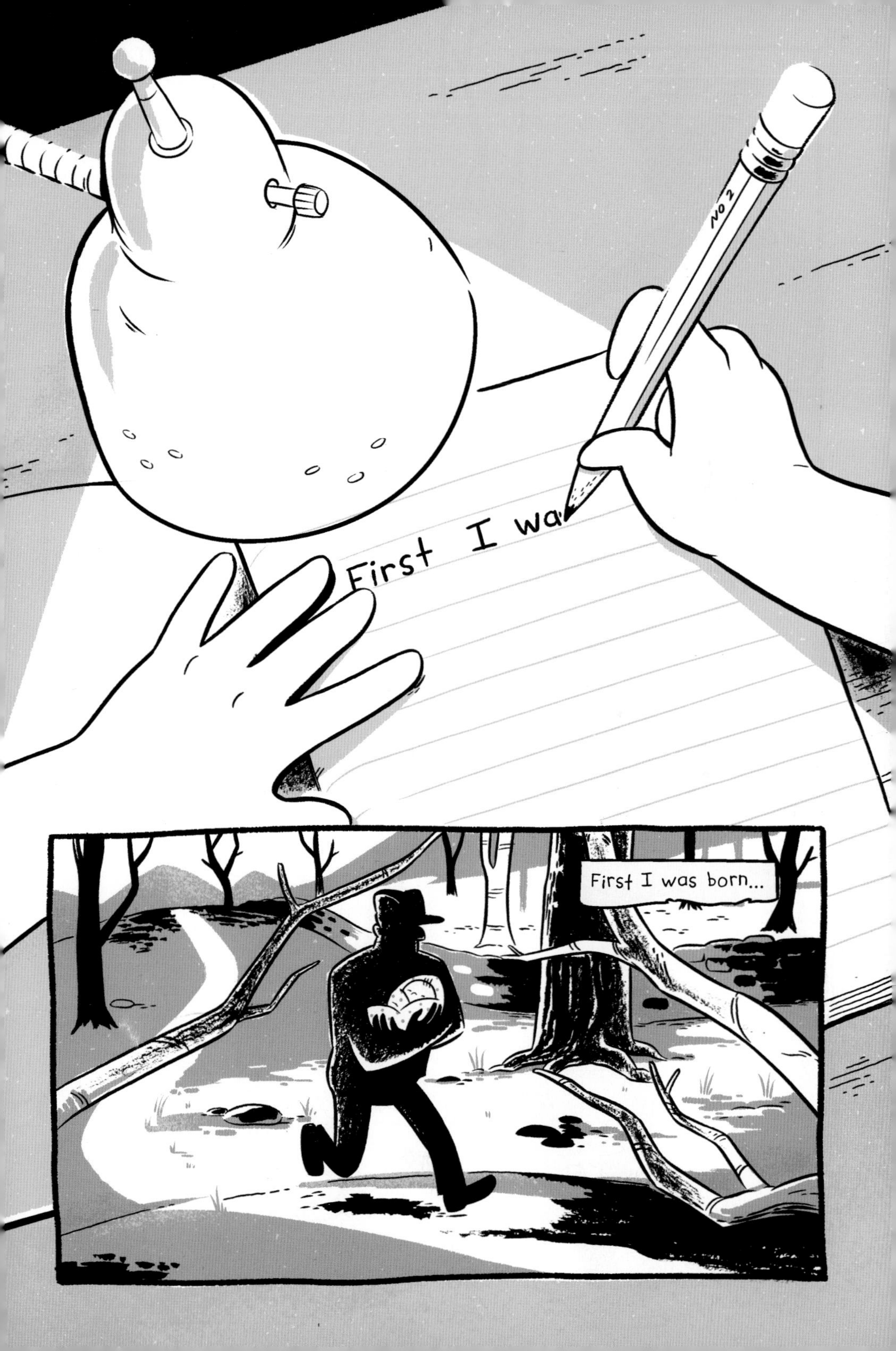
NO 2
First I wa
First I was born...

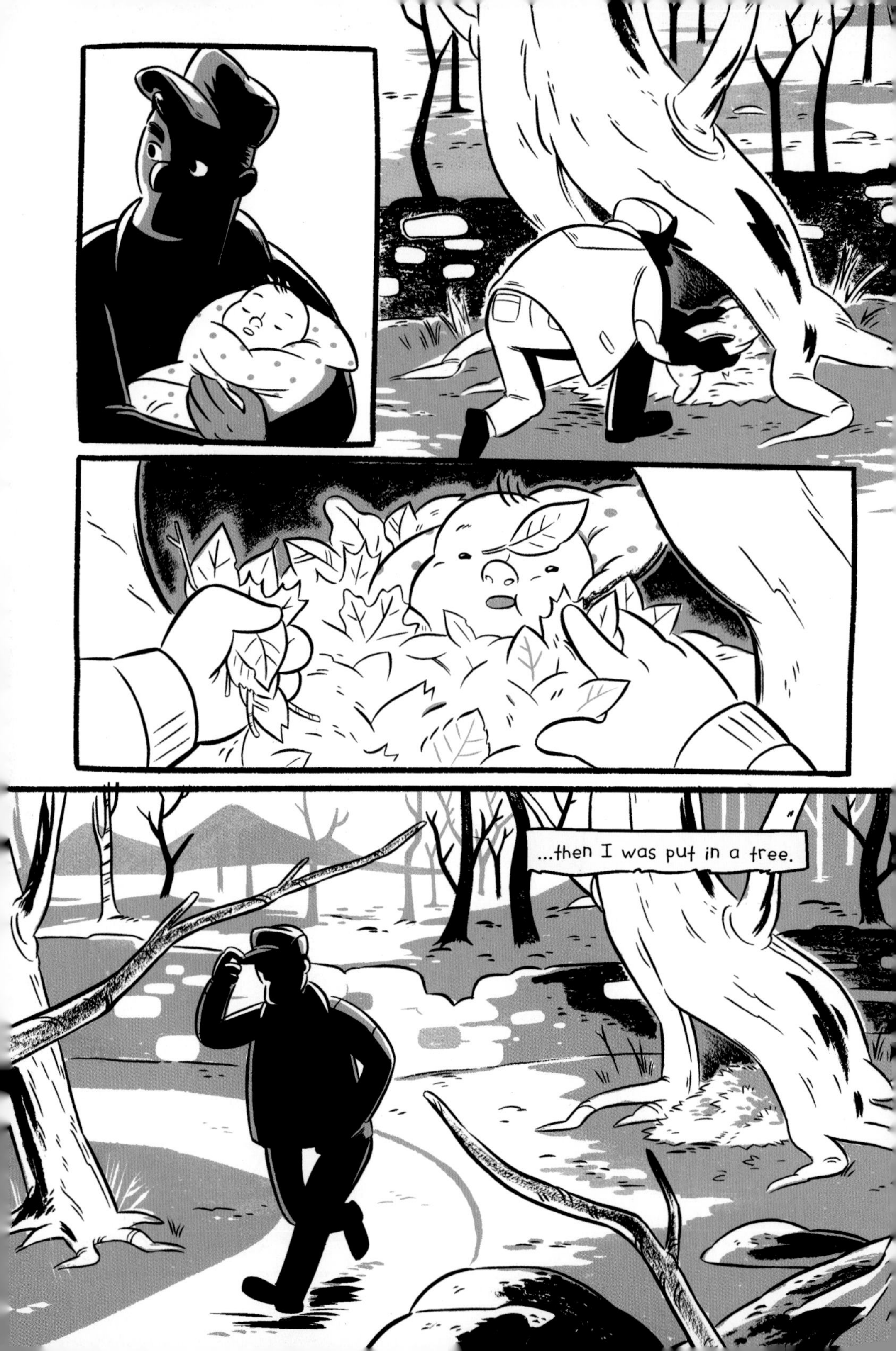
...then I was put in a tree.

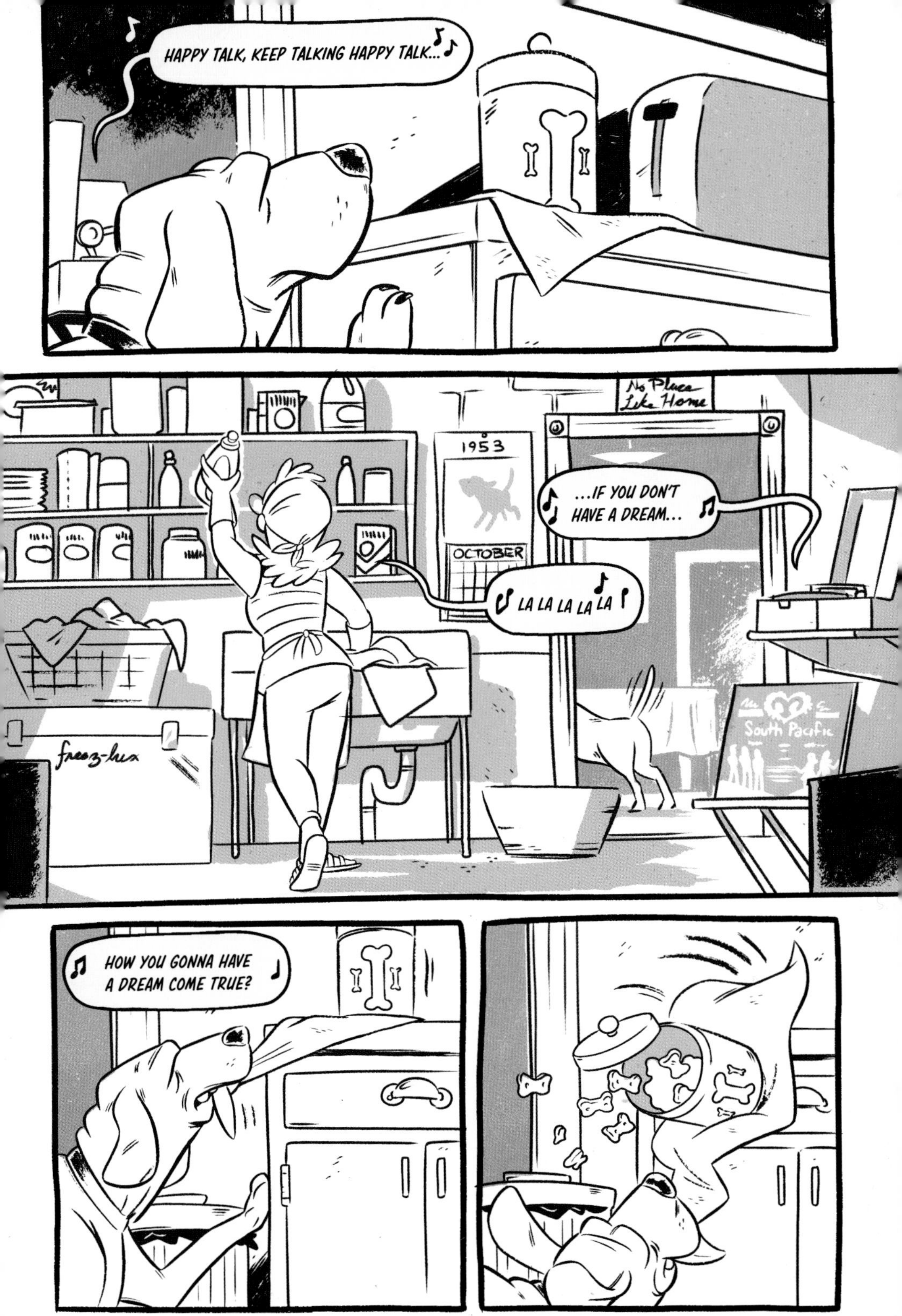
HAPPY TALK, KEEP TALKING HAPPY TALK...
No Place Like Home
1953
OCTOBER
...IF YOU DON'T HAVE A DREAM...
LA LA LA LA LA
South Pacific
HOW YOU GONNA HAVE A DREAM COME TRUE?

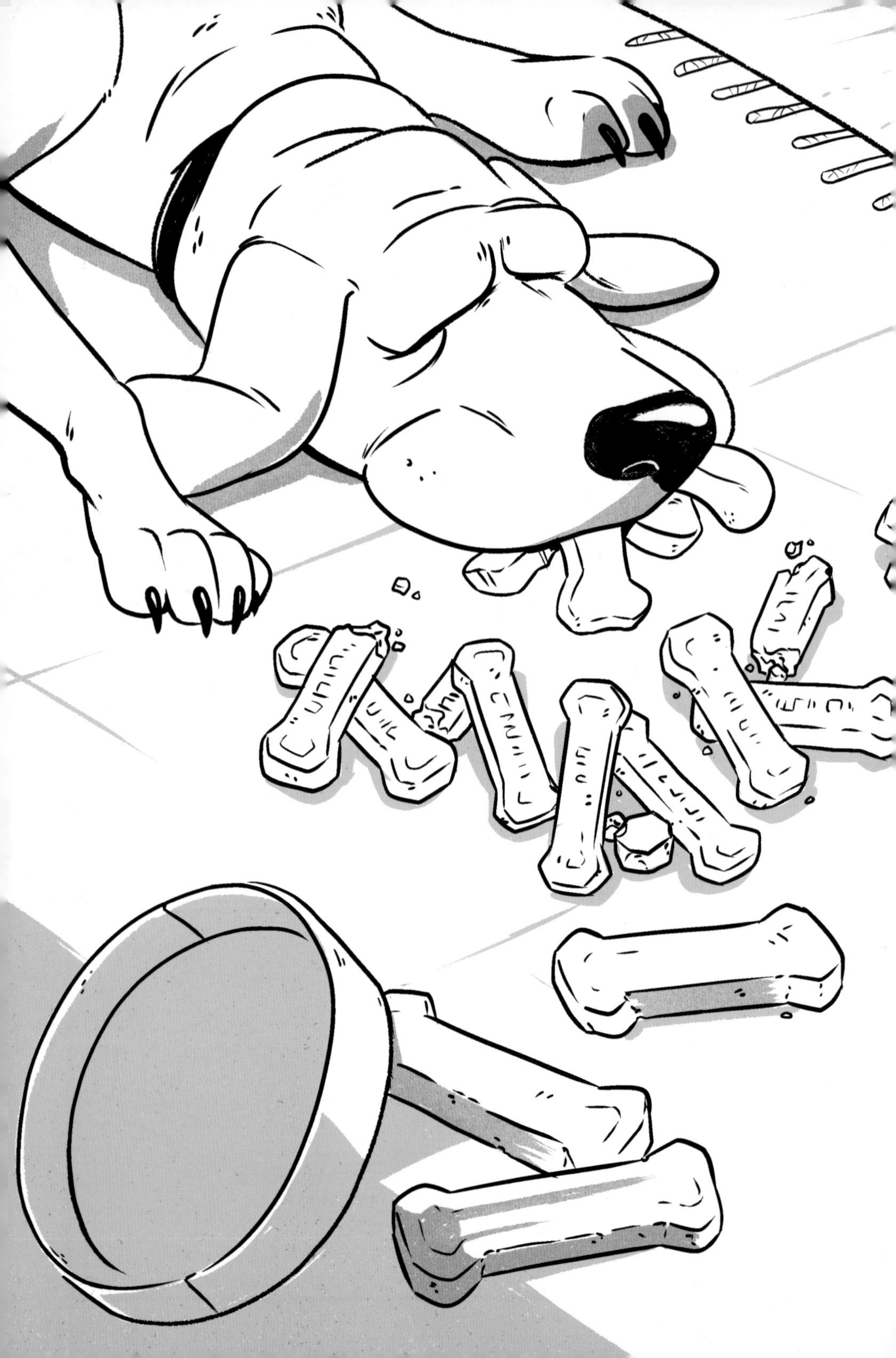

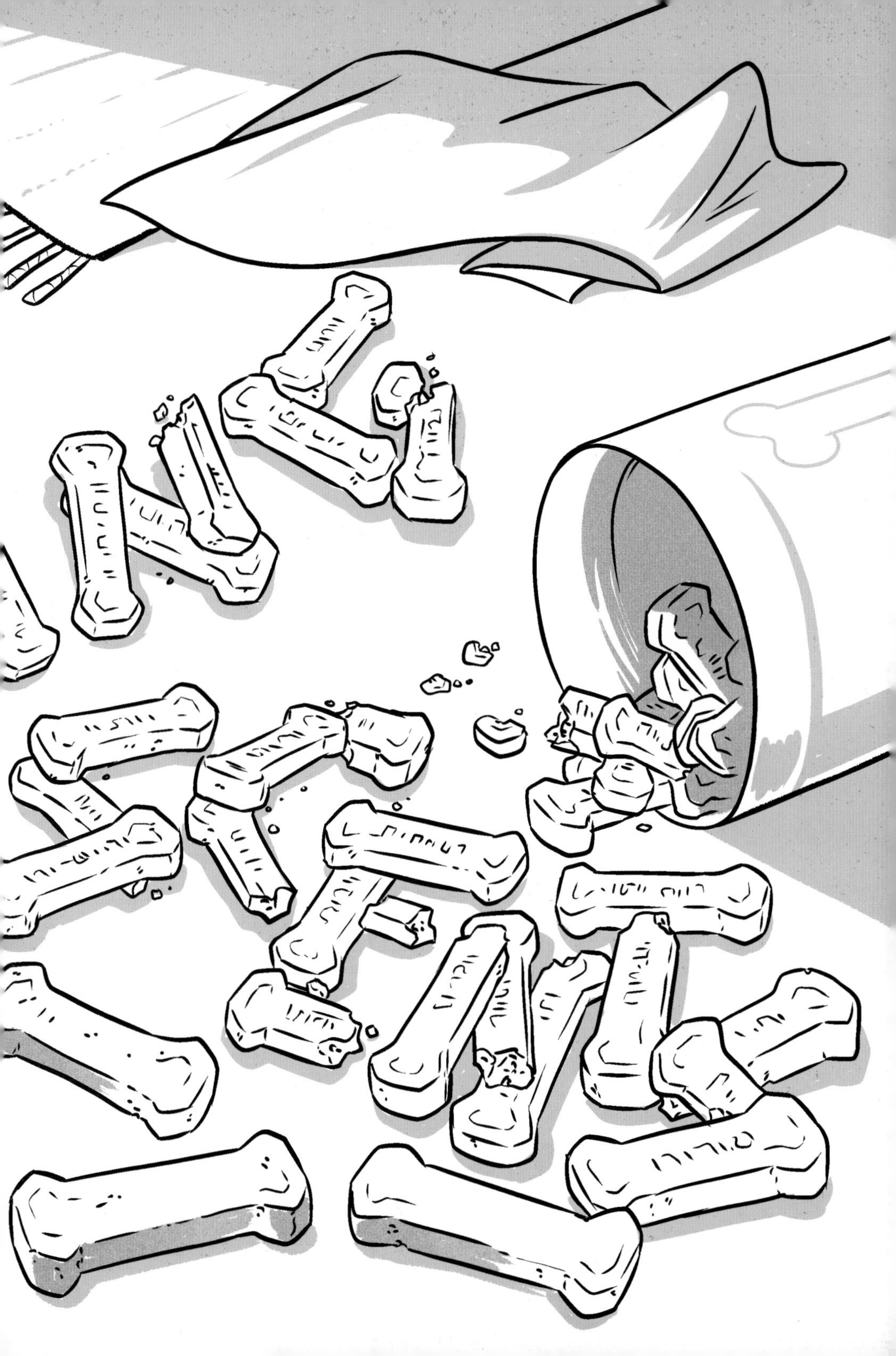

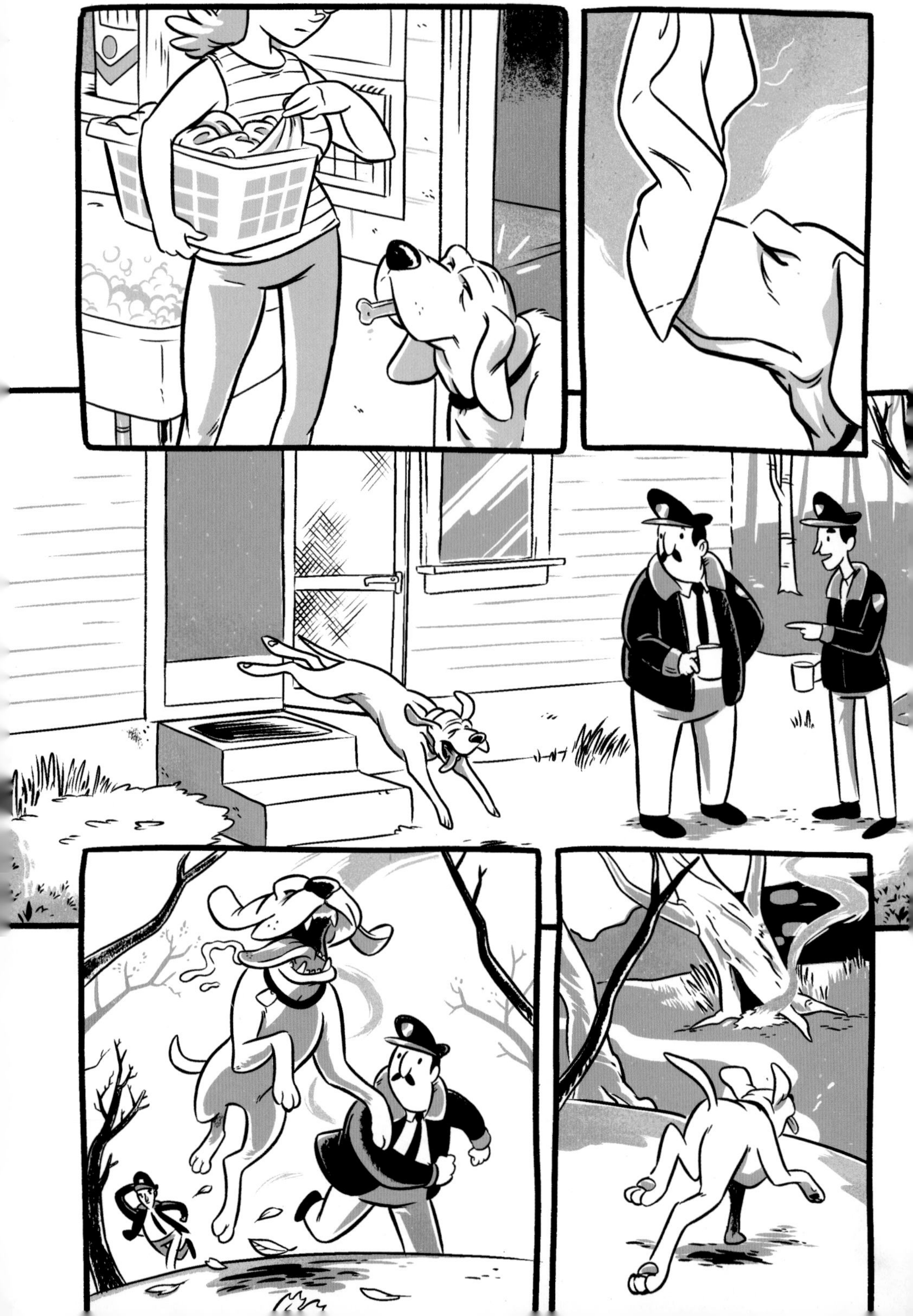

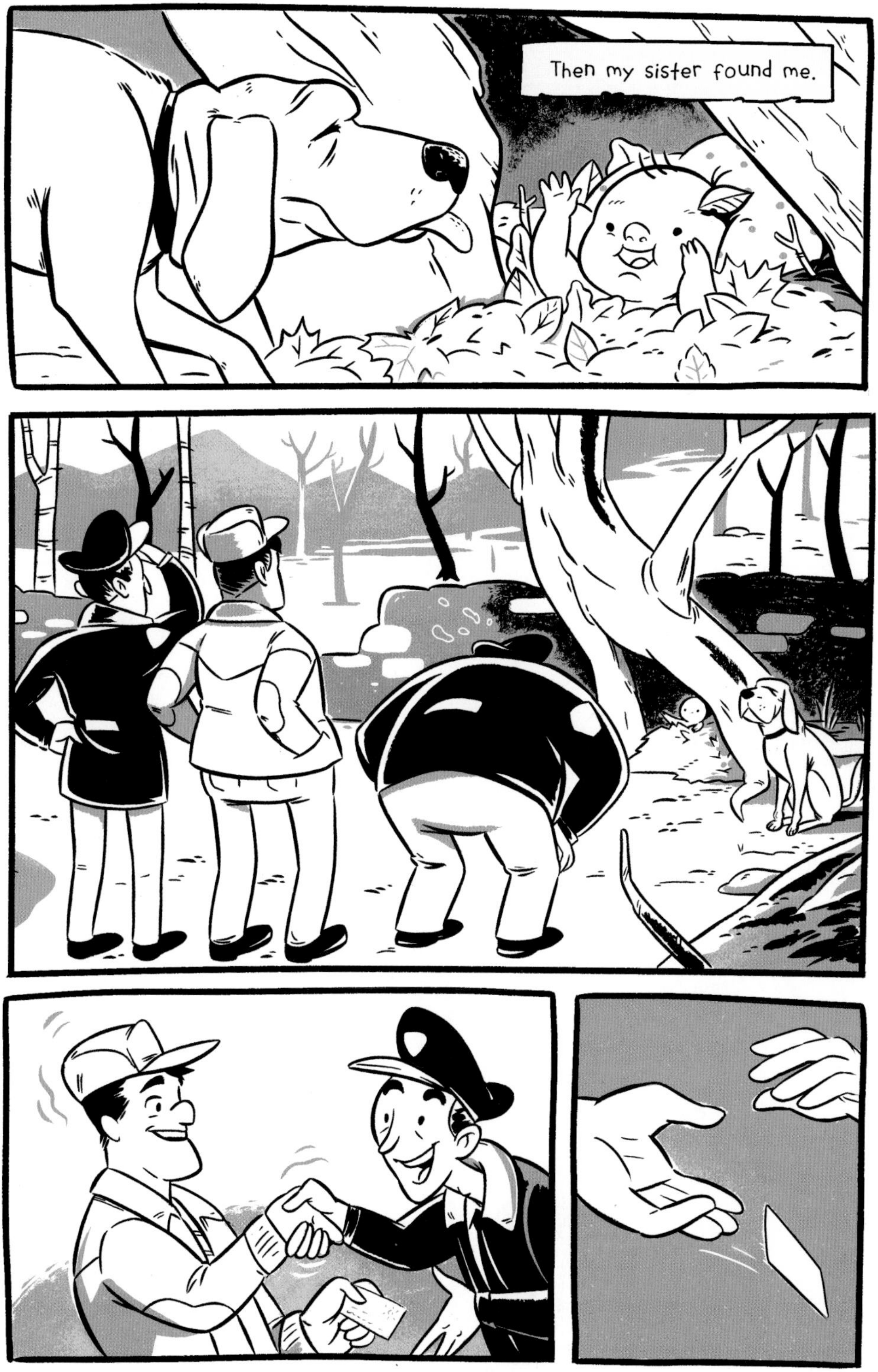
Then my sister found me.

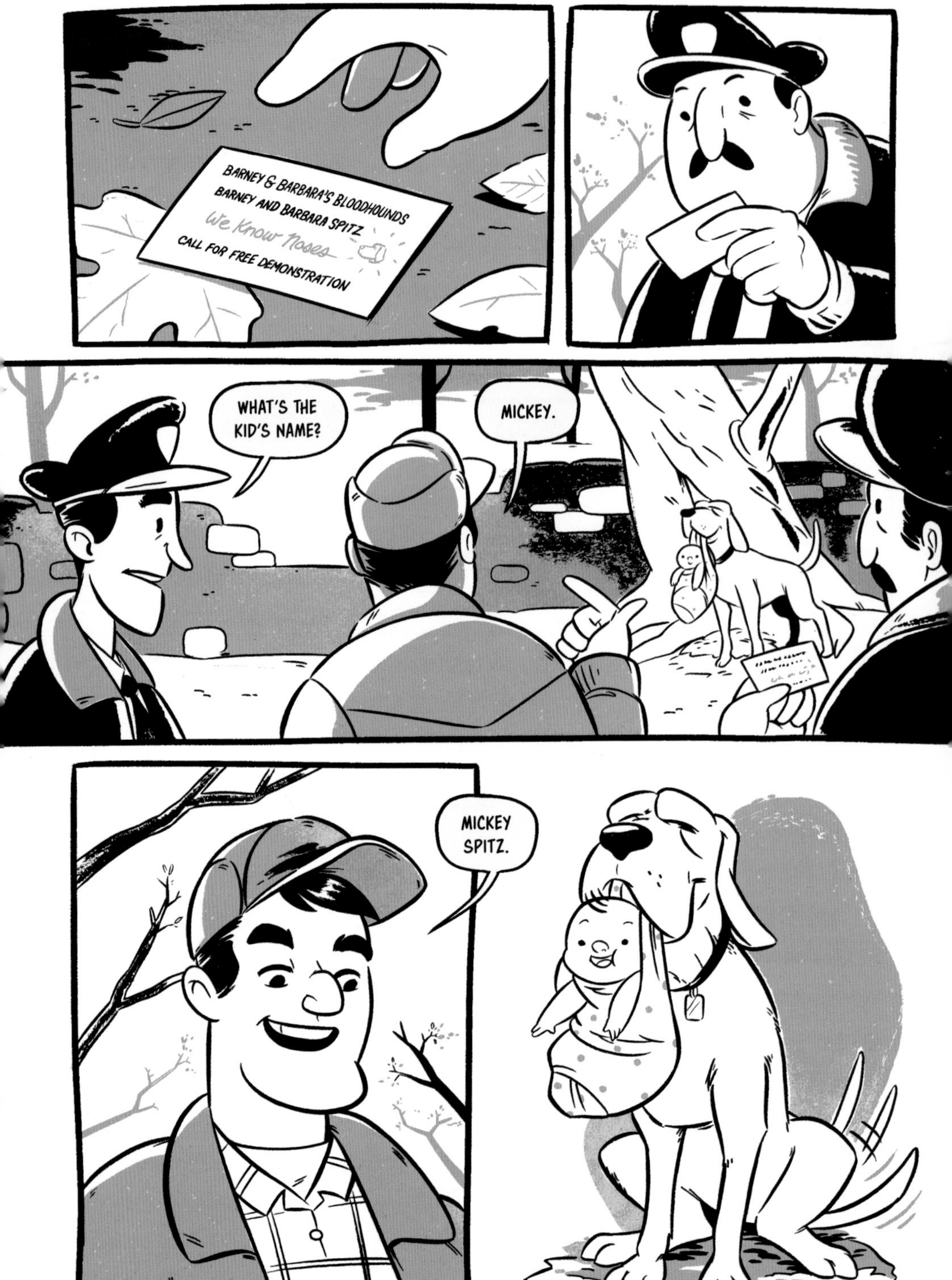
BARNEY & BARBARA'S BLOODHOUNDS
BARNEY AND BARBARA SPITZ
We Know Noses
CALL FOR FREE DEMONSTRATION
WHAT'S THE KID'S NAME?
MICKEY.
MICKEY SPITZ.

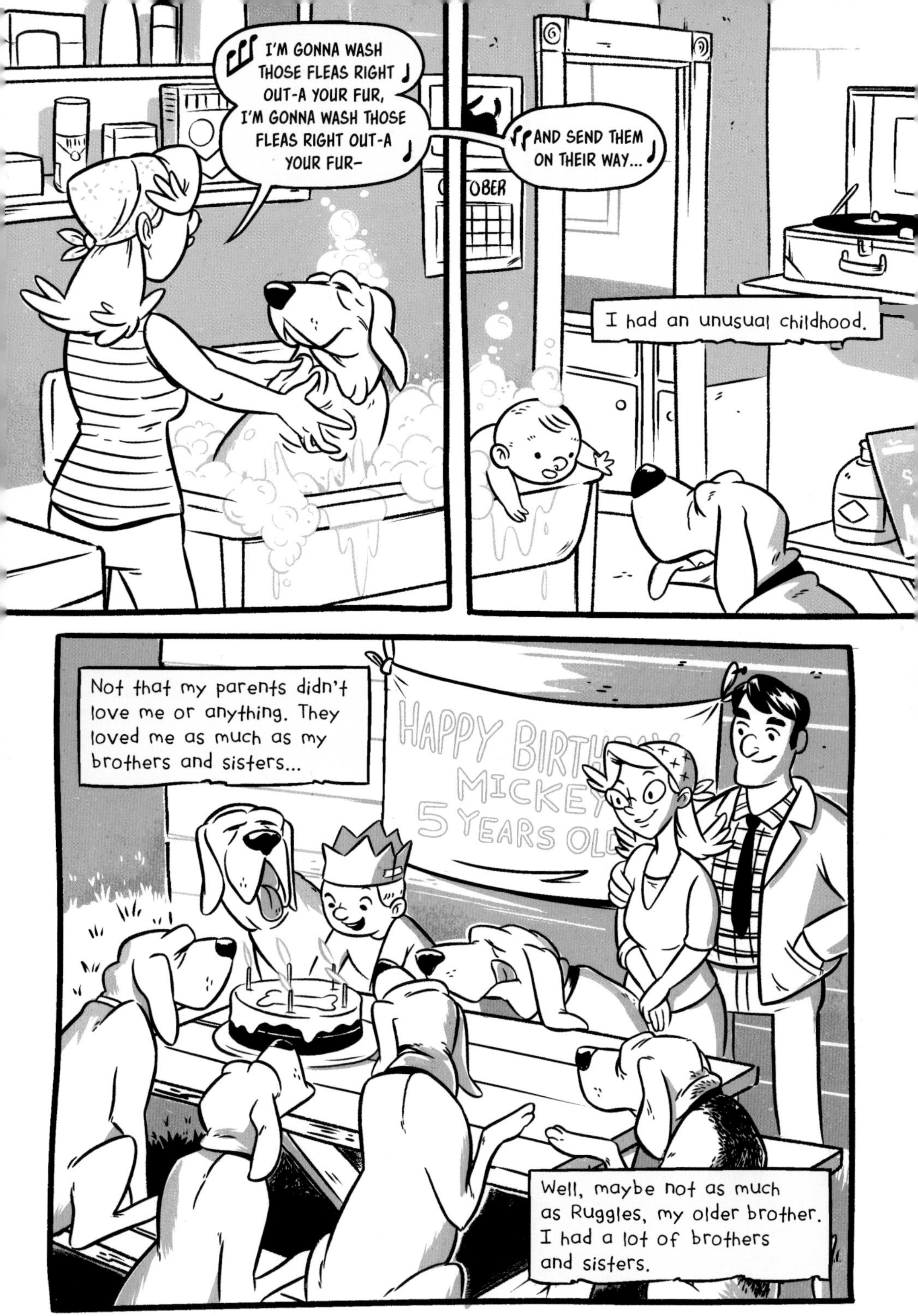
I'M GONNA WASH THOSE FLEAS RIGHT OUT-A YOUR FUR, I'M GONNA WASH THOSE FLEAS RIGHT OUT-A YOUR FUR–
AND SEND THEM ON THEIR WAY...
OCTOBER
I had an unusual childhood.
Not that my parents didn't love me or anything. They loved me as much as my brothers and sisters...
HAPPY BIRTH
MICKEY
5 YEARS OLD
Well, maybe not as much as Ruggles, my older brother. I had a lot of brothers and sisters.

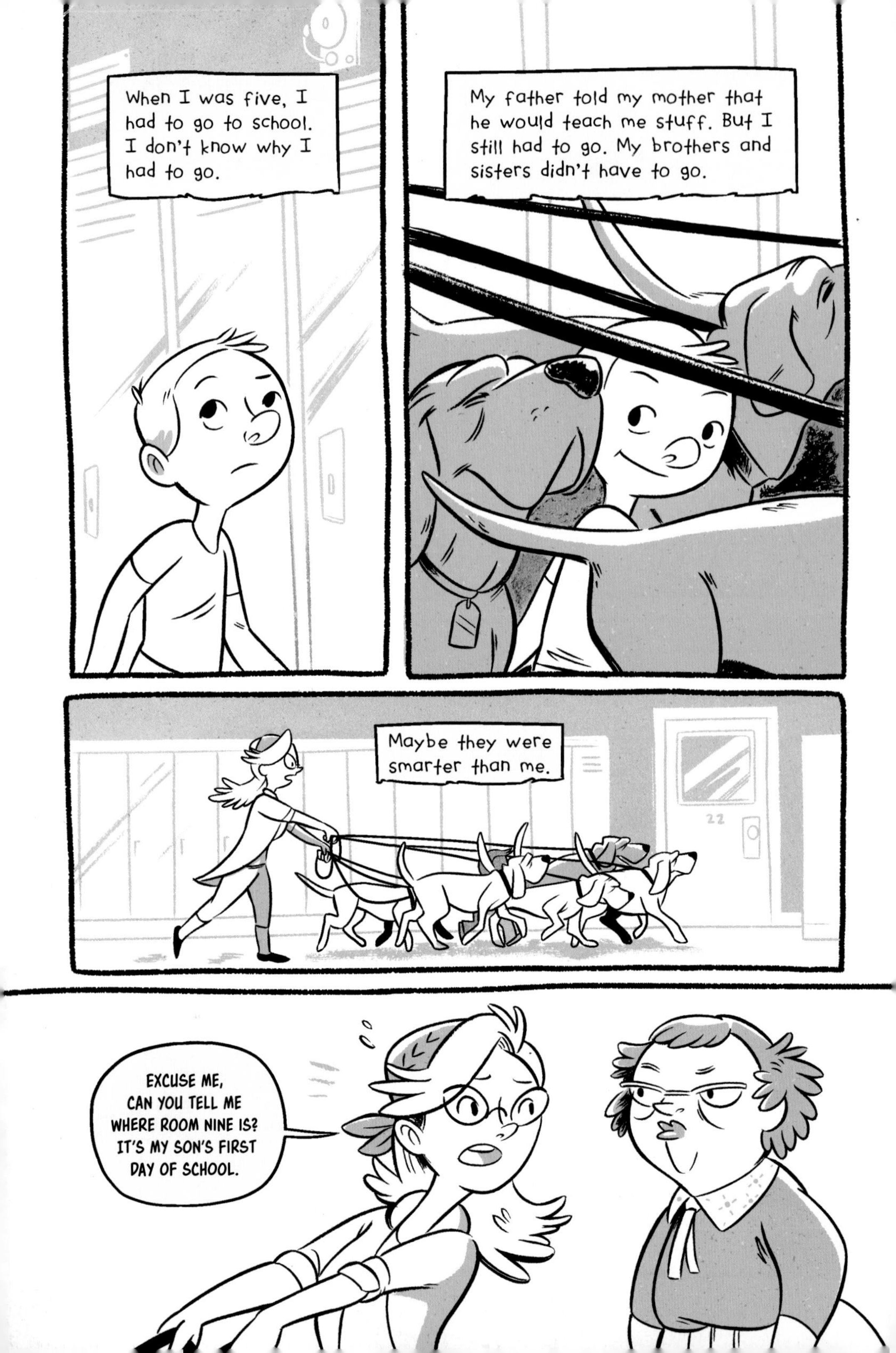
When I was five, I had to go to school. I don't know why I had to go.
My father told my mother that he would teach me stuff. But I still had to go. My brothers and sisters didn't have to go.
Maybe they were smarter than me.
22
EXCUSE ME, CAN YOU TELL ME WHERE ROOM NINE IS? IT'S MY SON'S FIRST DAY OF SCHOOL.

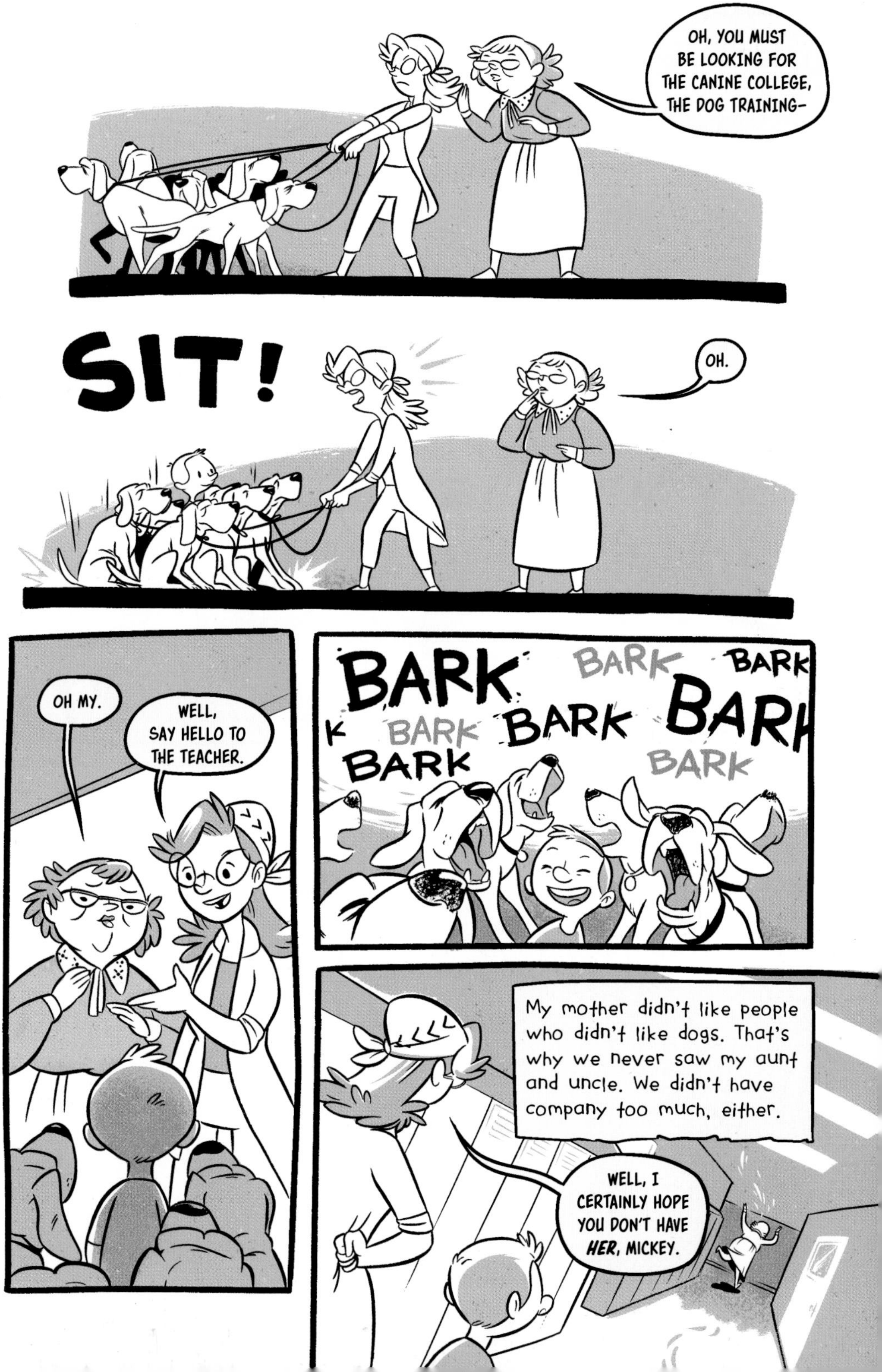
OH, YOU MUST BE LOOKING FOR THE CANINE COLLEGE, THE DOG TRAINING–
SIT!
OH.
OH MY.
WELL, SAY HELLO TO THE TEACHER.
BARK
BARK
BARK
BARK
BARK
BARK
BARK
BARK
My mother didn't like people who didn't like dogs. That's why we never saw my aunt and uncle. We didn't have company too much, either.
WELL, I CERTAINLY HOPE YOU DON'T HAVE *HER*, MICKEY.

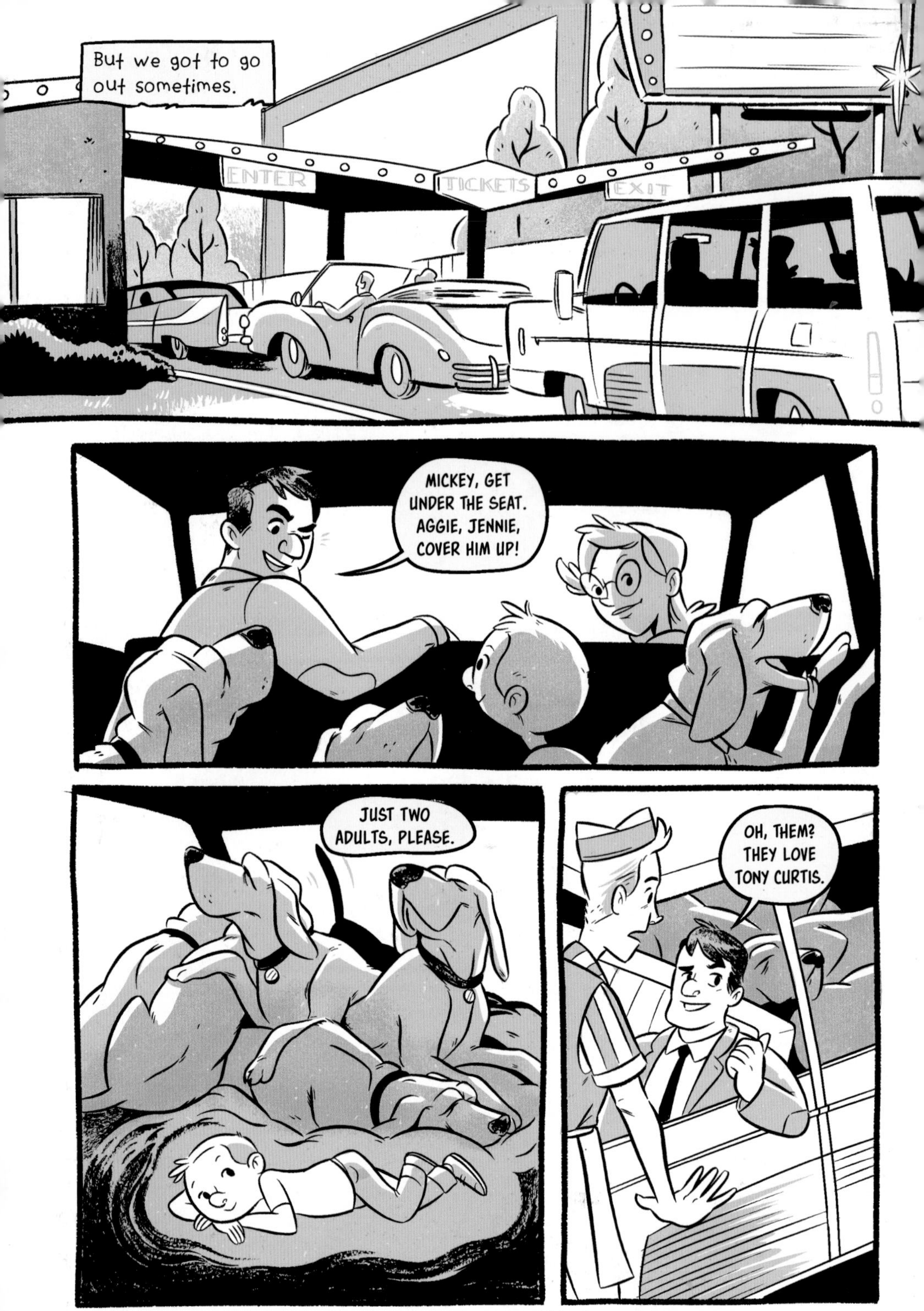
But we got to go out sometimes.
ENTER
TICKETS
EXIT
MICKEY, GET UNDER THE SEAT. AGGIE, JENNIE, COVER HIM UP!
JUST TWO ADULTS, PLEASE.
OH, THEM? THEY LOVE TONY CURTIS.

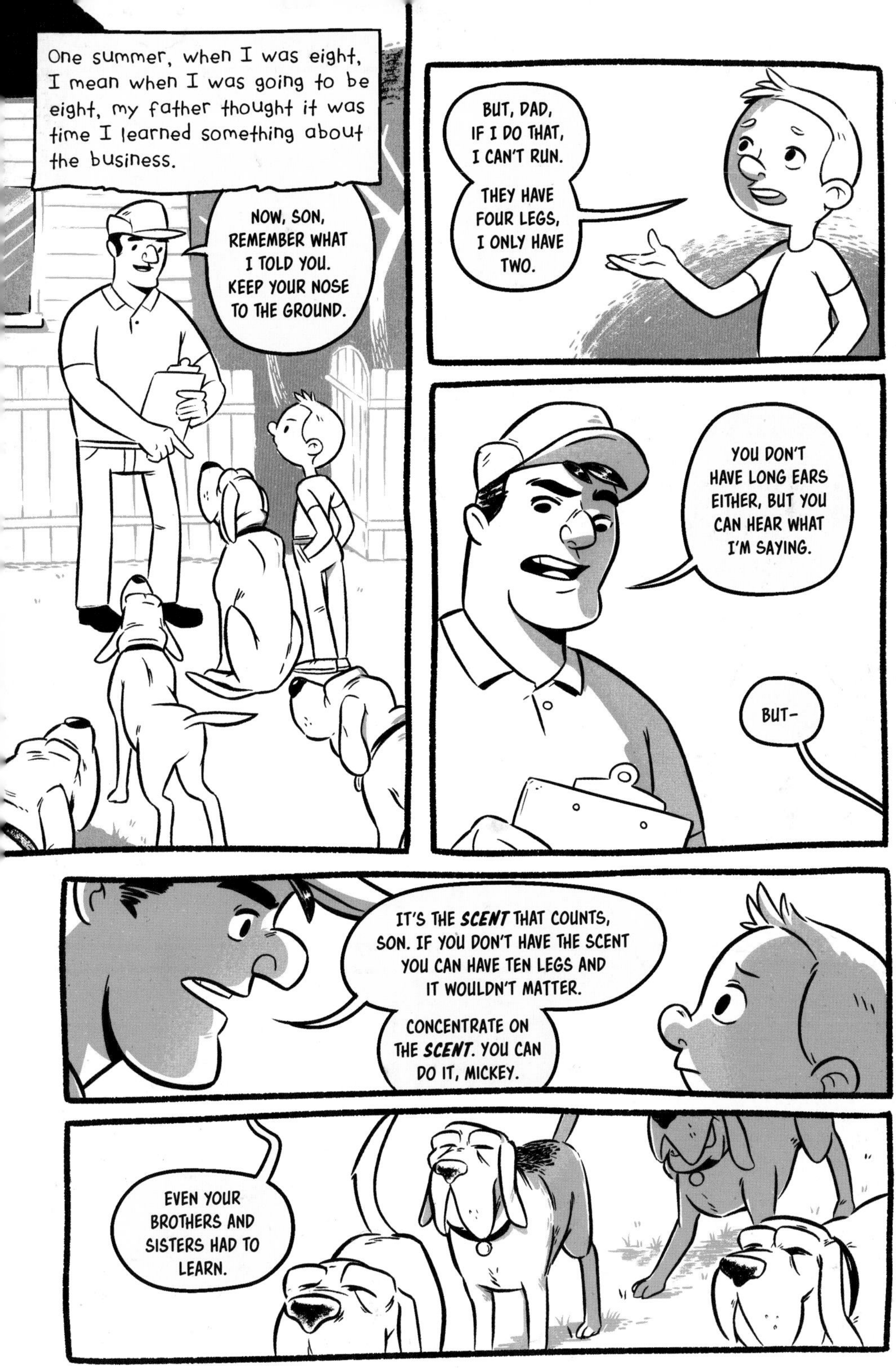
One summer, when I was eight, I mean when I was going to be eight, my father thought it was time I learned something about the business.
NOW, SON, REMEMBER WHAT I TOLD YOU. KEEP YOUR NOSE TO THE GROUND.
BUT, DAD, IF I DO THAT, I CAN'T RUN.
THEY HAVE FOUR LEGS, I ONLY HAVE TWO.
YOU DON'T HAVE LONG EARS EITHER, BUT YOU CAN HEAR WHAT I'M SAYING.
BUT-
IT'S THE *SCENT* THAT COUNTS, SON. IF YOU DON'T HAVE THE SCENT YOU CAN HAVE TEN LEGS AND IT WOULDN'T MATTER.
CONCENTRATE ON THE *SCENT*. YOU CAN DO IT, MICKEY.
EVEN YOUR BROTHERS AND SISTERS HAD TO LEARN.

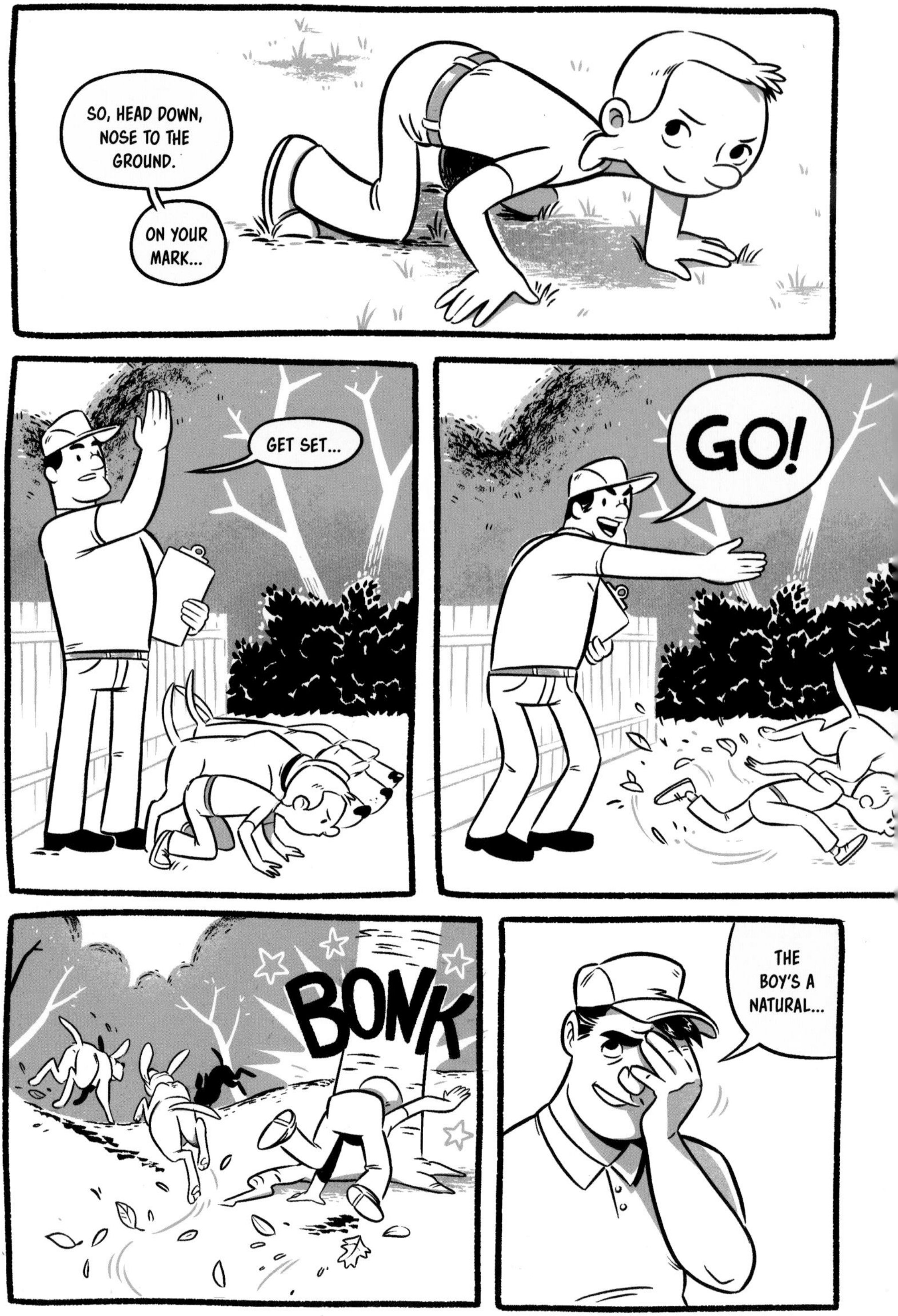
SO, HEAD DOWN, NOSE TO THE GROUND.
ON YOUR MARK...
GET SET...
GO!
BONK
THE BOY'S A NATURAL...

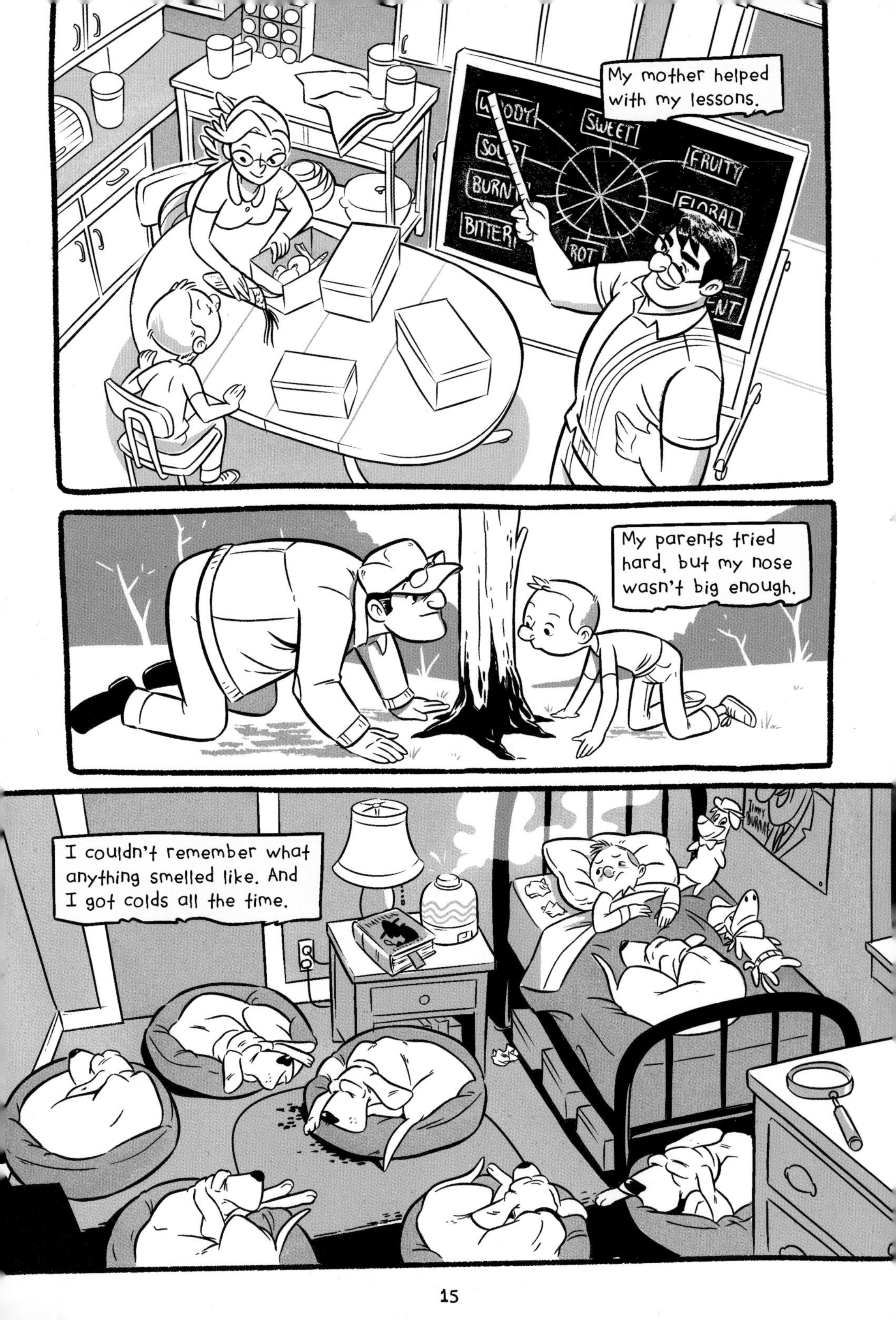
My mother helped with my lessons.
SWEET
FRUITY
My parents tried hard, but my nose wasn't big enough.
I couldn't remember what anything smelled like. And I got colds all the time.

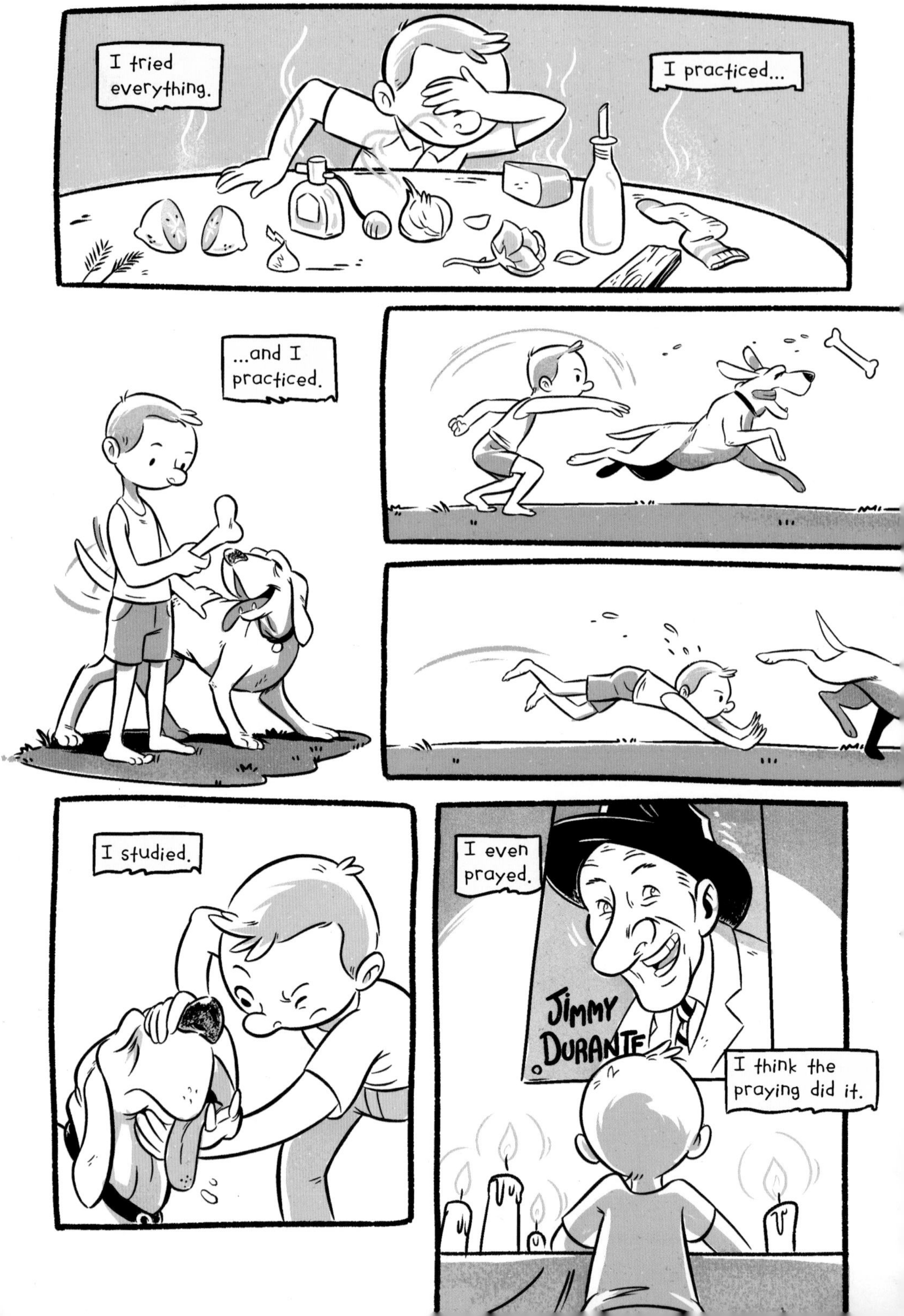
I tried everything.
I practiced...
...and I practiced.
I studied.
I even prayed.
JIMMY DURANTE
I think the praying did it.

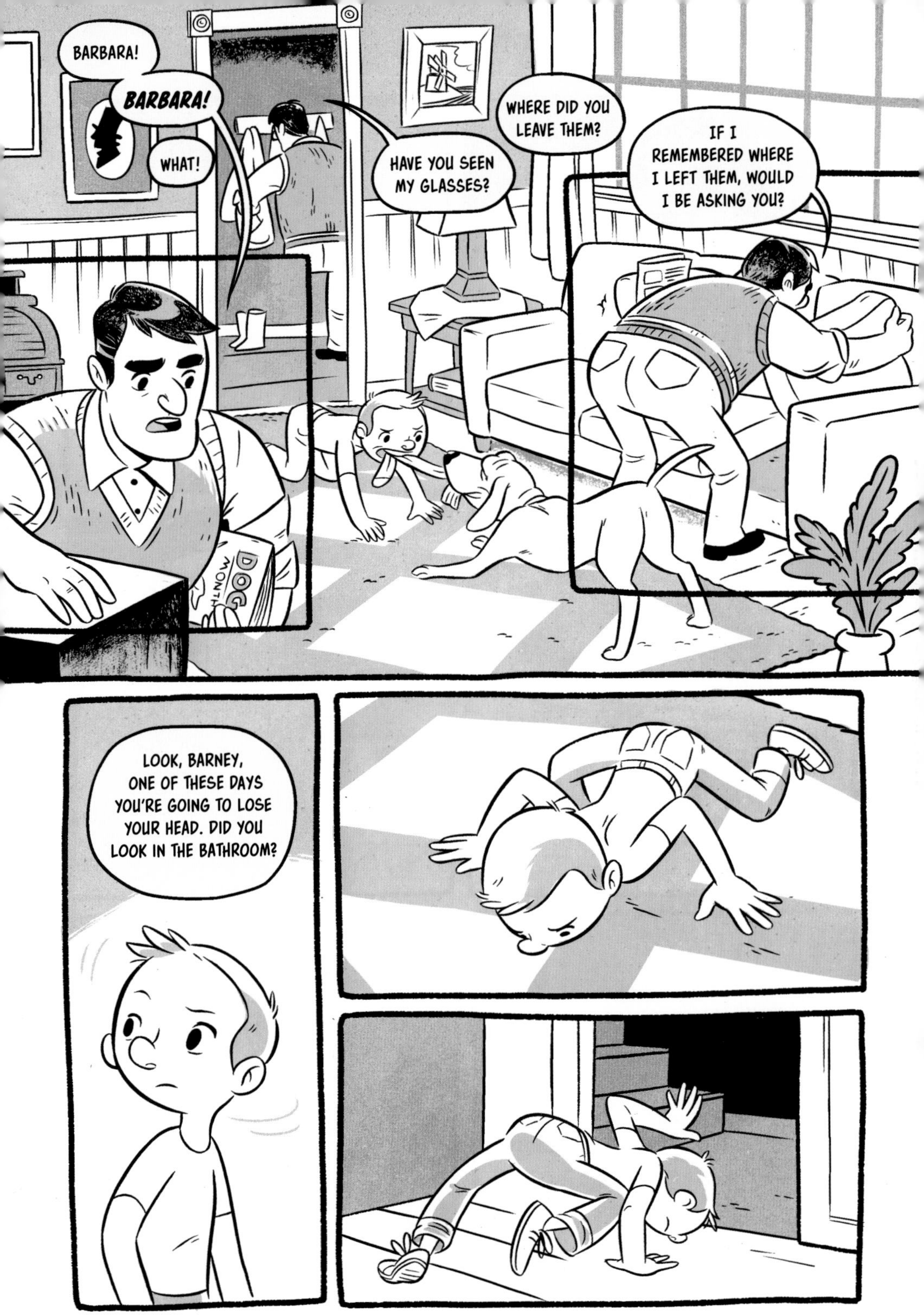
BARBARA!
BARBARA!
WHAT!
HAVE YOU SEEN MY GLASSES?
WHERE DID YOU LEAVE THEM?
IF I REMEMBERED WHERE I LEFT THEM, WOULD I BE ASKING YOU?
DOG MONTH
LOOK, BARNEY, ONE OF THESE DAYS YOU'RE GOING TO LOSE YOUR HEAD. DID YOU LOOK IN THE BATHROOM?

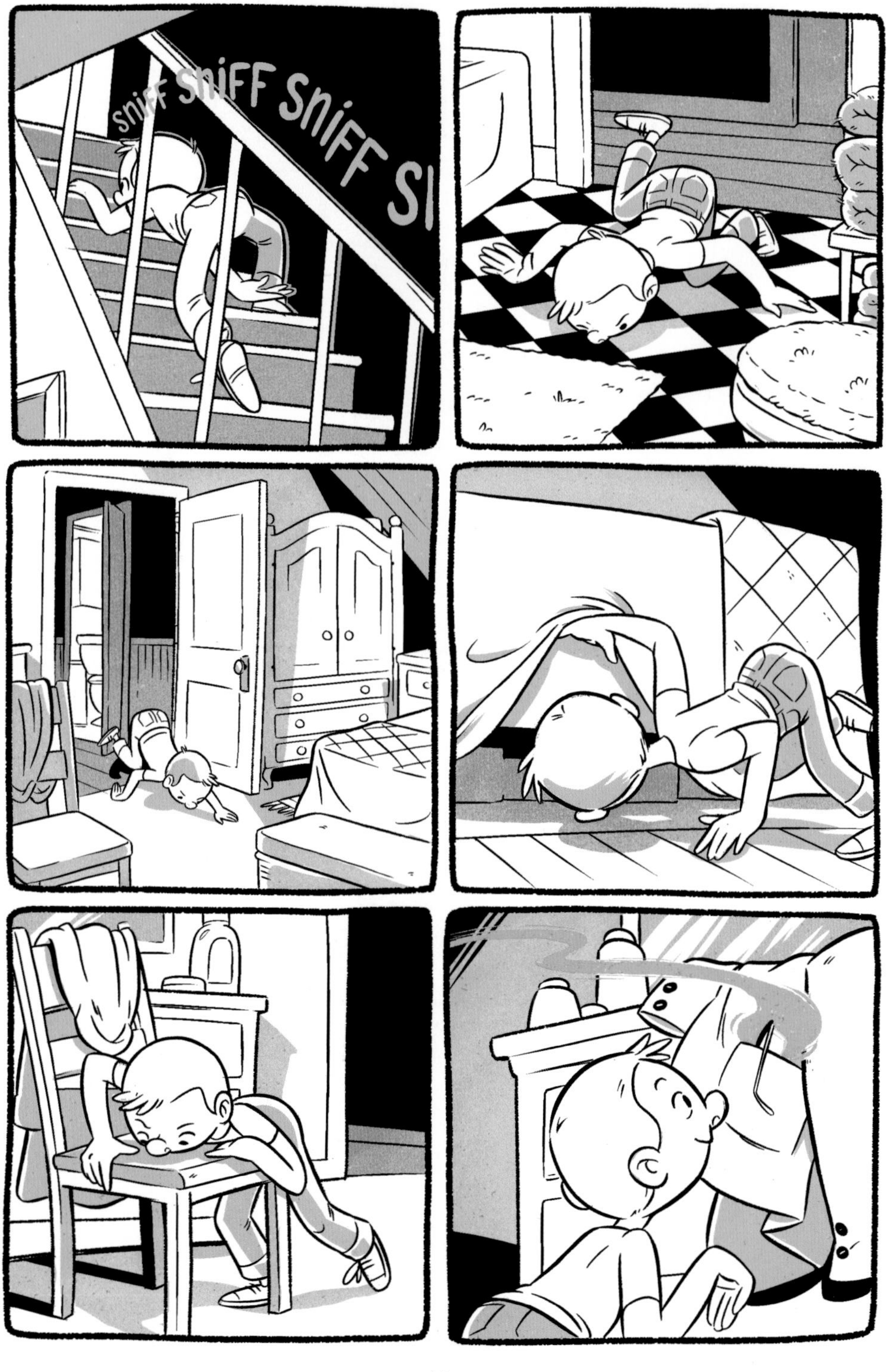
SNiFF SNiFF SNiFF SNiFF SI

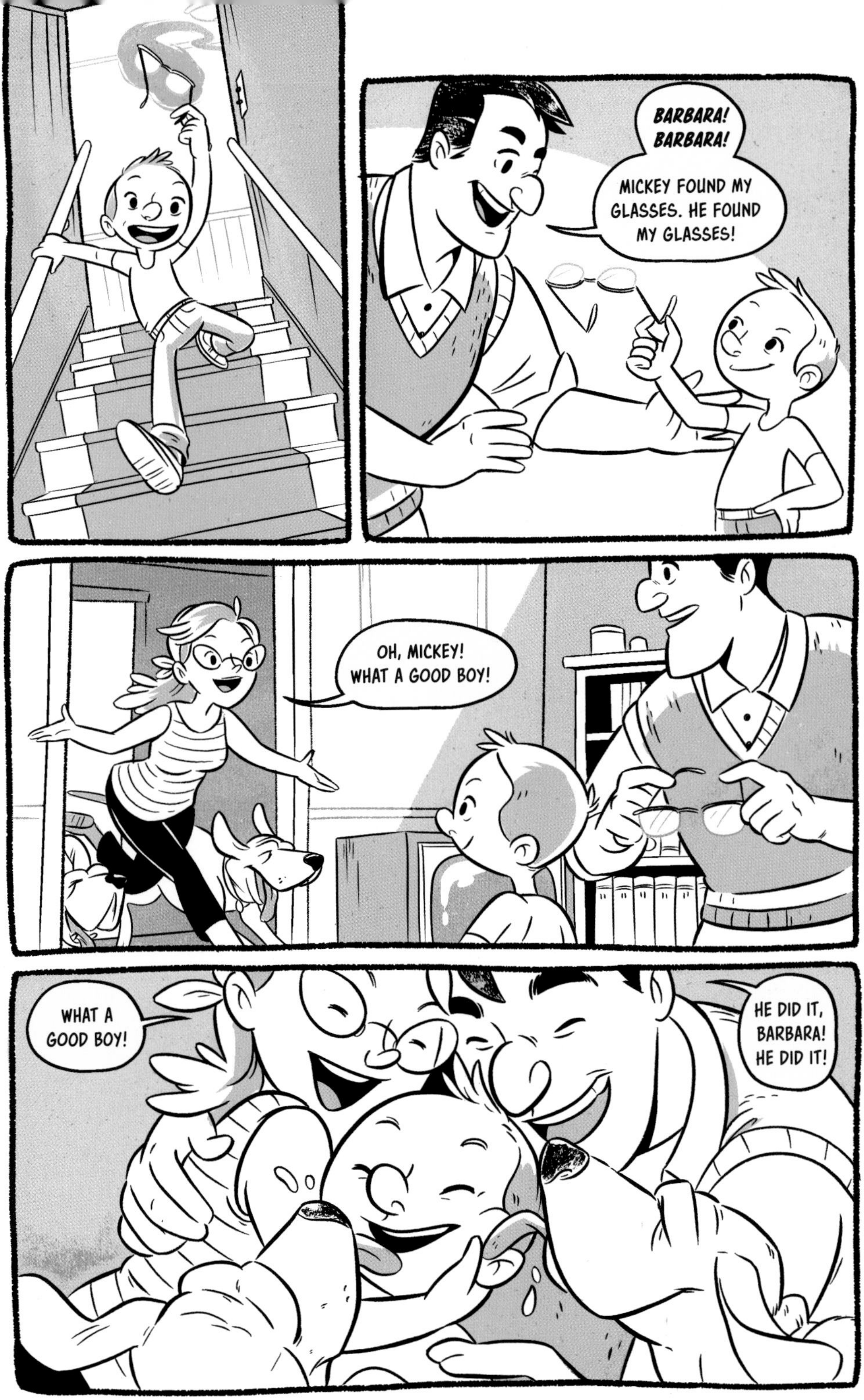
BARBARA! BARBARA!
MICKEY FOUND MY GLASSES. HE FOUND MY GLASSES!
OH, MICKEY! WHAT A GOOD BOY!
WHAT A GOOD BOY!
HE DID IT, BARBARA! HE DID IT!

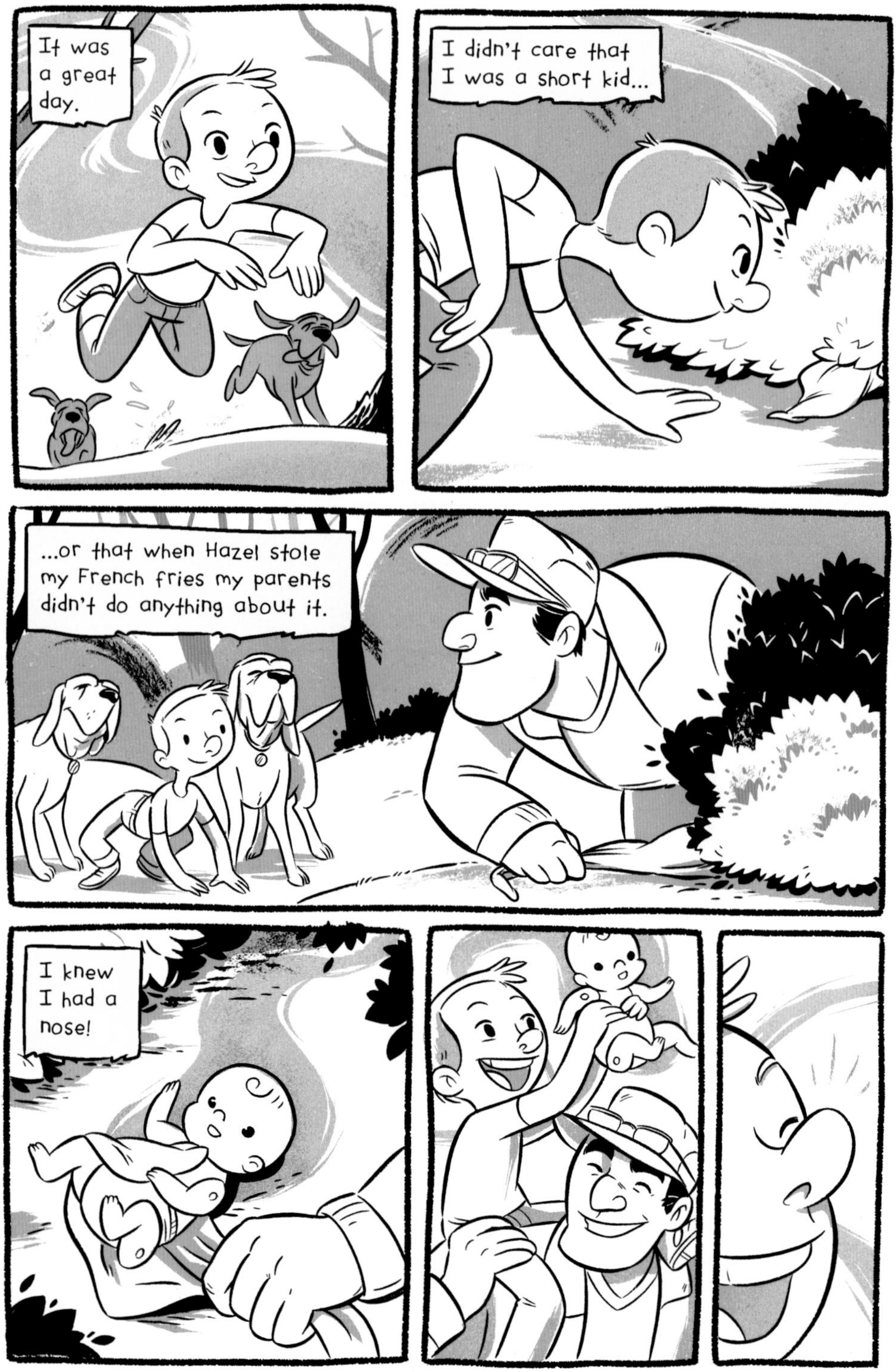
It was a great day.
I didn't care that I was a short kid...
...or that when Hazel stole my French fries my parents didn't do anything about it.
I knew I had a nose!

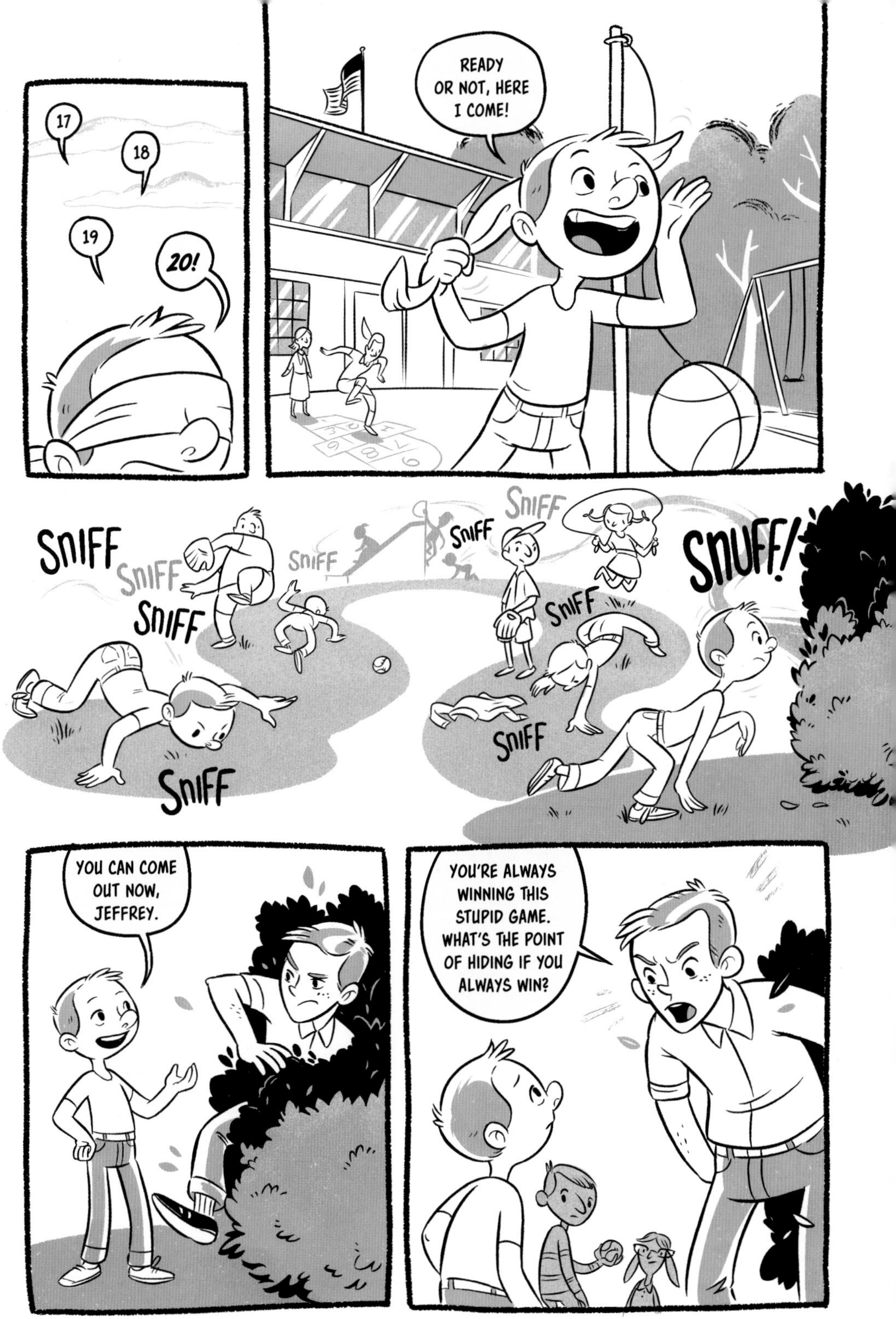
17
18
19
20!
READY OR NOT, HERE I COME!
SNIFF
SNIFF
SNIFF
SNIFF
SNIFF
SNIFF
SNIFF
SNIFF
SNIFF
SNUFF!
YOU CAN COME OUT NOW, JEFFREY.
YOU'RE ALWAYS WINNING THIS STUPID GAME. WHAT'S THE POINT OF HIDING IF YOU ALWAYS WIN?

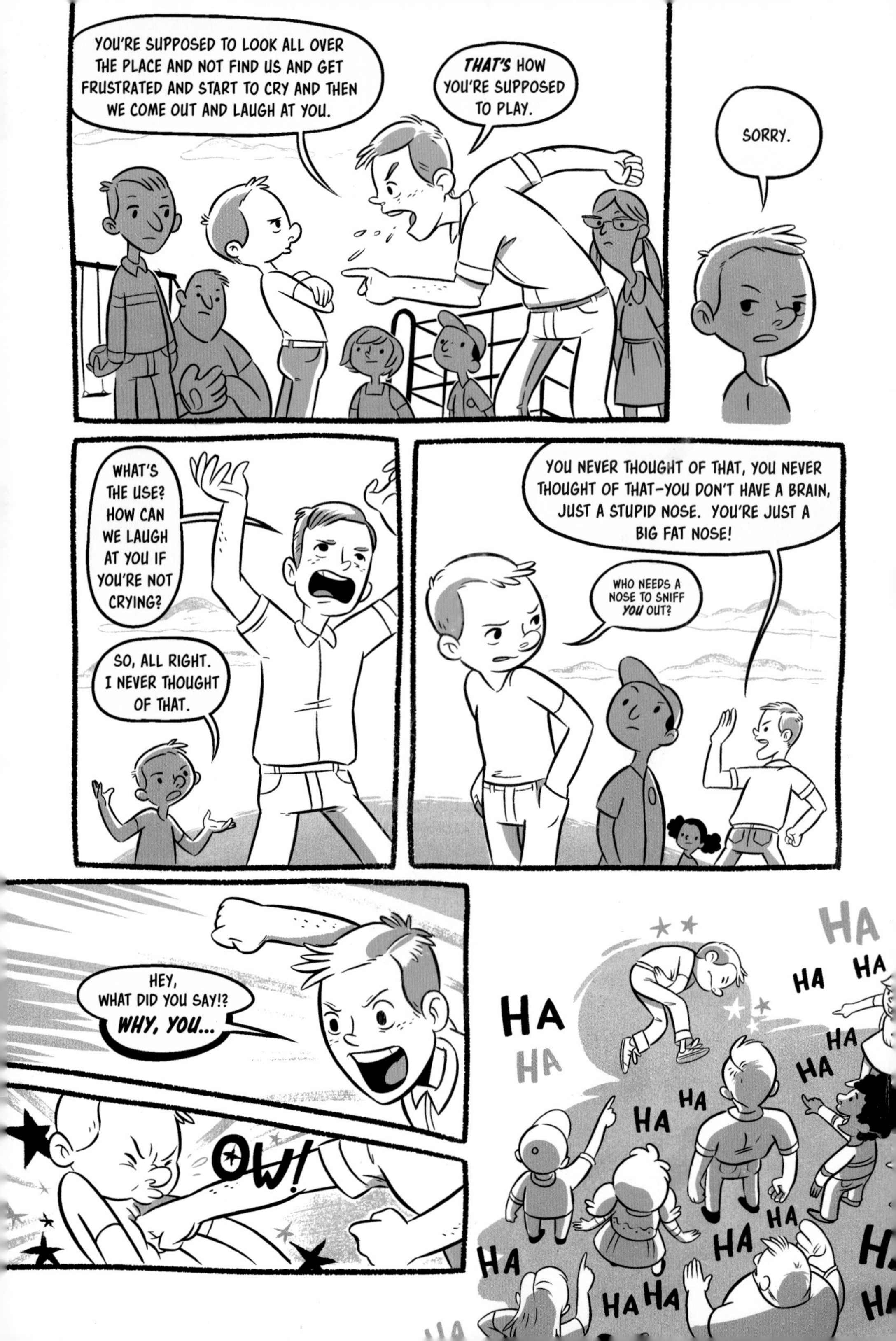

YOU'RE SUPPOSED TO LOOK ALL OVER THE PLACE AND NOT FIND US AND GET FRUSTRATED AND START TO CRY AND THEN WE COME OUT AND LAUGH AT YOU.
THAT'S HOW YOU'RE SUPPOSED TO PLAY.
SORRY.
WHAT'S THE USE? HOW CAN WE LAUGH AT YOU IF YOU'RE NOT CRYING?
SO, ALL RIGHT. I NEVER THOUGHT OF THAT.
YOU NEVER THOUGHT OF THAT, YOU NEVER THOUGHT OF THAT—YOU DON'T HAVE A BRAIN, JUST A STUPID NOSE. YOU'RE JUST A BIG FAT NOSE!
WHO NEEDS A NOSE TO SNIFF *YOU* OUT?
HEY, WHAT DID YOU SAY!? ***WHY, YOU...***
OW!
HA HA HA HA HA HA HA HA HA HA HA HA HA HA

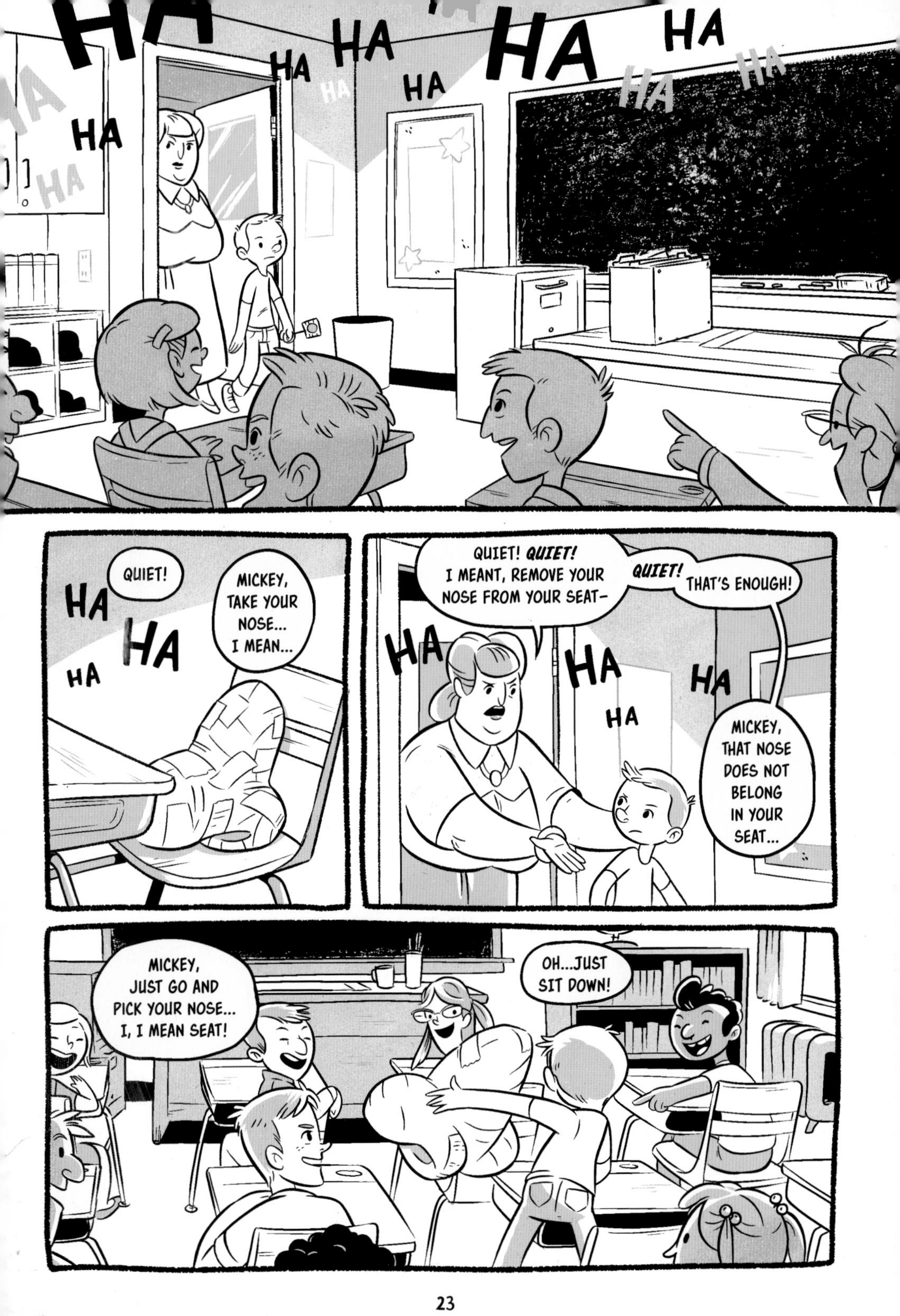
HA HA HA HA HA HA HA HA HA HA HA HA
QUIET!
HA HA HA
MICKEY, TAKE YOUR NOSE... I MEAN...
QUIET! *QUIET!* I MEANT, REMOVE YOUR NOSE FROM YOUR SEAT—
QUIET!
THAT'S ENOUGH!
HA HA HA HA
MICKEY, THAT NOSE DOES NOT BELONG IN YOUR SEAT...
MICKEY, JUST GO AND PICK YOUR NOSE... I, I MEAN SEAT!
OH...JUST SIT DOWN!

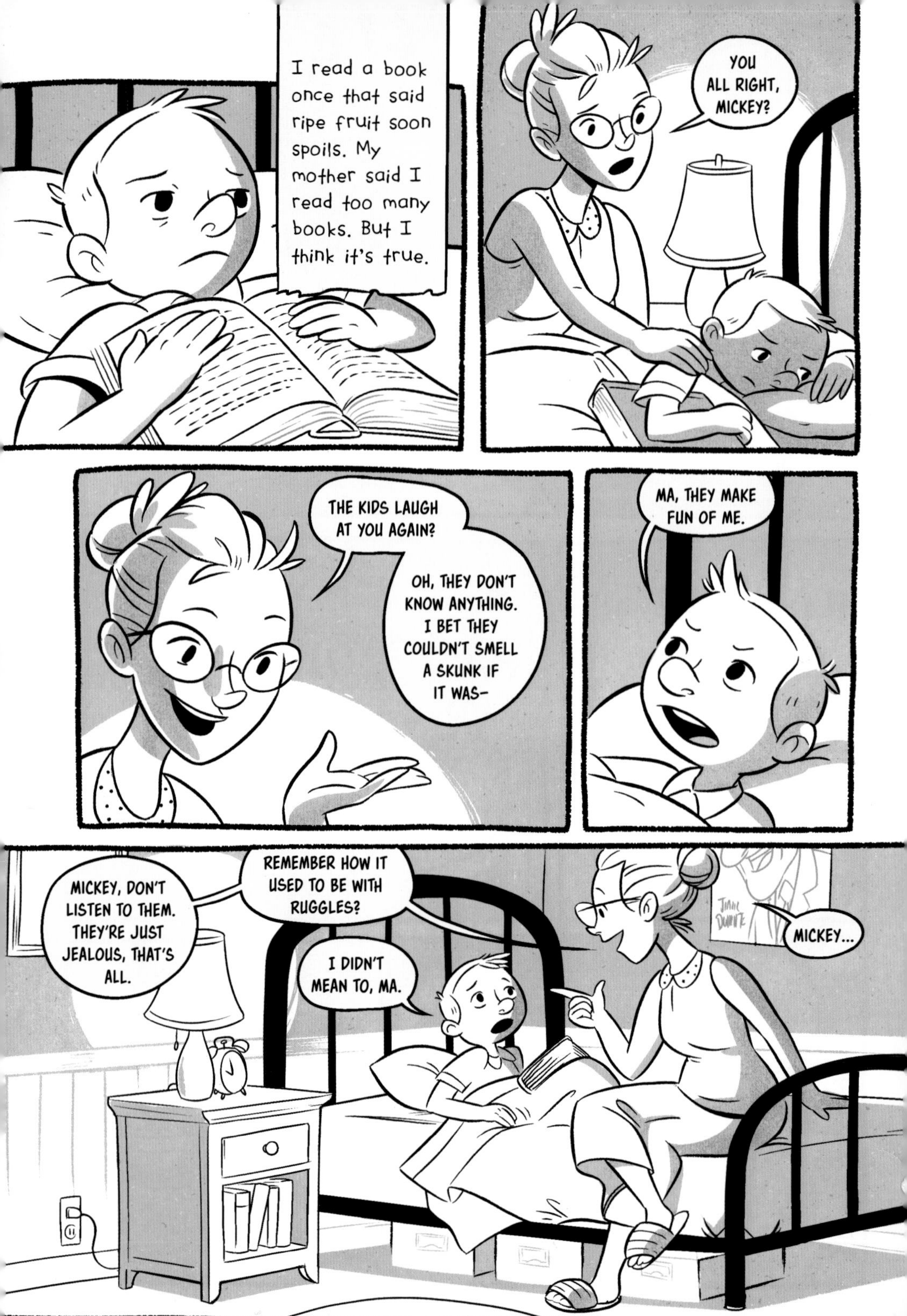

I read a book once that said ripe fruit soon spoils. My mother said I read too many books. But I think it's true.
YOU ALL RIGHT, MICKEY?
THE KIDS LAUGH AT YOU AGAIN?
OH, THEY DON'T KNOW ANYTHING. I BET THEY COULDN'T SMELL A SKUNK IF IT WAS-
MA, THEY MAKE FUN OF ME.
MICKEY, DON'T LISTEN TO THEM. THEY'RE JUST JEALOUS, THAT'S ALL.
REMEMBER HOW IT USED TO BE WITH RUGGLES?
I DIDN'T MEAN TO, MA.
MICKEY...

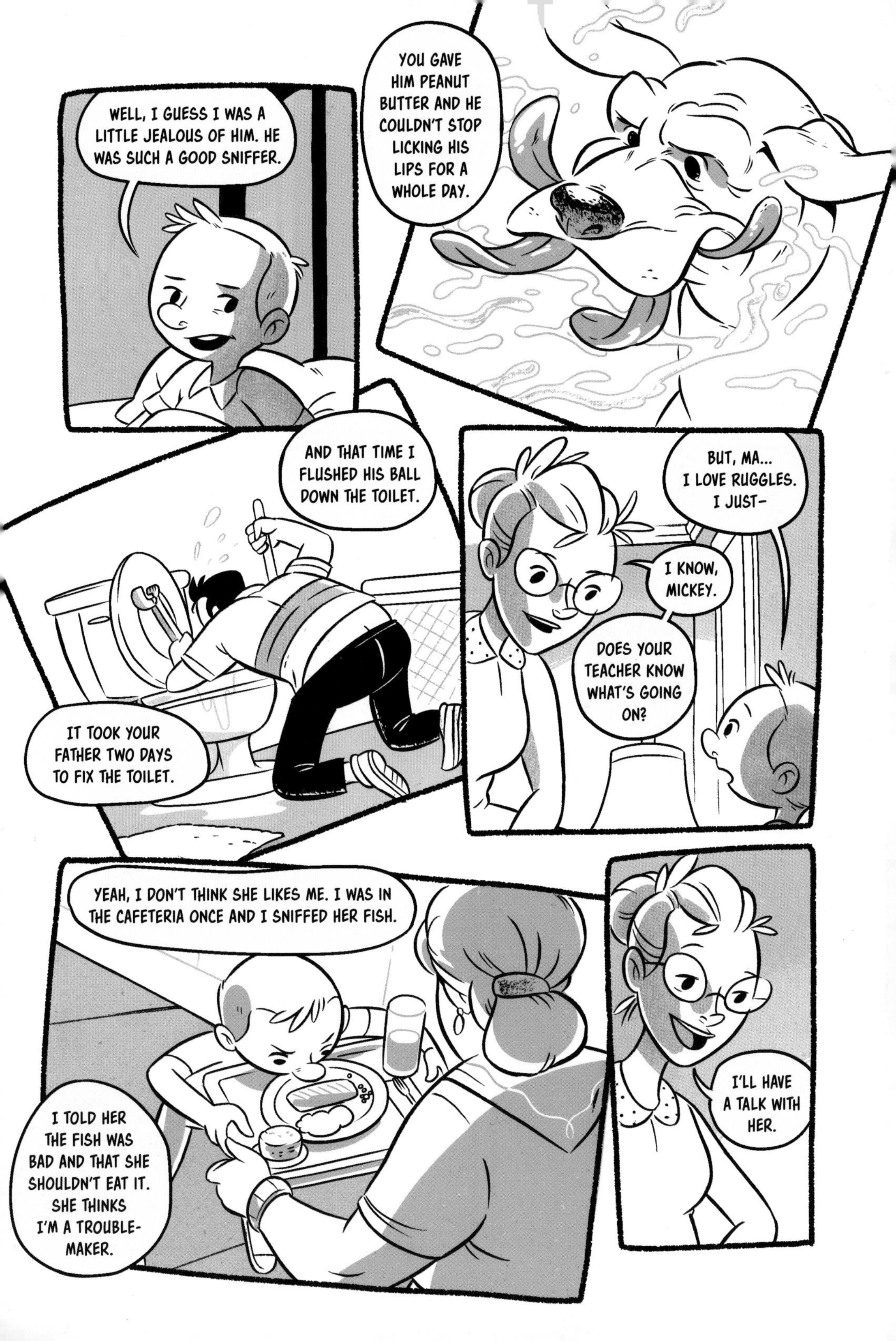
WELL, I GUESS I WAS A LITTLE JEALOUS OF HIM. HE WAS SUCH A GOOD SNIFFER.
YOU GAVE HIM PEANUT BUTTER AND HE COULDN'T STOP LICKING HIS LIPS FOR A WHOLE DAY.
AND THAT TIME I FLUSHED HIS BALL DOWN THE TOILET.
IT TOOK YOUR FATHER TWO DAYS TO FIX THE TOILET.
BUT, MA... I LOVE RUGGLES. I JUST–
I KNOW, MICKEY.
DOES YOUR TEACHER KNOW WHAT'S GOING ON?
YEAH, I DON'T THINK SHE LIKES ME. I WAS IN THE CAFETERIA ONCE AND I SNIFFED HER FISH.
I TOLD HER THE FISH WAS BAD AND THAT SHE SHOULDN'T EAT IT. SHE THINKS I'M A TROUBLE-MAKER.
I'LL HAVE A TALK WITH HER.

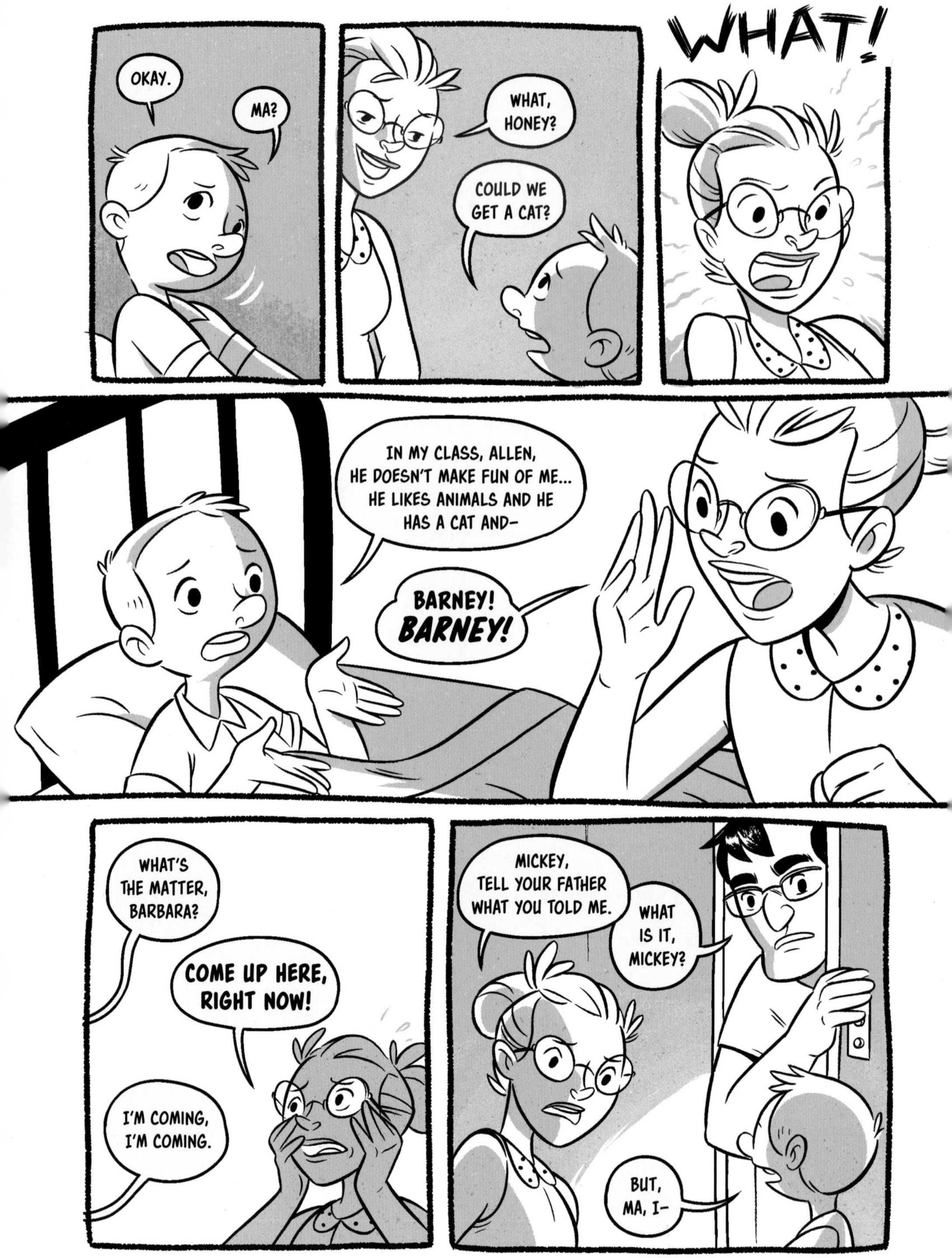
OKAY.
MA?
WHAT, HONEY?
COULD WE GET A CAT?
WHAT!
IN MY CLASS, ALLEN, HE DOESN'T MAKE FUN OF ME... HE LIKES ANIMALS AND HE HAS A CAT AND–
BARNEY! BARNEY!
WHAT'S THE MATTER, BARBARA?
COME UP HERE, RIGHT NOW!
I'M COMING, I'M COMING.
MICKEY, TELL YOUR FATHER WHAT YOU TOLD ME.
WHAT IS IT, MICKEY?
BUT, MA, I–

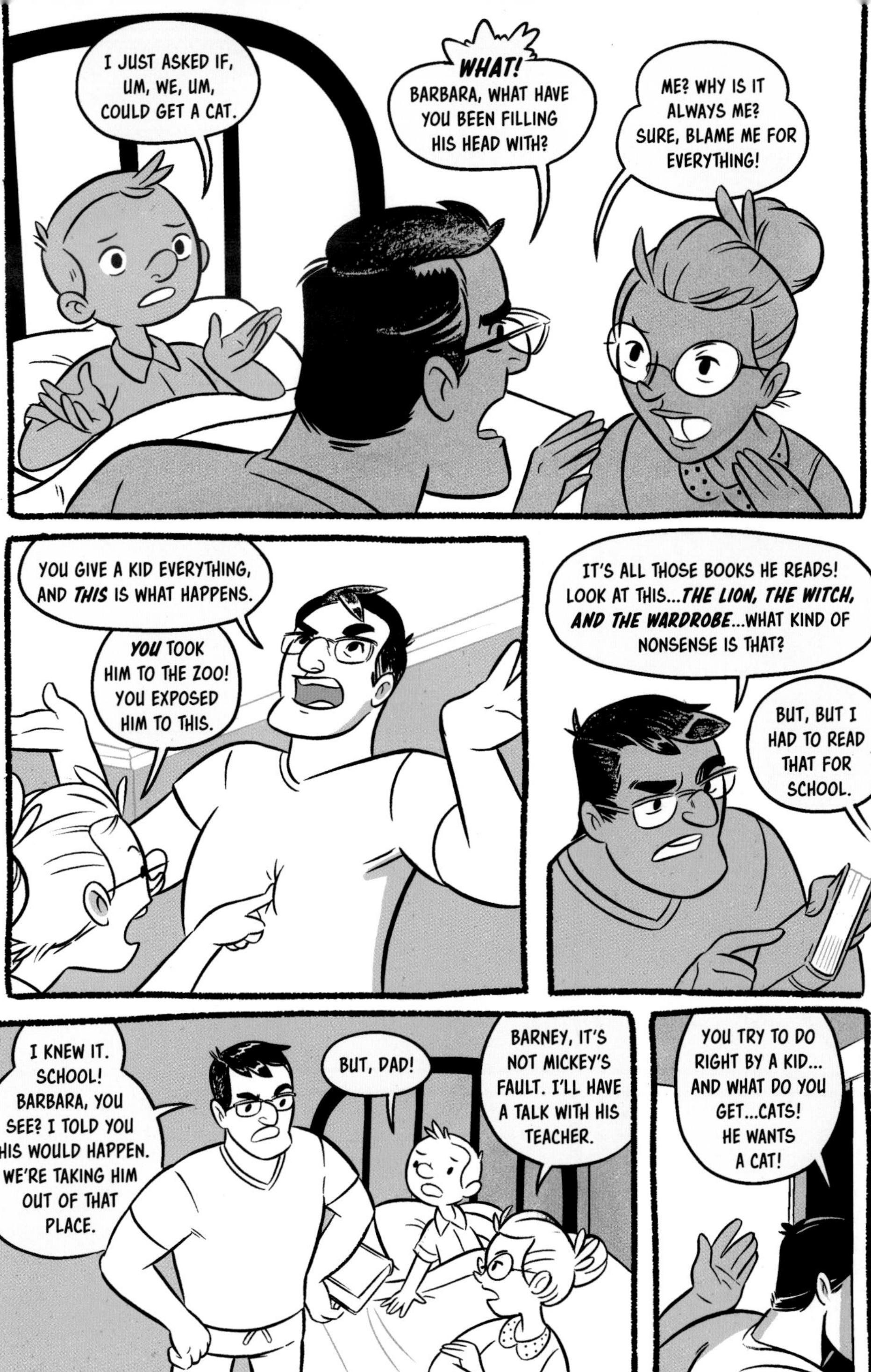
I JUST ASKED IF, UM, WE, UM, COULD GET A CAT.
WHAT! BARBARA, WHAT HAVE YOU BEEN FILLING HIS HEAD WITH?
ME? WHY IS IT ALWAYS ME? SURE, BLAME ME FOR EVERYTHING!
YOU GIVE A KID EVERYTHING, AND *THIS* IS WHAT HAPPENS.
YOU TOOK HIM TO THE ZOO! YOU EXPOSED HIM TO THIS.
IT'S ALL THOSE BOOKS HE READS! LOOK AT THIS...*THE LION, THE WITCH, AND THE WARDROBE*...WHAT KIND OF NONSENSE IS THAT?
BUT, BUT I HAD TO READ THAT FOR SCHOOL.
I KNEW IT. SCHOOL! BARBARA, YOU SEE? I TOLD YOU THIS WOULD HAPPEN. WE'RE TAKING HIM OUT OF THAT PLACE.
BUT, DAD!
BARNEY, IT'S NOT MICKEY'S FAULT. I'LL HAVE A TALK WITH HIS TEACHER.
YOU TRY TO DO RIGHT BY A KID... AND WHAT DO YOU GET...CATS! HE WANTS A CAT!

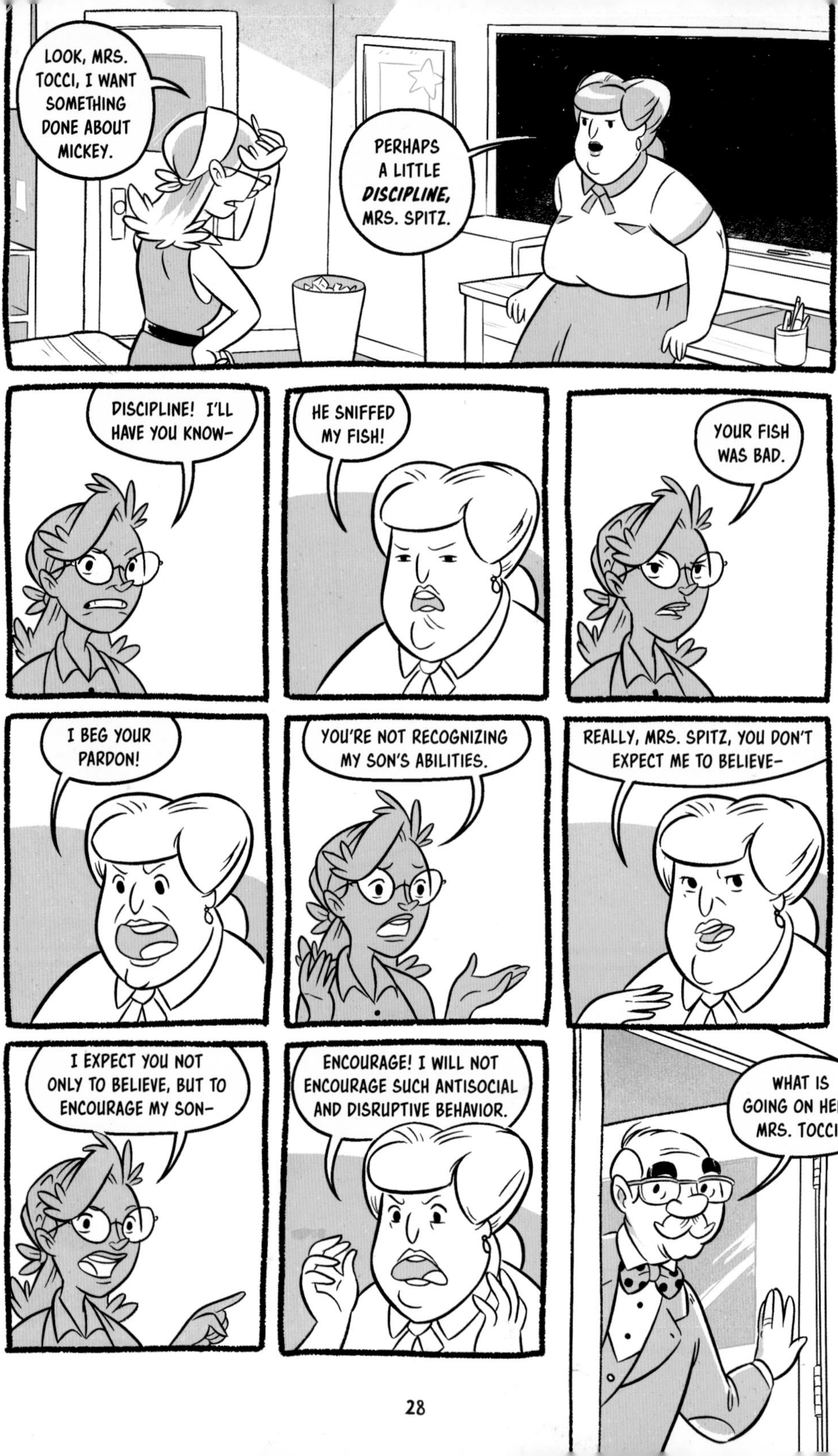
LOOK, MRS. TOCCI, I WANT SOMETHING DONE ABOUT MICKEY.
PERHAPS A LITTLE ***DISCIPLINE,*** MRS. SPITZ.
DISCIPLINE! I'LL HAVE YOU KNOW–
HE SNIFFED MY FISH!
YOUR FISH WAS BAD.
I BEG YOUR PARDON!
YOU'RE NOT RECOGNIZING MY SON'S ABILITIES.
REALLY, MRS. SPITZ, YOU DON'T EXPECT ME TO BELIEVE–
I EXPECT YOU NOT ONLY TO BELIEVE, BUT TO ENCOURAGE MY SON–
ENCOURAGE! I WILL NOT ENCOURAGE SUCH ANTISOCIAL AND DISRUPTIVE BEHAVIOR.
WHAT IS GOING ON HERE, MRS. TOCCI?

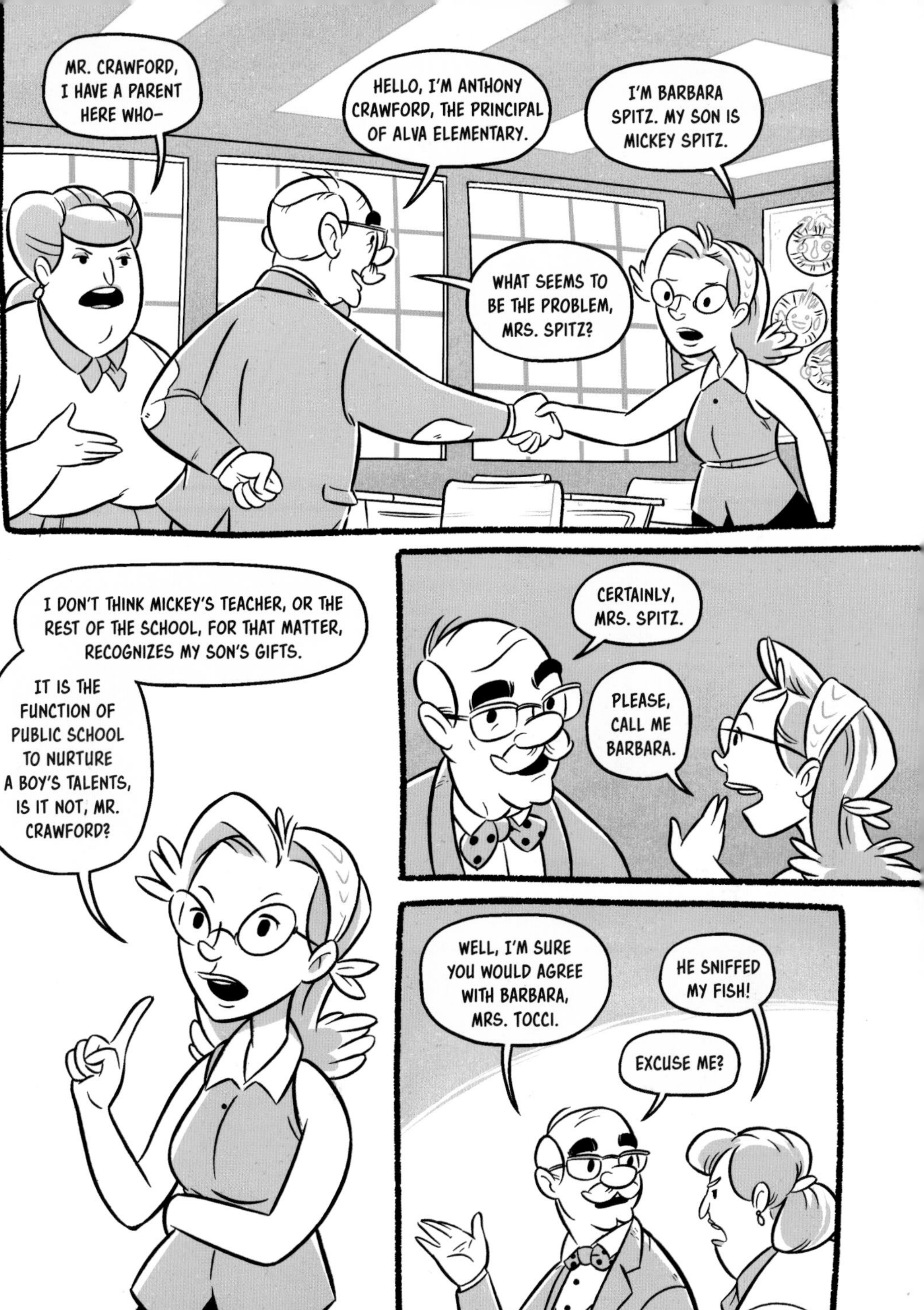
MR. CRAWFORD, I HAVE A PARENT HERE WHO–
HELLO, I'M ANTHONY CRAWFORD, THE PRINCIPAL OF ALVA ELEMENTARY.
I'M BARBARA SPITZ. MY SON IS MICKEY SPITZ.
WHAT SEEMS TO BE THE PROBLEM, MRS. SPITZ?
I DON'T THINK MICKEY'S TEACHER, OR THE REST OF THE SCHOOL, FOR THAT MATTER, RECOGNIZES MY SON'S GIFTS.
IT IS THE FUNCTION OF PUBLIC SCHOOL TO NURTURE A BOY'S TALENTS, IS IT NOT, MR. CRAWFORD?
CERTAINLY, MRS. SPITZ.
PLEASE, CALL ME BARBARA.
WELL, I'M SURE YOU WOULD AGREE WITH BARBARA, MRS. TOCCI.
HE SNIFFED MY FISH!
EXCUSE ME?

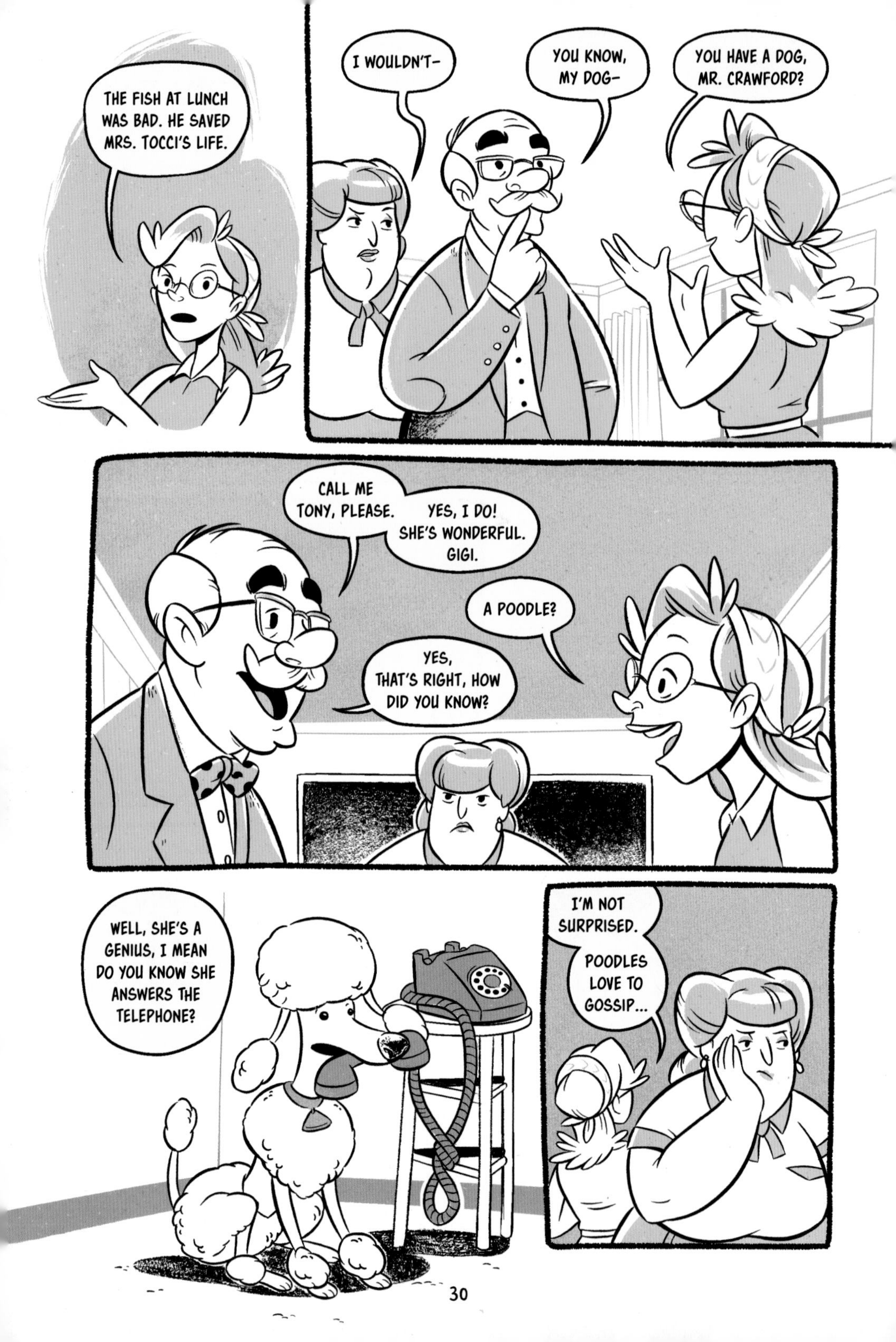
THE FISH AT LUNCH WAS BAD. HE SAVED MRS. TOCCI'S LIFE.
I WOULDN'T-
YOU KNOW, MY DOG-
YOU HAVE A DOG, MR. CRAWFORD?
CALL ME TONY, PLEASE.
YES, I DO! SHE'S WONDERFUL. GIGI.
A POODLE?
YES, THAT'S RIGHT, HOW DID YOU KNOW?
WELL, SHE'S A GENIUS, I MEAN DO YOU KNOW SHE ANSWERS THE TELEPHONE?
I'M NOT SURPRISED.
POODLES LOVE TO GOSSIP...

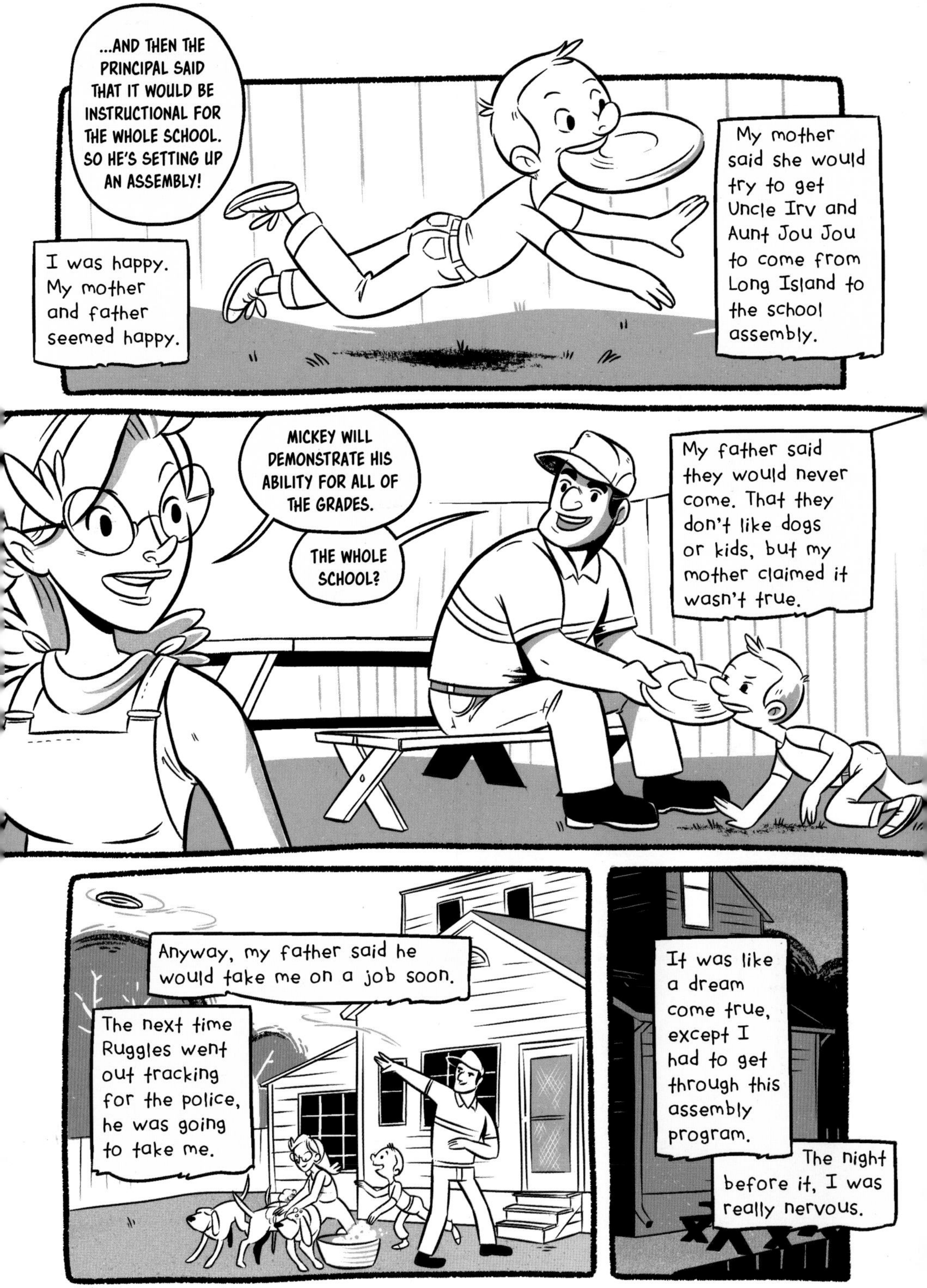
...AND THEN THE PRINCIPAL SAID THAT IT WOULD BE INSTRUCTIONAL FOR THE WHOLE SCHOOL. SO HE'S SETTING UP AN ASSEMBLY!
I was happy. My mother and father seemed happy.
My mother said she would try to get Uncle Irv and Aunt Jou Jou to come from Long Island to the school assembly.
MICKEY WILL DEMONSTRATE HIS ABILITY FOR ALL OF THE GRADES.
THE WHOLE SCHOOL?
My father said they would never come. That they don't like dogs or kids, but my mother claimed it wasn't true.
Anyway, my father said he would take me on a job soon.
The next time Ruggles went out tracking for the police, he was going to take me.
It was like a dream come true, except I had to get through this assembly program.
The night before it, I was really nervous.

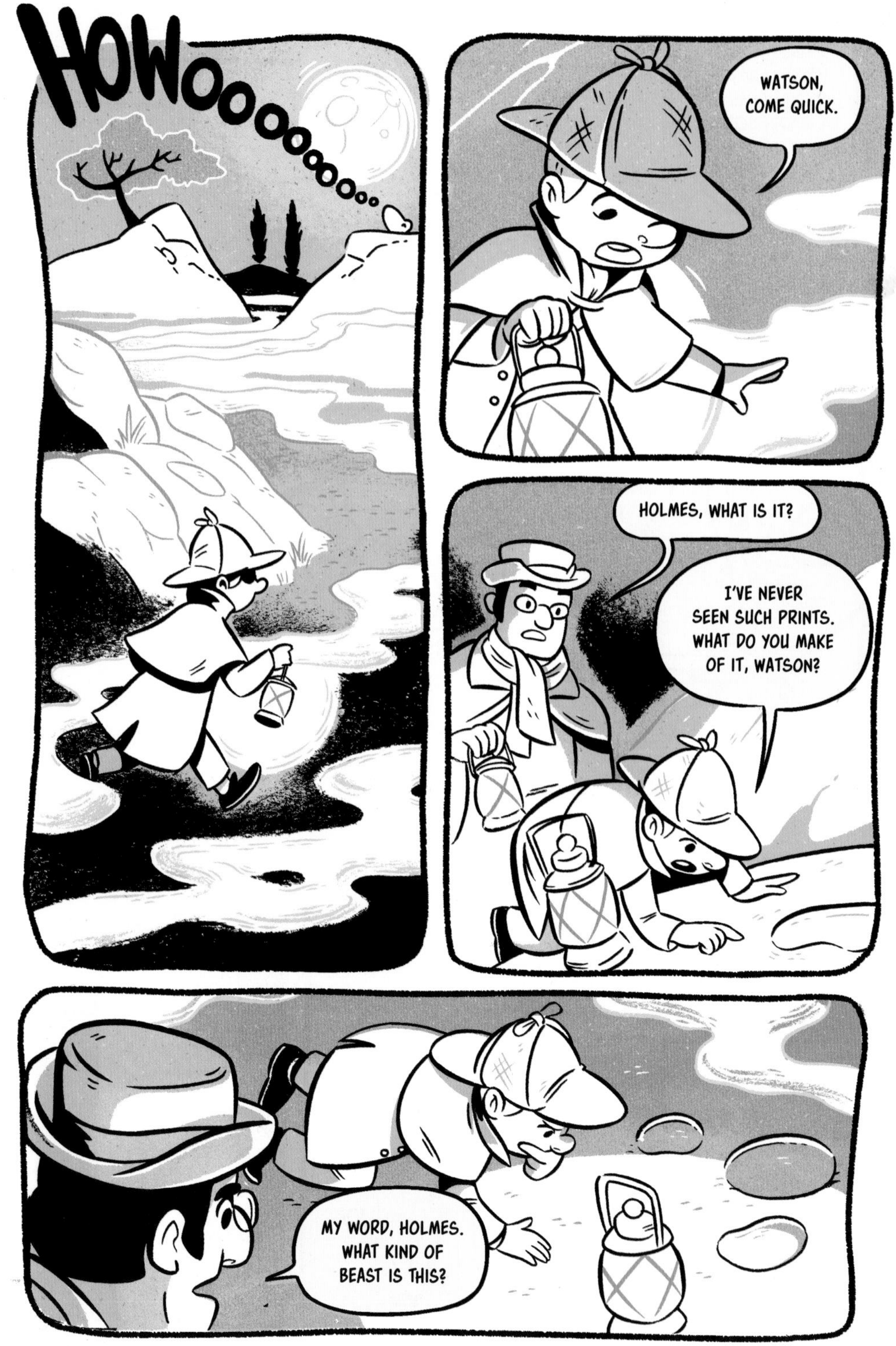
HOWOOOOOOOOOo
WATSON, COME QUICK.
HOLMES, WHAT IS IT?
I'VE NEVER SEEN SUCH PRINTS. WHAT DO YOU MAKE OF IT, WATSON?
MY WORD, HOLMES. WHAT KIND OF BEAST IS THIS?

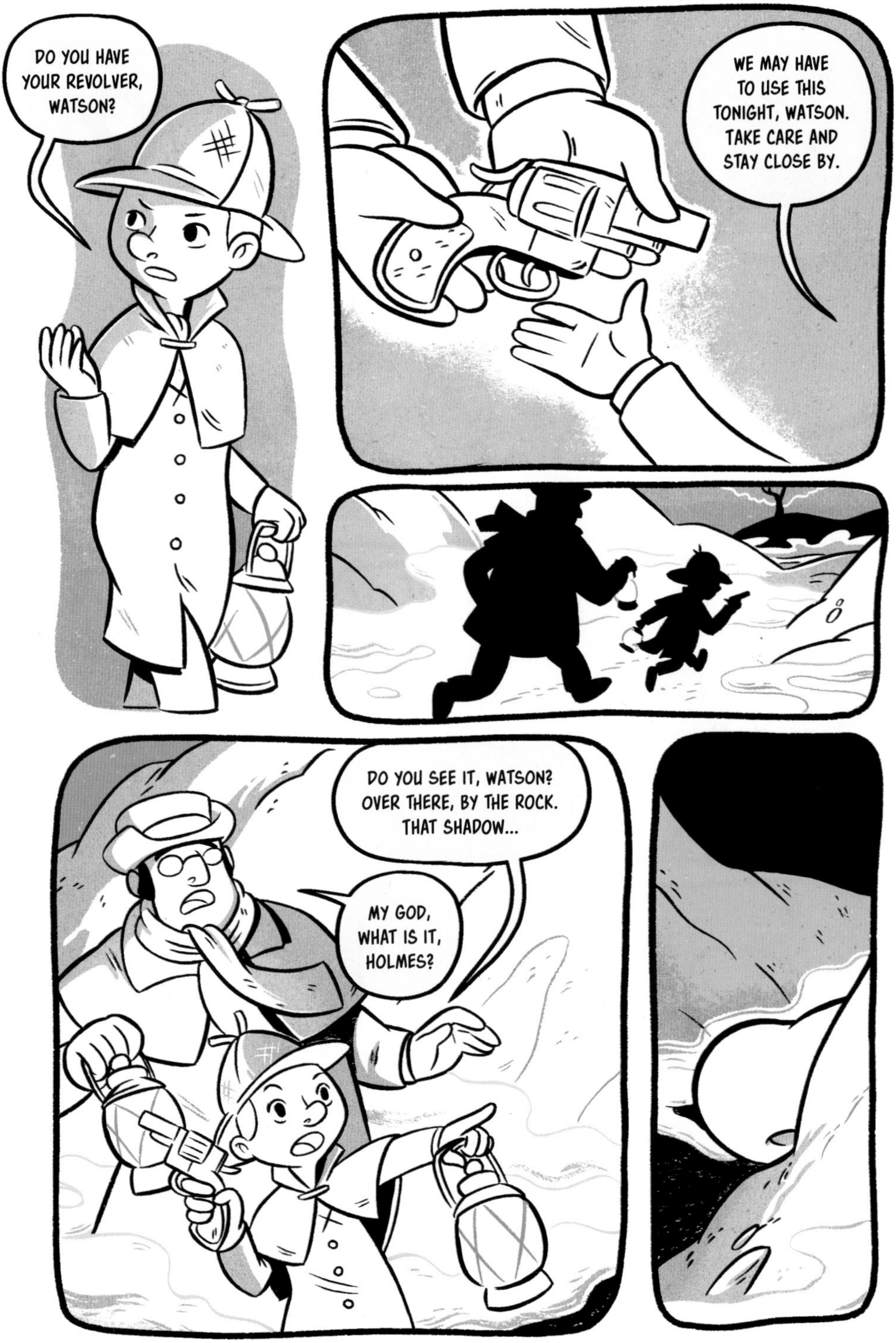
DO YOU HAVE YOUR REVOLVER, WATSON?
WE MAY HAVE TO USE THIS TONIGHT, WATSON. TAKE CARE AND STAY CLOSE BY.
DO YOU SEE IT, WATSON? OVER THERE, BY THE ROCK. THAT SHADOW...
MY GOD, WHAT IS IT, HOLMES?

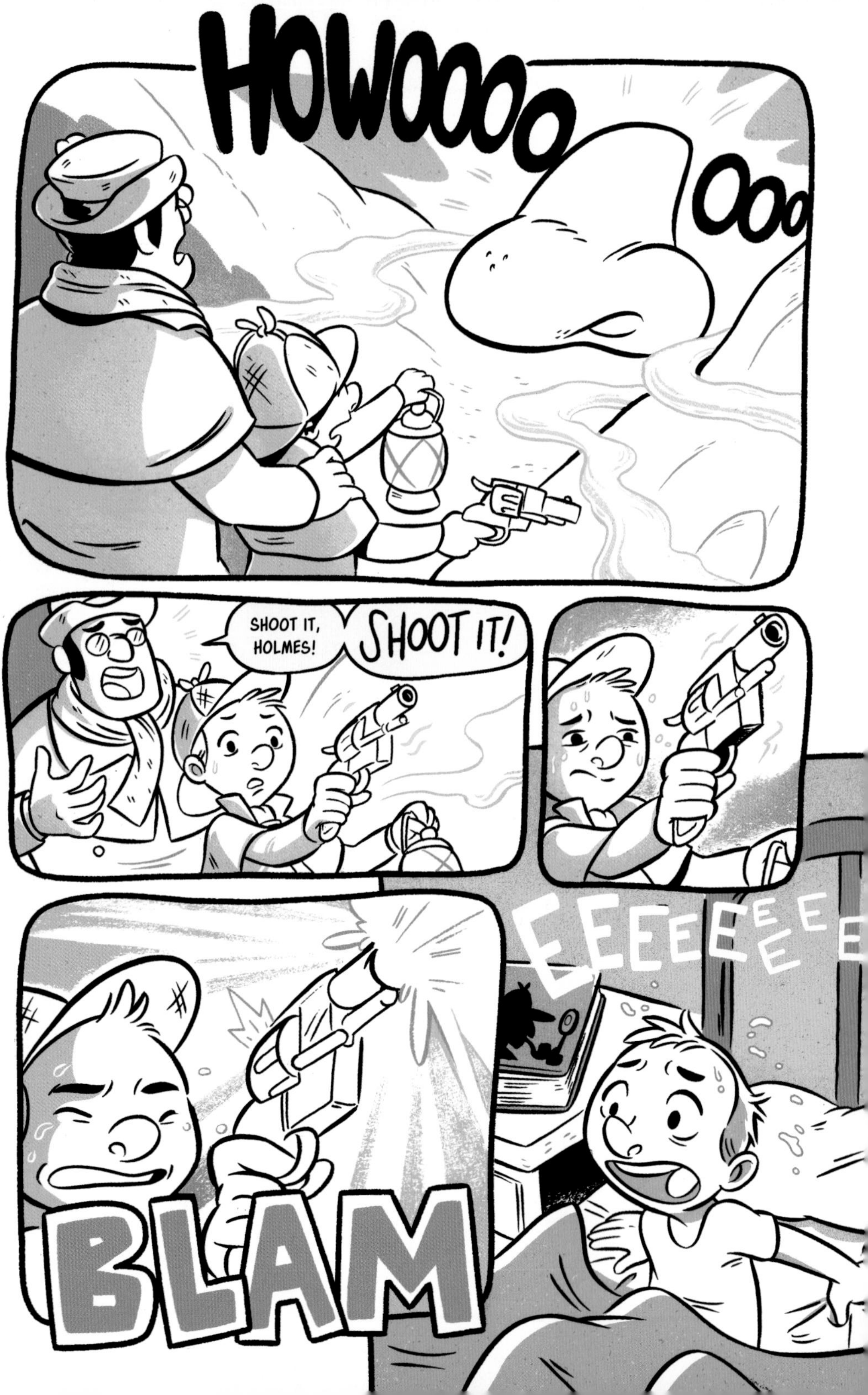
HOWOOOOOOOO
SHOOT IT, HOLMES!
SHOOT IT!
EEEEEEEEE
BLAM

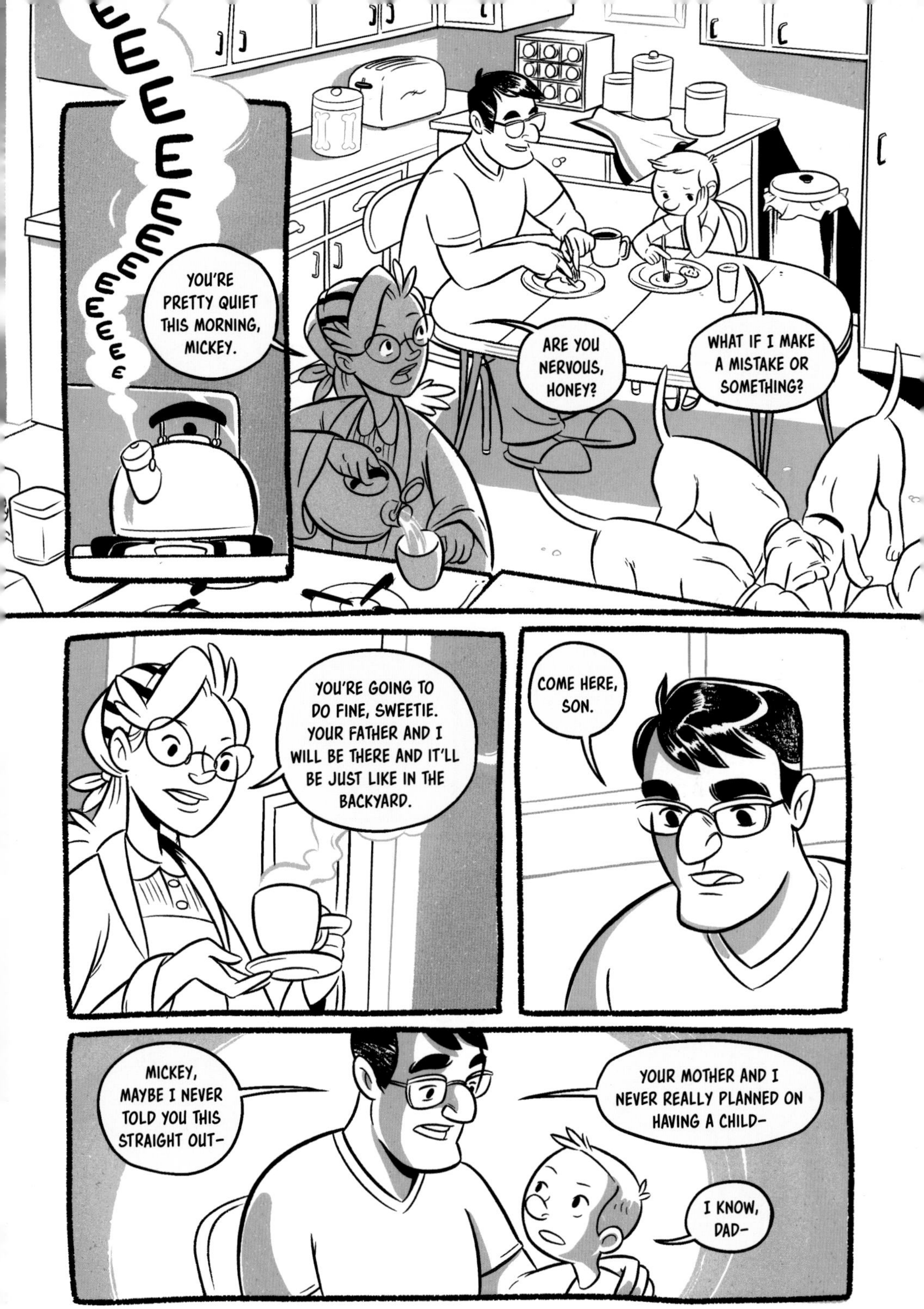
EEEEEEEEEEEEEEE
YOU'RE PRETTY QUIET THIS MORNING, MICKEY.
ARE YOU NERVOUS, HONEY?
WHAT IF I MAKE A MISTAKE OR SOMETHING?
YOU'RE GOING TO DO FINE, SWEETIE. YOUR FATHER AND I WILL BE THERE AND IT'LL BE JUST LIKE IN THE BACKYARD.
COME HERE, SON.
MICKEY, MAYBE I NEVER TOLD YOU THIS STRAIGHT OUT-
YOUR MOTHER AND I NEVER REALLY PLANNED ON HAVING A CHILD-
I KNOW, DAD-

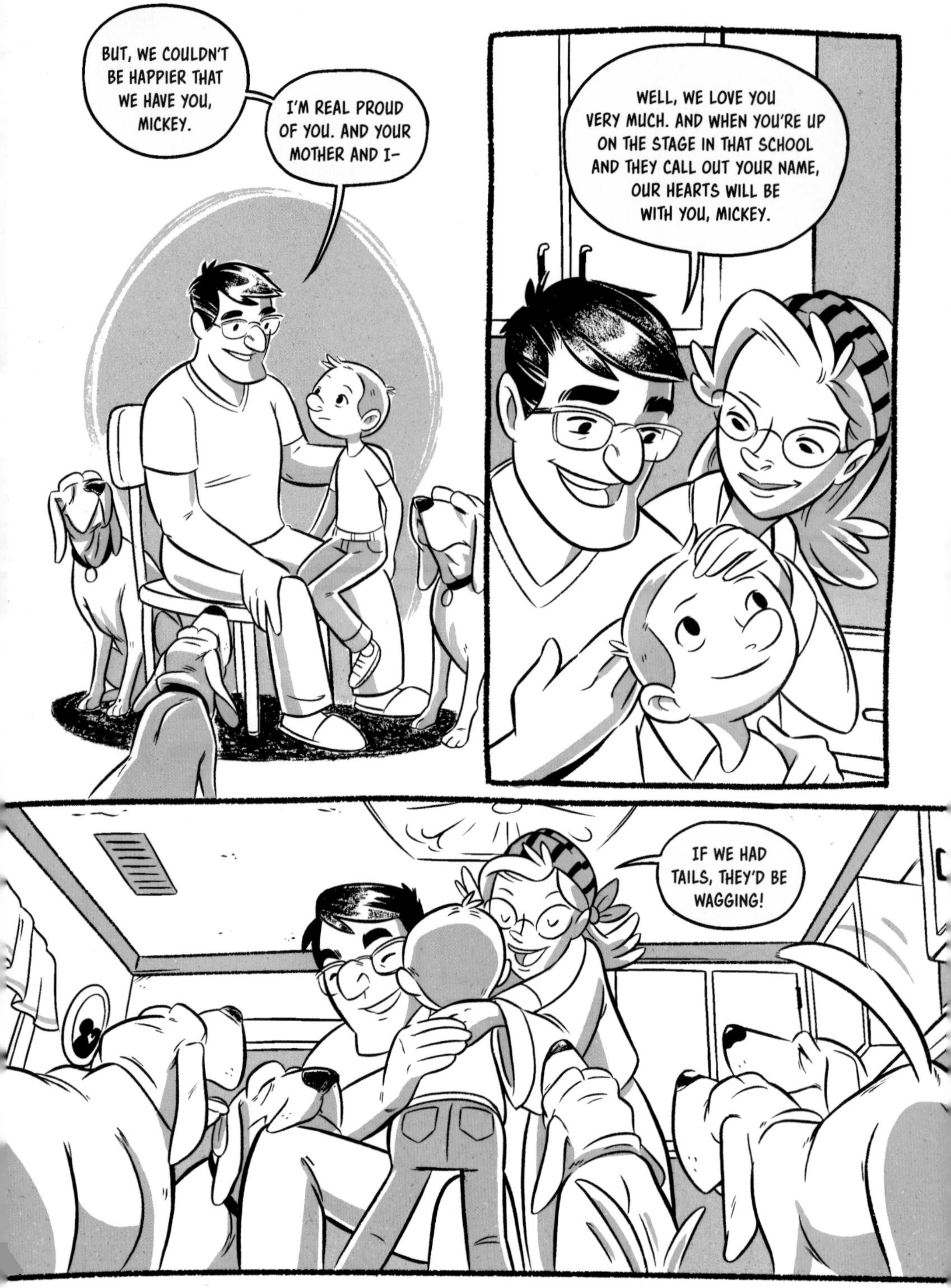
BUT, WE COULDN'T BE HAPPIER THAT WE HAVE YOU, MICKEY.
I'M REAL PROUD OF YOU. AND YOUR MOTHER AND I-
WELL, WE LOVE YOU VERY MUCH. AND WHEN YOU'RE UP ON THE STAGE IN THAT SCHOOL AND THEY CALL OUT YOUR NAME, OUR HEARTS WILL BE WITH YOU, MICKEY.
IF WE HAD TAILS, THEY'D BE WAGGING!

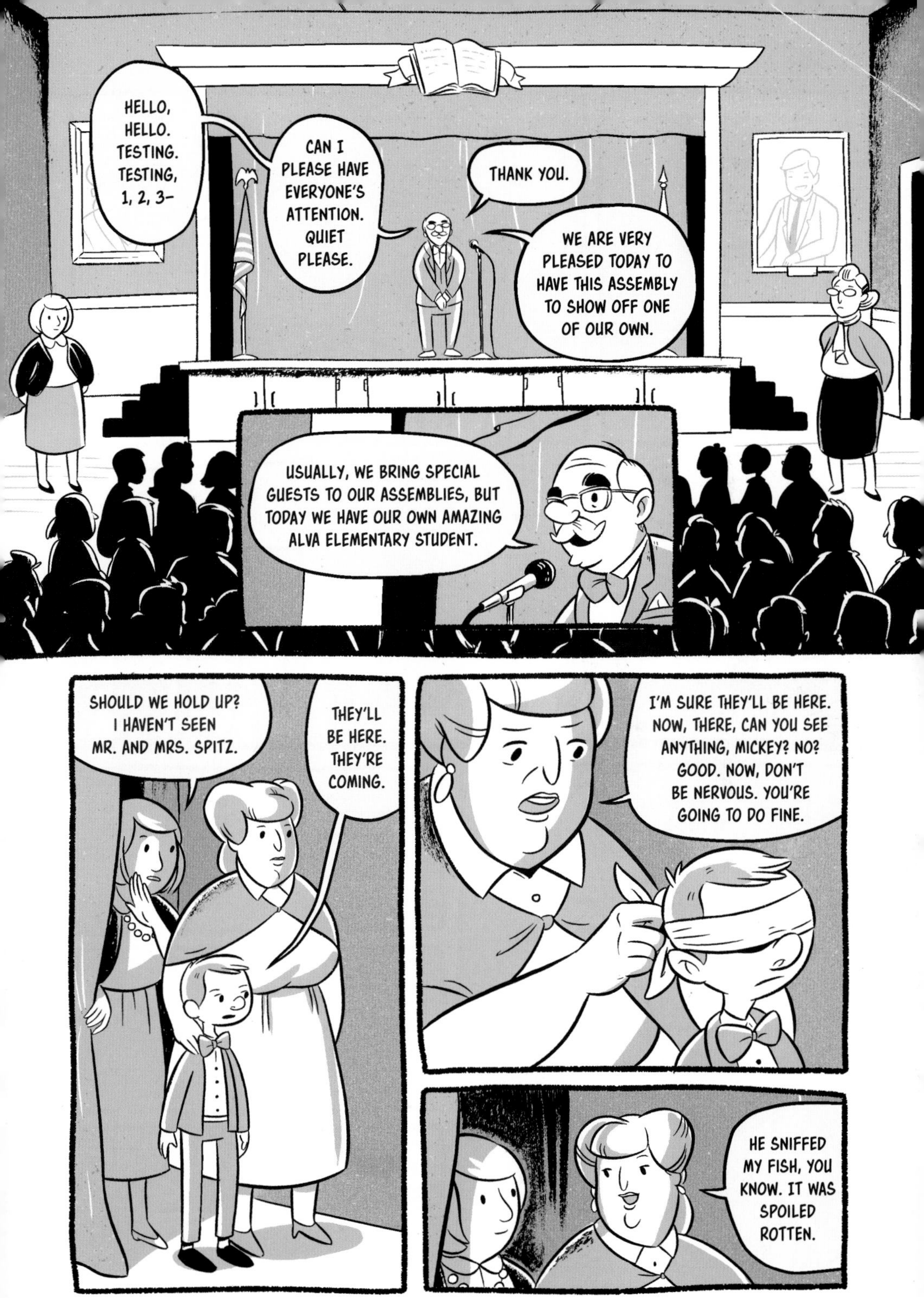

HELLO, HELLO. TESTING. TESTING, 1, 2, 3–
CAN I PLEASE HAVE EVERYONE'S ATTENTION. QUIET PLEASE.
THANK YOU.
WE ARE VERY PLEASED TODAY TO HAVE THIS ASSEMBLY TO SHOW OFF ONE OF OUR OWN.
USUALLY, WE BRING SPECIAL GUESTS TO OUR ASSEMBLIES, BUT TODAY WE HAVE OUR OWN AMAZING ALVA ELEMENTARY STUDENT.
SHOULD WE HOLD UP? I HAVEN'T SEEN MR. AND MRS. SPITZ.
THEY'LL BE HERE. THEY'RE COMING.
I'M SURE THEY'LL BE HERE. NOW, THERE, CAN YOU SEE ANYTHING, MICKEY? NO? GOOD. NOW, DON'T BE NERVOUS. YOU'RE GOING TO DO FINE.
HE SNIFFED MY FISH, YOU KNOW. IT WAS SPOILED ROTTEN.

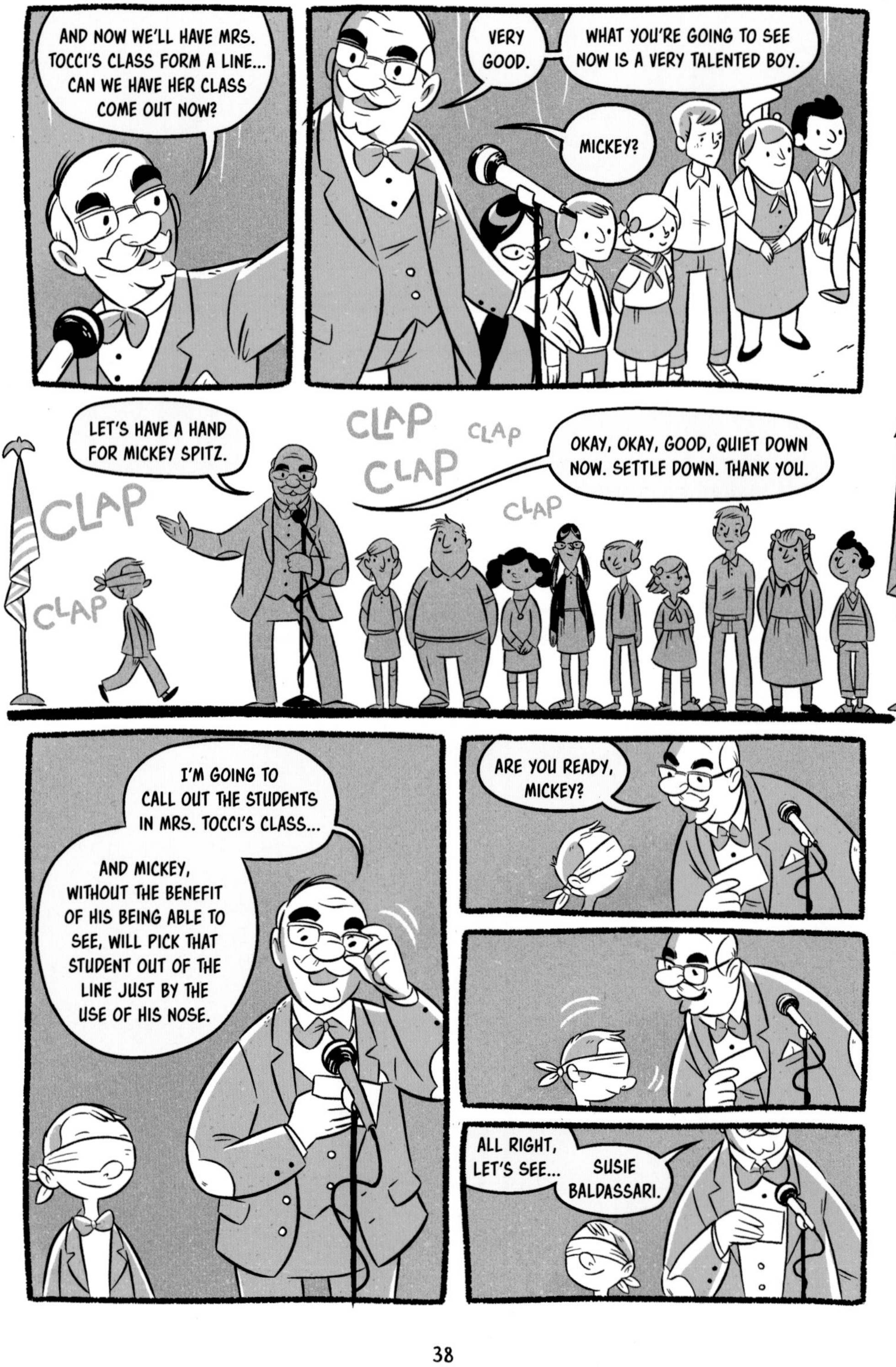
AND NOW WE'LL HAVE MRS. TOCCI'S CLASS FORM A LINE... CAN WE HAVE HER CLASS COME OUT NOW?
VERY GOOD.
WHAT YOU'RE GOING TO SEE NOW IS A VERY TALENTED BOY.
MICKEY?
LET'S HAVE A HAND FOR MICKEY SPITZ.
CLAP
CLAP
CLAP
CLAP
CLAP
CLAP
OKAY, OKAY, GOOD, QUIET DOWN NOW. SETTLE DOWN. THANK YOU.
I'M GOING TO CALL OUT THE STUDENTS IN MRS. TOCCI'S CLASS...
AND MICKEY, WITHOUT THE BENEFIT OF HIS BEING ABLE TO SEE, WILL PICK THAT STUDENT OUT OF THE LINE JUST BY THE USE OF HIS NOSE.
ARE YOU READY, MICKEY?
ALL RIGHT, LET'S SEE...
SUSIE BALDASSARI.

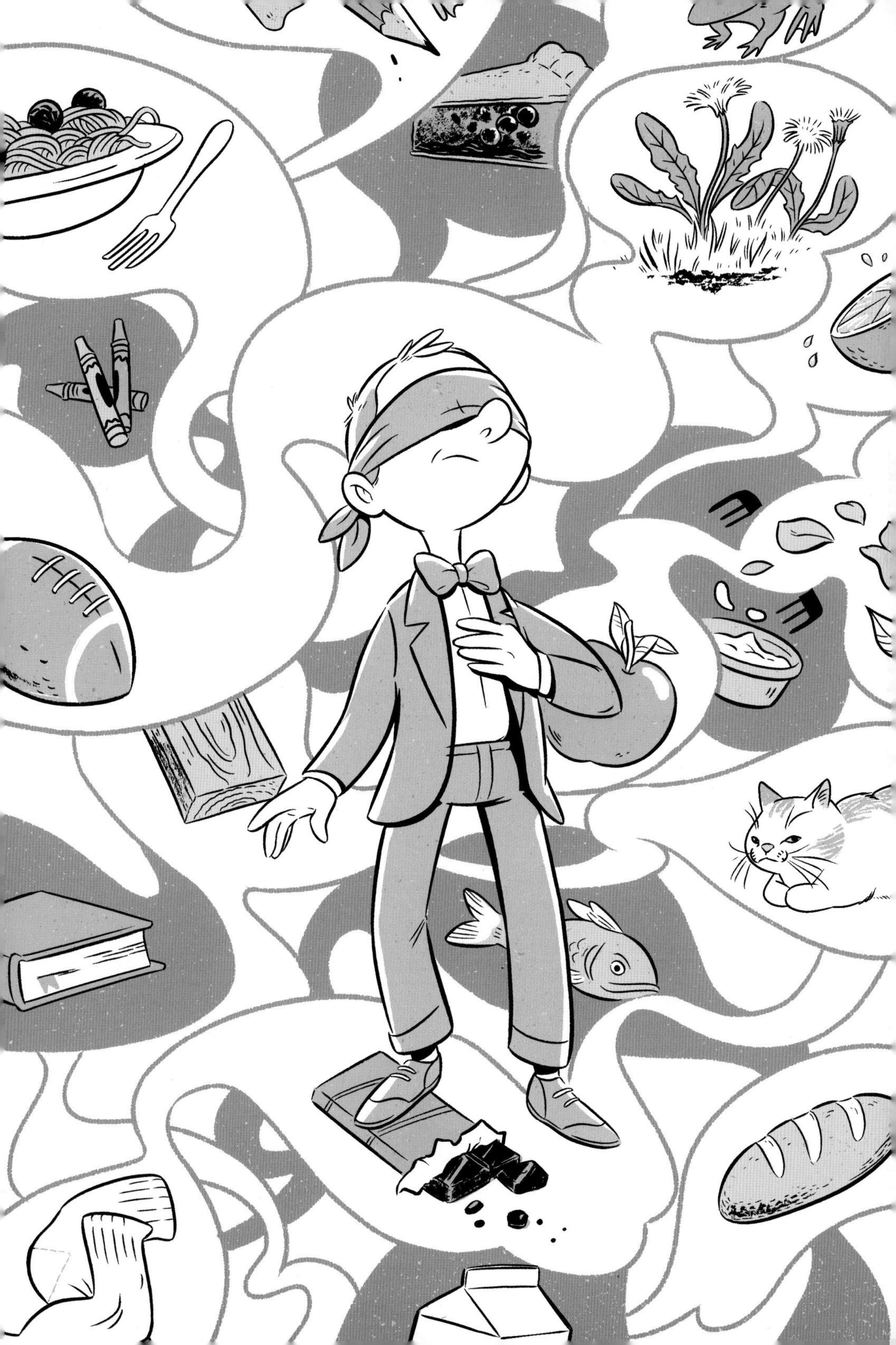

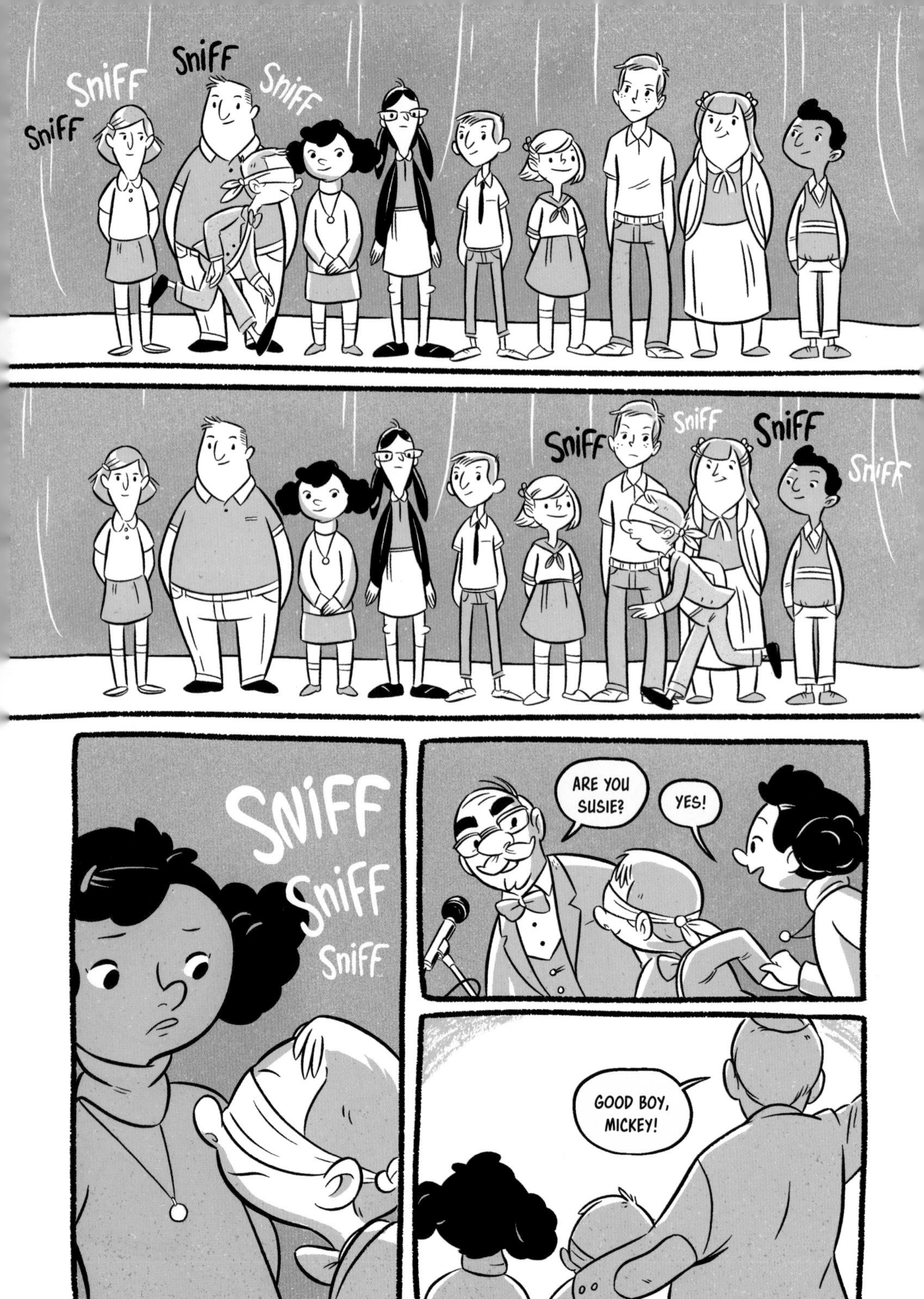
SNIFF
SNIFF
SNIFF
SNIFF
SNIFF
SNIFF
SNIFF
SNIFF
SNIFF
SNIFF
SNIFF
ARE YOU SUSIE?
YES!
GOOD BOY, MICKEY!

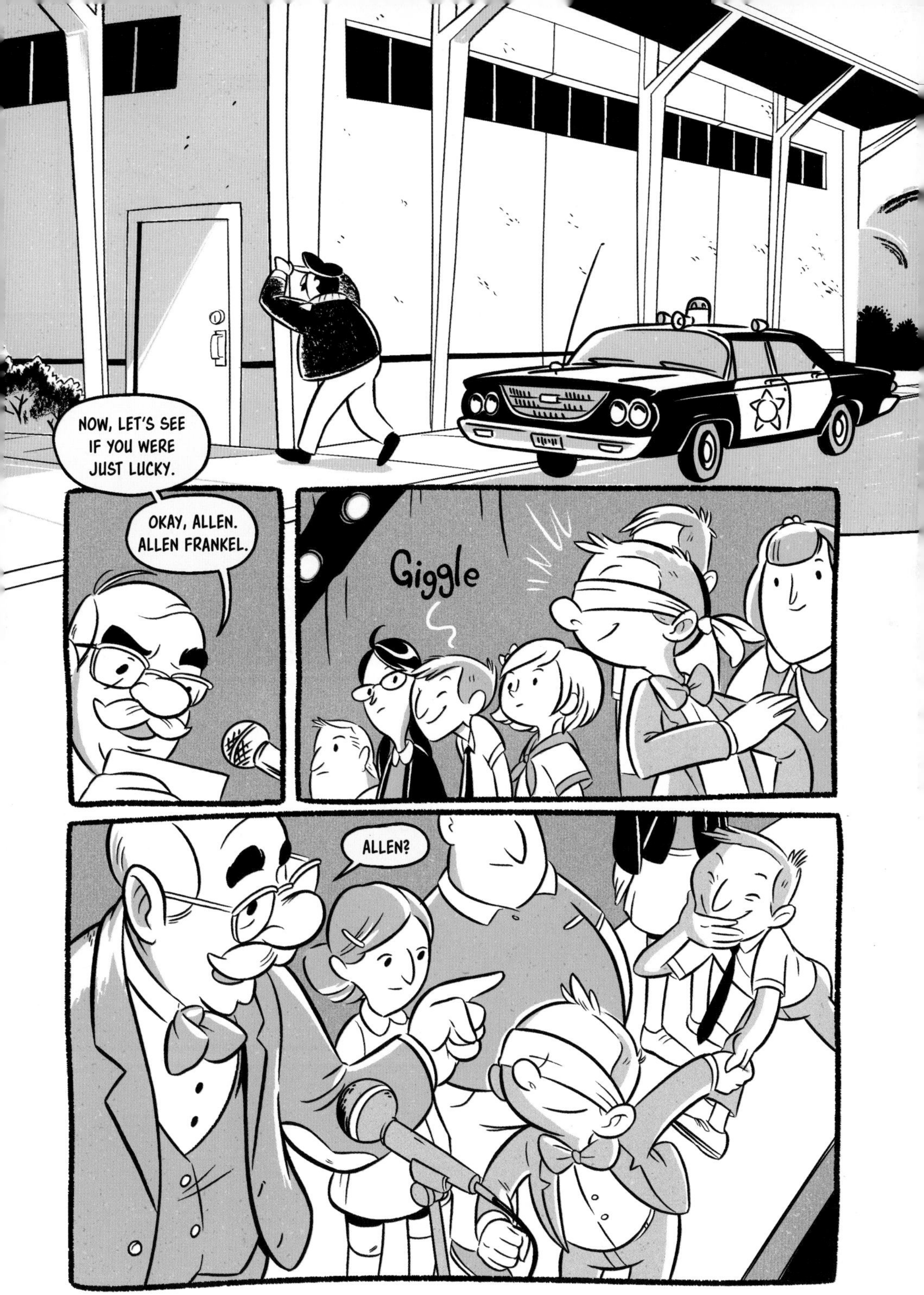
NOW, LET'S SEE IF YOU WERE JUST LUCKY.
OKAY, ALLEN. ALLEN FRANKEL.
Giggle
ALLEN?

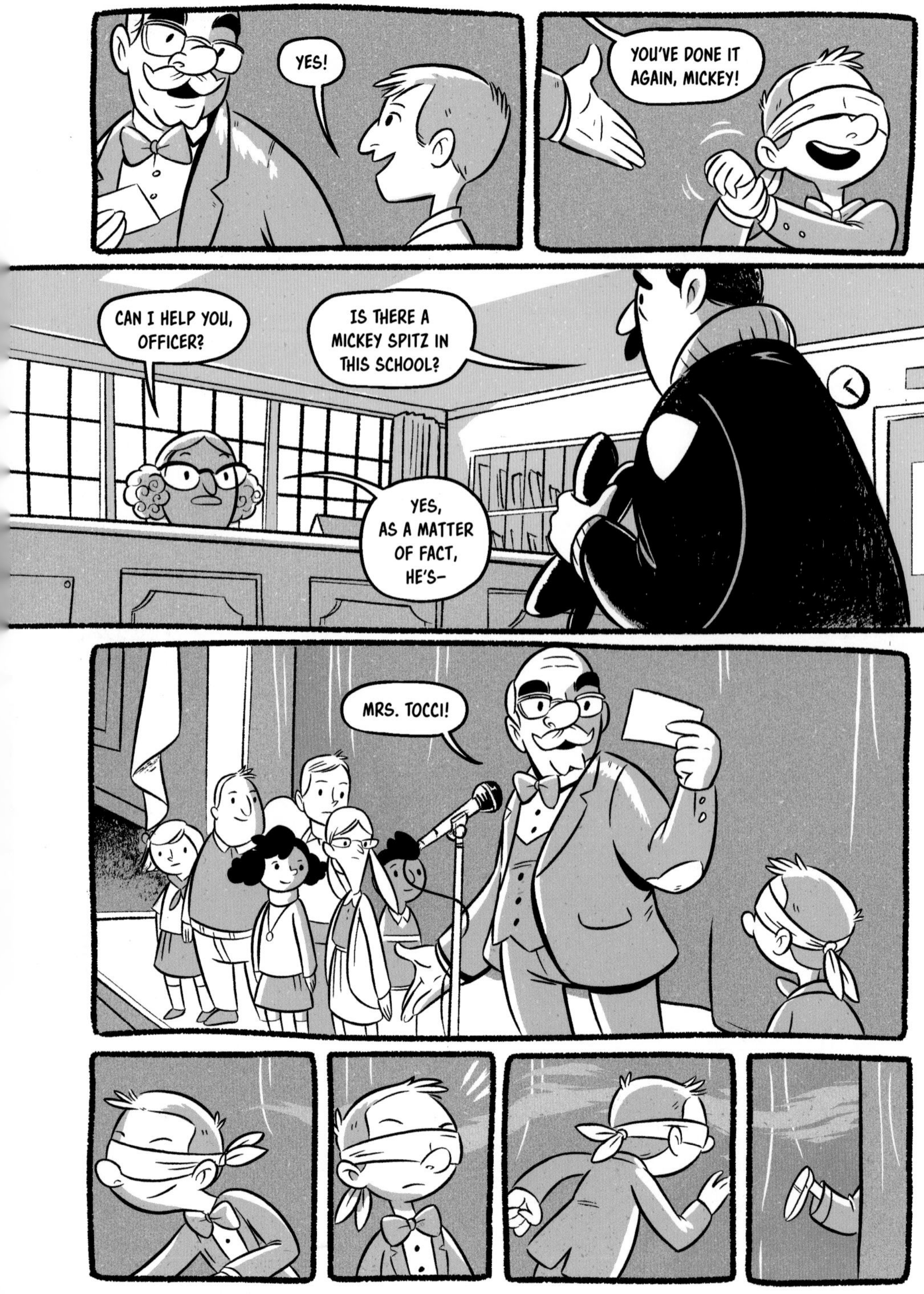
YES!
YOU'VE DONE IT AGAIN, MICKEY!
CAN I HELP YOU, OFFICER?
IS THERE A MICKEY SPITZ IN THIS SCHOOL?
YES, AS A MATTER OF FACT, HE'S–
MRS. TOCCI!

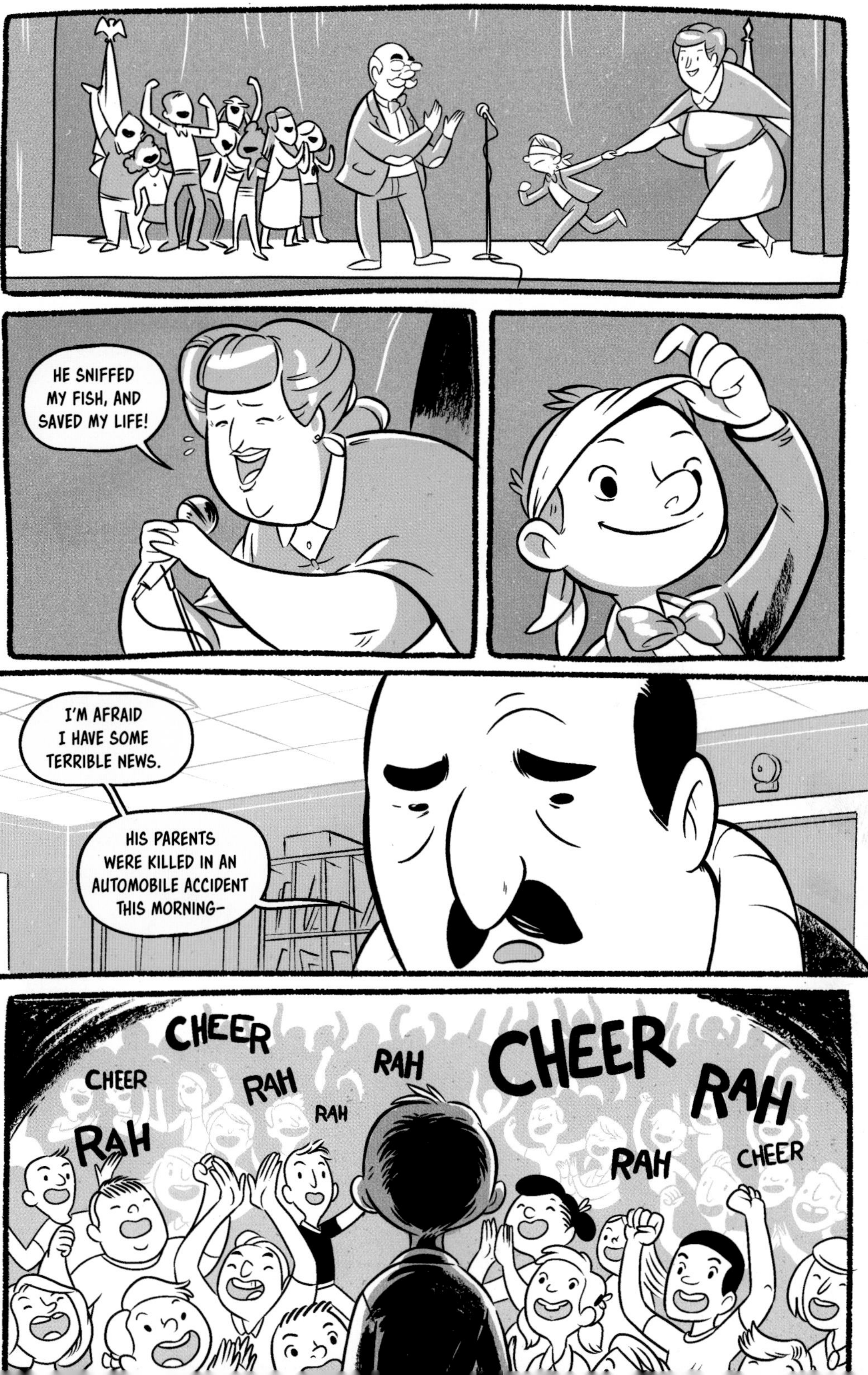
HE SNIFFED MY FISH, AND SAVED MY LIFE!
I'M AFRAID I HAVE SOME TERRIBLE NEWS.
HIS PARENTS WERE KILLED IN AN AUTOMOBILE ACCIDENT THIS MORNING–
CHEER
CHEER
RAH
RAH
RAH
RAH
CHEER
RAH
RAH
CHEER

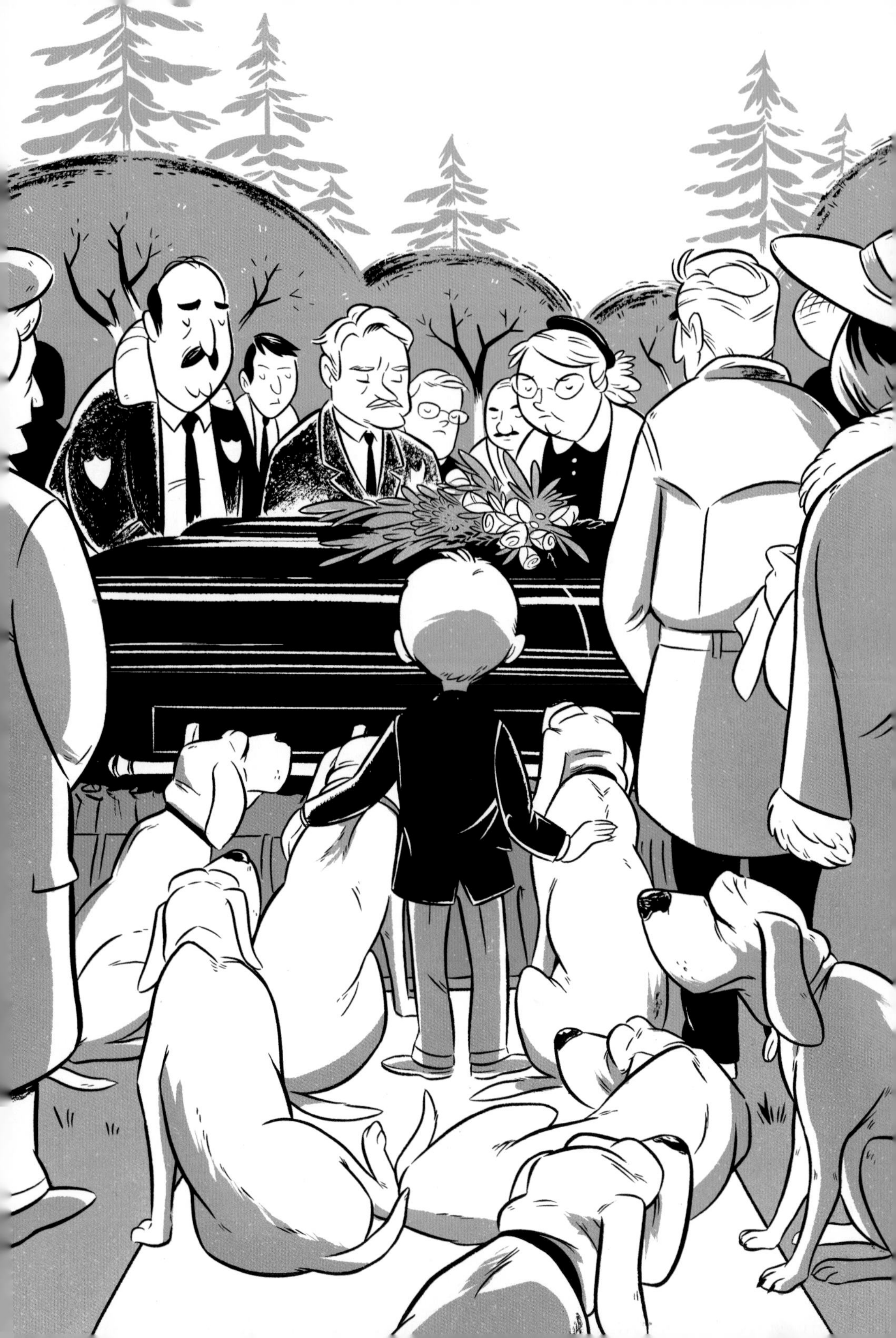

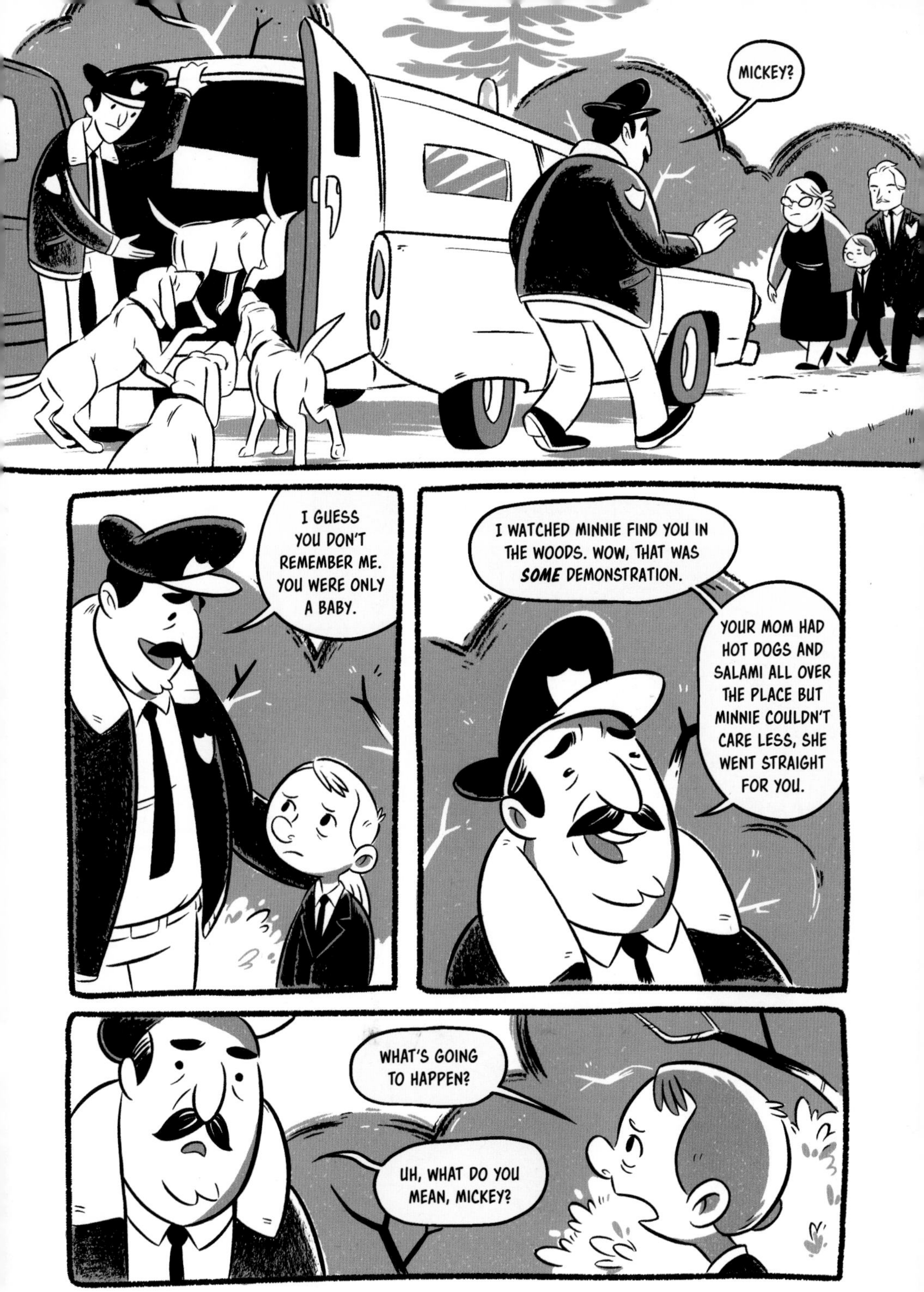
MICKEY?
I GUESS YOU DON'T REMEMBER ME. YOU WERE ONLY A BABY.
I WATCHED MINNIE FIND YOU IN THE WOODS. WOW, THAT WAS *SOME* DEMONSTRATION.
YOUR MOM HAD HOT DOGS AND SALAMI ALL OVER THE PLACE BUT MINNIE COULDN'T CARE LESS, SHE WENT STRAIGHT FOR YOU.
WHAT'S GOING TO HAPPEN?
UH, WHAT DO YOU MEAN, MICKEY?

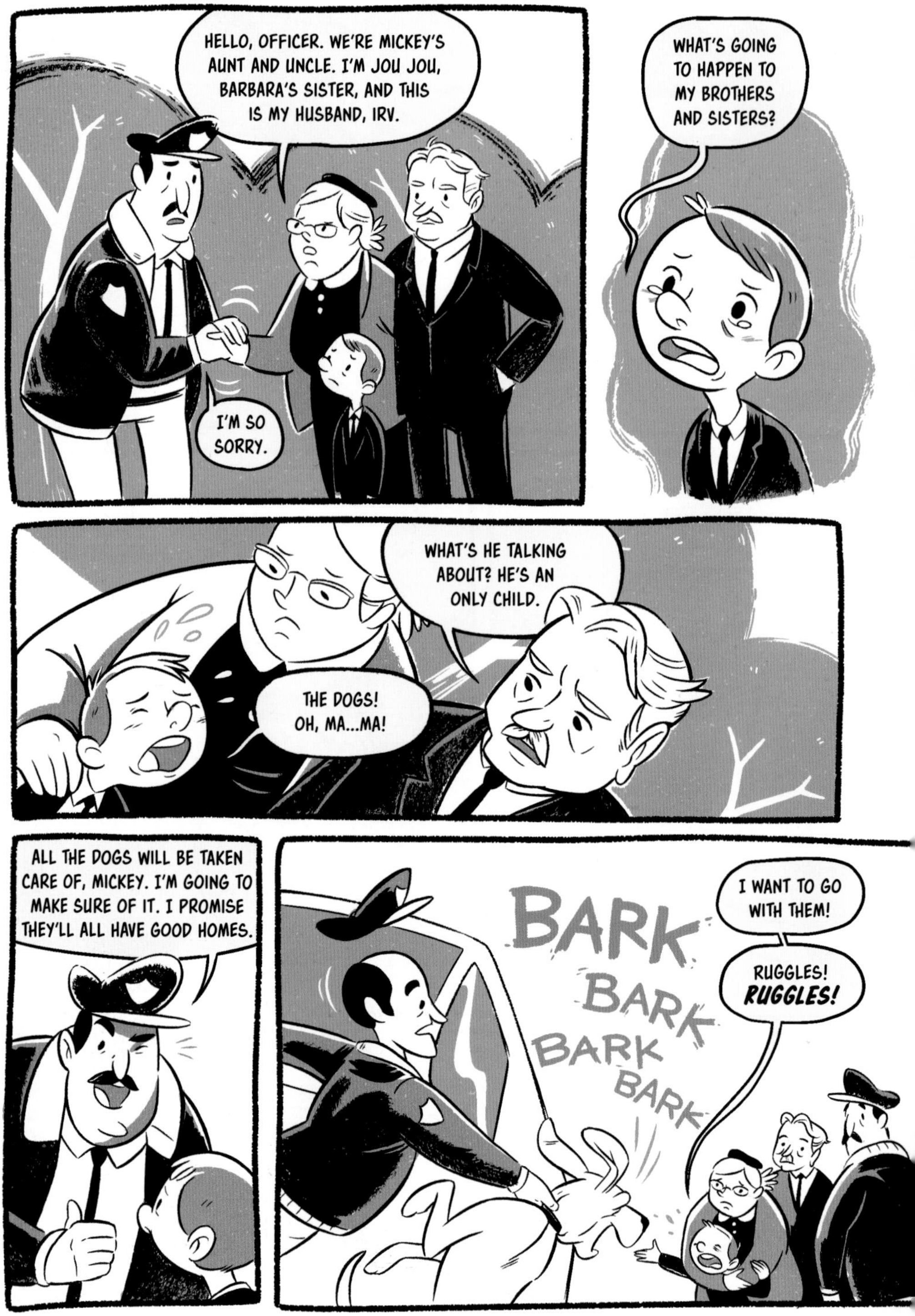

HELLO, OFFICER. WE'RE MICKEY'S AUNT AND UNCLE. I'M JOU JOU, BARBARA'S SISTER, AND THIS IS MY HUSBAND, IRV.
I'M SO SORRY.
WHAT'S GOING TO HAPPEN TO MY BROTHERS AND SISTERS?
WHAT'S HE TALKING ABOUT? HE'S AN ONLY CHILD.
THE DOGS! OH, MA...MA!
ALL THE DOGS WILL BE TAKEN CARE OF, MICKEY. I'M GOING TO MAKE SURE OF IT. I PROMISE THEY'LL ALL HAVE GOOD HOMES.
BARK
BARK
BARK
BARK
I WANT TO GO WITH THEM!
RUGGLES! ***RUGGLES!***

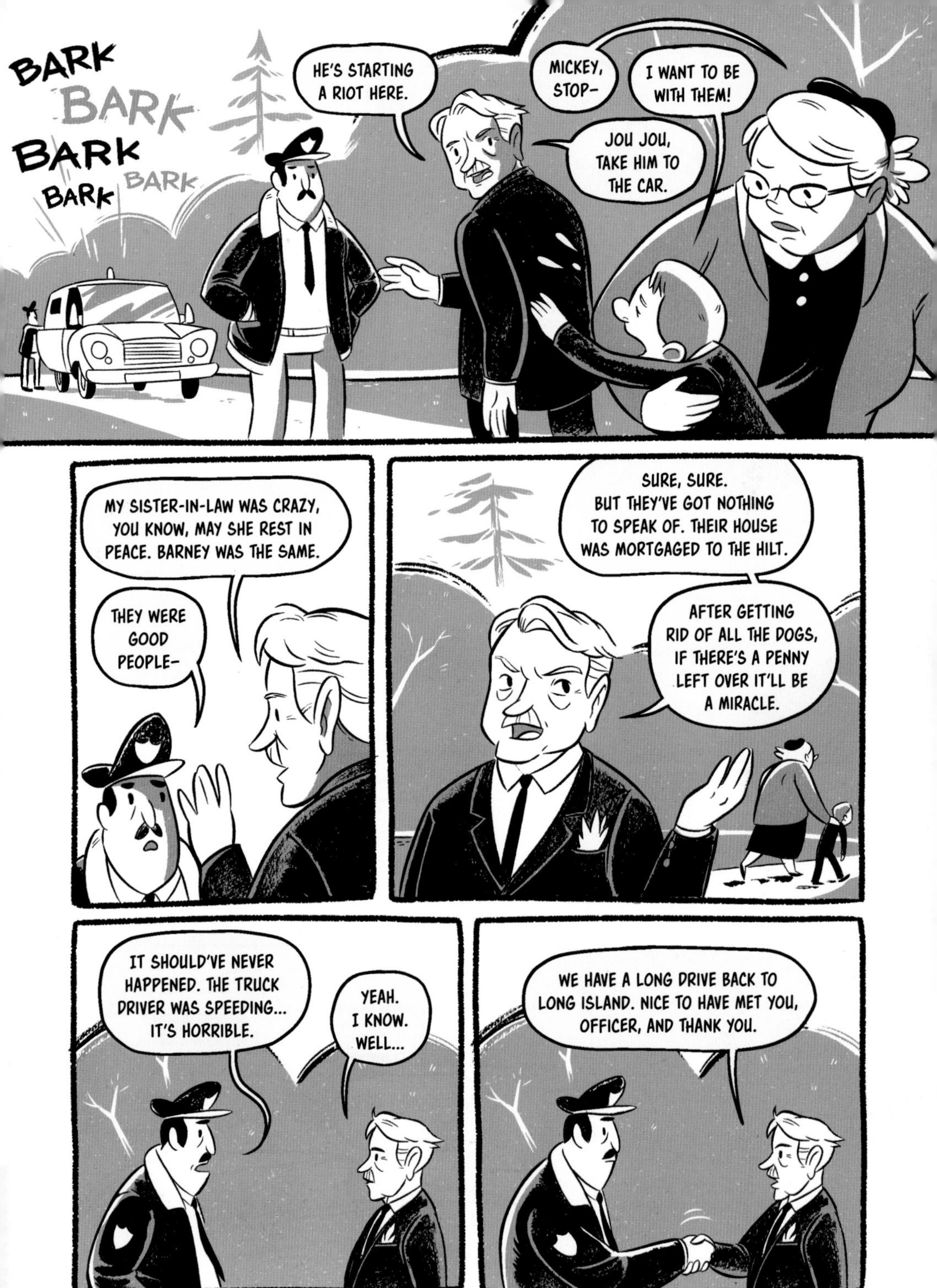
BARK BARK BARK BARK BARK
HE'S STARTING A RIOT HERE.
MICKEY, STOP–
I WANT TO BE WITH THEM!
JOU JOU, TAKE HIM TO THE CAR.
MY SISTER-IN-LAW WAS CRAZY, YOU KNOW, MAY SHE REST IN PEACE. BARNEY WAS THE SAME.
THEY WERE GOOD PEOPLE–
SURE, SURE. BUT THEY'VE GOT NOTHING TO SPEAK OF. THEIR HOUSE WAS MORTGAGED TO THE HILT.
AFTER GETTING RID OF ALL THE DOGS, IF THERE'S A PENNY LEFT OVER IT'LL BE A MIRACLE.
IT SHOULD'VE NEVER HAPPENED. THE TRUCK DRIVER WAS SPEEDING... IT'S HORRIBLE.
YEAH. I KNOW. WELL...
WE HAVE A LONG DRIVE BACK TO LONG ISLAND. NICE TO HAVE MET YOU, OFFICER, AND THANK YOU.

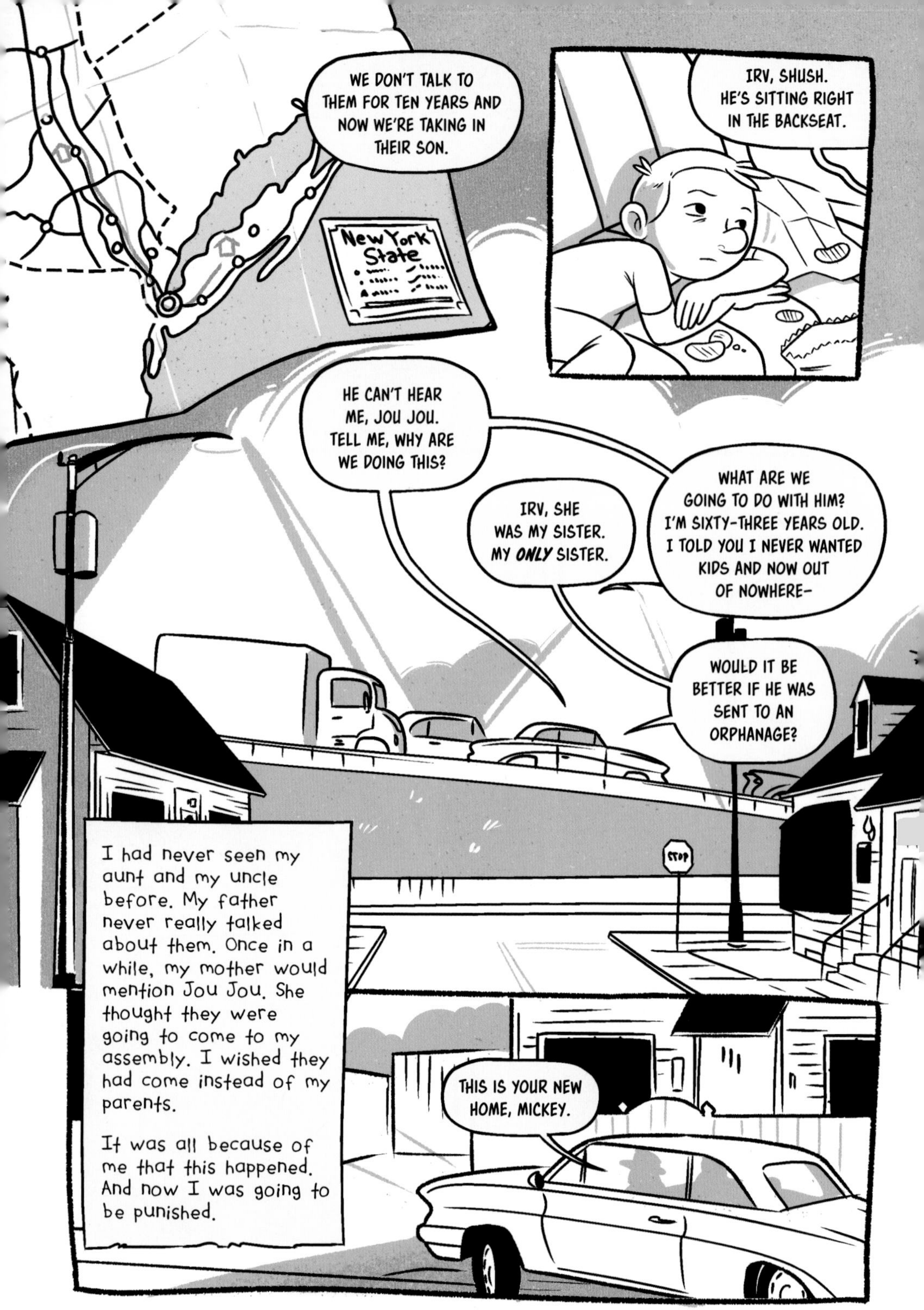
New York State
WE DON'T TALK TO THEM FOR TEN YEARS AND NOW WE'RE TAKING IN THEIR SON.
IRV, SHUSH. HE'S SITTING RIGHT IN THE BACKSEAT.
HE CAN'T HEAR ME, JOU JOU. TELL ME, WHY ARE WE DOING THIS?
WHAT ARE WE GOING TO DO WITH HIM? I'M SIXTY-THREE YEARS OLD. I TOLD YOU I NEVER WANTED KIDS AND NOW OUT OF NOWHERE-
IRV, SHE WAS MY SISTER. MY ONLY SISTER.
WOULD IT BE BETTER IF HE WAS SENT TO AN ORPHANAGE?
STOP
I had never seen my aunt and my uncle before. My father never really talked about them. Once in a while, my mother would mention Jou Jou. She thought they were going to come to my assembly. I wished they had come instead of my parents.
It was all because of me that this happened. And now I was going to be punished.
THIS IS YOUR NEW HOME, MICKEY.

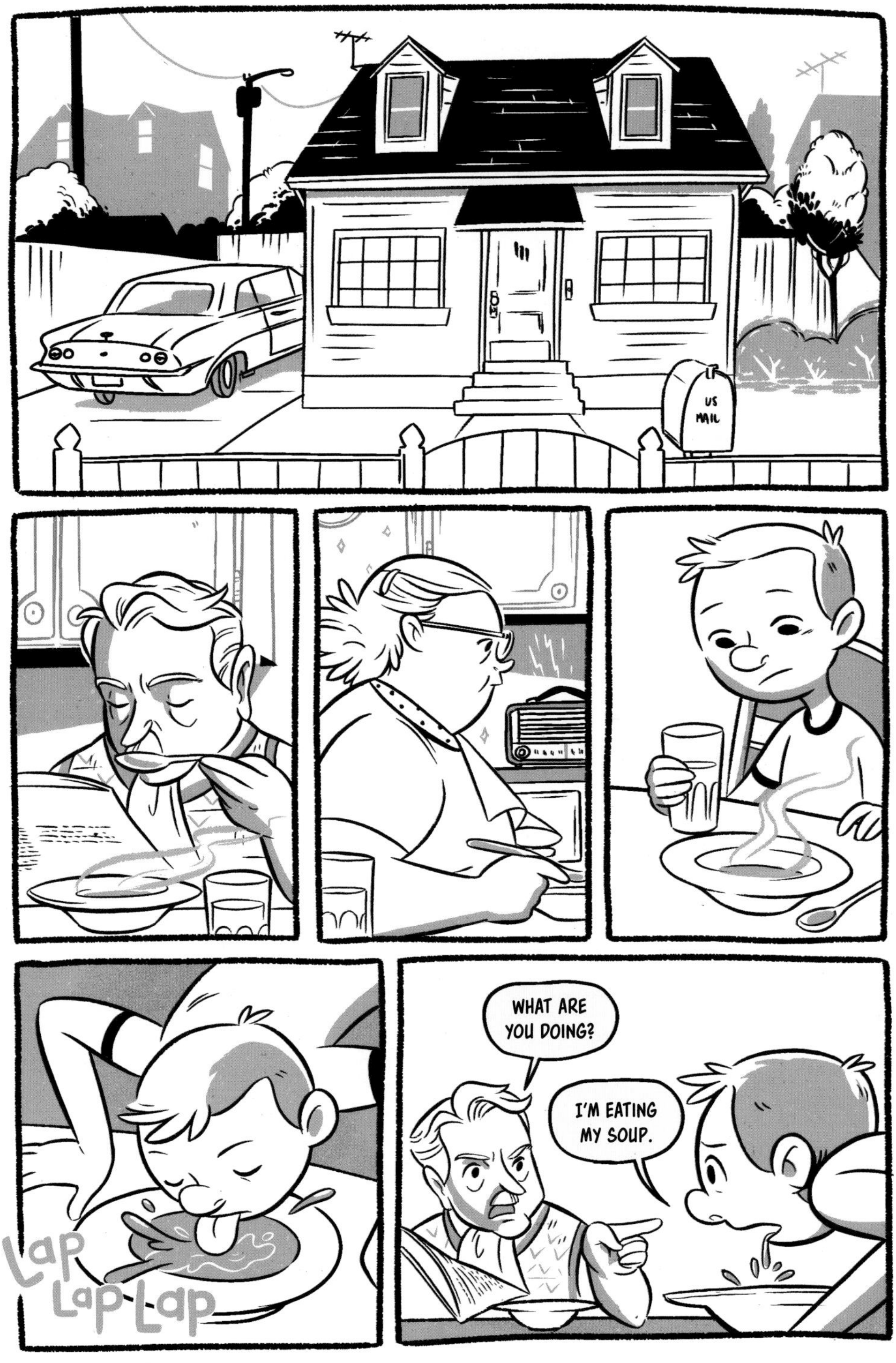
US
MAIL
LAP
LAP LAP
WHAT ARE YOU DOING?
I'M EATING MY SOUP.

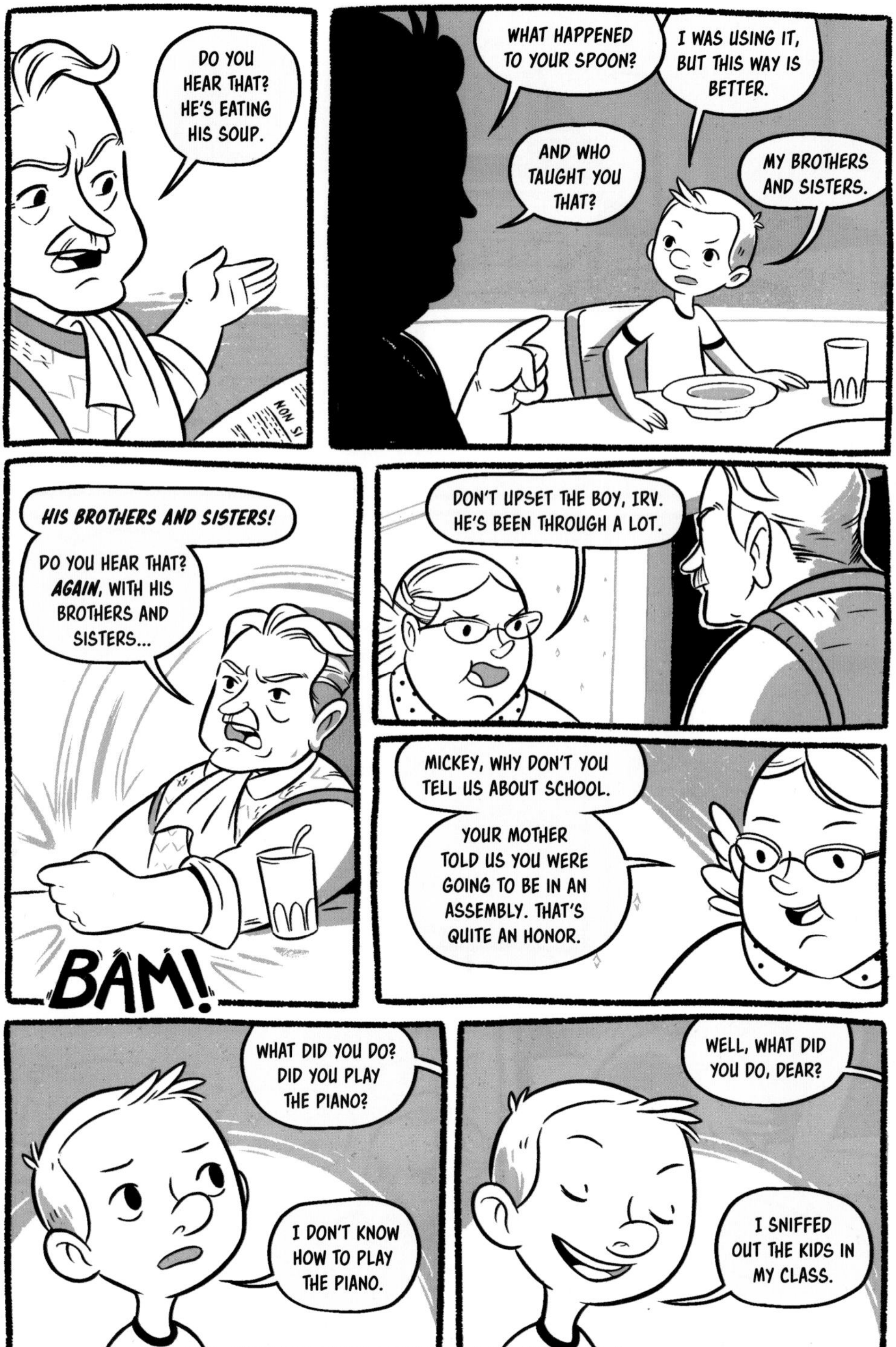
DO YOU HEAR THAT? HE'S EATING HIS SOUP.
WHAT HAPPENED TO YOUR SPOON?
I WAS USING IT, BUT THIS WAY IS BETTER.
AND WHO TAUGHT YOU THAT?
MY BROTHERS AND SISTERS.
HIS BROTHERS AND SISTERS!
DO YOU HEAR THAT? *AGAIN*, WITH HIS BROTHERS AND SISTERS...
BAM!
DON'T UPSET THE BOY, IRV. HE'S BEEN THROUGH A LOT.
MICKEY, WHY DON'T YOU TELL US ABOUT SCHOOL.
YOUR MOTHER TOLD US YOU WERE GOING TO BE IN AN ASSEMBLY. THAT'S QUITE AN HONOR.
WHAT DID YOU DO? DID YOU PLAY THE PIANO?
I DON'T KNOW HOW TO PLAY THE PIANO.
WELL, WHAT DID YOU DO, DEAR?
I SNIFFED OUT THE KIDS IN MY CLASS.

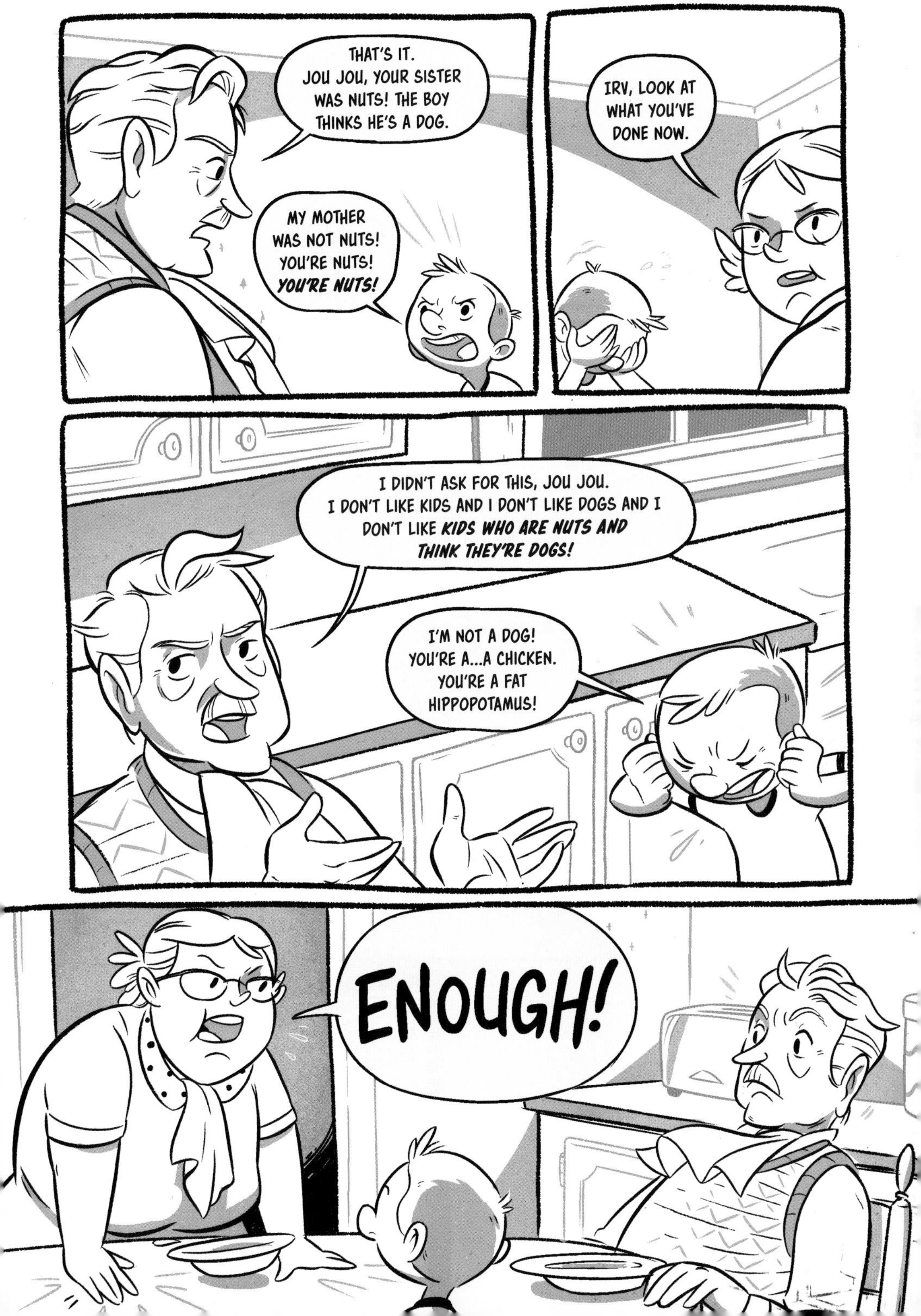
THAT'S IT.
JOU JOU, YOUR SISTER WAS NUTS! THE BOY THINKS HE'S A DOG.
MY MOTHER WAS NOT NUTS! YOU'RE NUTS! *YOU'RE NUTS!*
IRV, LOOK AT WHAT YOU'VE DONE NOW.
I DIDN'T ASK FOR THIS, JOU JOU. I DON'T LIKE KIDS AND I DON'T LIKE DOGS AND I DON'T LIKE *KIDS WHO ARE NUTS AND THINK THEY'RE DOGS!*
I'M NOT A DOG! YOU'RE A...A CHICKEN. YOU'RE A FAT HIPPOPOTAMUS!
ENOUGH!

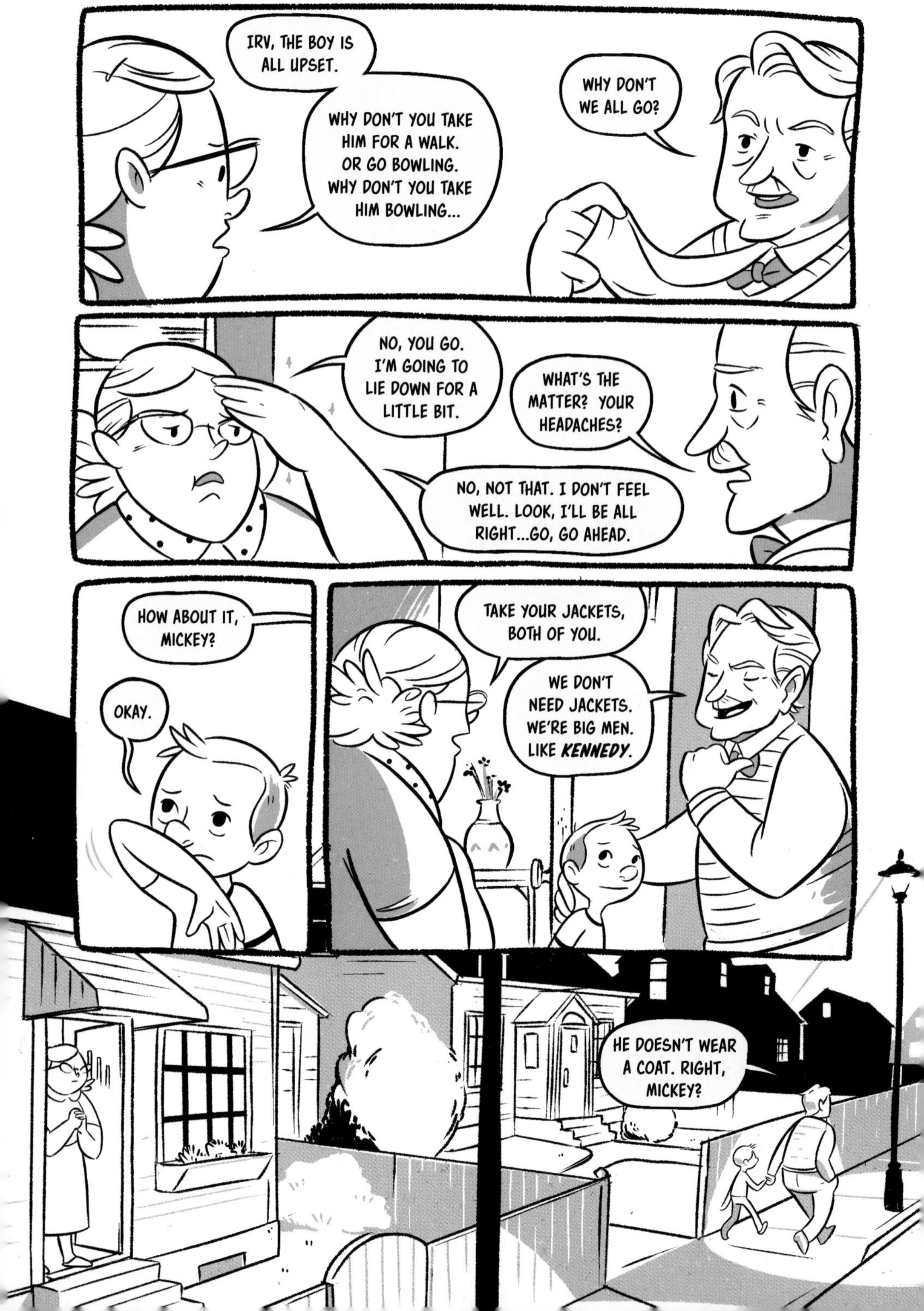
IRV, THE BOY IS ALL UPSET.
WHY DON'T YOU TAKE HIM FOR A WALK. OR GO BOWLING. WHY DON'T YOU TAKE HIM BOWLING...
WHY DON'T WE ALL GO?
NO, YOU GO. I'M GOING TO LIE DOWN FOR A LITTLE BIT.
WHAT'S THE MATTER? YOUR HEADACHES?
NO, NOT THAT. I DON'T FEEL WELL. LOOK, I'LL BE ALL RIGHT...GO, GO AHEAD.
HOW ABOUT IT, MICKEY?
OKAY.
TAKE YOUR JACKETS, BOTH OF YOU.
WE DON'T NEED JACKETS. WE'RE BIG MEN. LIKE *KENNEDY*.
HE DOESN'T WEAR A COAT. RIGHT, MICKEY?

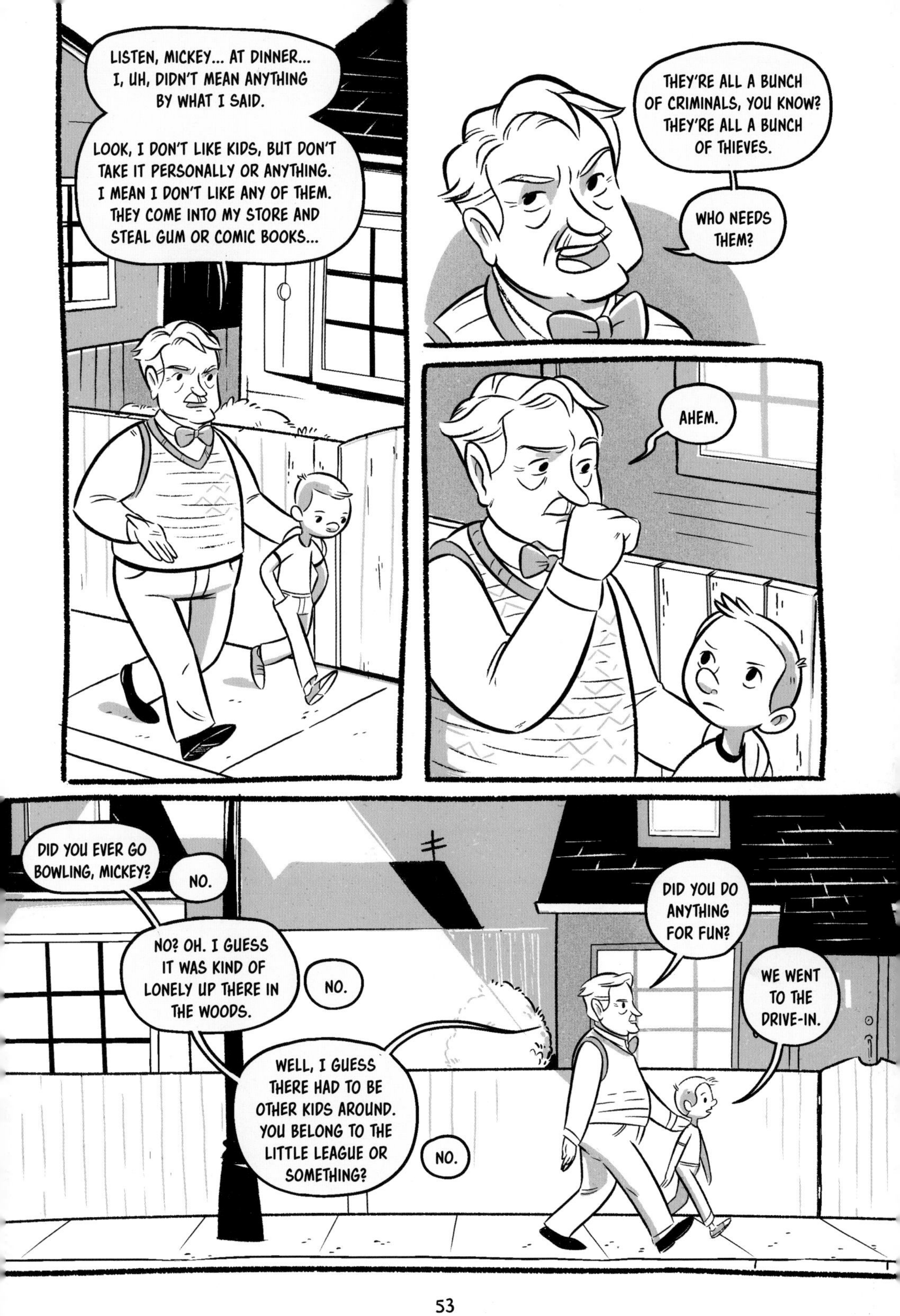
LISTEN, MICKEY... AT DINNER... I, UH, DIDN'T MEAN ANYTHING BY WHAT I SAID.
LOOK, I DON'T LIKE KIDS, BUT DON'T TAKE IT PERSONALLY OR ANYTHING. I MEAN I DON'T LIKE ANY OF THEM. THEY COME INTO MY STORE AND STEAL GUM OR COMIC BOOKS...
THEY'RE ALL A BUNCH OF CRIMINALS, YOU KNOW? THEY'RE ALL A BUNCH OF THIEVES.
WHO NEEDS THEM?
AHEM.
DID YOU EVER GO BOWLING, MICKEY?
NO.
NO? OH. I GUESS IT WAS KIND OF LONELY UP THERE IN THE WOODS.
NO.
WELL, I GUESS THERE HAD TO BE OTHER KIDS AROUND. YOU BELONG TO THE LITTLE LEAGUE OR SOMETHING?
NO.
DID YOU DO ANYTHING FOR FUN?
WE WENT TO THE DRIVE-IN.

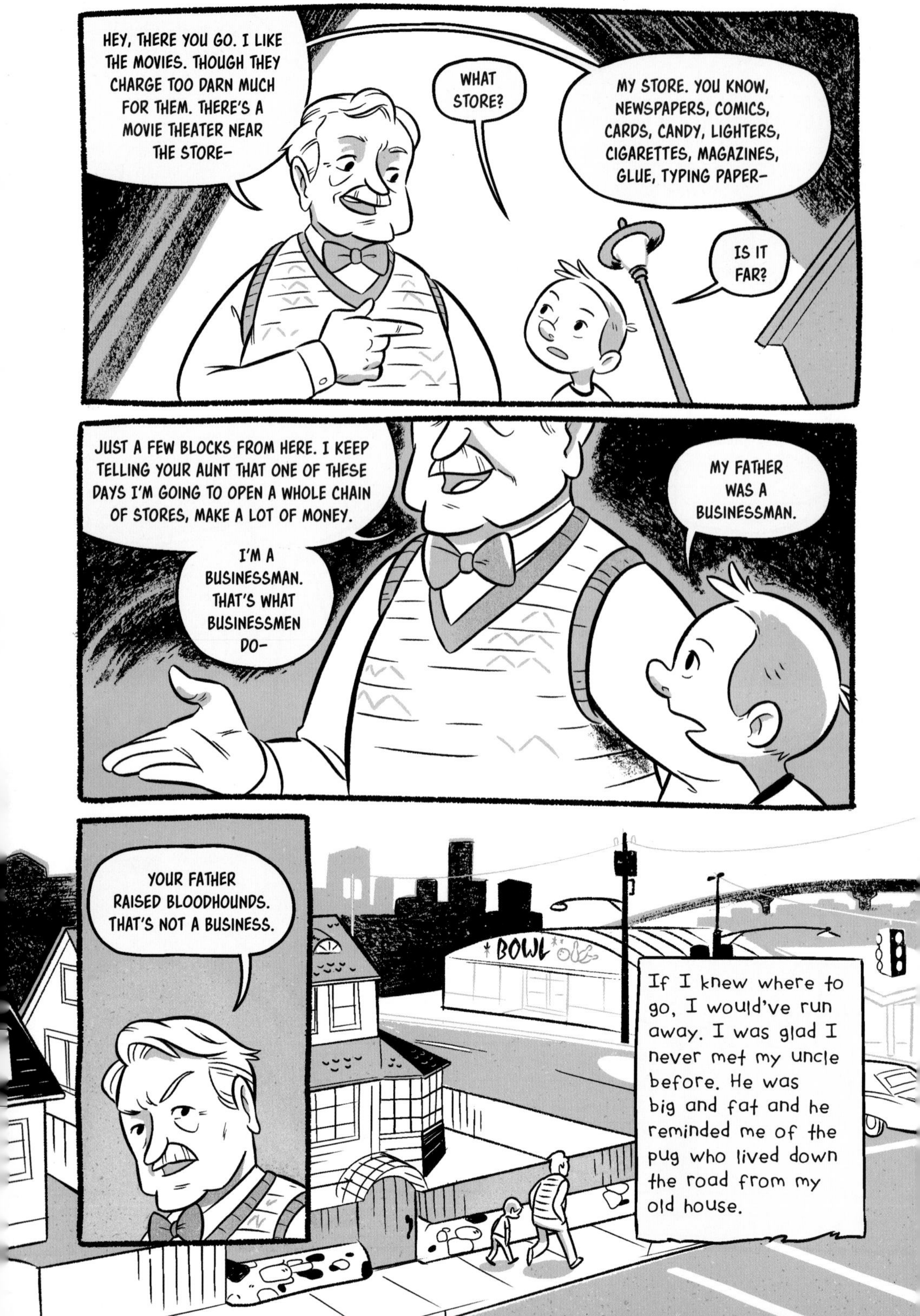
HEY, THERE YOU GO. I LIKE THE MOVIES. THOUGH THEY CHARGE TOO DARN MUCH FOR THEM. THERE'S A MOVIE THEATER NEAR THE STORE-
WHAT STORE?
MY STORE. YOU KNOW, NEWSPAPERS, COMICS, CARDS, CANDY, LIGHTERS, CIGARETTES, MAGAZINES, GLUE, TYPING PAPER-
IS IT FAR?
JUST A FEW BLOCKS FROM HERE. I KEEP TELLING YOUR AUNT THAT ONE OF THESE DAYS I'M GOING TO OPEN A WHOLE CHAIN OF STORES, MAKE A LOT OF MONEY.
I'M A BUSINESSMAN. THAT'S WHAT BUSINESSMEN DO-
MY FATHER WAS A BUSINESSMAN.
YOUR FATHER RAISED BLOODHOUNDS. THAT'S NOT A BUSINESS.
BOWL
If I knew where to go, I would've run away. I was glad I never met my uncle before. He was big and fat and he reminded me of the pug who lived down the road from my old house.

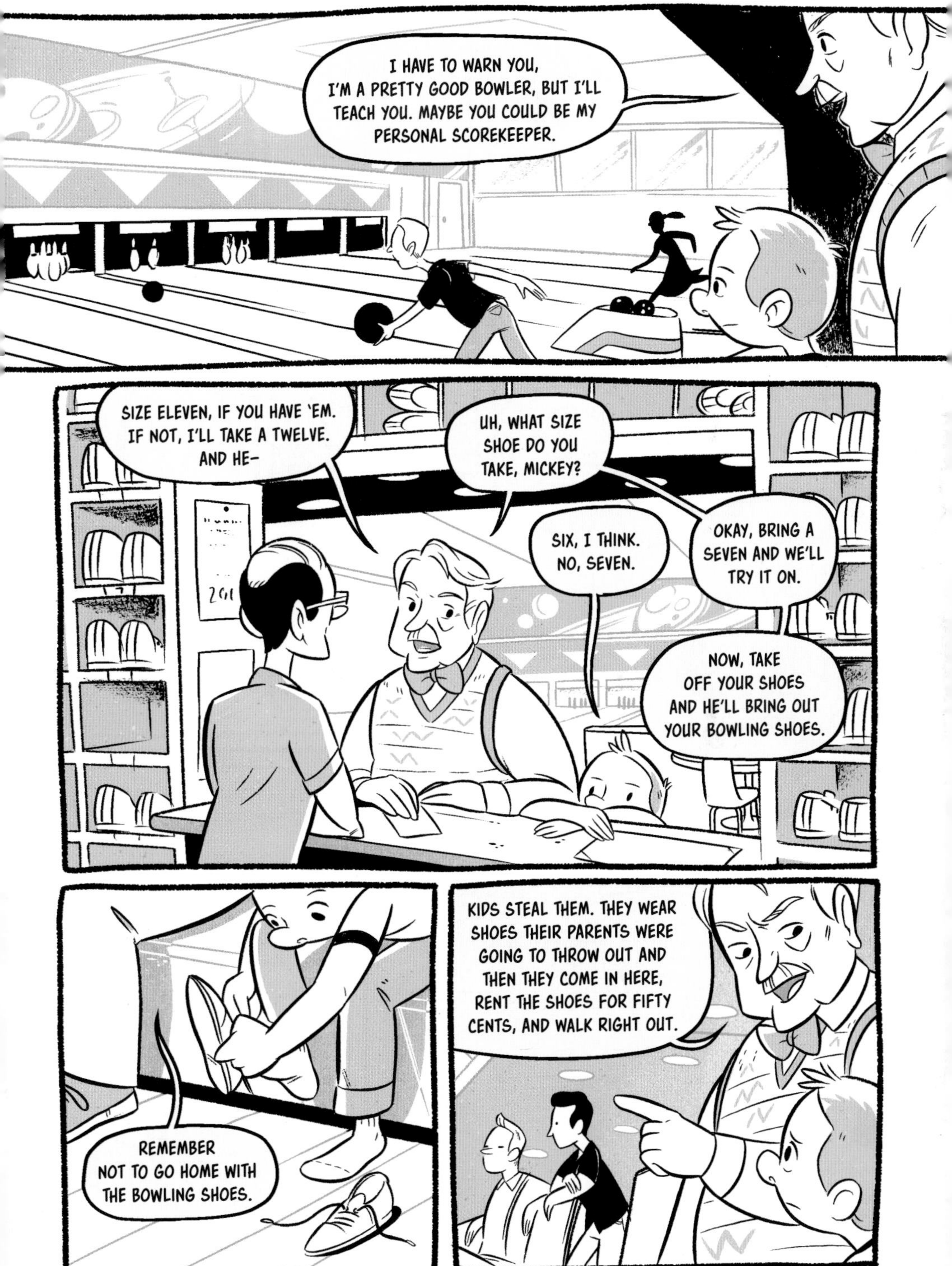
I HAVE TO WARN YOU, I'M A PRETTY GOOD BOWLER, BUT I'LL TEACH YOU. MAYBE YOU COULD BE MY PERSONAL SCOREKEEPER.
SIZE ELEVEN, IF YOU HAVE 'EM. IF NOT, I'LL TAKE A TWELVE. AND HE–
UH, WHAT SIZE SHOE DO YOU TAKE, MICKEY?
SIX, I THINK. NO, SEVEN.
OKAY, BRING A SEVEN AND WE'LL TRY IT ON.
NOW, TAKE OFF YOUR SHOES AND HE'LL BRING OUT YOUR BOWLING SHOES.
REMEMBER NOT TO GO HOME WITH THE BOWLING SHOES.
KIDS STEAL THEM. THEY WEAR SHOES THEIR PARENTS WERE GOING TO THROW OUT AND THEN THEY COME IN HERE, RENT THE SHOES FOR FIFTY CENTS, AND WALK RIGHT OUT.

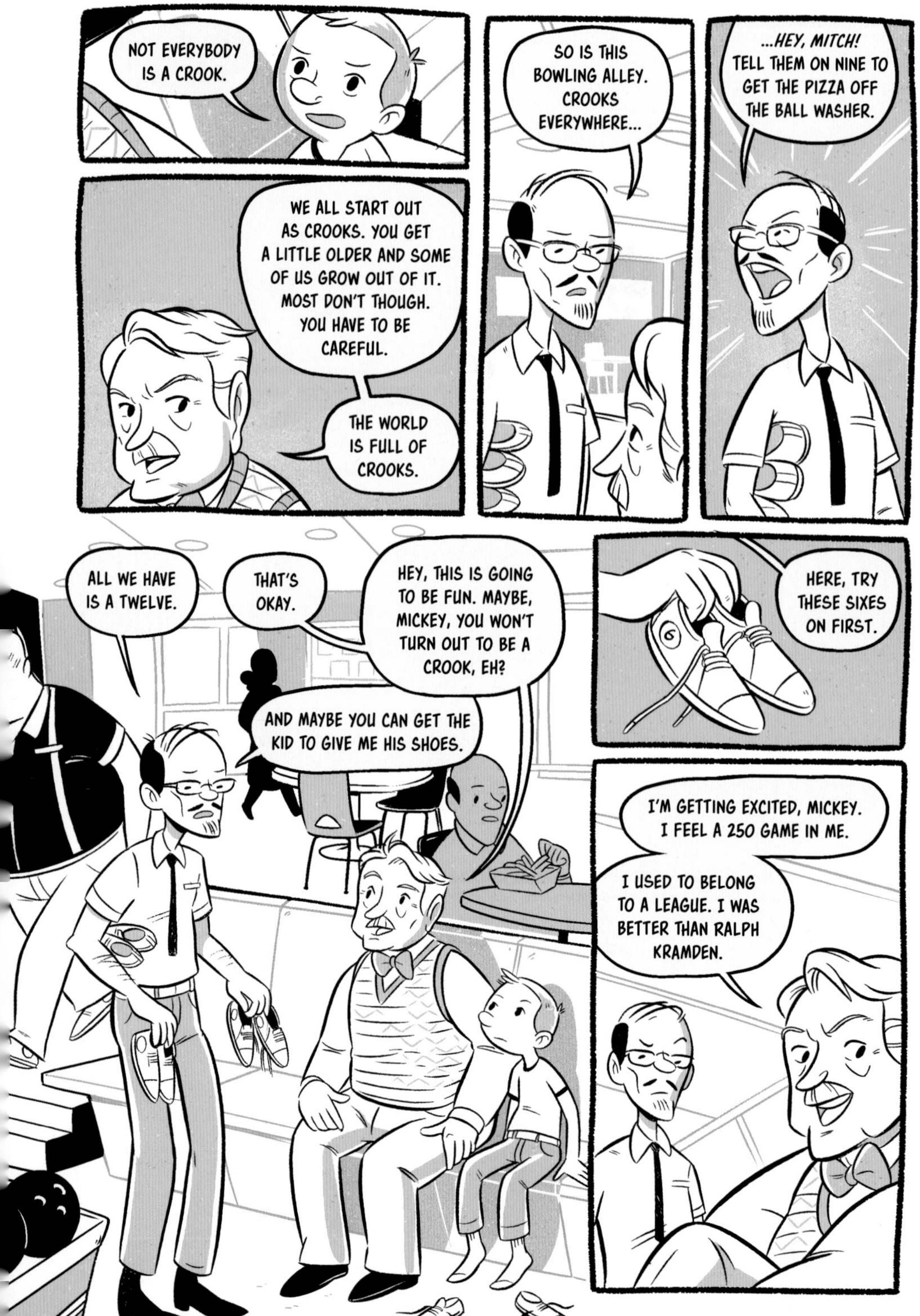
NOT EVERYBODY IS A CROOK.
WE ALL START OUT AS CROOKS. YOU GET A LITTLE OLDER AND SOME OF US GROW OUT OF IT. MOST DON'T THOUGH. YOU HAVE TO BE CAREFUL.
THE WORLD IS FULL OF CROOKS.
SO IS THIS BOWLING ALLEY. CROOKS EVERYWHERE...
...HEY, MITCH! TELL THEM ON NINE TO GET THE PIZZA OFF THE BALL WASHER.
ALL WE HAVE IS A TWELVE.
THAT'S OKAY.
HEY, THIS IS GOING TO BE FUN. MAYBE, MICKEY, YOU WON'T TURN OUT TO BE A CROOK, EH?
AND MAYBE YOU CAN GET THE KID TO GIVE ME HIS SHOES.
HERE, TRY THESE SIXES ON FIRST.
I'M GETTING EXCITED, MICKEY. I FEEL A 250 GAME IN ME.
I USED TO BELONG TO A LEAGUE. I WAS BETTER THAN RALPH KRAMDEN.

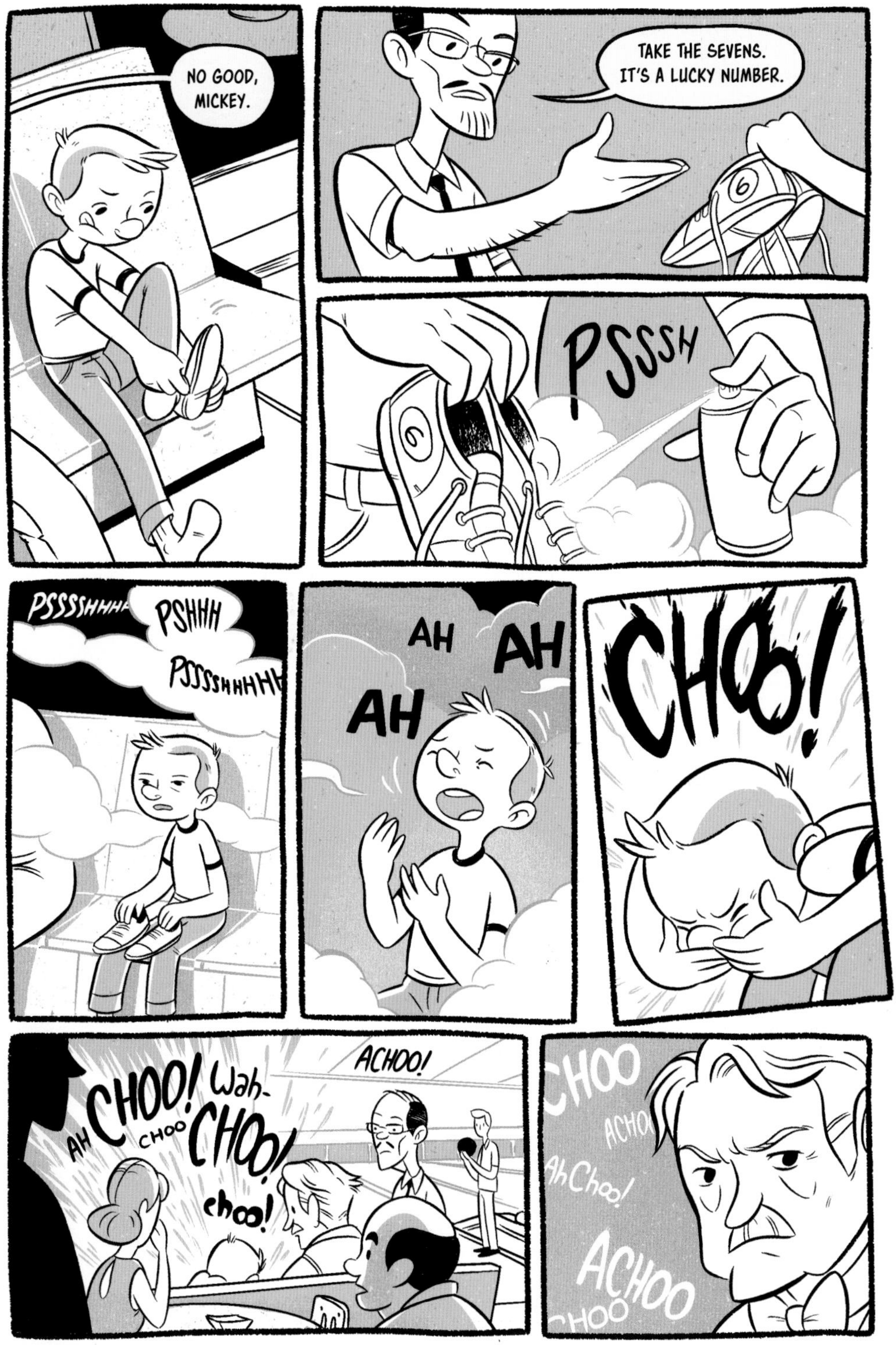

NO GOOD, MICKEY.
TAKE THE SEVENS. IT'S A LUCKY NUMBER.
PSSSH
PSSSSHHHH
PSHHH
PSSSSHHHHH
AH
AH
AH
CHOO!
ACHOO!
AH CHOO!
CHOO
Wah-CHOO!
choo!
CHOO
ACHOO
AhChoo!
ACHOO
CHOO

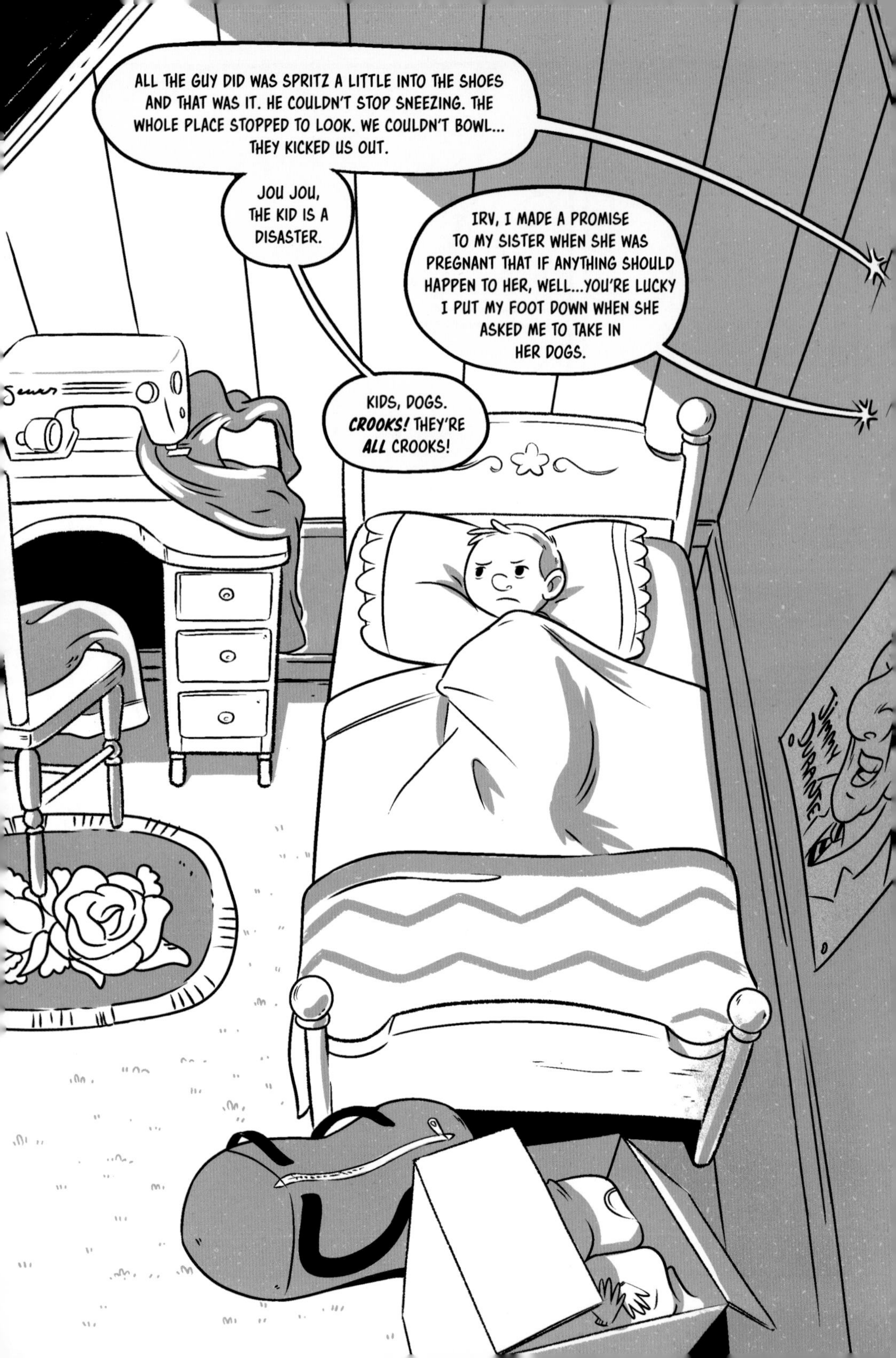
ALL THE GUY DID WAS SPRITZ A LITTLE INTO THE SHOES AND THAT WAS IT. HE COULDN'T STOP SNEEZING. THE WHOLE PLACE STOPPED TO LOOK. WE COULDN'T BOWL... THEY KICKED US OUT.
JOU JOU, THE KID IS A DISASTER.
IRV, I MADE A PROMISE TO MY SISTER WHEN SHE WAS PREGNANT THAT IF ANYTHING SHOULD HAPPEN TO HER, WELL...YOU'RE LUCKY I PUT MY FOOT DOWN WHEN SHE ASKED ME TO TAKE IN HER DOGS.
KIDS, DOGS. ***CROOKS!*** THEY'RE ***ALL*** CROOKS!
JIMMY DURANTE

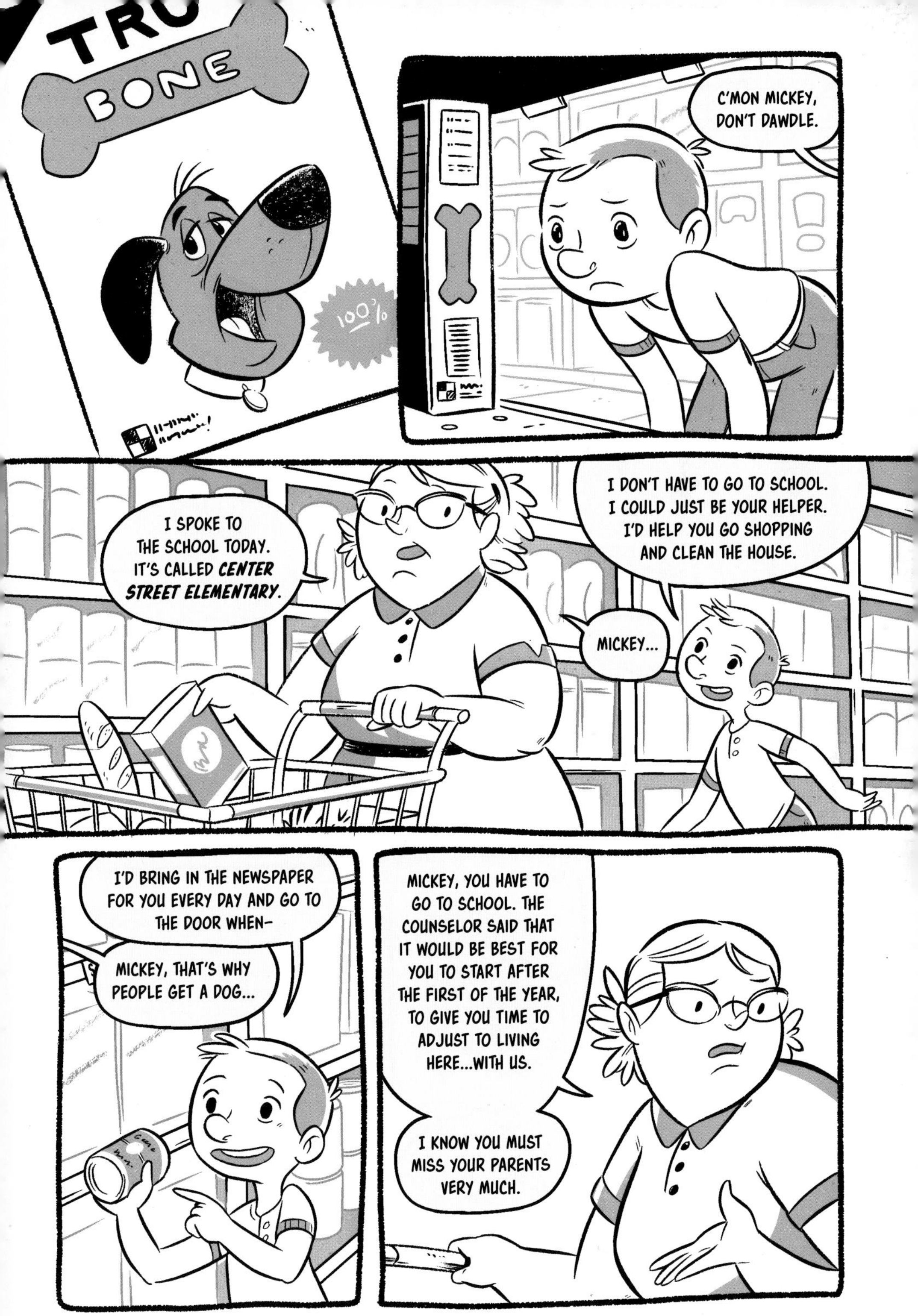
TRU
BONE
100%
C'MON MICKEY, DON'T DAWDLE.
I SPOKE TO THE SCHOOL TODAY. IT'S CALLED *CENTER STREET ELEMENTARY*.
I DON'T HAVE TO GO TO SCHOOL. I COULD JUST BE YOUR HELPER. I'D HELP YOU GO SHOPPING AND CLEAN THE HOUSE.
MICKEY...
I'D BRING IN THE NEWSPAPER FOR YOU EVERY DAY AND GO TO THE DOOR WHEN–
MICKEY, THAT'S WHY PEOPLE GET A DOG...
MICKEY, YOU HAVE TO GO TO SCHOOL. THE COUNSELOR SAID THAT IT WOULD BE BEST FOR YOU TO START AFTER THE FIRST OF THE YEAR, TO GIVE YOU TIME TO ADJUST TO LIVING HERE...WITH US.
I KNOW YOU MUST MISS YOUR PARENTS VERY MUCH.

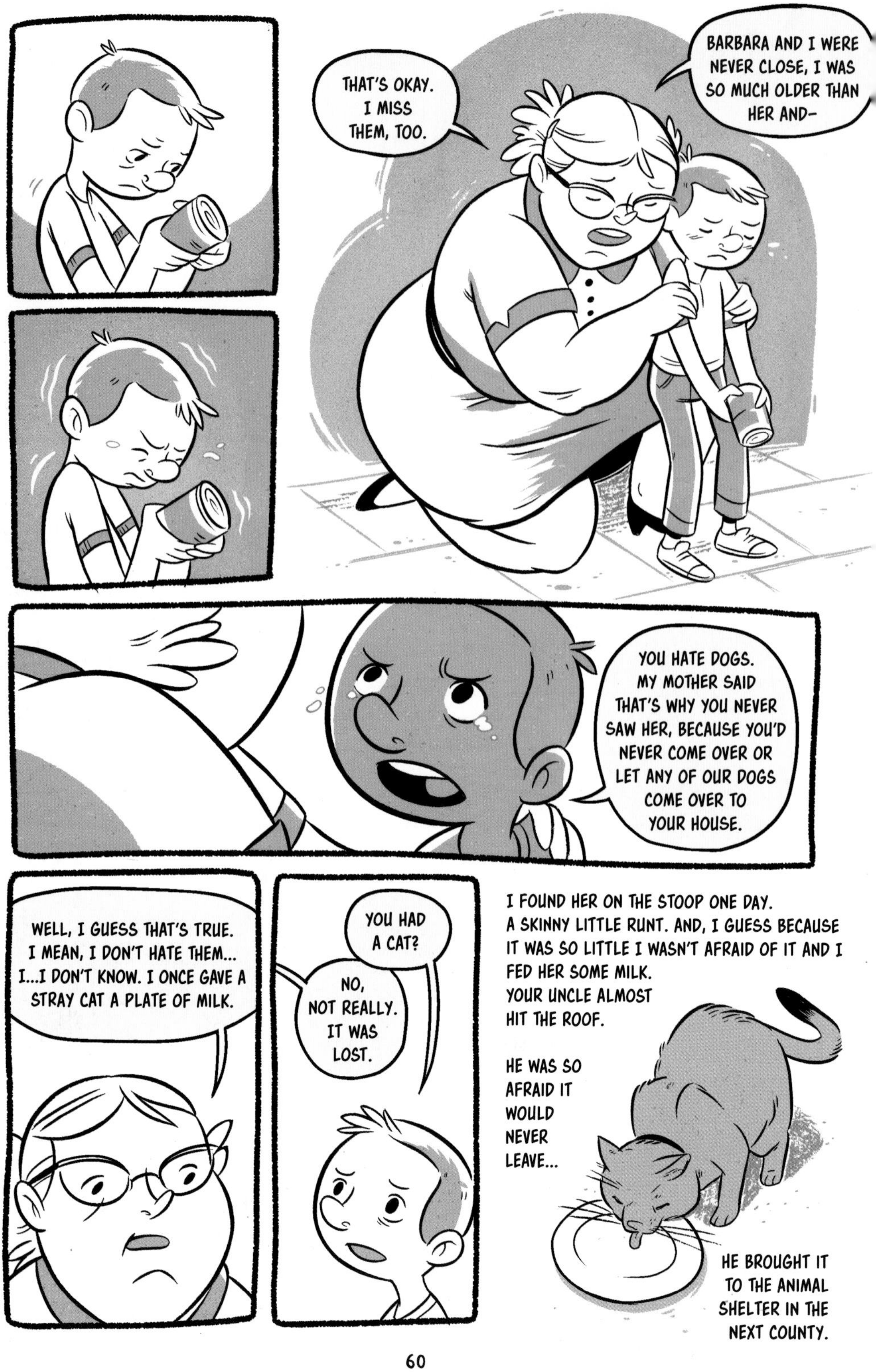
THAT'S OKAY. I MISS THEM, TOO.
BARBARA AND I WERE NEVER CLOSE, I WAS SO MUCH OLDER THAN HER AND–
YOU HATE DOGS. MY MOTHER SAID THAT'S WHY YOU NEVER SAW HER, BECAUSE YOU'D NEVER COME OVER OR LET ANY OF OUR DOGS COME OVER TO YOUR HOUSE.
WELL, I GUESS THAT'S TRUE. I MEAN, I DON'T HATE THEM... I...I DON'T KNOW. I ONCE GAVE A STRAY CAT A PLATE OF MILK.
YOU HAD A CAT?
NO, NOT REALLY. IT WAS LOST.
I FOUND HER ON THE STOOP ONE DAY. A SKINNY LITTLE RUNT. AND, I GUESS BECAUSE IT WAS SO LITTLE I WASN'T AFRAID OF IT AND I FED HER SOME MILK. YOUR UNCLE ALMOST HIT THE ROOF.
HE WAS SO AFRAID IT WOULD NEVER LEAVE...
HE BROUGHT IT TO THE ANIMAL SHELTER IN THE NEXT COUNTY.

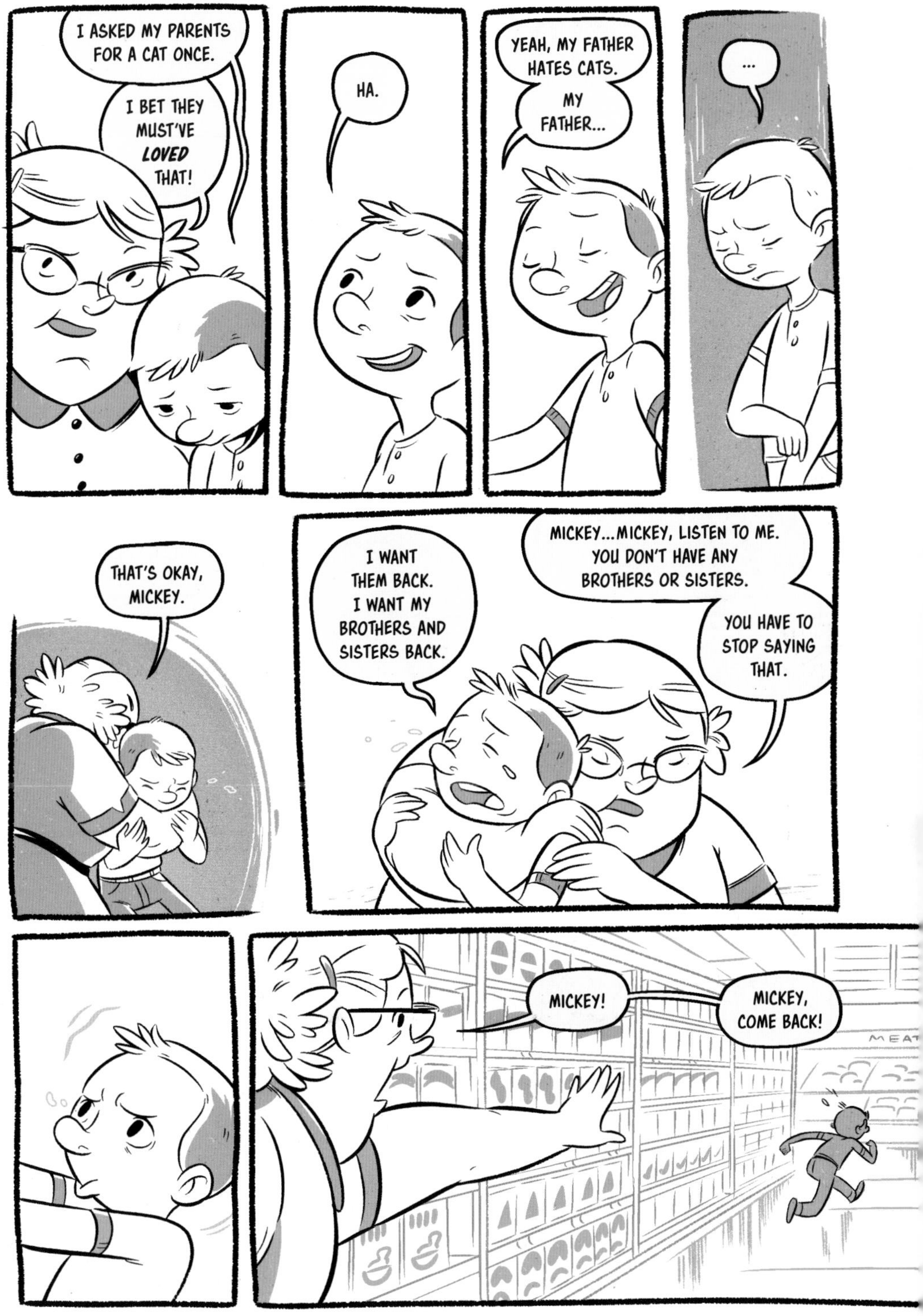
I ASKED MY PARENTS FOR A CAT ONCE.
I BET THEY MUST'VE ***LOVED*** THAT!
HA.
YEAH, MY FATHER HATES CATS.
MY FATHER...
...
THAT'S OKAY, MICKEY.
I WANT THEM BACK. I WANT MY BROTHERS AND SISTERS BACK.
MICKEY...MICKEY, LISTEN TO ME. YOU DON'T HAVE ANY BROTHERS OR SISTERS.
YOU HAVE TO STOP SAYING THAT.
MICKEY!
MICKEY, COME BACK!
MEAT

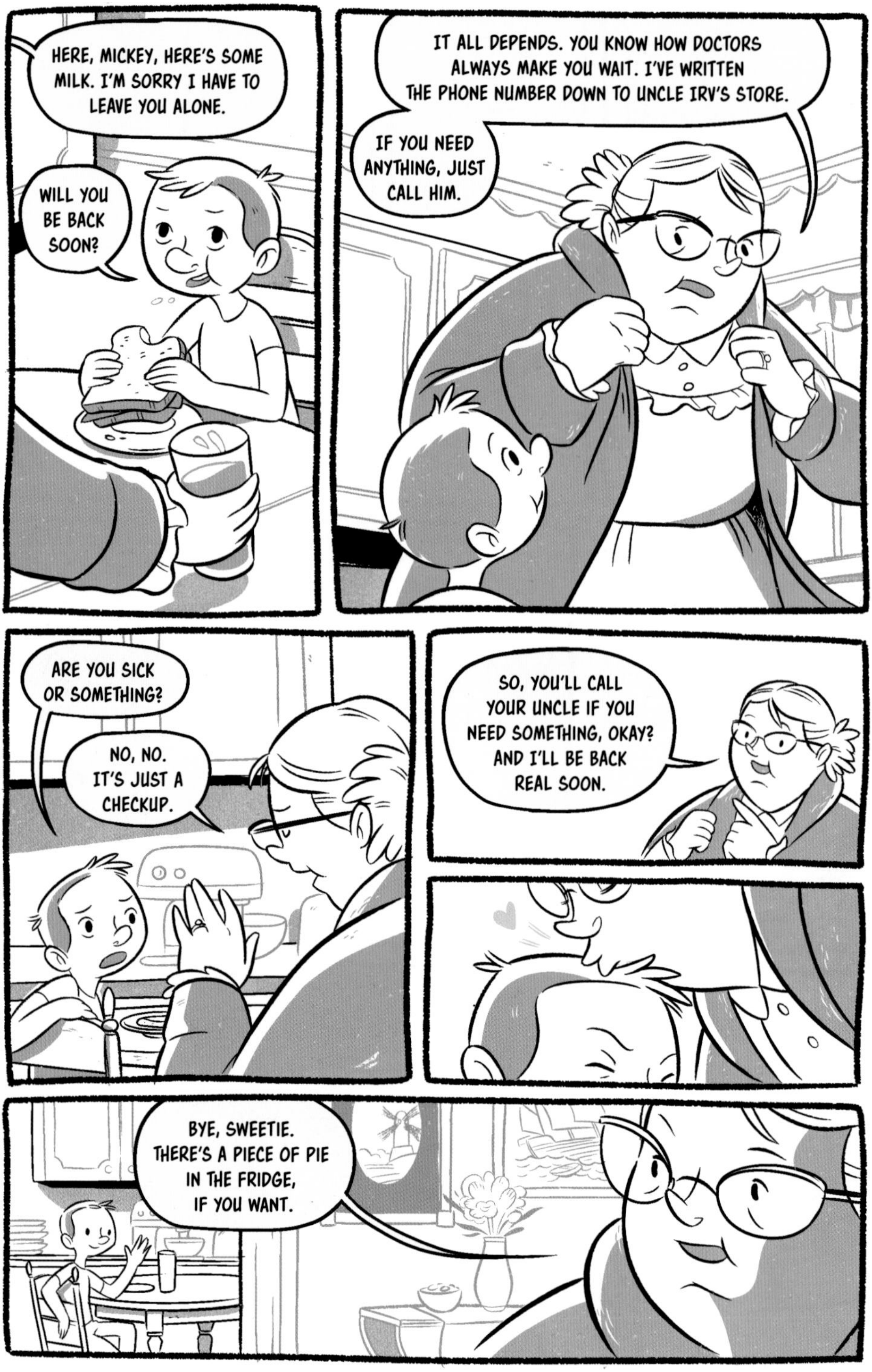
HERE, MICKEY, HERE'S SOME MILK. I'M SORRY I HAVE TO LEAVE YOU ALONE.
WILL YOU BE BACK SOON?
IT ALL DEPENDS. YOU KNOW HOW DOCTORS ALWAYS MAKE YOU WAIT. I'VE WRITTEN THE PHONE NUMBER DOWN TO UNCLE IRV'S STORE.
IF YOU NEED ANYTHING, JUST CALL HIM.
ARE YOU SICK OR SOMETHING?
NO, NO. IT'S JUST A CHECKUP.
SO, YOU'LL CALL YOUR UNCLE IF YOU NEED SOMETHING, OKAY? AND I'LL BE BACK REAL SOON.
BYE, SWEETIE. THERE'S A PIECE OF PIE IN THE FRIDGE, IF YOU WANT.

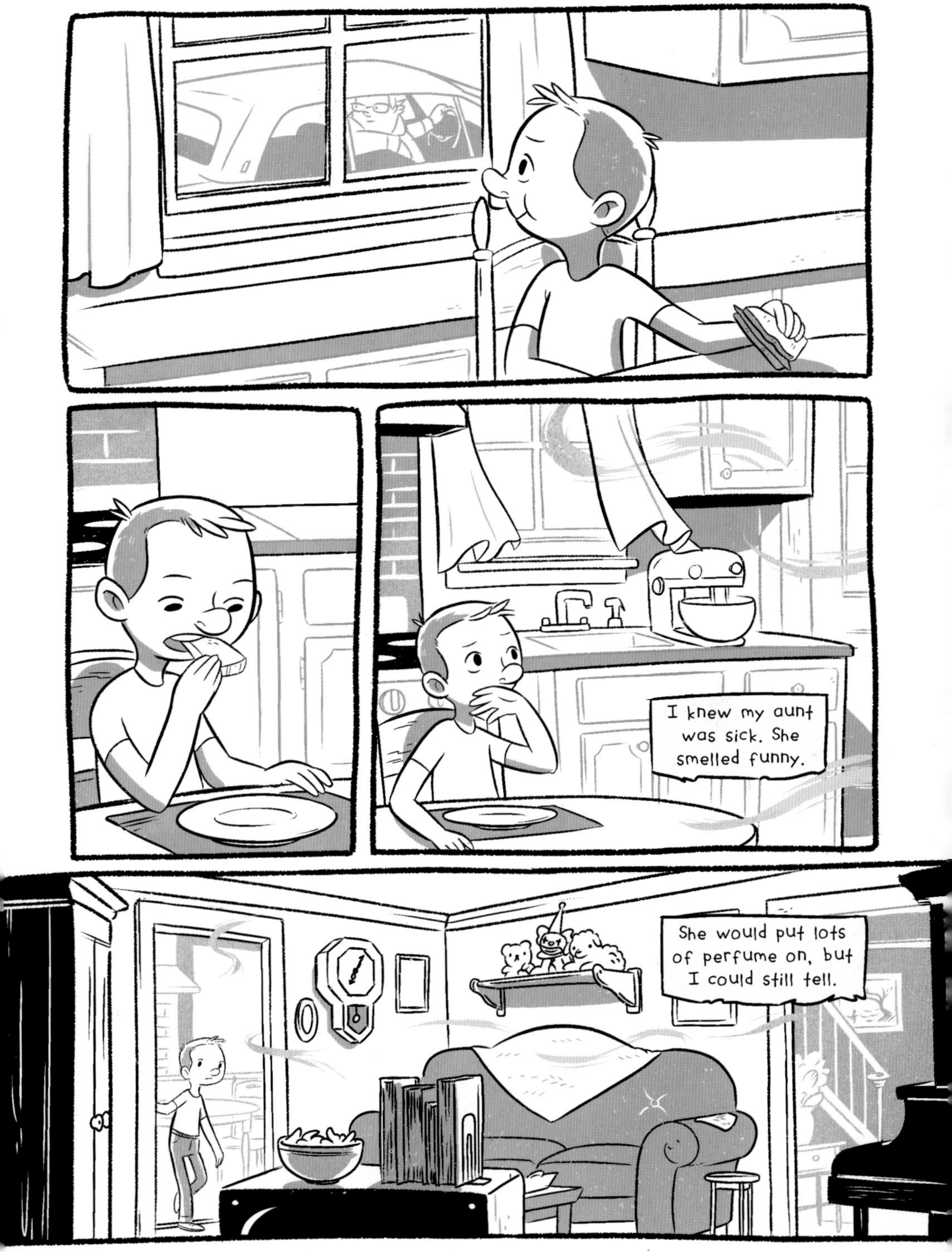
I knew my aunt was sick. She smelled funny.
She would put lots of perfume on, but I could still tell.

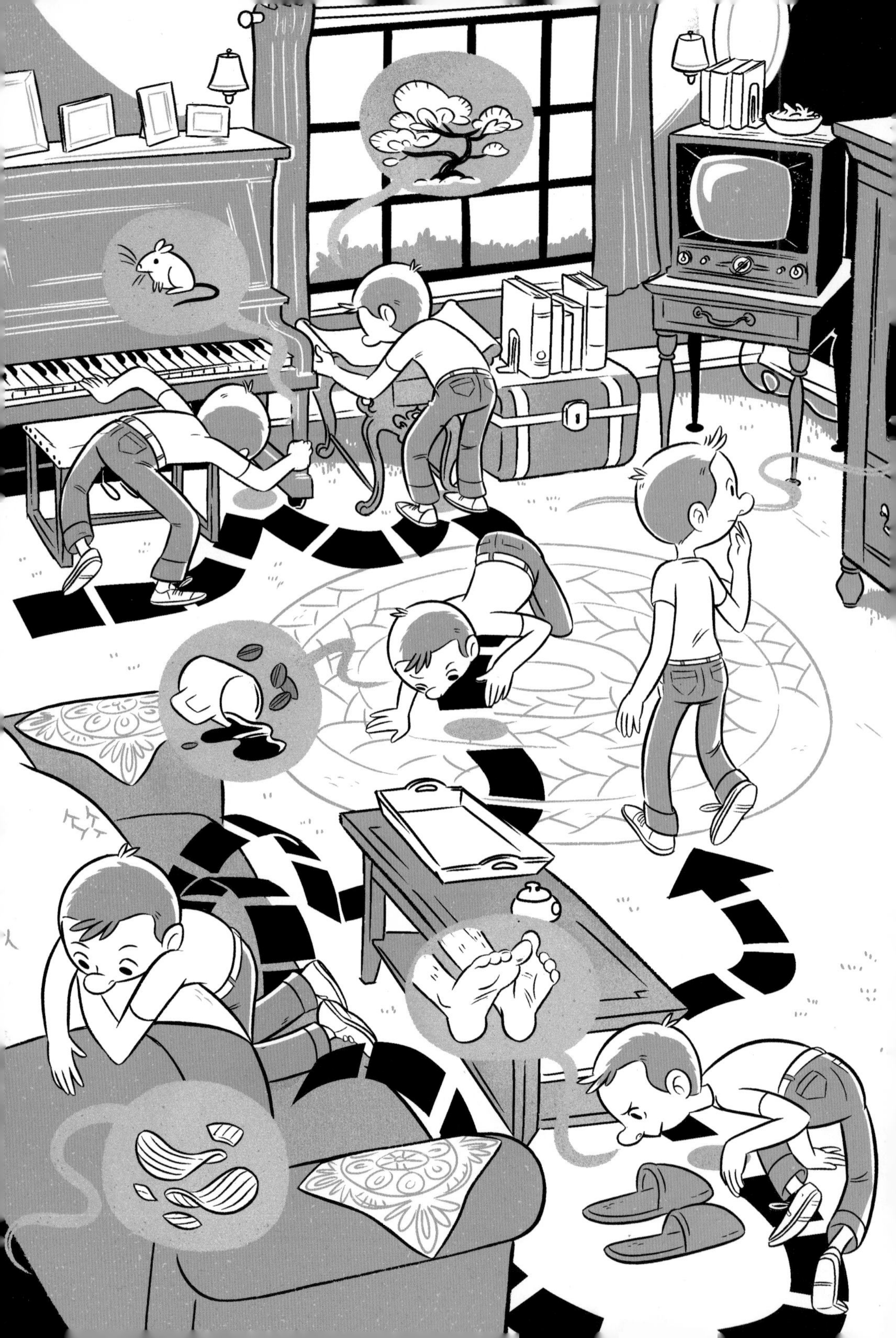

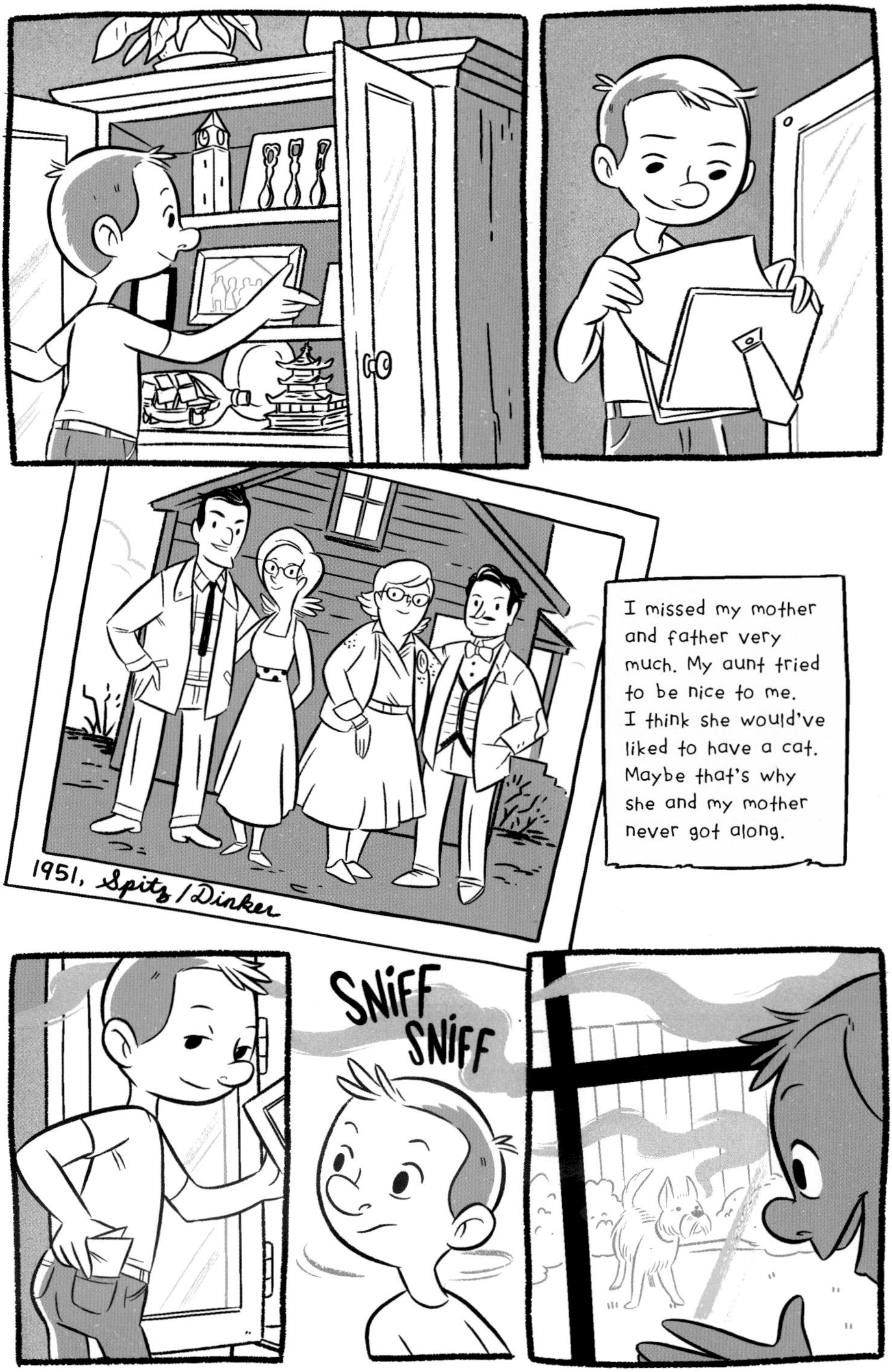
1951, Spitz / Dinker
I missed my mother and father very much. My aunt tried to be nice to me. I think she would've liked to have a cat. Maybe that's why she and my mother never got along.
SNIFF SNIFF

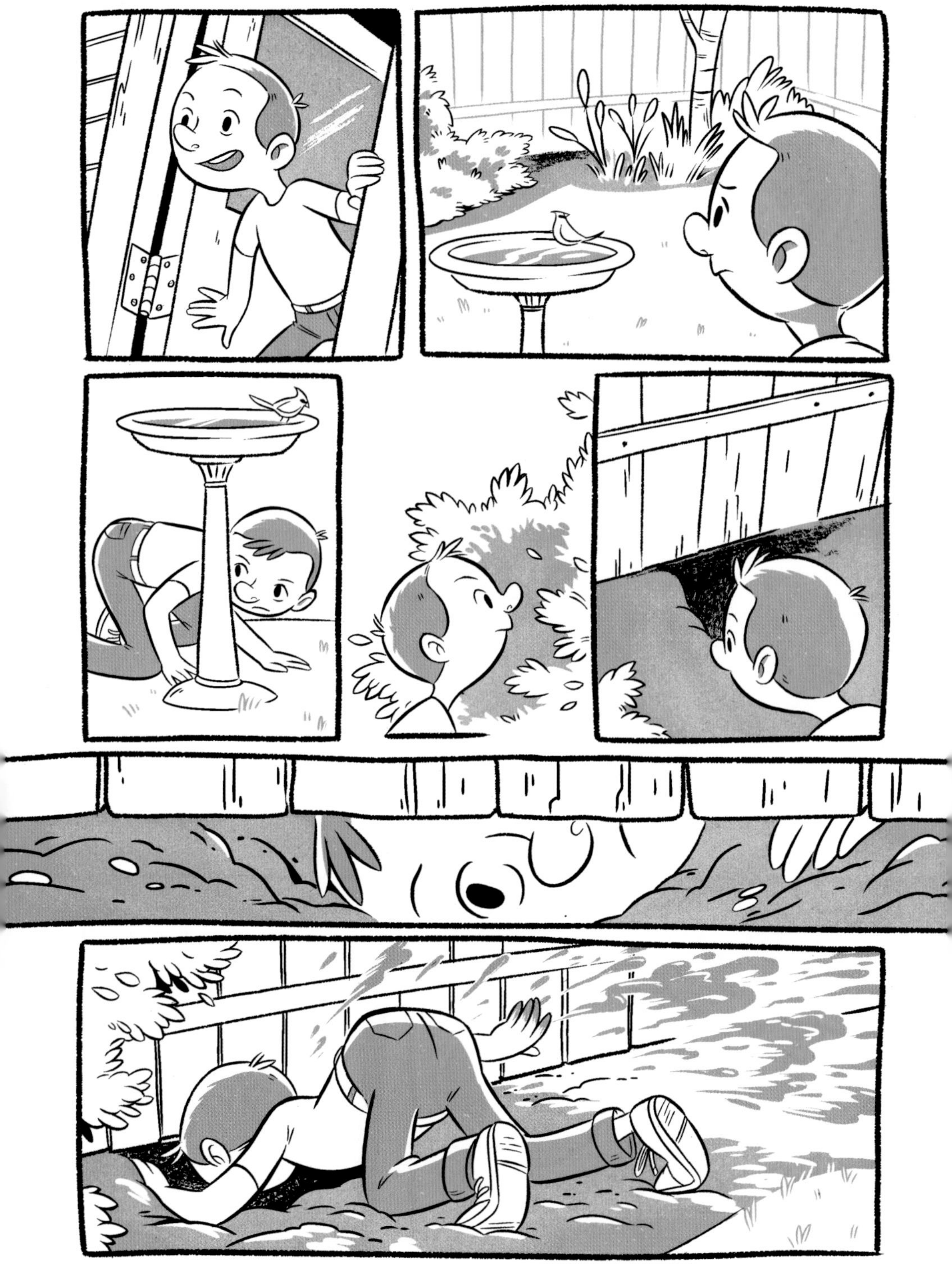

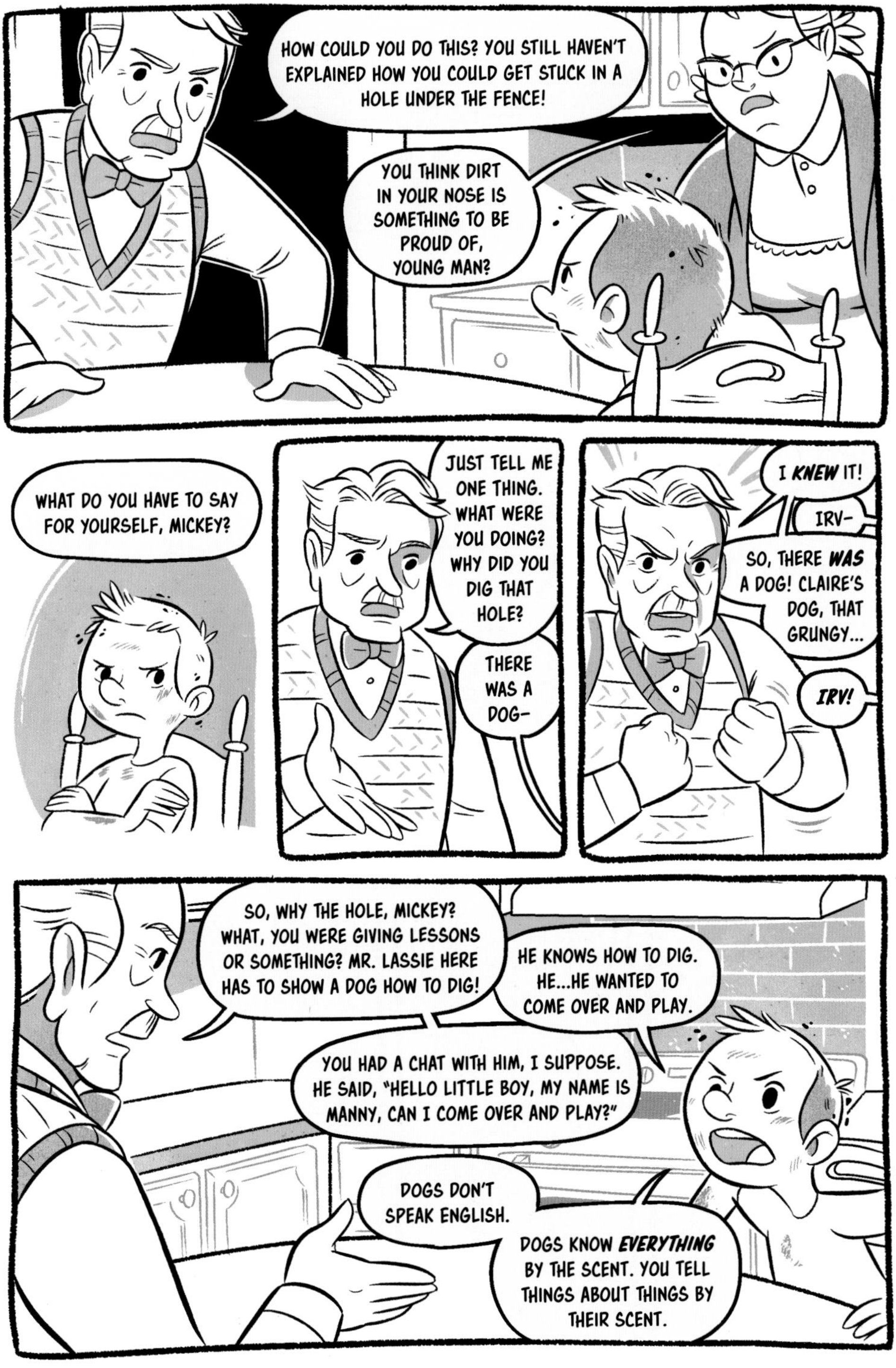
HOW COULD YOU DO THIS? YOU STILL HAVEN'T EXPLAINED HOW YOU COULD GET STUCK IN A HOLE UNDER THE FENCE!
YOU THINK DIRT IN YOUR NOSE IS SOMETHING TO BE PROUD OF, YOUNG MAN?
WHAT DO YOU HAVE TO SAY FOR YOURSELF, MICKEY?
JUST TELL ME ONE THING. WHAT WERE YOU DOING? WHY DID YOU DIG THAT HOLE?
THERE WAS A DOG-
I *KNEW* IT!
IRV-
SO, THERE *WAS* A DOG! CLAIRE'S DOG, THAT GRUNGY...
IRV!
SO, WHY THE HOLE, MICKEY? WHAT, YOU WERE GIVING LESSONS OR SOMETHING? MR. LASSIE HERE HAS TO SHOW A DOG HOW TO DIG!
HE KNOWS HOW TO DIG. HE...HE WANTED TO COME OVER AND PLAY.
YOU HAD A CHAT WITH HIM, I SUPPOSE. HE SAID, "HELLO LITTLE BOY, MY NAME IS MANNY, CAN I COME OVER AND PLAY?"
DOGS DON'T SPEAK ENGLISH.
DOGS KNOW *EVERYTHING* BY THE SCENT. YOU TELL THINGS ABOUT THINGS BY THEIR SCENT.

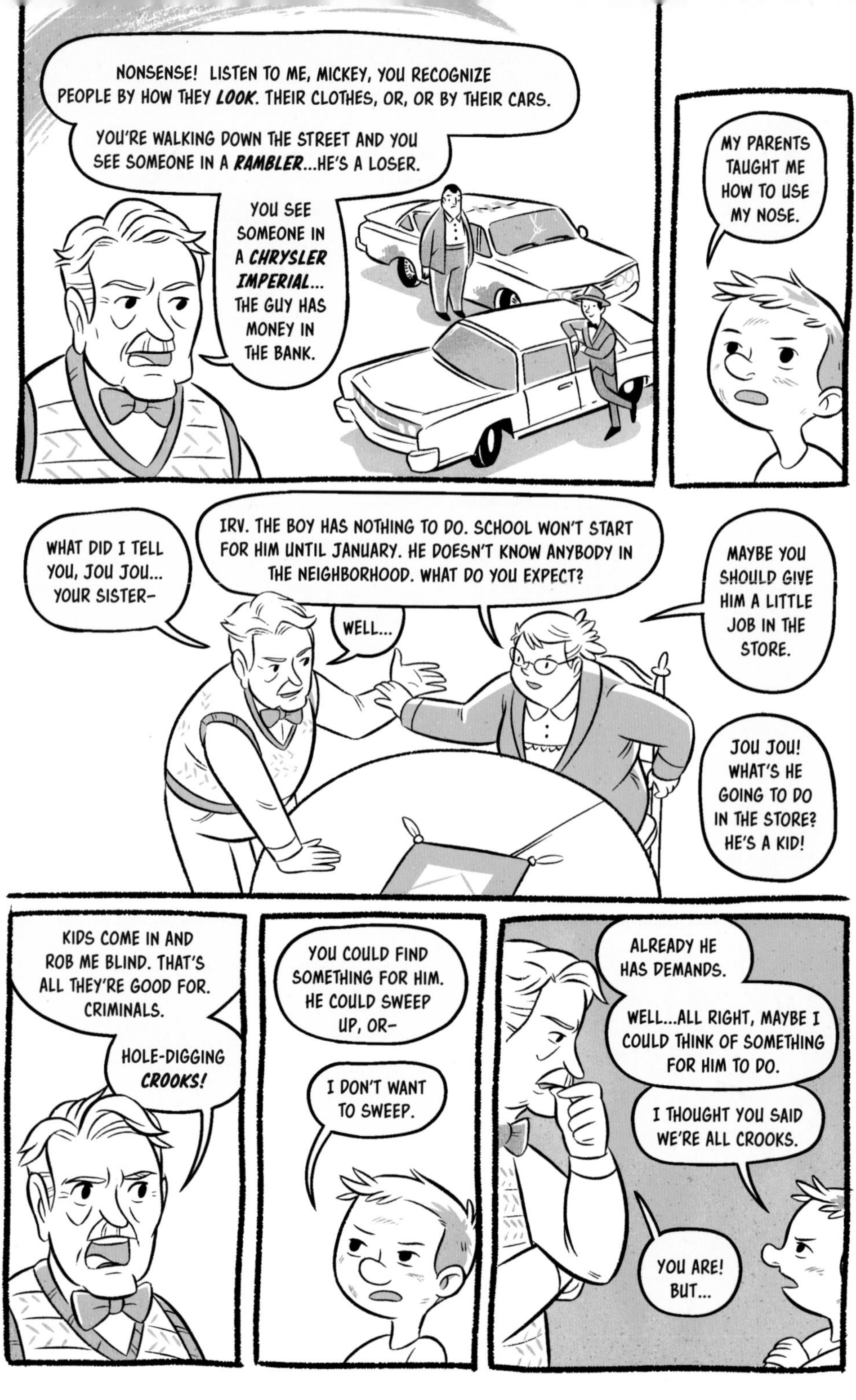
NONSENSE! LISTEN TO ME, MICKEY, YOU RECOGNIZE PEOPLE BY HOW THEY *LOOK*. THEIR CLOTHES, OR, OR BY THEIR CARS.
YOU'RE WALKING DOWN THE STREET AND YOU SEE SOMEONE IN A *RAMBLER*...HE'S A LOSER.
YOU SEE SOMEONE IN A *CHRYSLER IMPERIAL*... THE GUY HAS MONEY IN THE BANK.
MY PARENTS TAUGHT ME HOW TO USE MY NOSE.
WHAT DID I TELL YOU, JOU JOU... YOUR SISTER–
IRV. THE BOY HAS NOTHING TO DO. SCHOOL WON'T START FOR HIM UNTIL JANUARY. HE DOESN'T KNOW ANYBODY IN THE NEIGHBORHOOD. WHAT DO YOU EXPECT?
WELL...
MAYBE YOU SHOULD GIVE HIM A LITTLE JOB IN THE STORE.
JOU JOU! WHAT'S HE GOING TO DO IN THE STORE? HE'S A KID!
KIDS COME IN AND ROB ME BLIND. THAT'S ALL THEY'RE GOOD FOR. CRIMINALS.
HOLE-DIGGING *CROOKS!*
YOU COULD FIND SOMETHING FOR HIM. HE COULD SWEEP UP, OR–
I DON'T WANT TO SWEEP.
ALREADY HE HAS DEMANDS.
WELL...ALL RIGHT, MAYBE I COULD THINK OF SOMETHING FOR HIM TO DO.
I THOUGHT YOU SAID WE'RE ALL CROOKS.
YOU ARE! BUT...

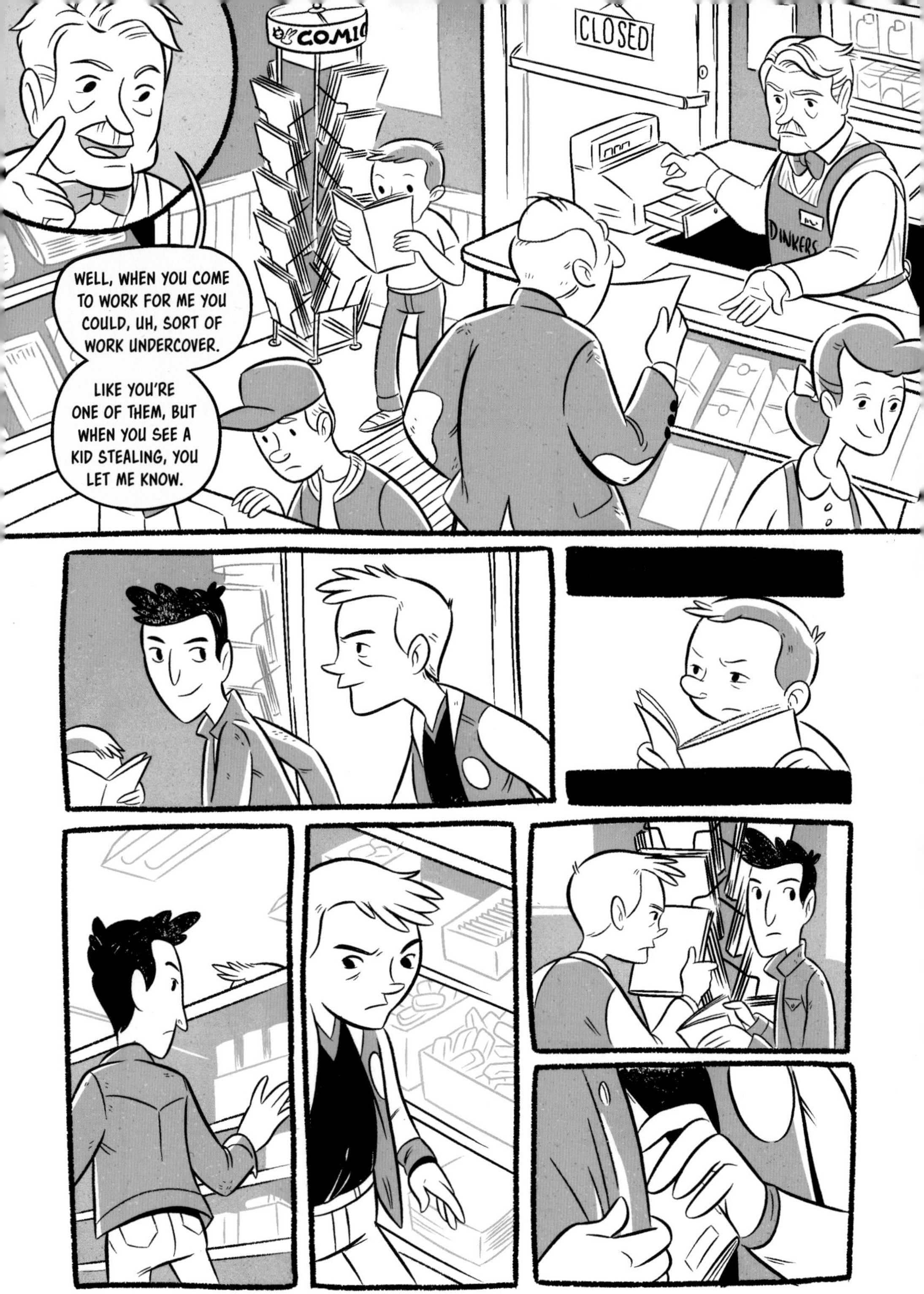
COMIC
CLOSED
DINKERS
WELL, WHEN YOU COME TO WORK FOR ME YOU COULD, UH, SORT OF WORK UNDERCOVER.
LIKE YOU'RE ONE OF THEM, BUT WHEN YOU SEE A KID STEALING, YOU LET ME KNOW.

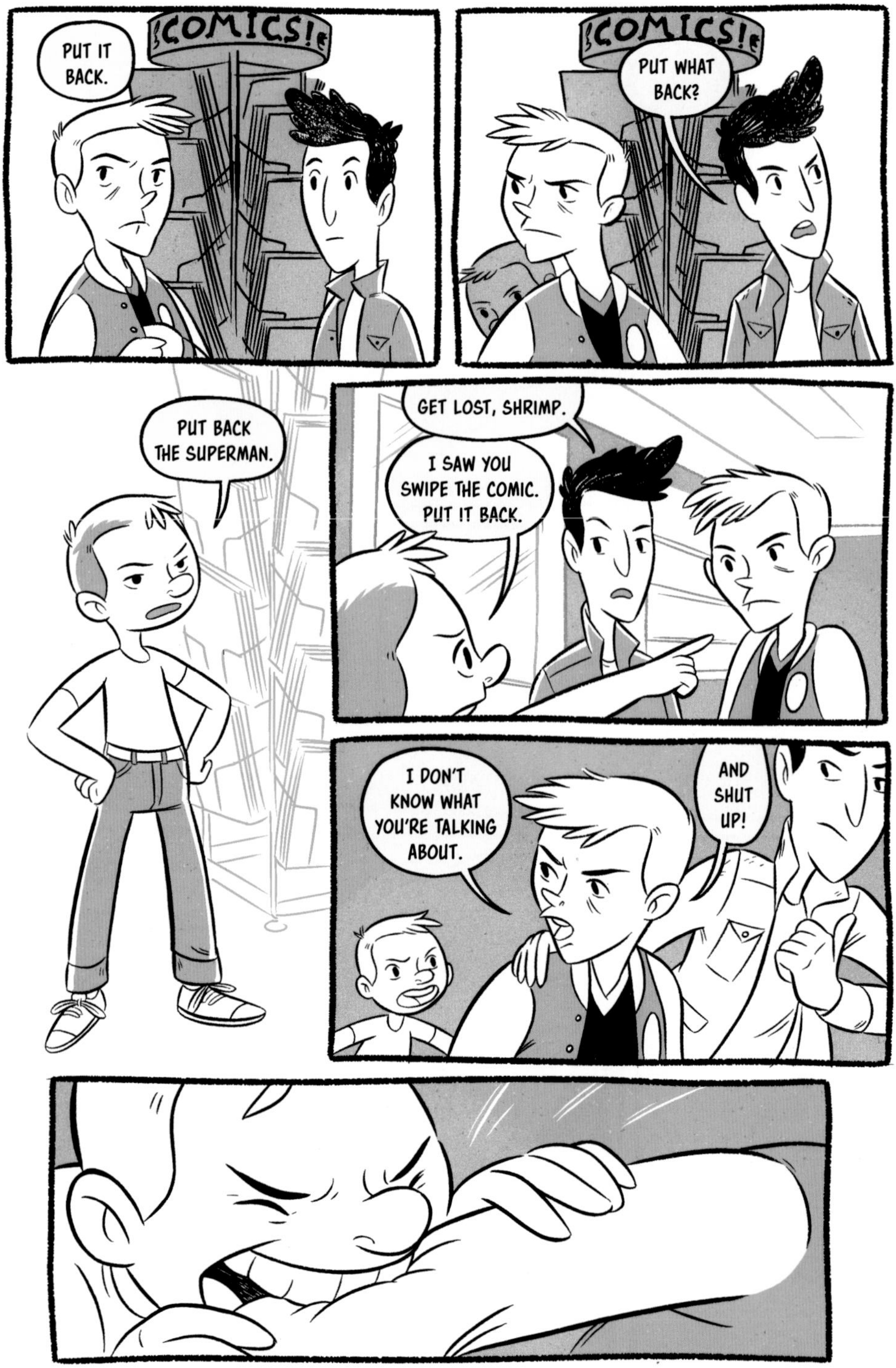
COMICS!
PUT IT BACK.
COMICS!
PUT WHAT BACK?
PUT BACK THE SUPERMAN.
GET LOST, SHRIMP.
I SAW YOU SWIPE THE COMIC. PUT IT BACK.
I DON'T KNOW WHAT YOU'RE TALKING ABOUT.
AND SHUT UP!

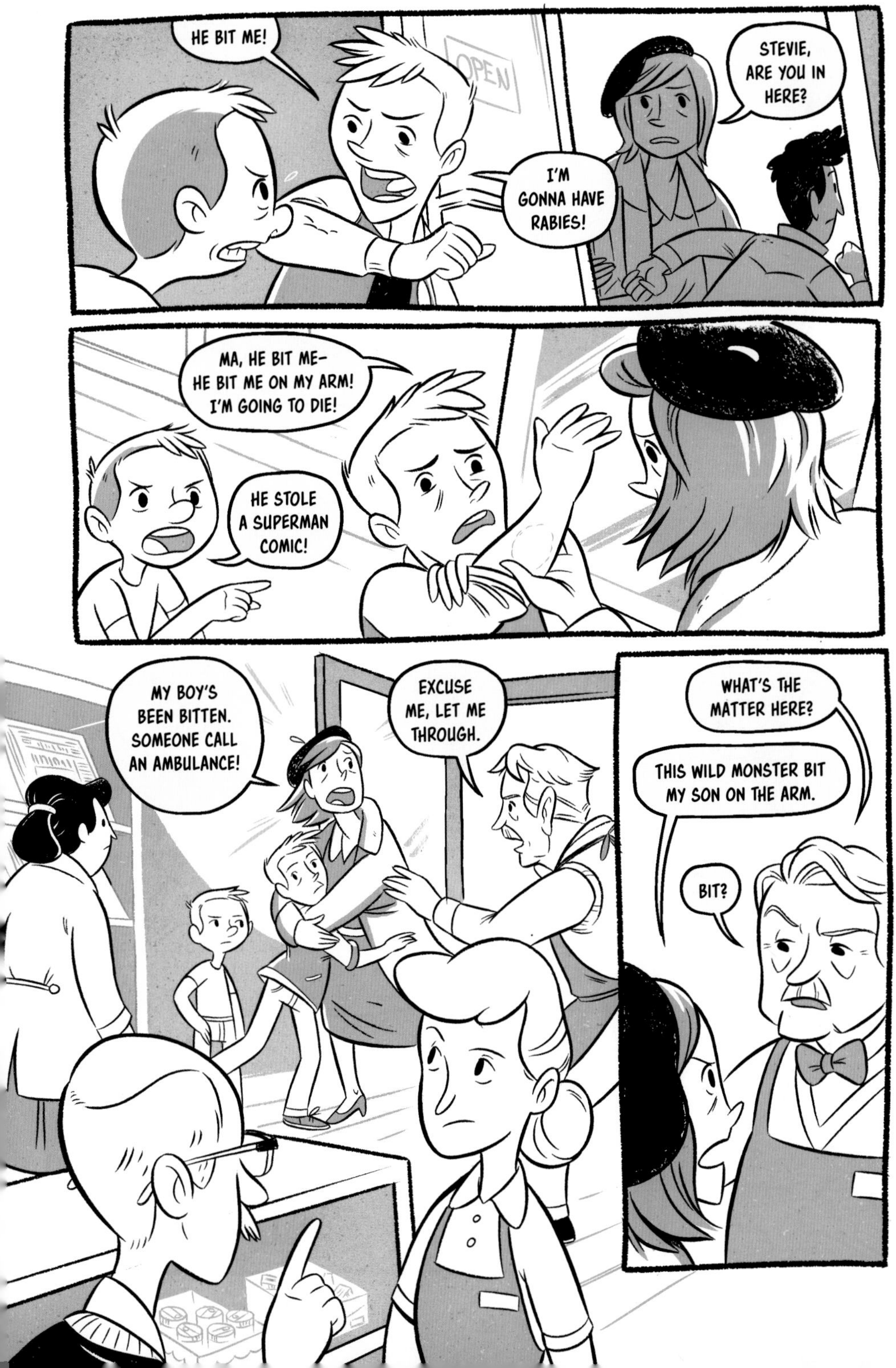
HE BIT ME!
OPEN
I'M GONNA HAVE RABIES!
STEVIE, ARE YOU IN HERE?
MA, HE BIT ME– HE BIT ME ON MY ARM! I'M GOING TO DIE!
HE STOLE A SUPERMAN COMIC!
MY BOY'S BEEN BITTEN. SOMEONE CALL AN AMBULANCE!
EXCUSE ME, LET ME THROUGH.
WHAT'S THE MATTER HERE?
THIS WILD MONSTER BIT MY SON ON THE ARM.
BIT?

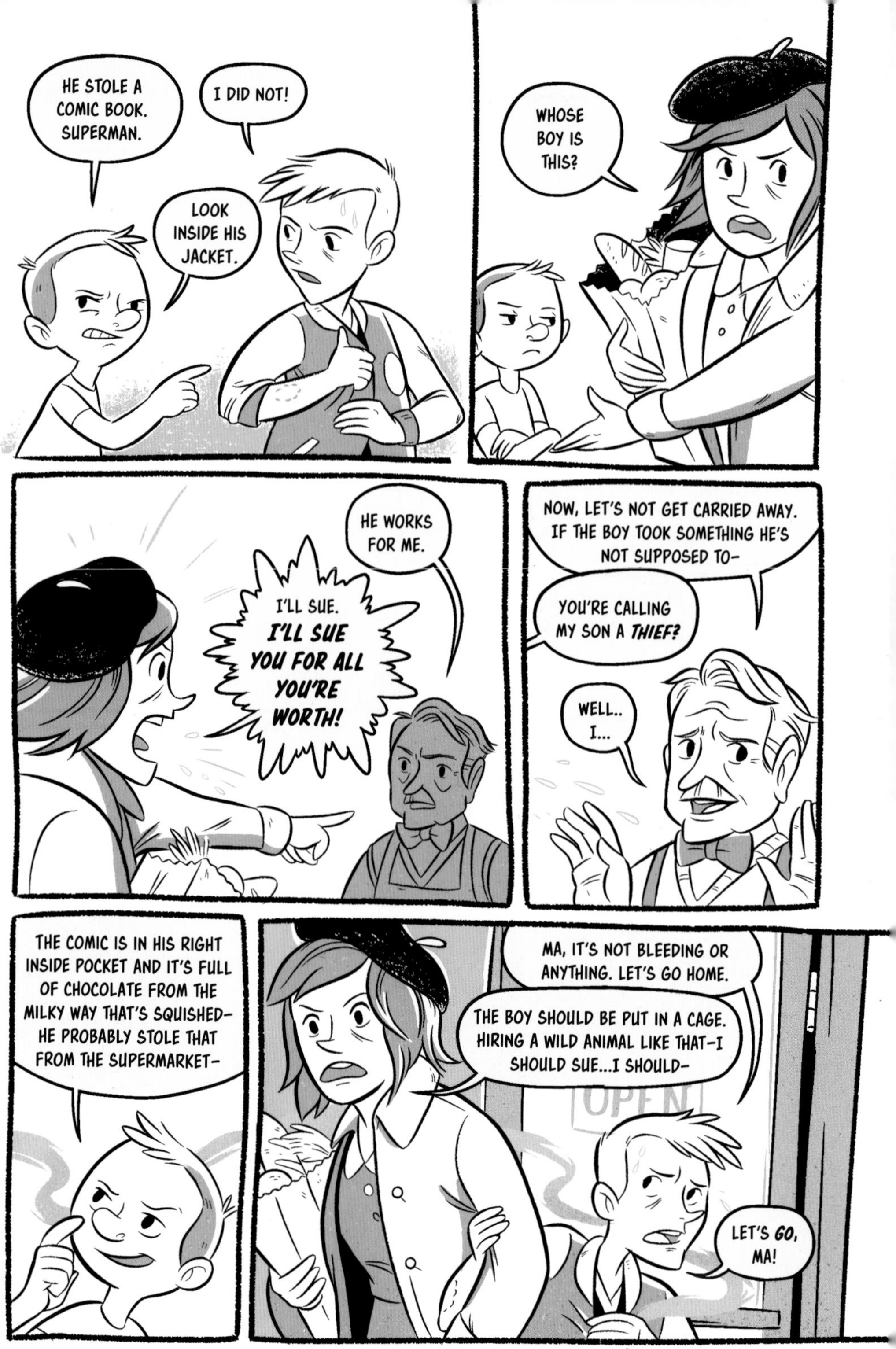

HE STOLE A COMIC BOOK. SUPERMAN.
I DID NOT!
LOOK INSIDE HIS JACKET.
WHOSE BOY IS THIS?
HE WORKS FOR ME.
I'LL SUE. *I'LL SUE YOU FOR ALL YOU'RE WORTH!*
NOW, LET'S NOT GET CARRIED AWAY. IF THE BOY TOOK SOMETHING HE'S NOT SUPPOSED TO–
YOU'RE CALLING MY SON A *THIEF?*
WELL.. I...
THE COMIC IS IN HIS RIGHT INSIDE POCKET AND IT'S FULL OF CHOCOLATE FROM THE MILKY WAY THAT'S SQUISHED– HE PROBABLY STOLE THAT FROM THE SUPERMARKET–
MA, IT'S NOT BLEEDING OR ANYTHING. LET'S GO HOME.
THE BOY SHOULD BE PUT IN A CAGE. HIRING A WILD ANIMAL LIKE THAT–I SHOULD SUE...I SHOULD–
OPEN
LET'S *GO*, MA!

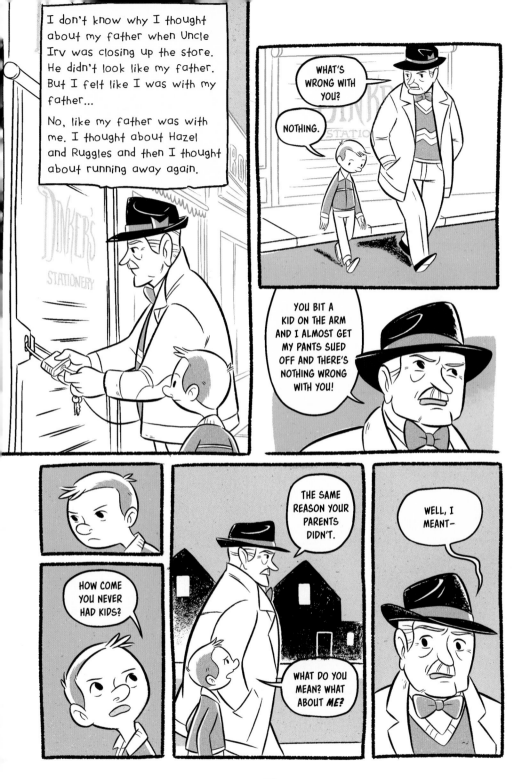

I don't know why I thought about my father when Uncle Irv was closing up the store. He didn't look like my father. But I felt like I was with my father...

No, like my father was with me. I thought about Hazel and Ruggles and then I thought about running away again.

WHAT'S WRONG WITH YOU?

NOTHING.

YOU BIT A KID ON THE ARM AND I ALMOST GET MY PANTS SUED OFF AND THERE'S NOTHING WRONG WITH YOU!

HOW COME YOU NEVER HAD KIDS?

THE SAME REASON YOUR PARENTS DIDN'T.

WHAT DO YOU MEAN? WHAT ABOUT ME?

WELL, I MEANT—

73

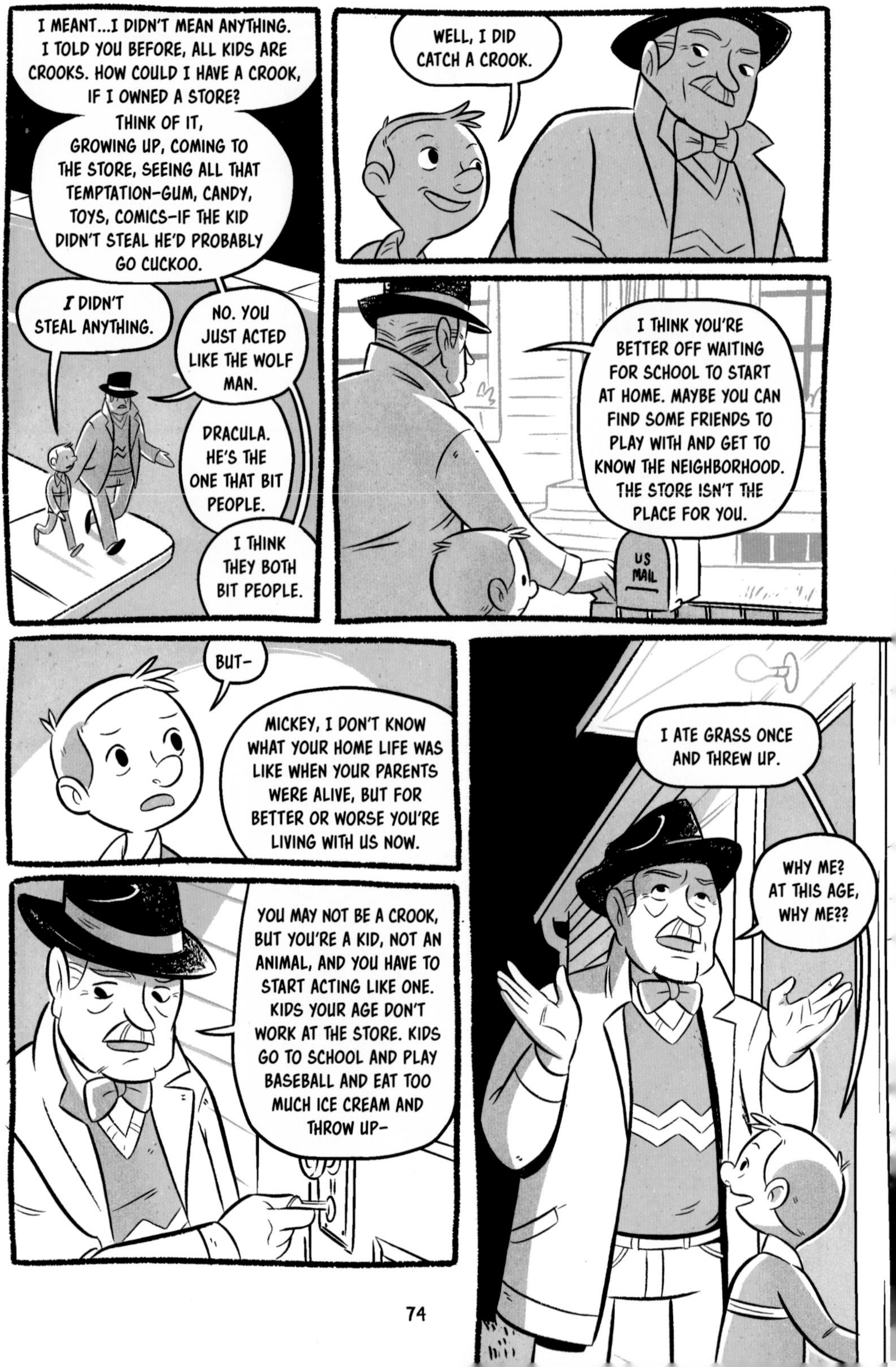

I MEANT...I DIDN'T MEAN ANYTHING. I TOLD YOU BEFORE, ALL KIDS ARE CROOKS. HOW COULD I HAVE A CROOK, IF I OWNED A STORE?
THINK OF IT, GROWING UP, COMING TO THE STORE, SEEING ALL THAT TEMPTATION–GUM, CANDY, TOYS, COMICS–IF THE KID DIDN'T STEAL HE'D PROBABLY GO CUCKOO.
I DIDN'T STEAL ANYTHING.
NO. YOU JUST ACTED LIKE THE WOLF MAN.
DRACULA. HE'S THE ONE THAT BIT PEOPLE.
I THINK THEY BOTH BIT PEOPLE.
WELL, I DID CATCH A CROOK.
I THINK YOU'RE BETTER OFF WAITING FOR SCHOOL TO START AT HOME. MAYBE YOU CAN FIND SOME FRIENDS TO PLAY WITH AND GET TO KNOW THE NEIGHBORHOOD. THE STORE ISN'T THE PLACE FOR YOU.
US MAIL
BUT–
MICKEY, I DON'T KNOW WHAT YOUR HOME LIFE WAS LIKE WHEN YOUR PARENTS WERE ALIVE, BUT FOR BETTER OR WORSE YOU'RE LIVING WITH US NOW.
YOU MAY NOT BE A CROOK, BUT YOU'RE A KID, NOT AN ANIMAL, AND YOU HAVE TO START ACTING LIKE ONE. KIDS YOUR AGE DON'T WORK AT THE STORE. KIDS GO TO SCHOOL AND PLAY BASEBALL AND EAT TOO MUCH ICE CREAM AND THROW UP–
I ATE GRASS ONCE AND THREW UP.
WHY ME? AT THIS AGE, WHY ME??

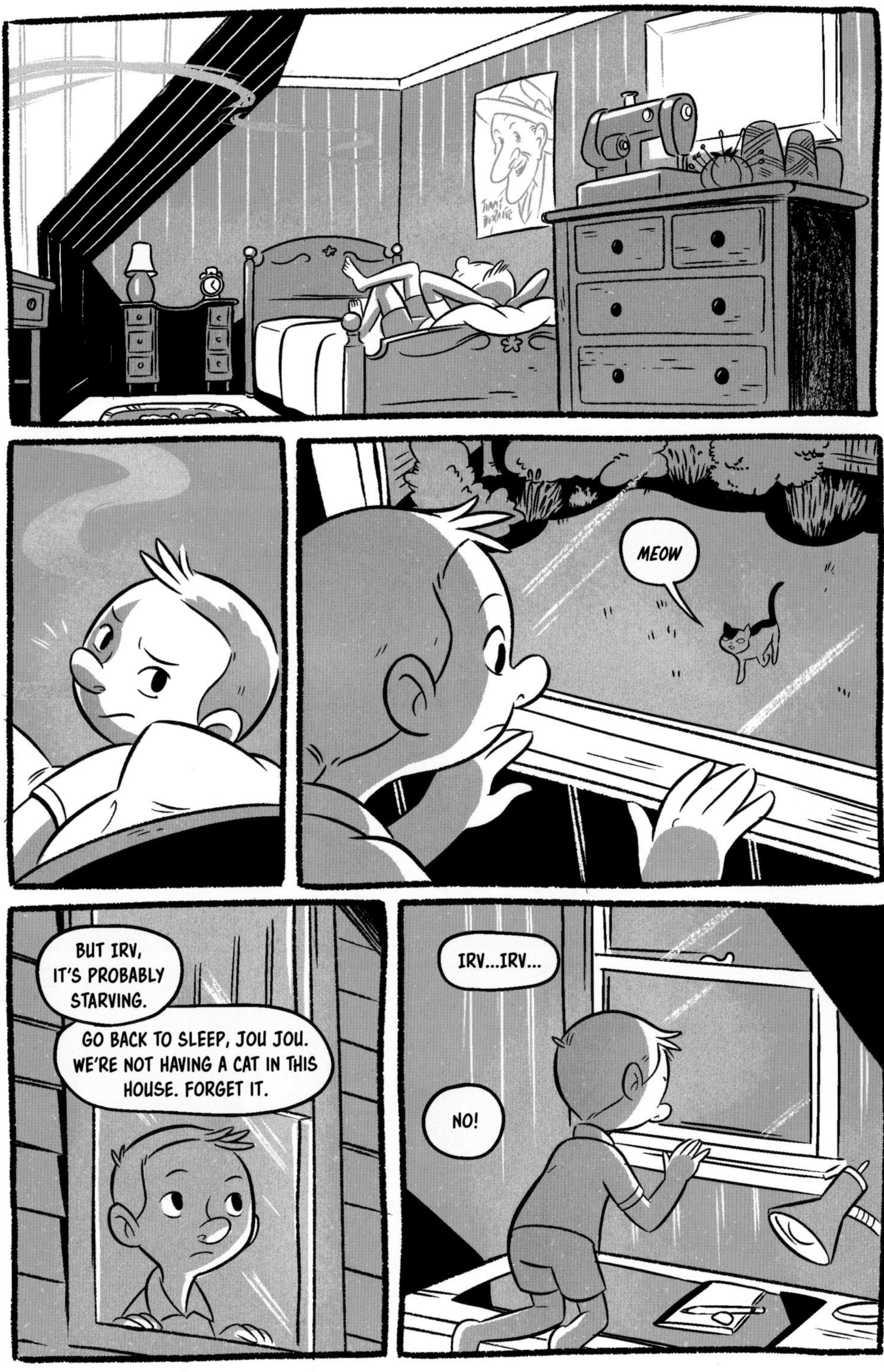
TIMMY BURNSIDE
MEOW
BUT IRV, IT'S PROBABLY STARVING.
GO BACK TO SLEEP, JOU JOU. WE'RE NOT HAVING A CAT IN THIS HOUSE. FORGET IT.
IRV...IRV...
NO!

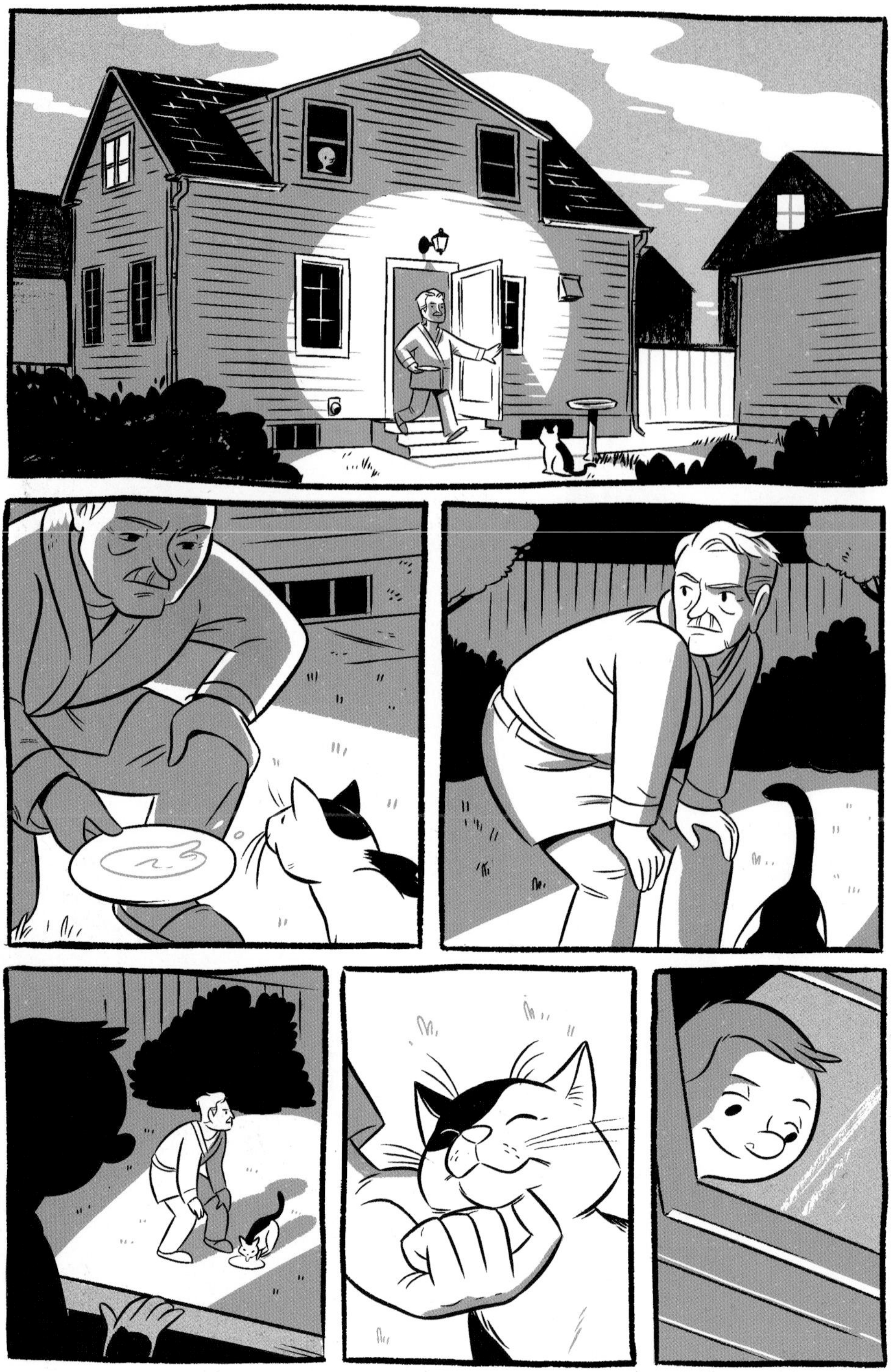

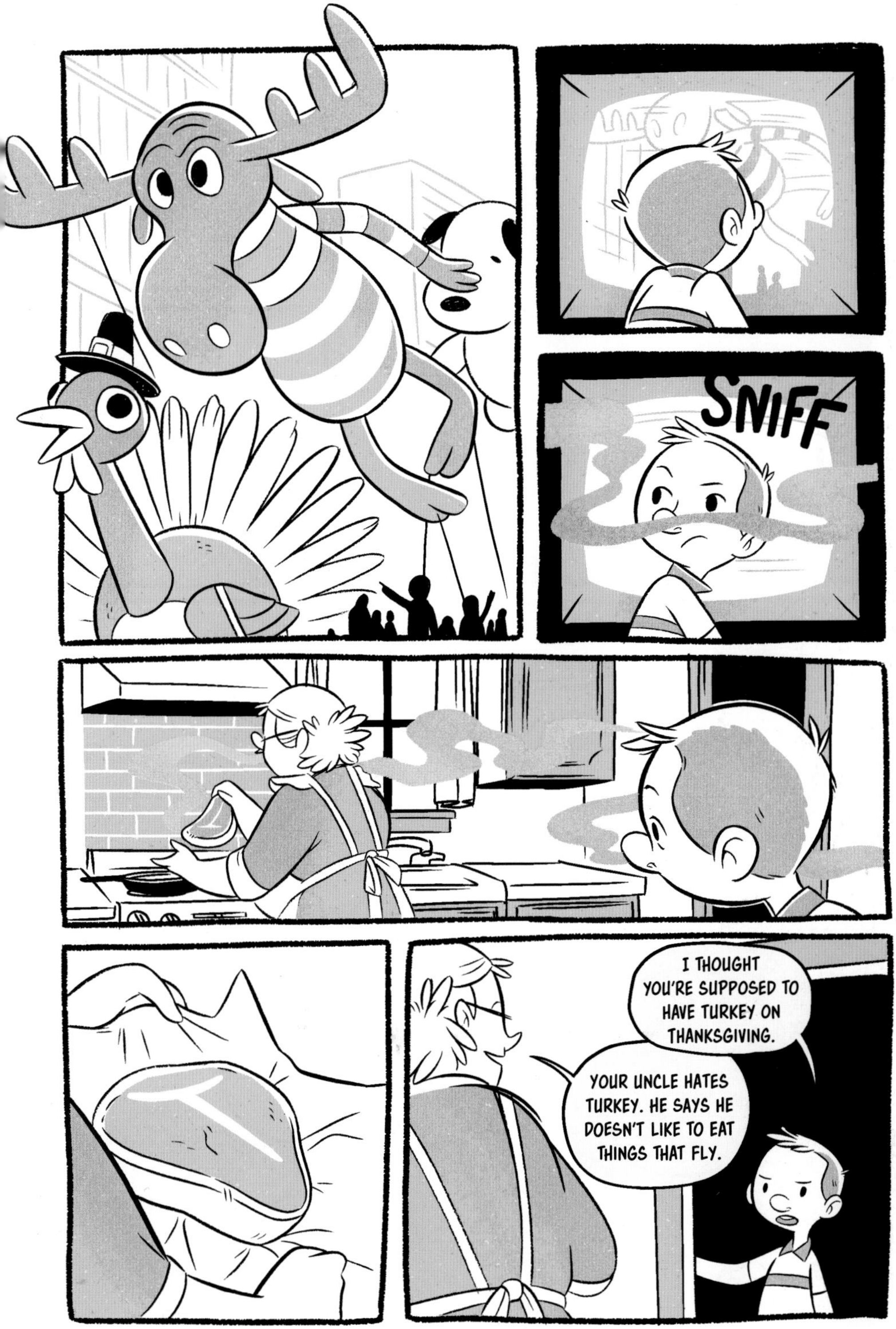
SNIFF
I THOUGHT YOU'RE SUPPOSED TO HAVE TURKEY ON THANKSGIVING.
YOUR UNCLE HATES TURKEY. HE SAYS HE DOESN'T LIKE TO EAT THINGS THAT FLY.

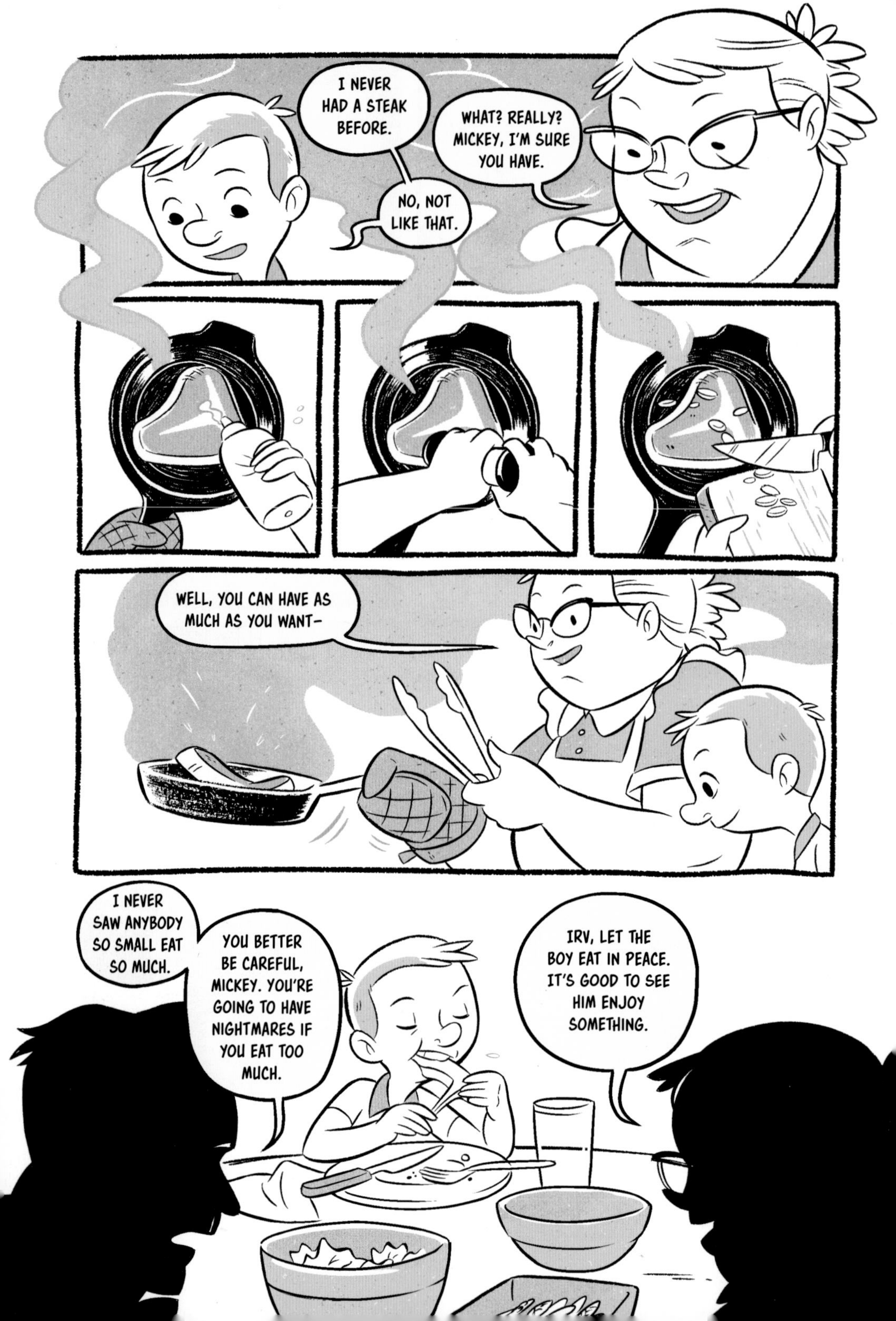
I NEVER HAD A STEAK BEFORE.
WHAT? REALLY? MICKEY, I'M SURE YOU HAVE.
NO, NOT LIKE THAT.
WELL, YOU CAN HAVE AS MUCH AS YOU WANT–
I NEVER SAW ANYBODY SO SMALL EAT SO MUCH.
YOU BETTER BE CAREFUL, MICKEY. YOU'RE GOING TO HAVE NIGHTMARES IF YOU EAT TOO MUCH.
IRV, LET THE BOY EAT IN PEACE. IT'S GOOD TO SEE HIM ENJOY SOMETHING.

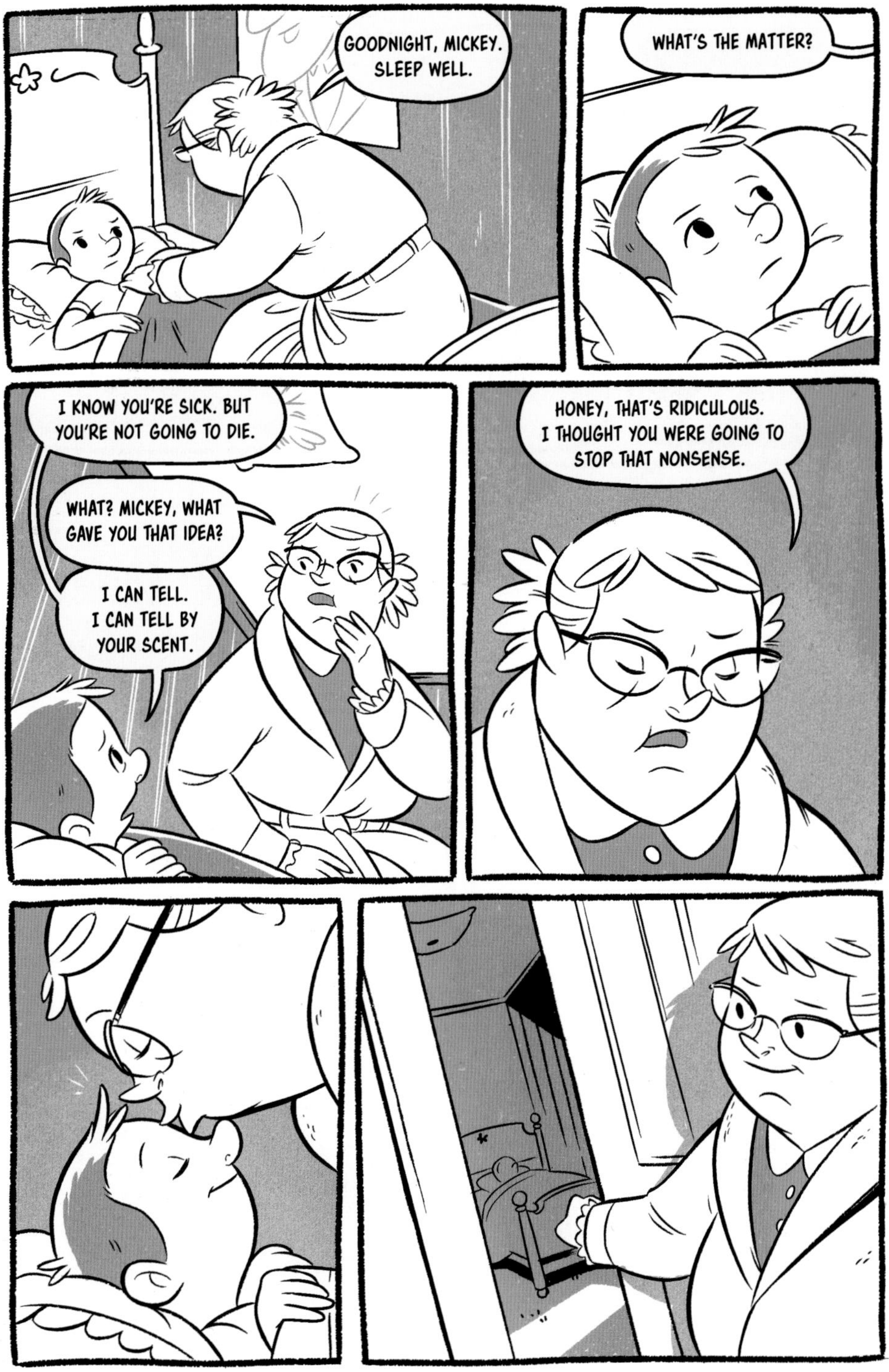
GOODNIGHT, MICKEY. SLEEP WELL.
WHAT'S THE MATTER?
I KNOW YOU'RE SICK. BUT YOU'RE NOT GOING TO DIE.
WHAT? MICKEY, WHAT GAVE YOU THAT IDEA?
I CAN TELL. I CAN TELL BY YOUR SCENT.
HONEY, THAT'S RIDICULOUS. I THOUGHT YOU WERE GOING TO STOP THAT NONSENSE.

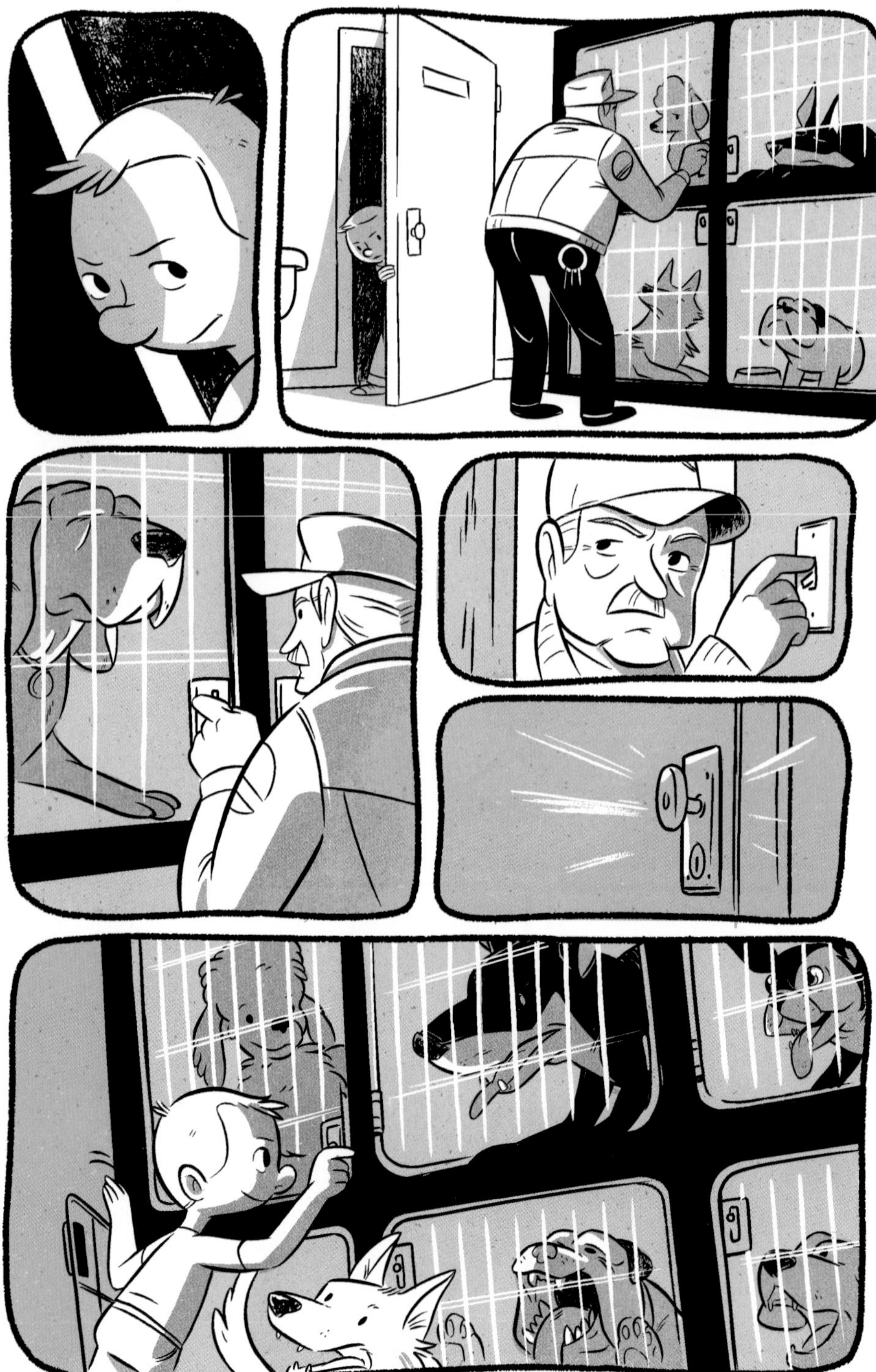

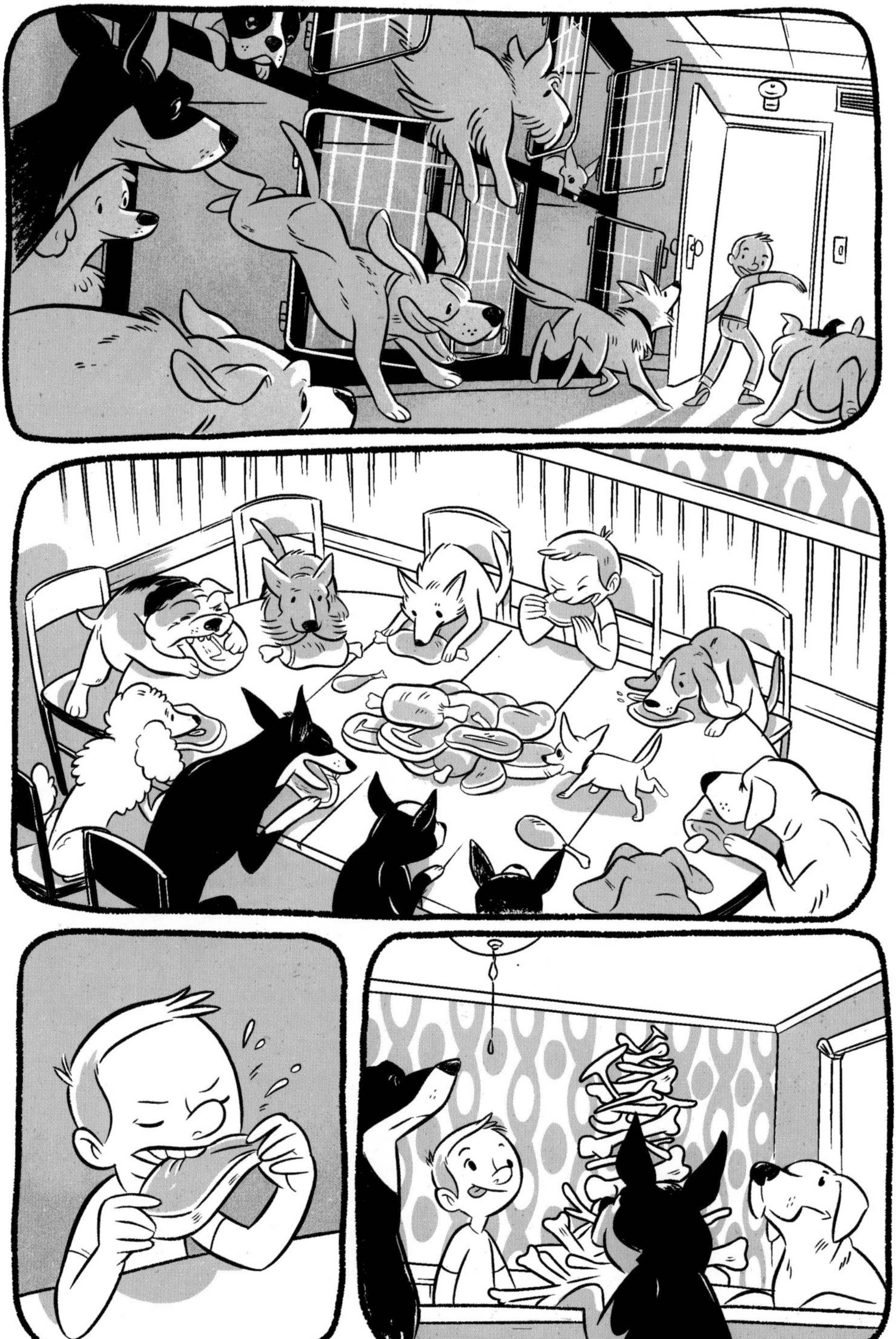

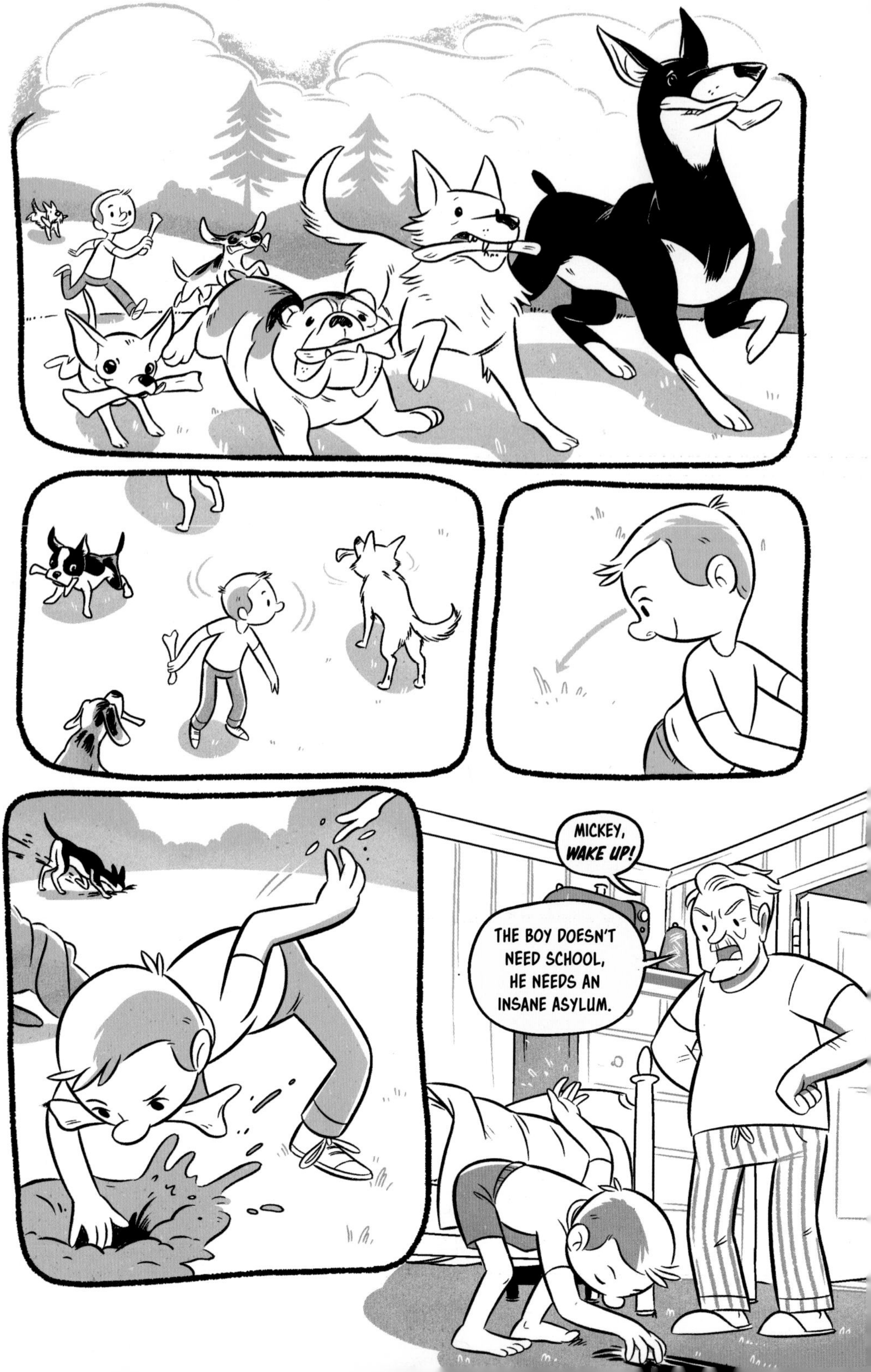
MICKEY, WAKE UP!
THE BOY DOESN'T NEED SCHOOL, HE NEEDS AN INSANE ASYLUM.

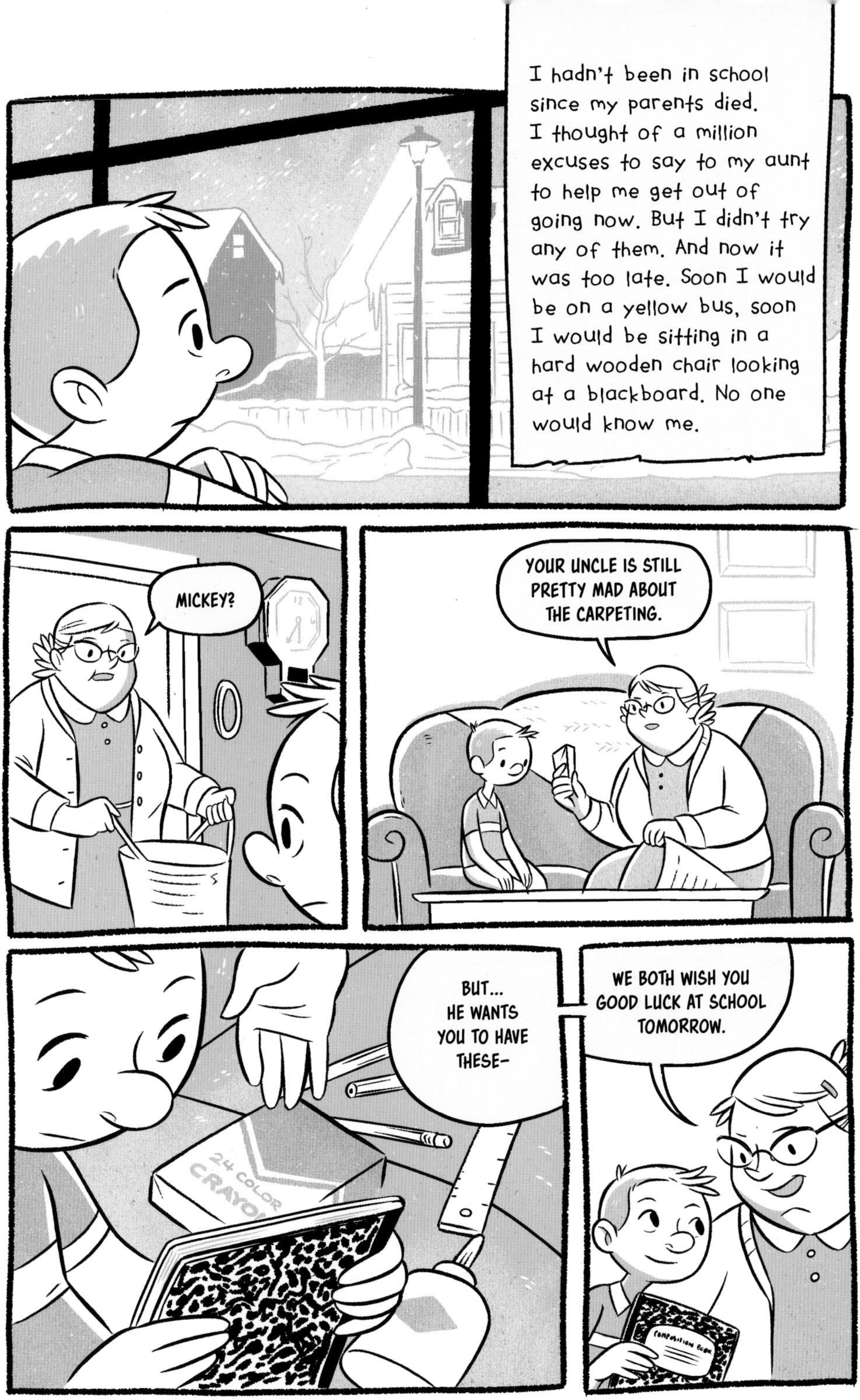
I hadn't been in school since my parents died. I thought of a million excuses to say to my aunt to help me get out of going now. But I didn't try any of them. And now it was too late. Soon I would be on a yellow bus, soon I would be sitting in a hard wooden chair looking at a blackboard. No one would know me.
MICKEY?
YOUR UNCLE IS STILL PRETTY MAD ABOUT THE CARPETING.
BUT... HE WANTS YOU TO HAVE THESE-
WE BOTH WISH YOU GOOD LUCK AT SCHOOL TOMORROW.
24 COLOR CRAYO

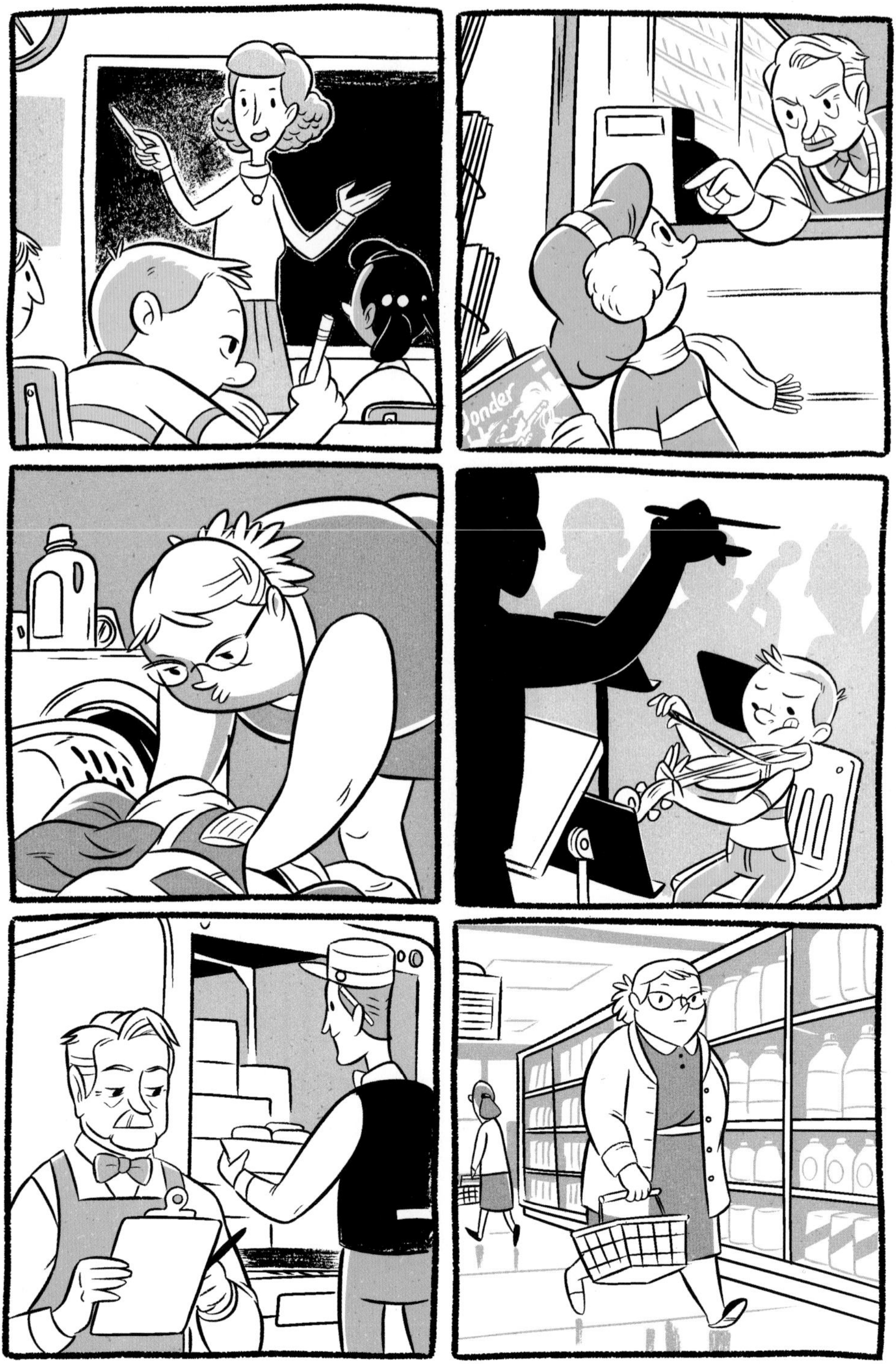

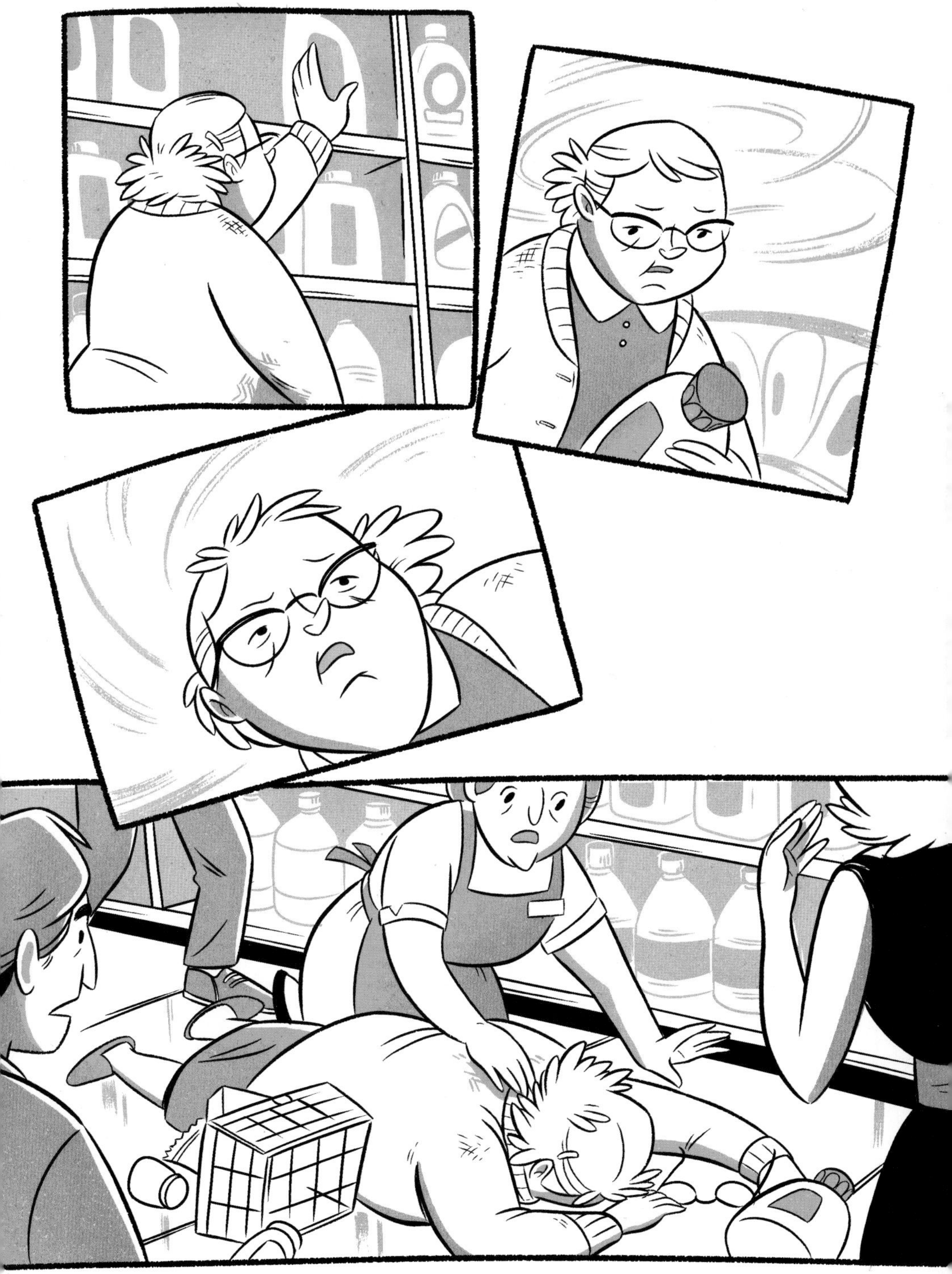

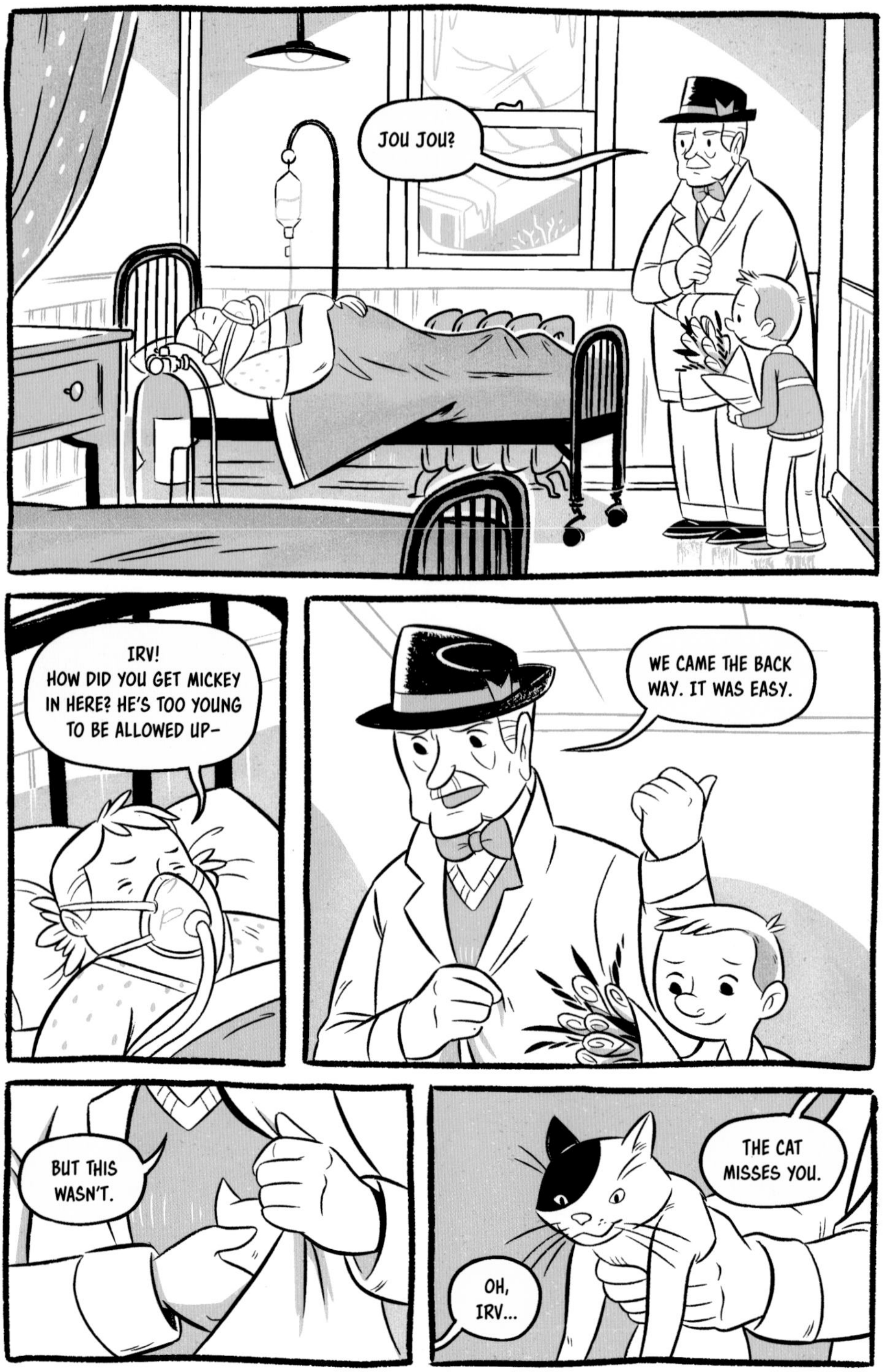
JOU JOU?
IRV!
HOW DID YOU GET MICKEY
IN HERE? HE'S TOO YOUNG
TO BE ALLOWED UP-
WE CAME THE BACK
WAY. IT WAS EASY.
BUT THIS
WASN'T.
THE CAT
MISSES YOU.
OH,
IRV...

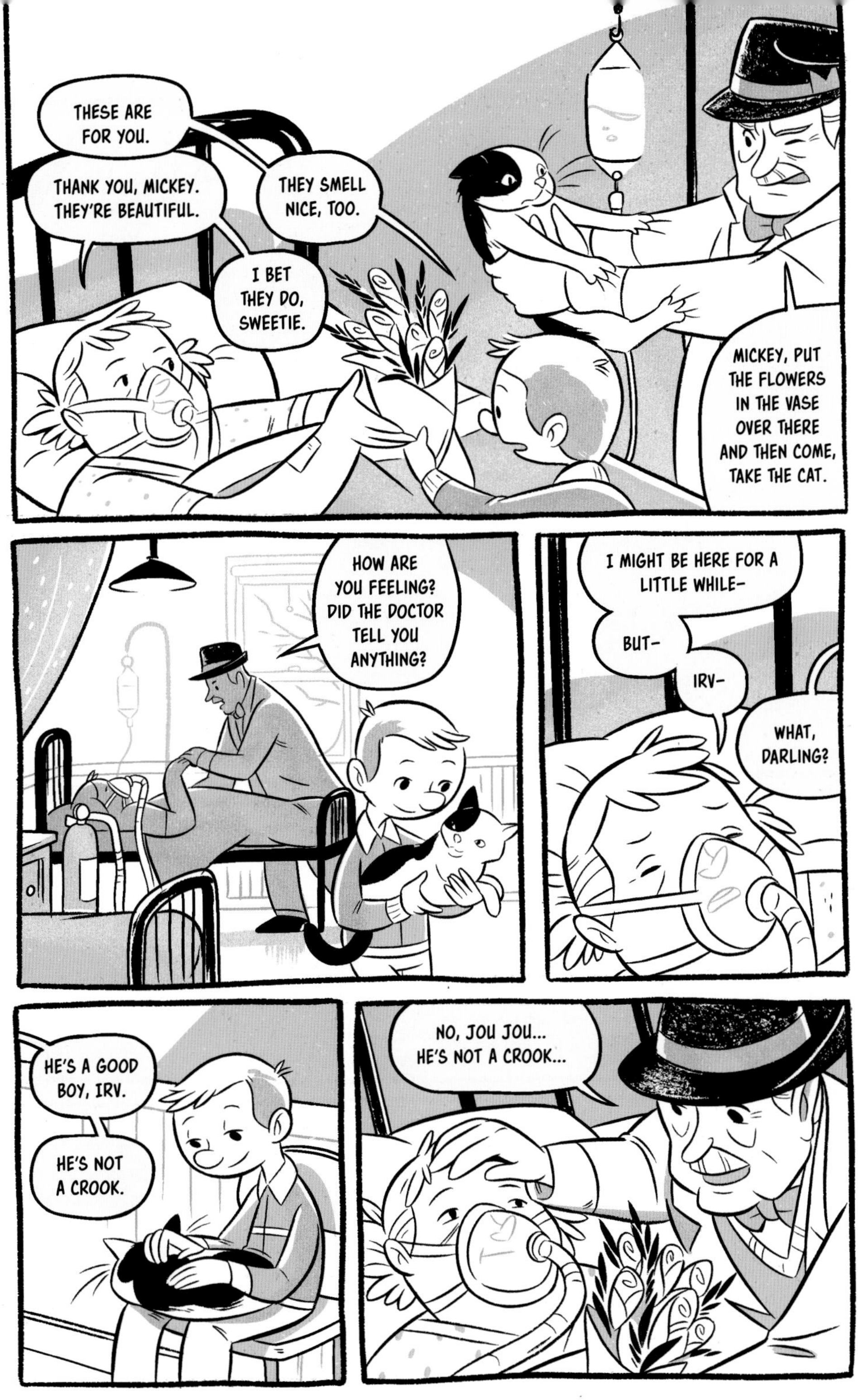
THESE ARE FOR YOU.
THANK YOU, MICKEY. THEY'RE BEAUTIFUL.
THEY SMELL NICE, TOO.
I BET THEY DO, SWEETIE.
MICKEY, PUT THE FLOWERS IN THE VASE OVER THERE AND THEN COME, TAKE THE CAT.
HOW ARE YOU FEELING? DID THE DOCTOR TELL YOU ANYTHING?
I MIGHT BE HERE FOR A LITTLE WHILE–
BUT–
IRV–
WHAT, DARLING?
HE'S A GOOD BOY, IRV.
HE'S NOT A CROOK.
NO, JOU JOU... HE'S NOT A CROOK...

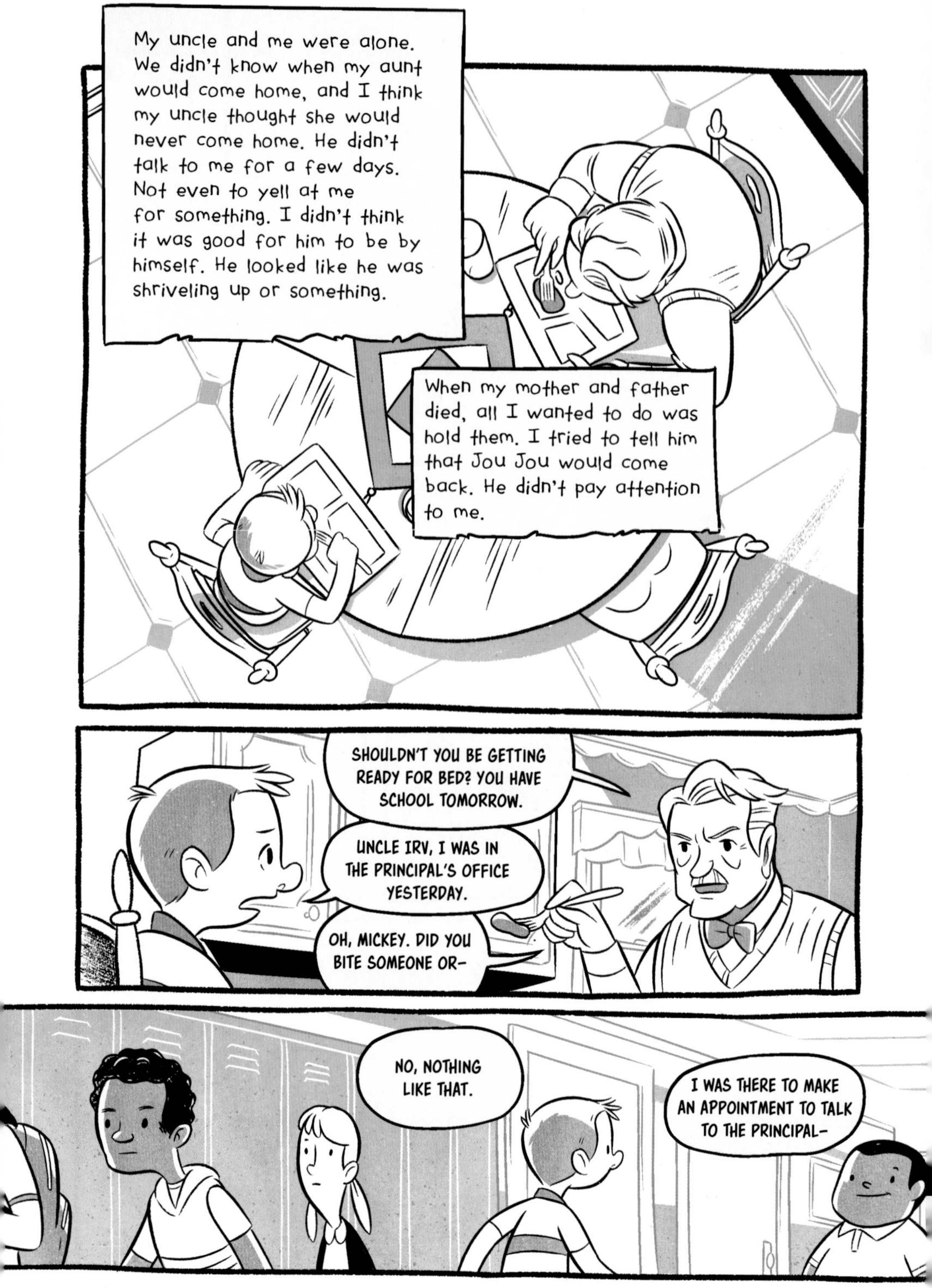
My uncle and me were alone. We didn't know when my aunt would come home, and I think my uncle thought she would never come home. He didn't talk to me for a few days. Not even to yell at me for something. I didn't think it was good for him to be by himself. He looked like he was shriveling up or something.
When my mother and father died, all I wanted to do was hold them. I tried to tell him that Jou Jou would come back. He didn't pay attention to me.
SHOULDN'T YOU BE GETTING READY FOR BED? YOU HAVE SCHOOL TOMORROW.
UNCLE IRV, I WAS IN THE PRINCIPAL'S OFFICE YESTERDAY.
OH, MICKEY. DID YOU BITE SOMEONE OR-
NO, NOTHING LIKE THAT.
I WAS THERE TO MAKE AN APPOINTMENT TO TALK TO THE PRINCIPAL-

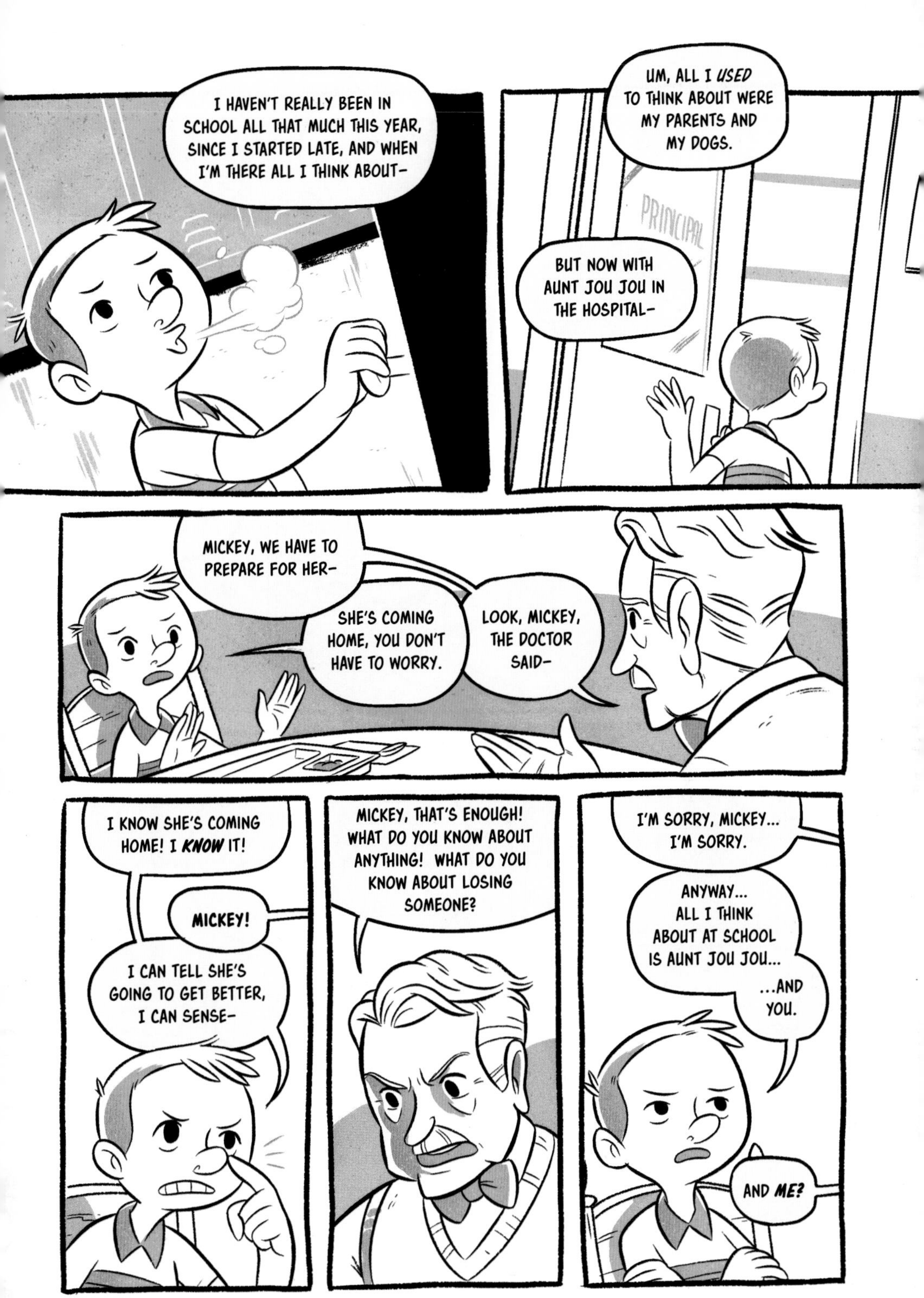
I HAVEN'T REALLY BEEN IN SCHOOL ALL THAT MUCH THIS YEAR, SINCE I STARTED LATE, AND WHEN I'M THERE ALL I THINK ABOUT-
UM, ALL I *USED* TO THINK ABOUT WERE MY PARENTS AND MY DOGS.
PRINCIPAL
BUT NOW WITH AUNT JOU JOU IN THE HOSPITAL-
MICKEY, WE HAVE TO PREPARE FOR HER-
SHE'S COMING HOME, YOU DON'T HAVE TO WORRY.
LOOK, MICKEY, THE DOCTOR SAID-
I KNOW SHE'S COMING HOME! I ***KNOW*** IT!
MICKEY!
I CAN TELL SHE'S GOING TO GET BETTER, I CAN SENSE-
MICKEY, THAT'S ENOUGH! WHAT DO YOU KNOW ABOUT ANYTHING! WHAT DO YOU KNOW ABOUT LOSING SOMEONE?
I'M SORRY, MICKEY... I'M SORRY.
ANYWAY... ALL I THINK ABOUT AT SCHOOL IS AUNT JOU JOU...
...AND YOU.
AND ***ME?***

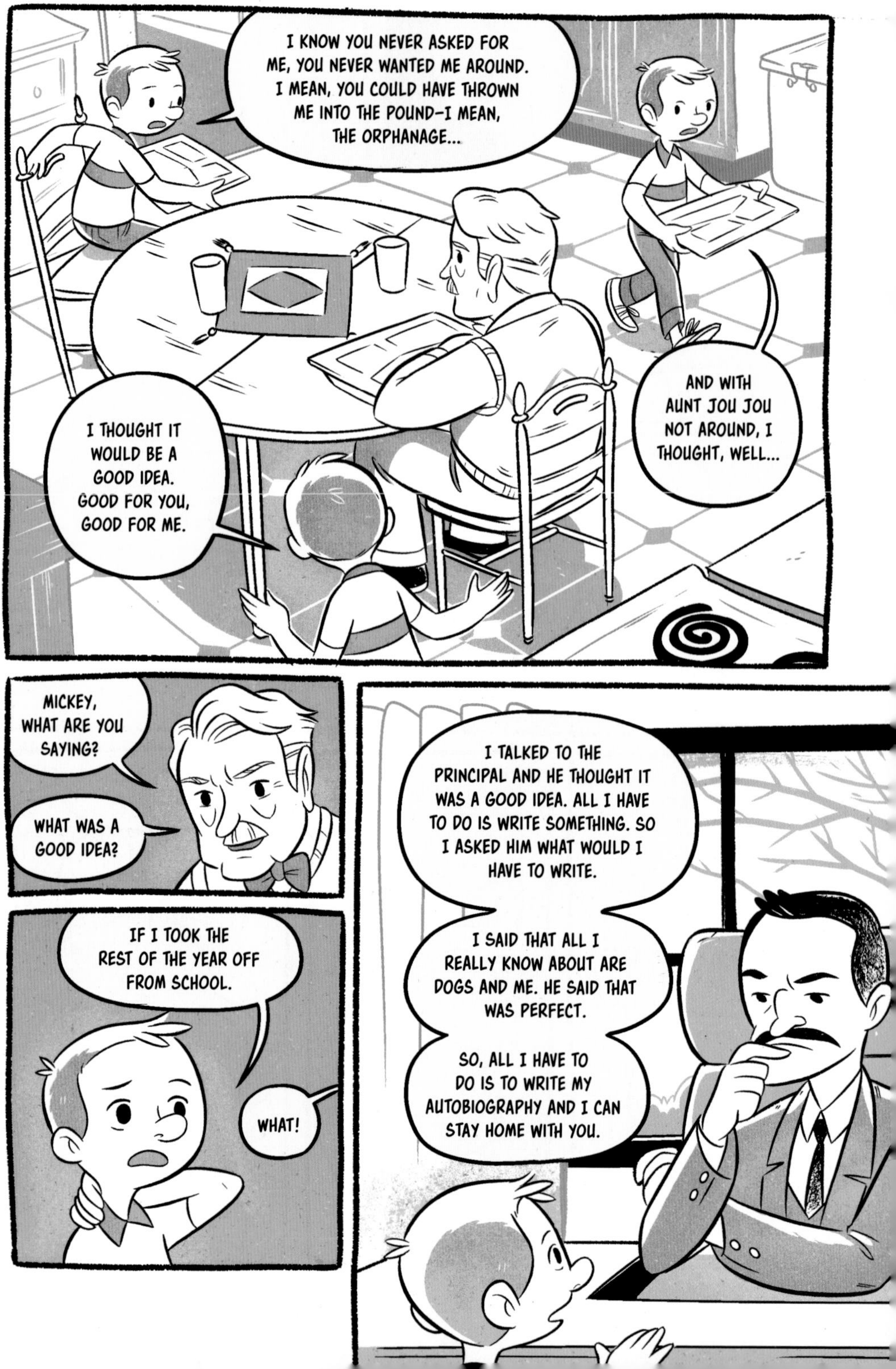
I KNOW YOU NEVER ASKED FOR ME, YOU NEVER WANTED ME AROUND. I MEAN, YOU COULD HAVE THROWN ME INTO THE POUND—I MEAN, THE ORPHANAGE...
AND WITH AUNT JOU JOU NOT AROUND, I THOUGHT, WELL...
I THOUGHT IT WOULD BE A GOOD IDEA. GOOD FOR YOU, GOOD FOR ME.
MICKEY, WHAT ARE YOU SAYING?
WHAT WAS A GOOD IDEA?
IF I TOOK THE REST OF THE YEAR OFF FROM SCHOOL.
WHAT!
I TALKED TO THE PRINCIPAL AND HE THOUGHT IT WAS A GOOD IDEA. ALL I HAVE TO DO IS WRITE SOMETHING. SO I ASKED HIM WHAT WOULD I HAVE TO WRITE.
I SAID THAT ALL I REALLY KNOW ABOUT ARE DOGS AND ME. HE SAID THAT WAS PERFECT.
SO, ALL I HAVE TO DO IS TO WRITE MY AUTOBIOGRAPHY AND I CAN STAY HOME WITH YOU.

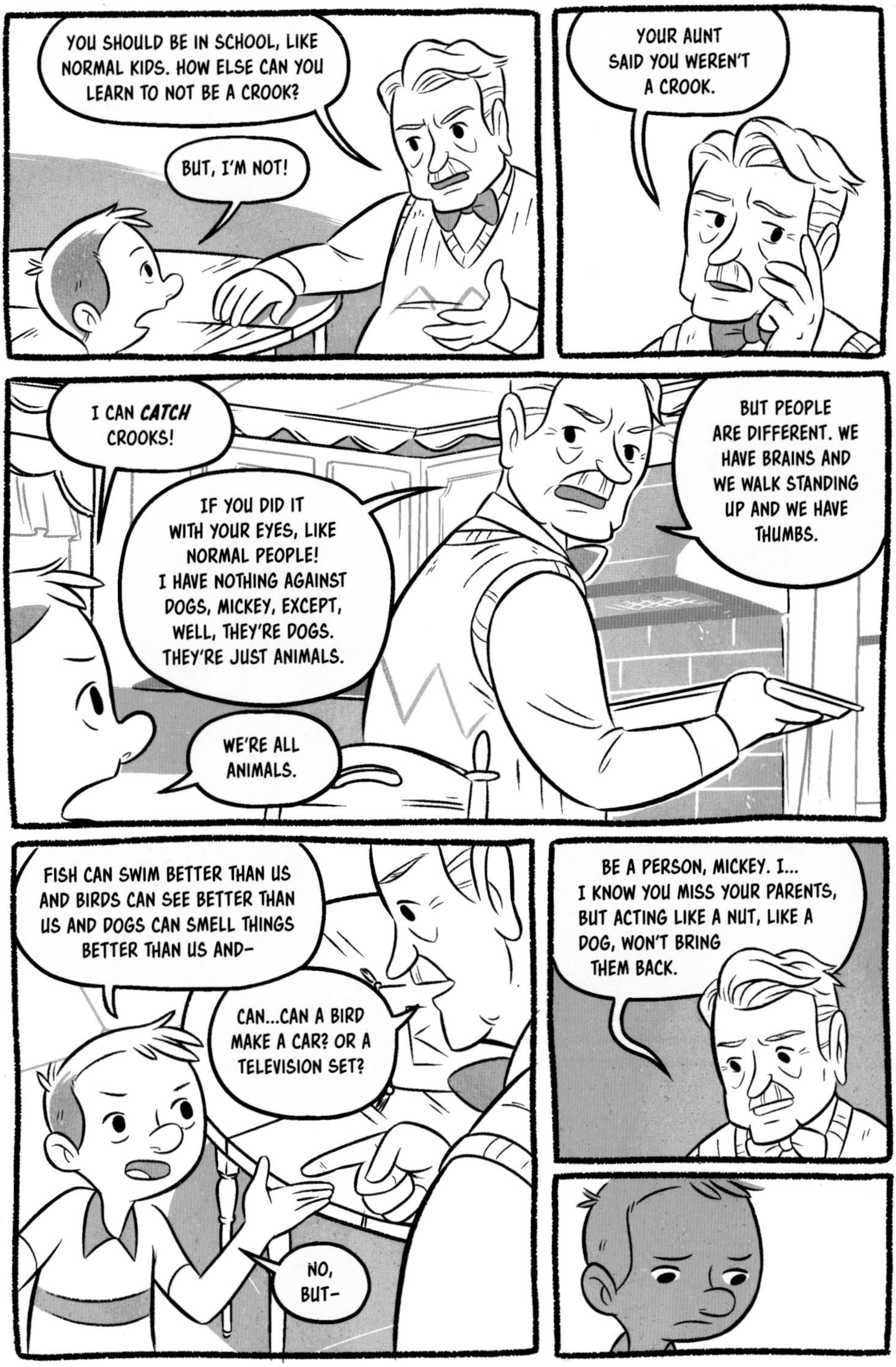
YOU SHOULD BE IN SCHOOL, LIKE NORMAL KIDS. HOW ELSE CAN YOU LEARN TO NOT BE A CROOK?
BUT, I'M NOT!
YOUR AUNT SAID YOU WEREN'T A CROOK.
I CAN *CATCH* CROOKS!
IF YOU DID IT WITH YOUR EYES, LIKE NORMAL PEOPLE! I HAVE NOTHING AGAINST DOGS, MICKEY, EXCEPT, WELL, THEY'RE DOGS. THEY'RE JUST ANIMALS.
WE'RE ALL ANIMALS.
BUT PEOPLE ARE DIFFERENT. WE HAVE BRAINS AND WE WALK STANDING UP AND WE HAVE THUMBS.
FISH CAN SWIM BETTER THAN US AND BIRDS CAN SEE BETTER THAN US AND DOGS CAN SMELL THINGS BETTER THAN US AND-
CAN...CAN A BIRD MAKE A CAR? OR A TELEVISION SET?
NO, BUT-
BE A PERSON, MICKEY. I... I KNOW YOU MISS YOUR PARENTS, BUT ACTING LIKE A NUT, LIKE A DOG, WON'T BRING THEM BACK.

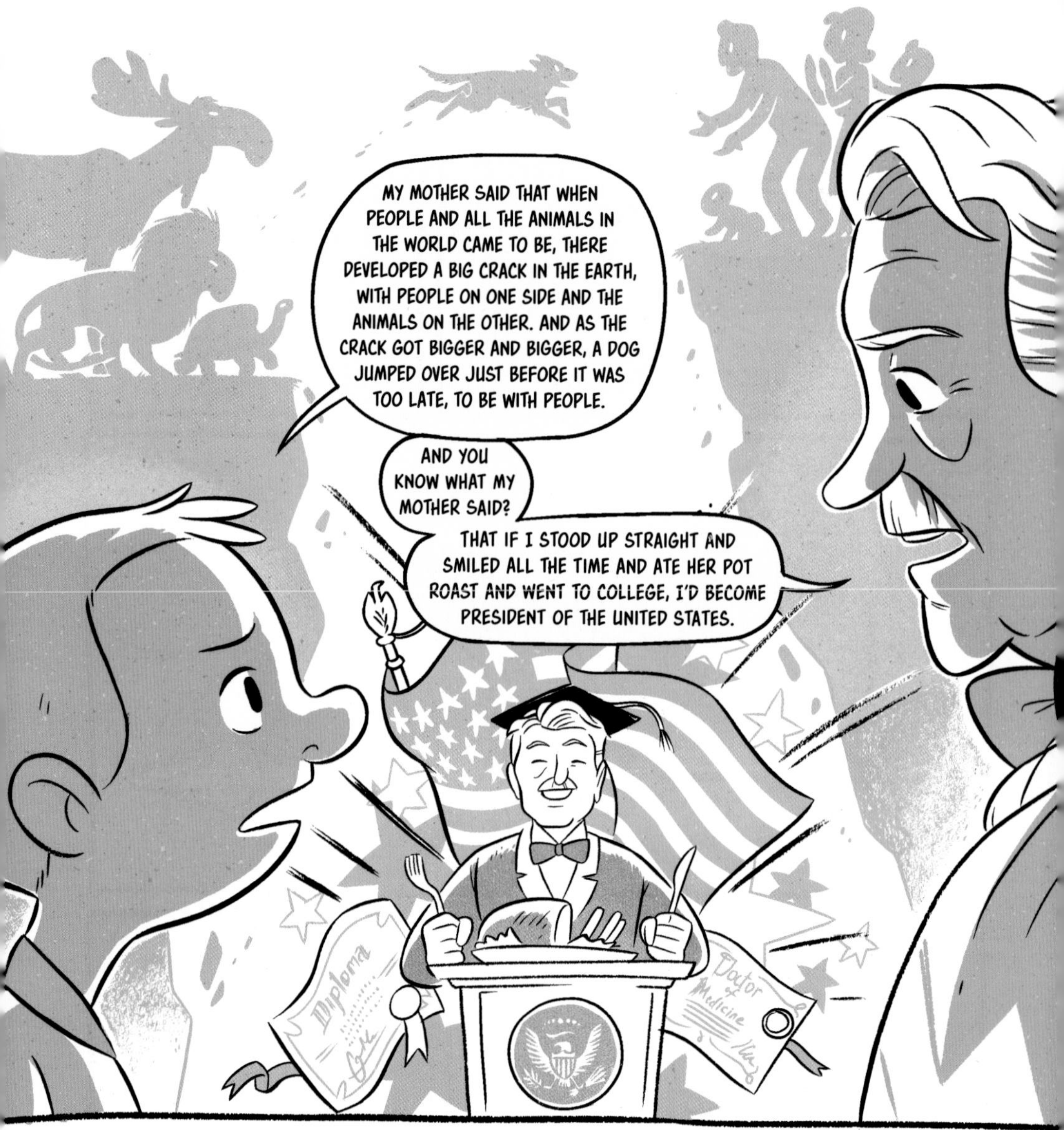
MY MOTHER SAID THAT WHEN PEOPLE AND ALL THE ANIMALS IN THE WORLD CAME TO BE, THERE DEVELOPED A BIG CRACK IN THE EARTH, WITH PEOPLE ON ONE SIDE AND THE ANIMALS ON THE OTHER. AND AS THE CRACK GOT BIGGER AND BIGGER, A DOG JUMPED OVER JUST BEFORE IT WAS TOO LATE, TO BE WITH PEOPLE.
AND YOU KNOW WHAT MY MOTHER SAID?
THAT IF I STOOD UP STRAIGHT AND SMILED ALL THE TIME AND ATE HER POT ROAST AND WENT TO COLLEGE, I'D BECOME PRESIDENT OF THE UNITED STATES.
Diploma
Doctor of Medicine

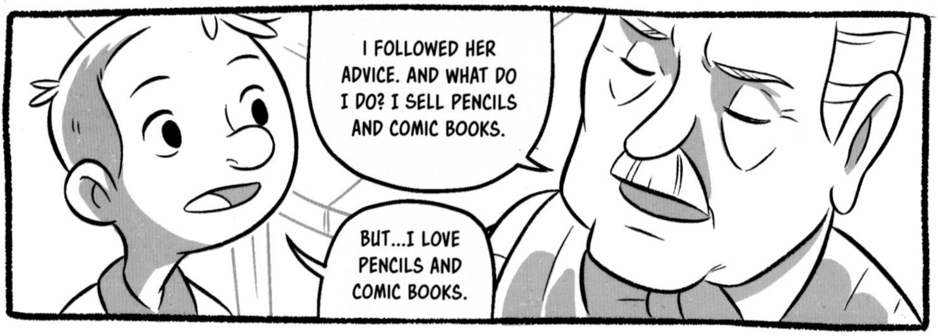
I FOLLOWED HER ADVICE. AND WHAT DO I DO? I SELL PENCILS AND COMIC BOOKS.
BUT...I LOVE PENCILS AND COMIC BOOKS.

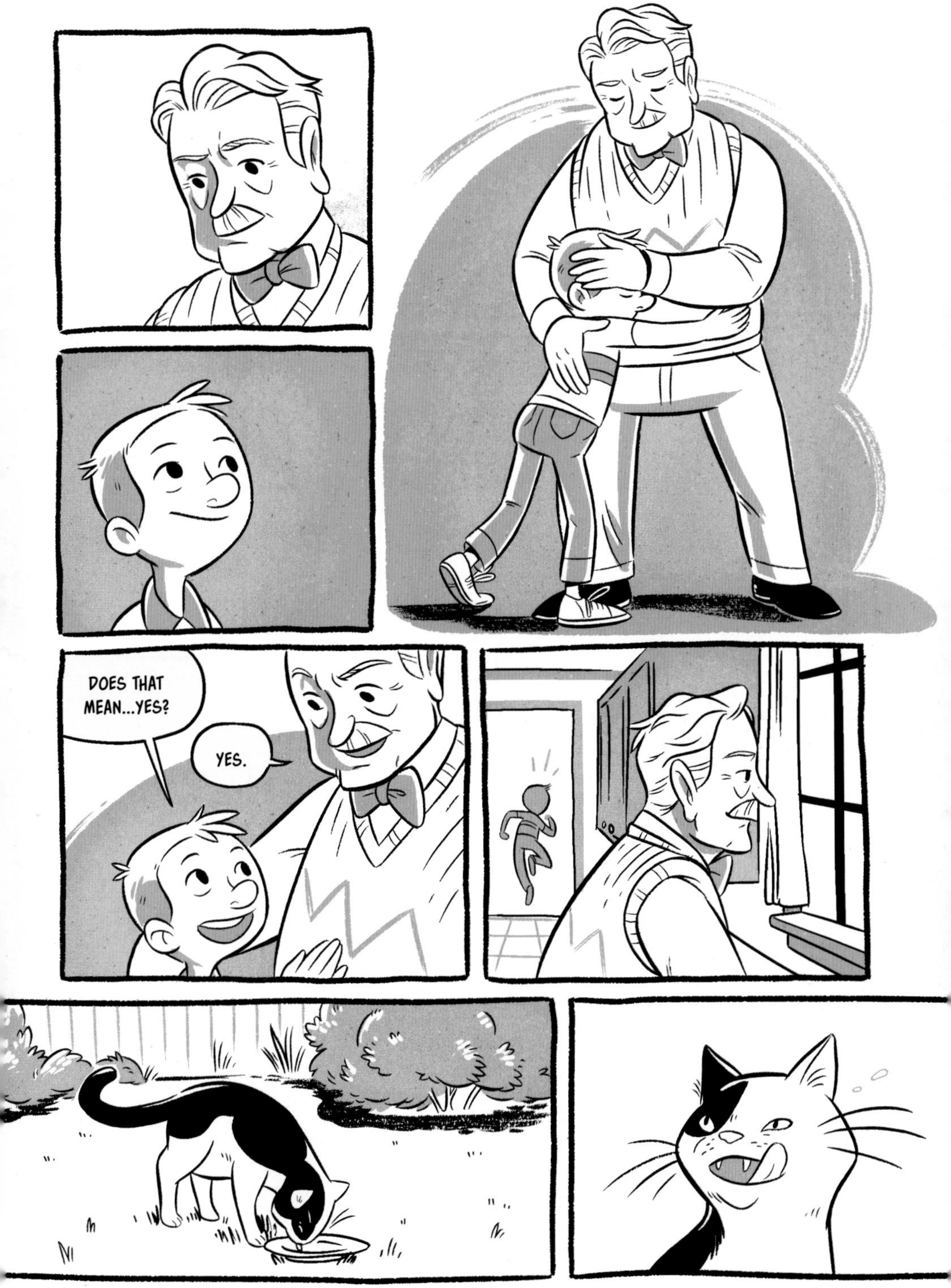

DOES THAT MEAN...YES?
YES.

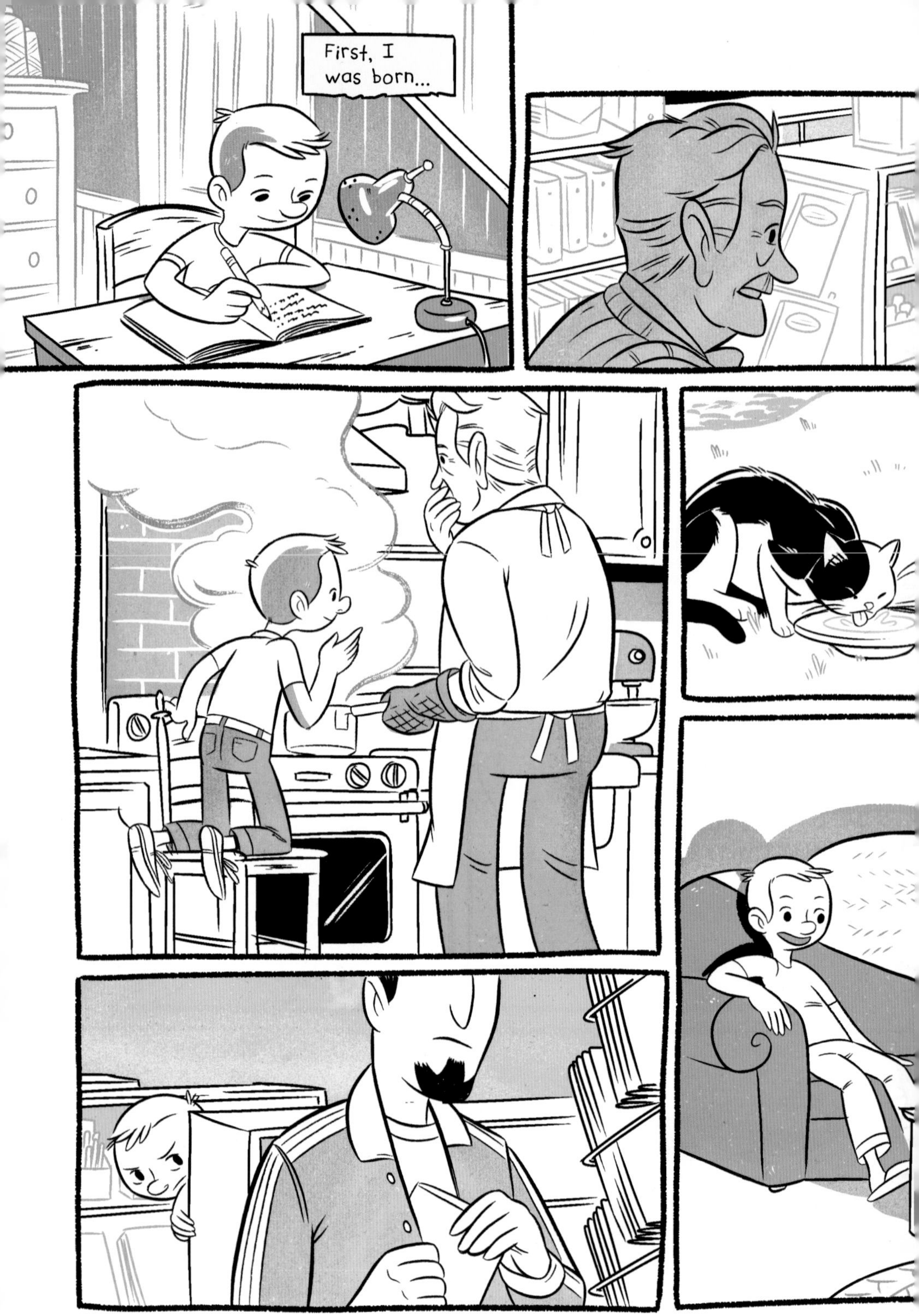
First, I was born...

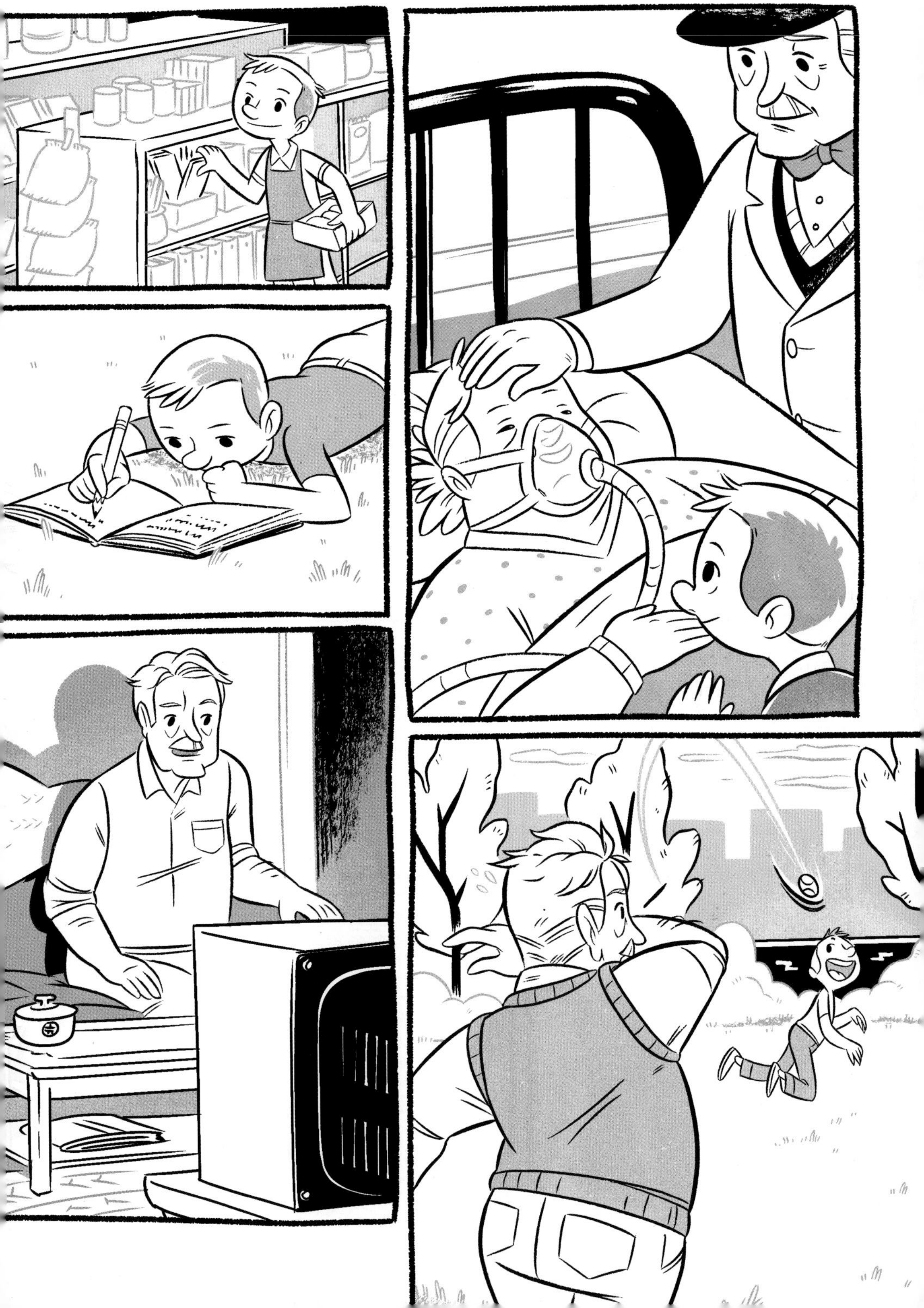

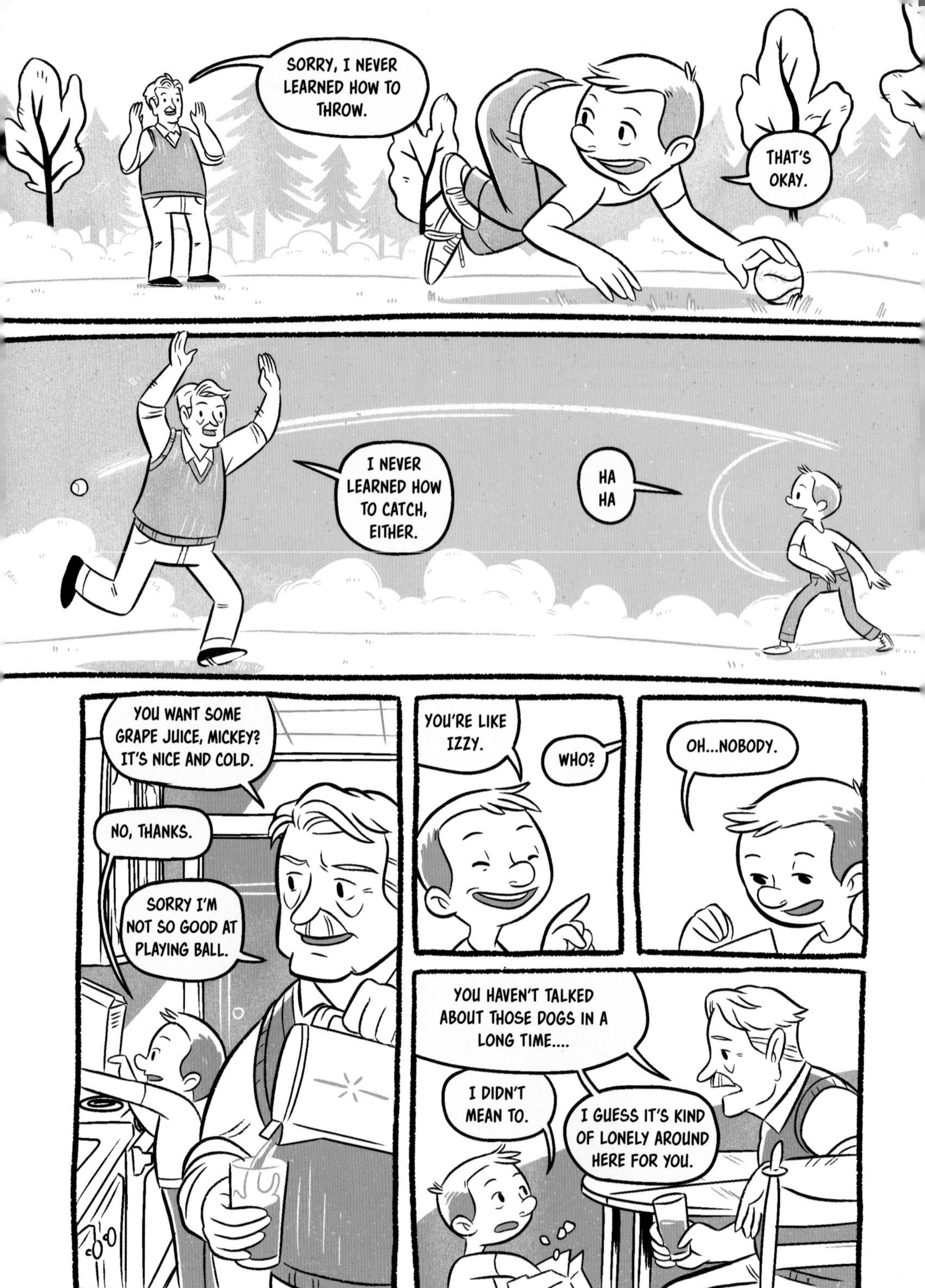
SORRY, I NEVER LEARNED HOW TO THROW.
THAT'S OKAY.
I NEVER LEARNED HOW TO CATCH, EITHER.
HA HA
YOU WANT SOME GRAPE JUICE, MICKEY? IT'S NICE AND COLD.
NO, THANKS.
SORRY I'M NOT SO GOOD AT PLAYING BALL.
YOU'RE LIKE IZZY.
WHO?
OH...NOBODY.
YOU HAVEN'T TALKED ABOUT THOSE DOGS IN A LONG TIME....
I DIDN'T MEAN TO.
I GUESS IT'S KIND OF LONELY AROUND HERE FOR YOU.

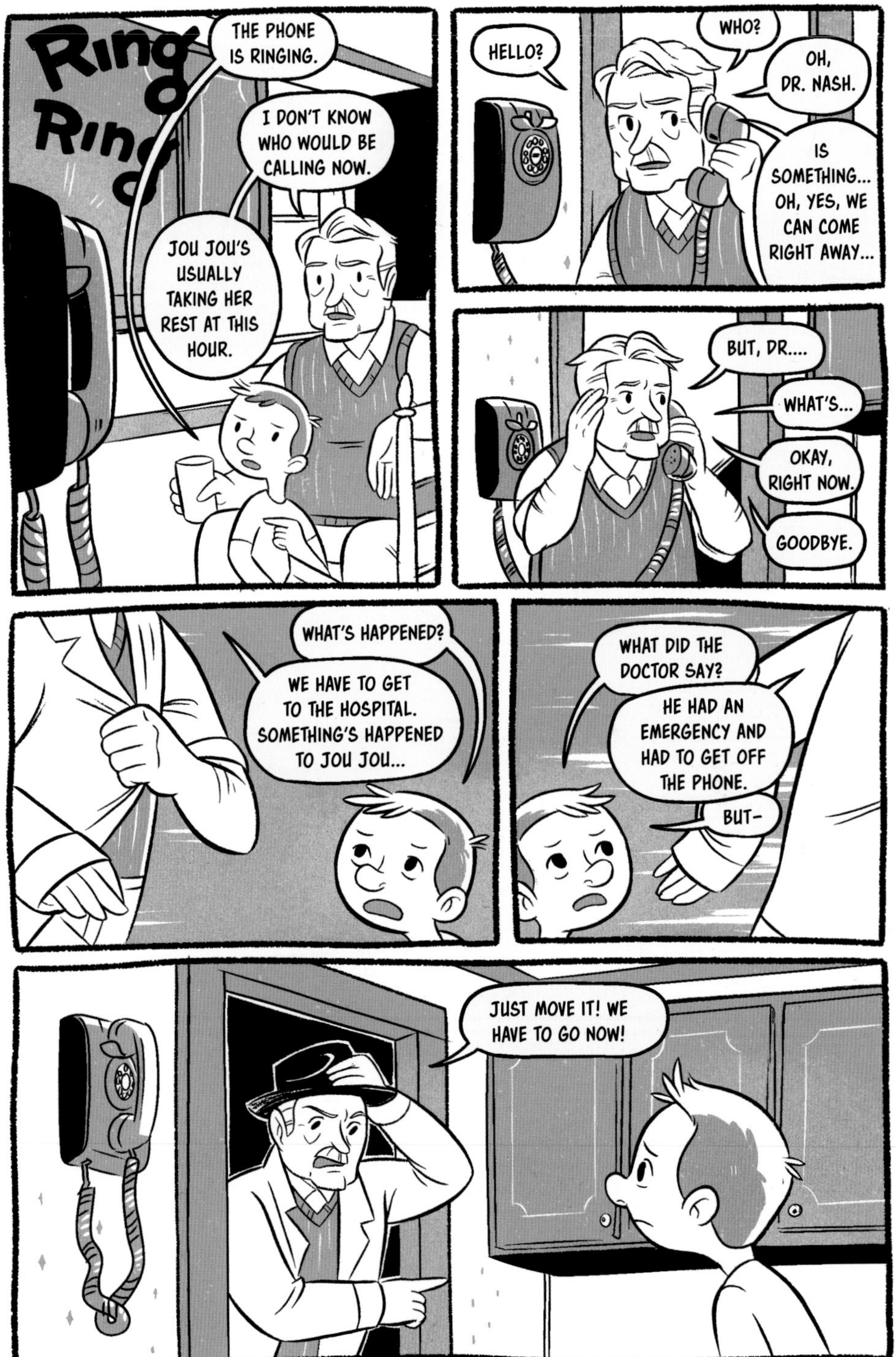
Ring
Ring
THE PHONE IS RINGING.
I DON'T KNOW WHO WOULD BE CALLING NOW.
JOU JOU'S USUALLY TAKING HER REST AT THIS HOUR.
HELLO?
WHO?
OH, DR. NASH.
IS SOMETHING... OH, YES, WE CAN COME RIGHT AWAY...
BUT, DR....
WHAT'S...
OKAY, RIGHT NOW.
GOODBYE.
WHAT'S HAPPENED?
WE HAVE TO GET TO THE HOSPITAL. SOMETHING'S HAPPENED TO JOU JOU...
WHAT DID THE DOCTOR SAY?
HE HAD AN EMERGENCY AND HAD TO GET OFF THE PHONE.
BUT-
JUST MOVE IT! WE HAVE TO GO NOW!

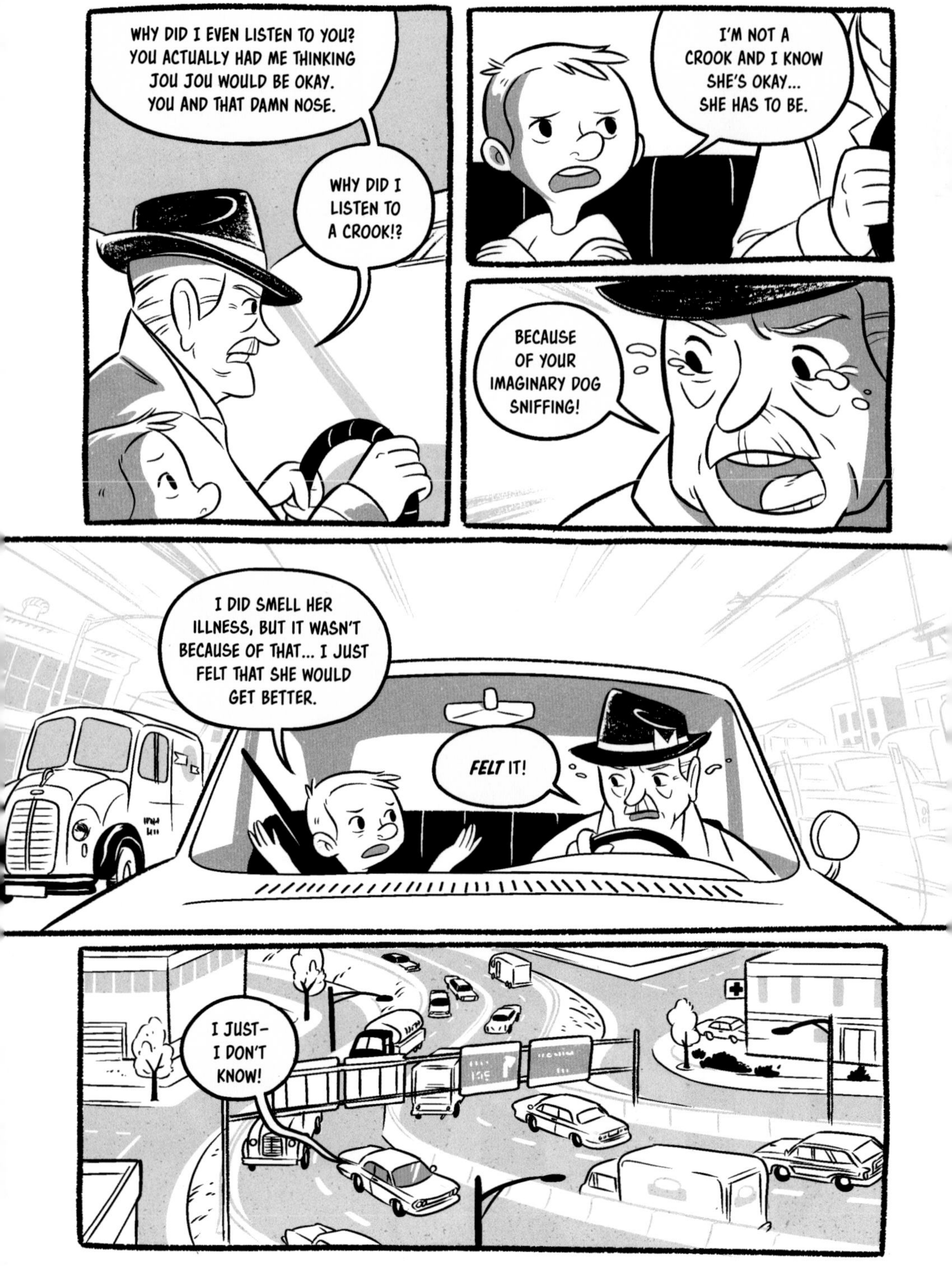
WHY DID I EVEN LISTEN TO YOU? YOU ACTUALLY HAD ME THINKING JOU JOU WOULD BE OKAY. YOU AND THAT DAMN NOSE.
WHY DID I LISTEN TO A CROOK!?
I'M NOT A CROOK AND I KNOW SHE'S OKAY... SHE HAS TO BE.
BECAUSE OF YOUR IMAGINARY DOG SNIFFING!
I DID SMELL HER ILLNESS, BUT IT WASN'T BECAUSE OF THAT... I JUST FELT THAT SHE WOULD GET BETTER.
FELT IT!
I JUST- I DON'T KNOW!

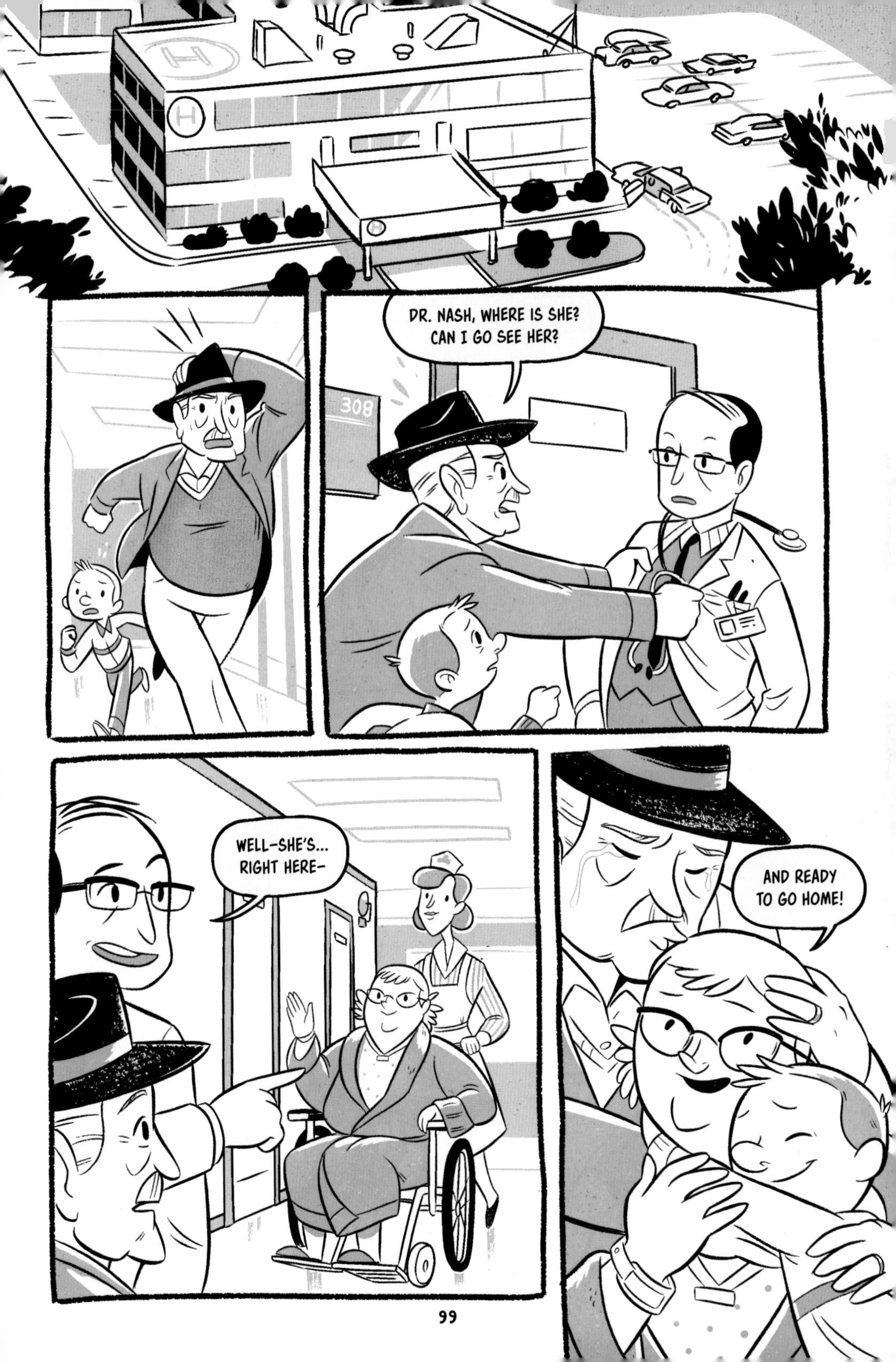
308
DR. NASH, WHERE IS SHE? CAN I GO SEE HER?
WELL–SHE'S... RIGHT HERE–
AND READY TO GO HOME!

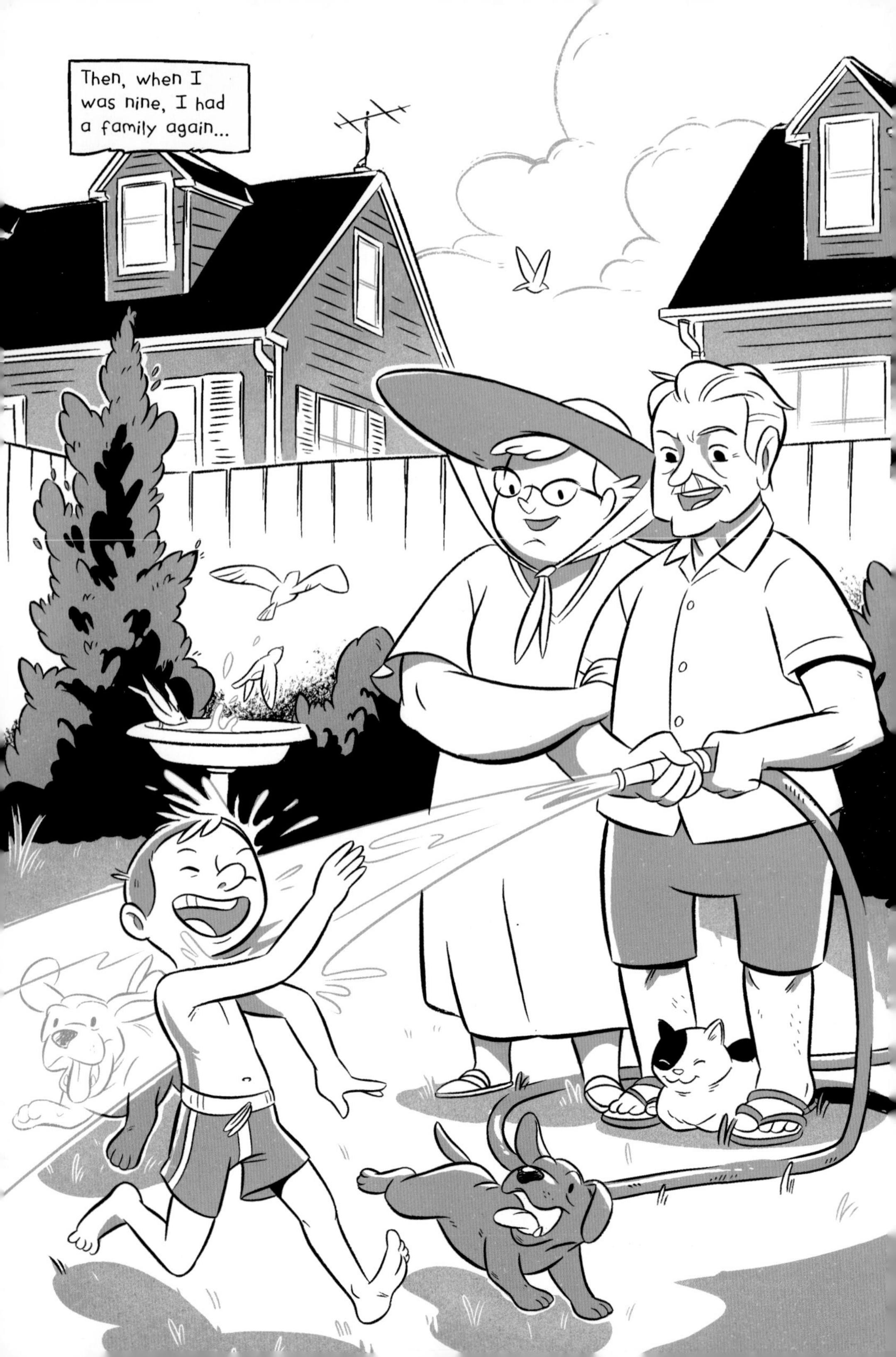
Then, when I was nine, I had a family again...

THE MAKING OF Making scents

With Artists
Shelli Paroline
& Braden Lamb

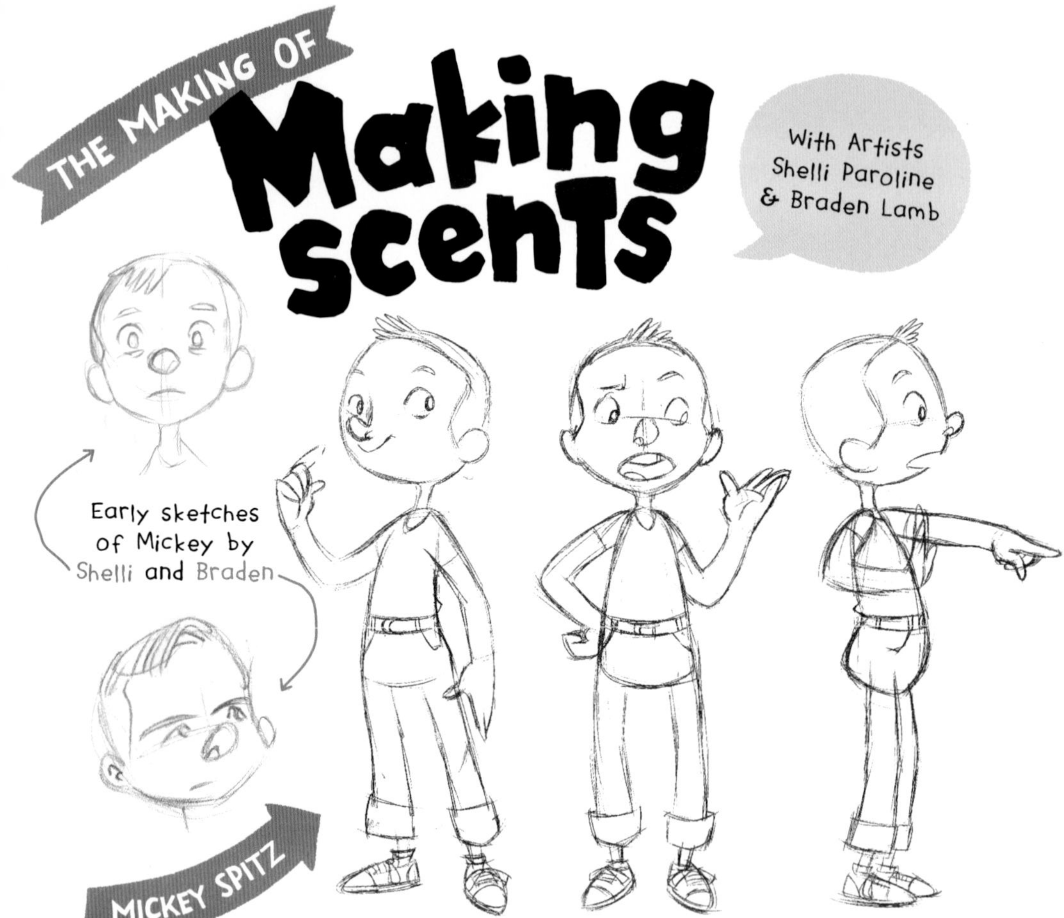

Early sketches of Mickey by Shelli and Braden
MICKEY SPITZ

Character Art

Art development began with some character designs for Mickey and his family. This is similar to animation model sheets or turn-arounds.

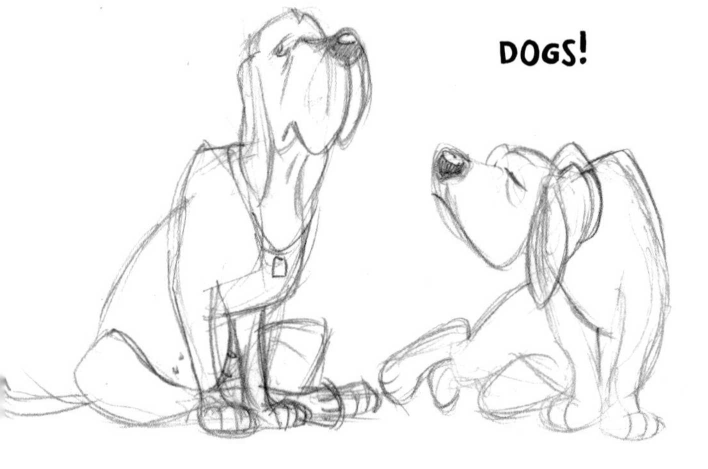

DOGS!

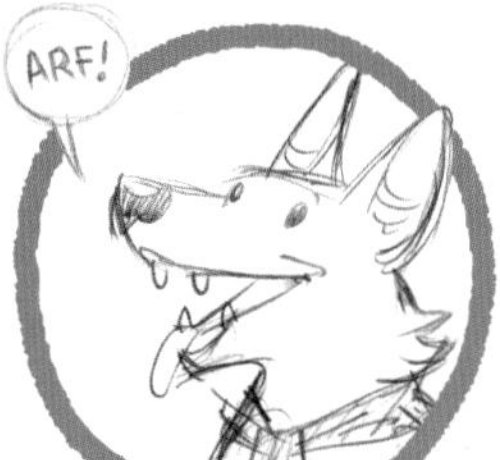

ARF!

Our dog Biggs also appears in the book. Can you spot him?

MORE CHARACTER ART!

BARBARA SPITZ

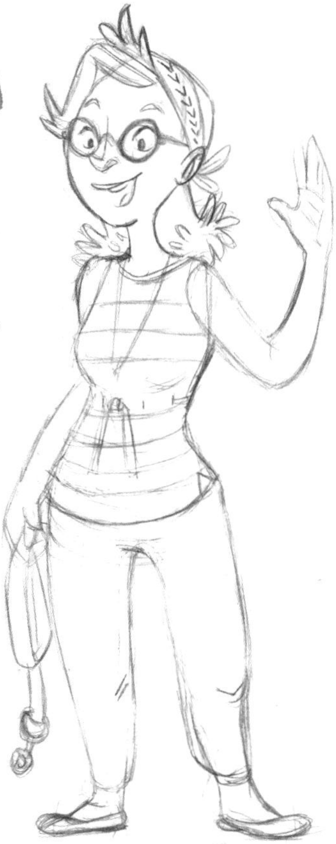

BARNEY SPITZ

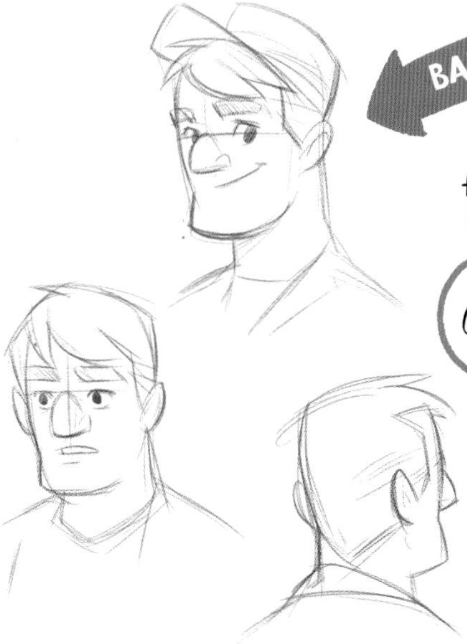

It was important that each character had a unique nose.

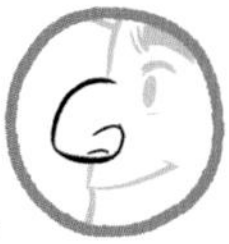

Dad's nose

Mom's nose

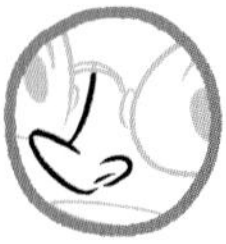

AUNT JOU JOU & UNCLE IRV

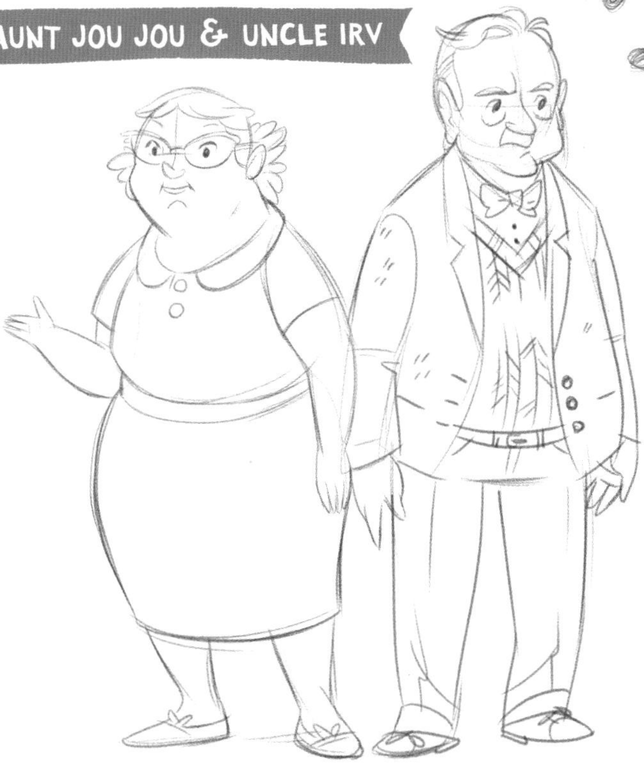

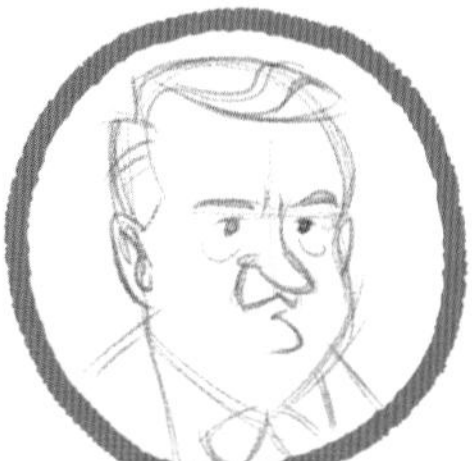

Early Irv sketch

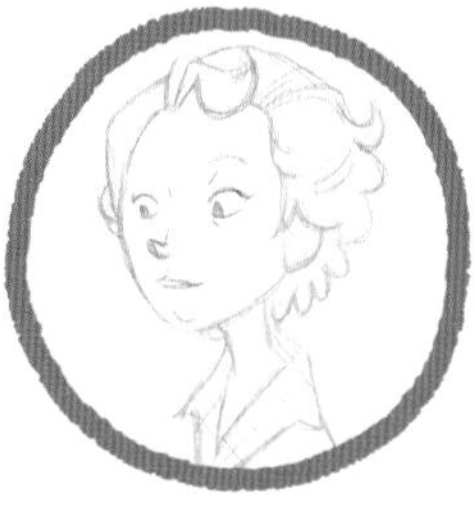

Early Jou Jou sketch

MAKING A COMIC PAGE

It all starts with Arthur Yorinks's script, which looks like this. Usually, comic scripts are written a little differently, describing how many panels appear on a page and what is in each panel. This script is more like a screenplay for film, but it gives us dialogue, setting, and action, which is all we need to turn Arthur's words into comics!

EXT. SCHOOLYARD/ALVA ELEMENTARY SCHOOL - FALL DAY

The white cloth is now a handkerchief wrapped around MICKEY's eyes. MICKEY is playing hide-and-seek with an assortment of school kids in the school yard.

MICKEY

Eighteen, nineteen, twenty! Ready or not, here I come!

MICKEY rips off the blindfold, drops to all fours, and begins to sniff the ground. He sniffs all over the school yard stopping right at a clump of bushes.

MICKEY (CONT'D)

You can come out now, Jeffrey.

JEFFREY, a school mate, angrily comes from behind the bushes.

JEFFREY

You're always winning this stupid game.
What's the point of hiding if you always win?

A BUNCH OF KIDS have gathered around.

JEFFREY (CONT'D)

You're supposed to look all over the place and not find us and get frustrated and start to cry and then we come out and laugh at you. That's how you're supposed to play.

MICKEY

Sorry.

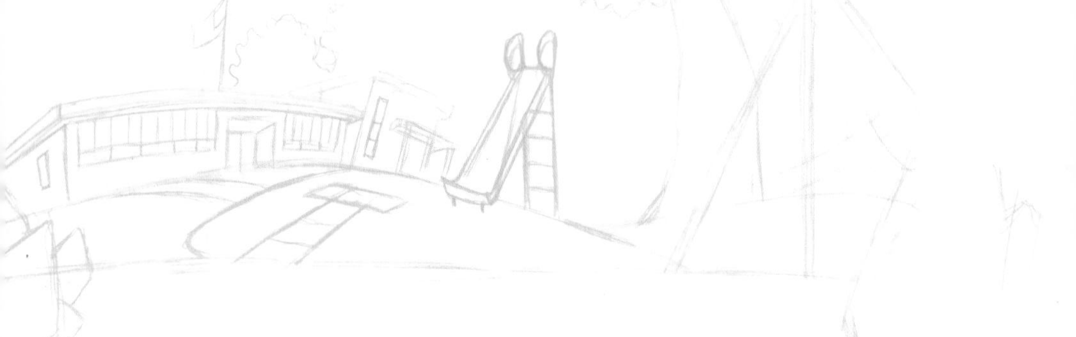

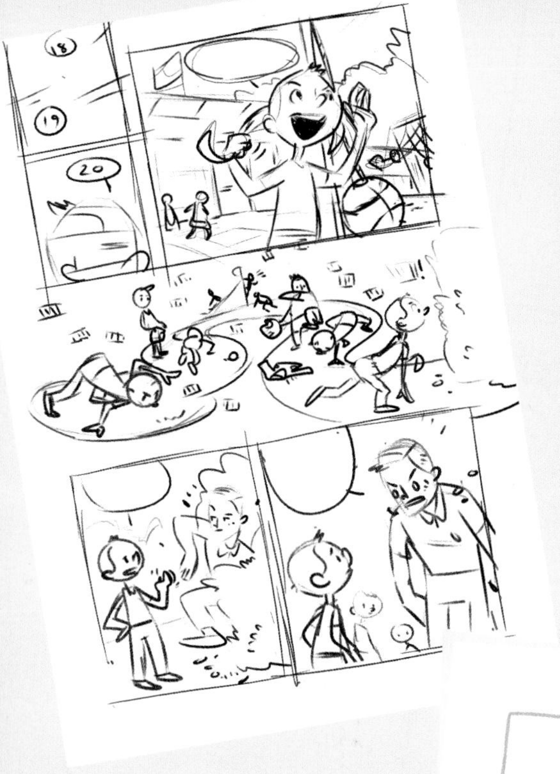
18
19
20

Thumbnails

The art process begins with a simple drawing to plan the layout of the page—and it is the most important stage! Think of it as a rough draft. The thumbnail doesn't look perfect, but we need to see that there's room for the dialogue, the action is clear, and the storytelling flows along. If one of these components isn't working, it's easier to redo a quick sketch than a detailed drawing.

TOOLS

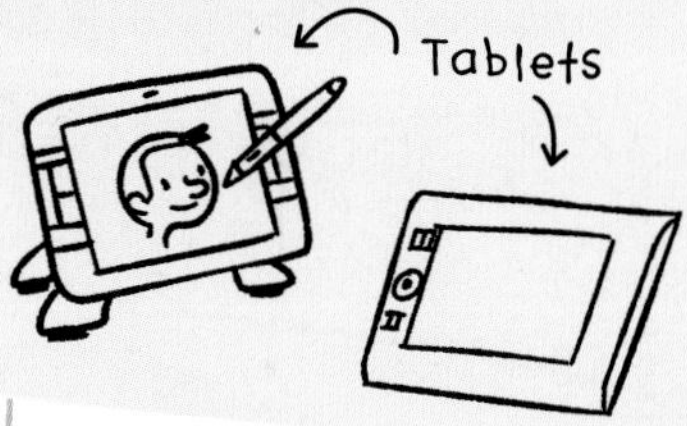
Tablets

Pencils

Once we're happy with the rough draft, we move on to the details of the drawing: getting expressions right, refining a pose, and adding backgrounds. We pencil on the computer, which makes it easy to delete, resize, or flip parts of the drawing if necessary. (Watch those two boys playing catch!) Once this is done, we print it out in light blue ink onto a large piece of Bristol paper.

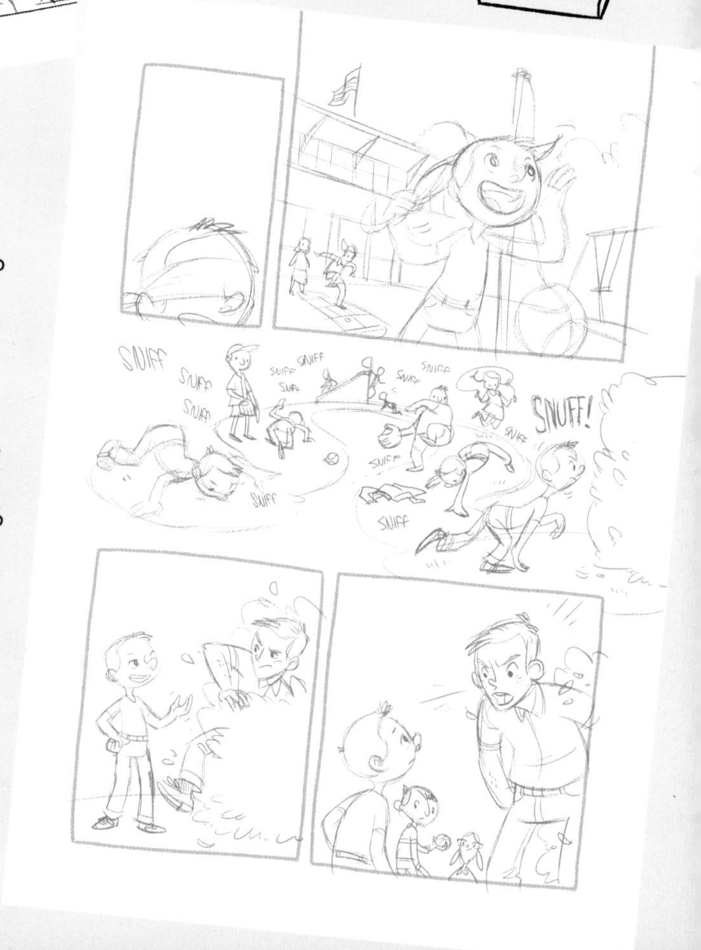
SNIFF
SNIFF
SNIFF
SNIFF
SNIFF
SNUFF!
SNIFF
SNIFF
SNIFF

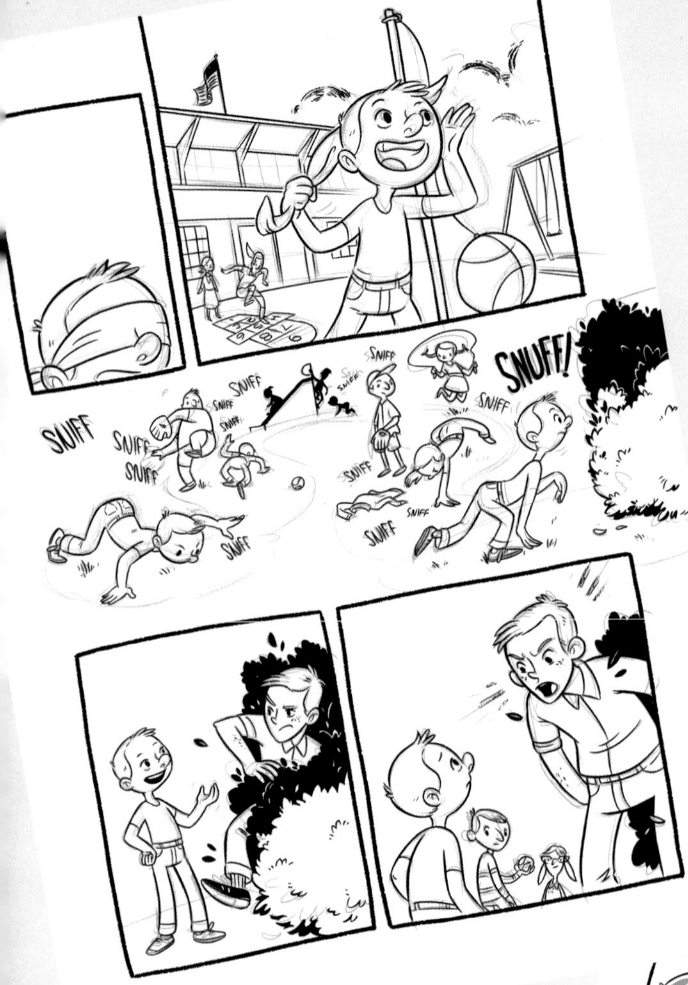
SNIFF
SNIFF
SNIFF
SNIFF
SNIFF
SNIFF
SNIFF
SNIFF
SNUFF!

Inks

We use watercolor brushes to ink over our pencils. Every other stage of this book uses digital tools, but traditional inking gets the right look for the 50's style and setting of Making Scents. We scan this back into the computer, filtering out the blue pencils, and leaving only the black lines.

TOOLS

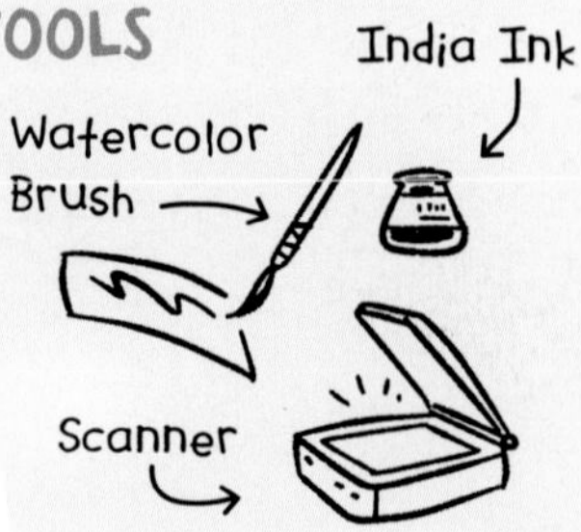
India Ink
Watercolor Brush
Scanner

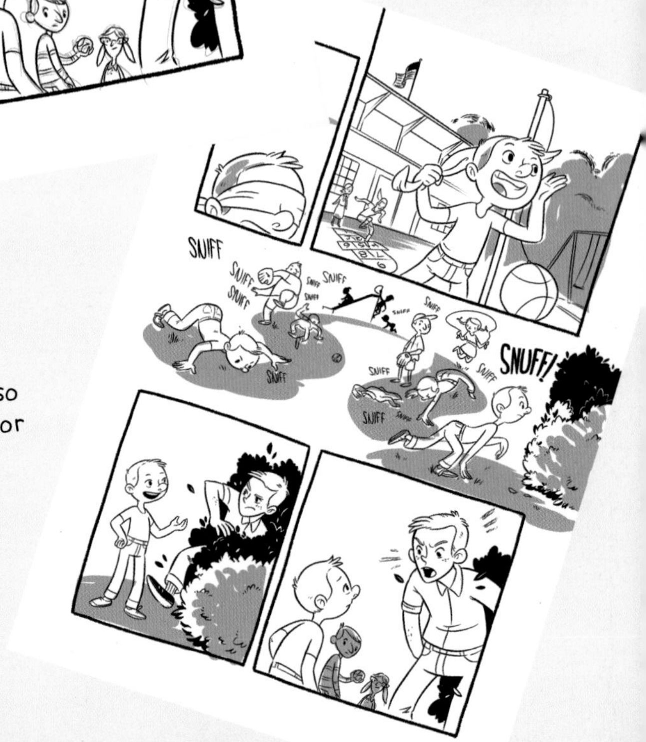
SNIFF
SNIFF
SNIFF
SNIFF
SNIFF
SNUFF!

Color Test

Color has "weight," so we quickly lay in color to see if the page looks balanced.

Colors

Using one main color simplifies our palette, but it's also limiting. We have to choose what the color means in each case—shadow, contrast, distance, or mood. We also like to break the mold to make different colors count—like a sudden burst of pink to represent scents that Mickey smells.

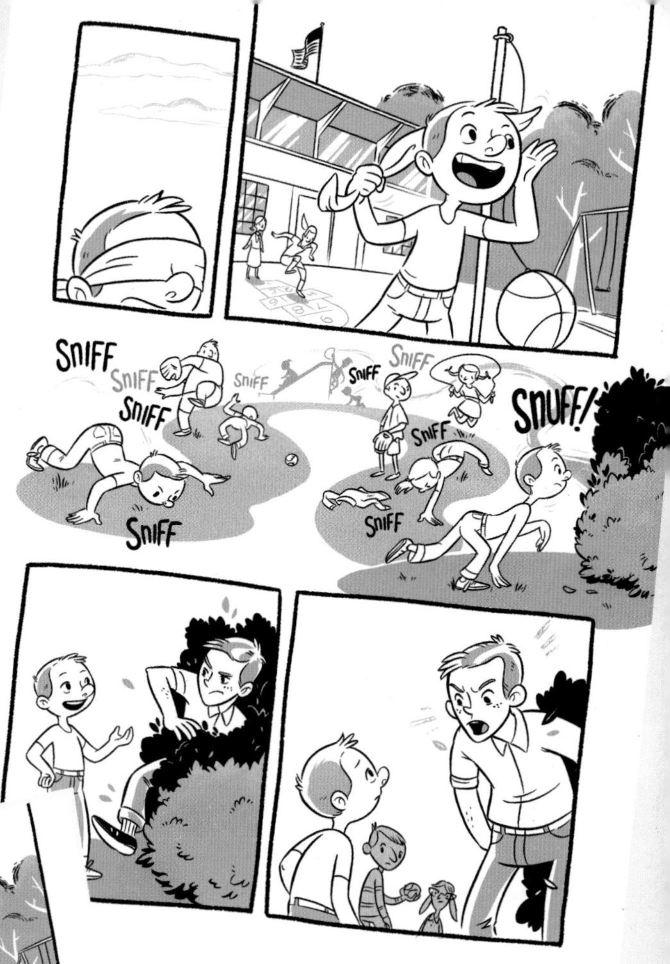
SNIFF
SNIFF
SNIFF
SNIFF
SNIFF
SNIFF
SNIFF
SNUFF!
SNIFF
SNIFF

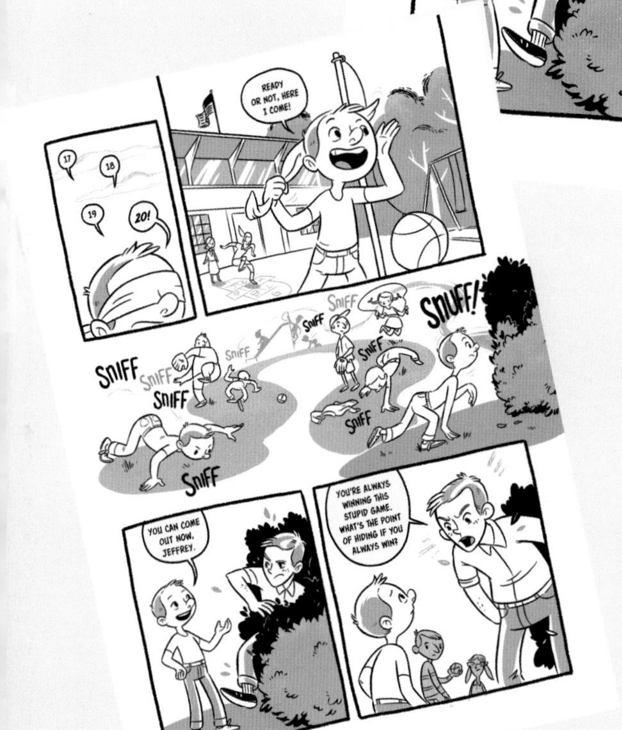
17
18
19
20!
READY OR NOT, HERE I COME!
SNIFF
SNIFF
SNIFF
SNIFF
SNIFF
SNIFF
SNIFF
SNUFF!
SNIFF
SNIFF
YOU CAN COME OUT NOW, JEFFREY.
YOU'RE ALWAYS WINNING THIS STUPID GAME. WHAT'S THE POINT OF HIDING IF YOU ALWAYS WIN?
21

Lettering

We planned out the word balloons back in our thumbnails and finally add the character dialogue at this stage. The editor and the author have a chance to make any final changes to the words, so digital tools are helpful here.

ARTHUR YORINKS

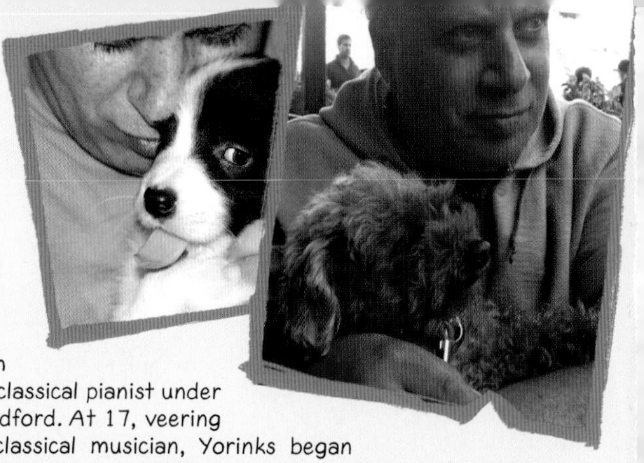

has written and directed for opera, theater, dance, film, and radio and is the author of over thirty-five acclaimed and award-winning books, including *Hey, Al*, a children's book, which earned the Caldecott Medal in 1987.

Born on Long Island, New York, from the age of 6, Yorinks studied to be a classical pianist under former Juilliard professor Robert Bedford. At 17, veering from a potential profession as a classical musician, Yorinks began over four decades of writing and working in the performing arts, and in his wide-ranging career became known for his collaborations with a broad spectrum of celebrated artists.

In the field of opera, Yorinks was Philip Glass's librettist for the operas *The Juniper Tree* and *The Fall of the House of Usher*, both of which have been performed all over the world.

Among his many published works for adults and children, his writings have been hailed as "one of the most distinctive prose styles in children's literature." Through his forty years of picture-book making, he has teamed up with many famed illustrators, including Maurice Sendak, William Steig, Mort Drucker, David Small, and Richard Egielski.

Bill Ott in *The New York Times* once hailed Yorinks's body of work as "some of the best humor to appear since Woody Allen was writing for *The New Yorker*..." His book, *Mommy?*, was a *New York Times* bestseller. Mr. Yorinks lives in New York City and continues to write and direct.

SHELLI PAROLINE

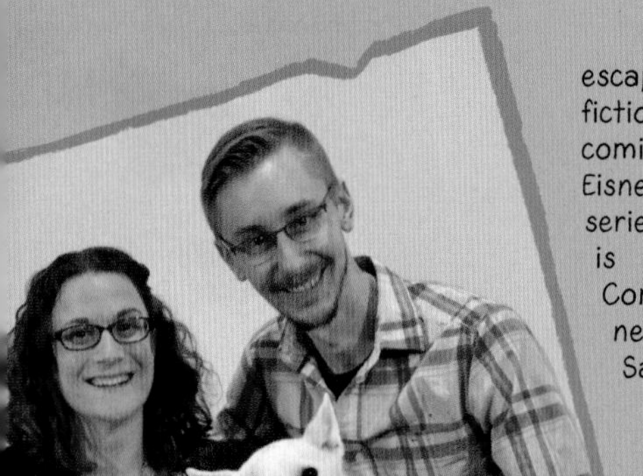

escaped early on into the world of cartoons and science fiction and from there launched into a career creating comics. She and her husband, Braden Lamb, form an Eisner Award–winning art team, collaborating on such series as Adventure Time and The Midas Flesh. Shelli is co-director of the Massachusetts Independent Comics Expo, an annual event highlighting the best in new and local sequential art. She lives and works in Salem, Massachusetts.

BRADEN LAMB

grew up in Seattle, studied film in upstate New York, and learned about epic sagas in Iceland and Norway. He now lives and works in Salem, Massachusetts, with his wife and art partner, Shelli Paroline. Braden is also the colorist for several *New York Times* bestselling–graphic novels, including *Sisters*, *The Baby-Sitters Club*, and *Broxo*.

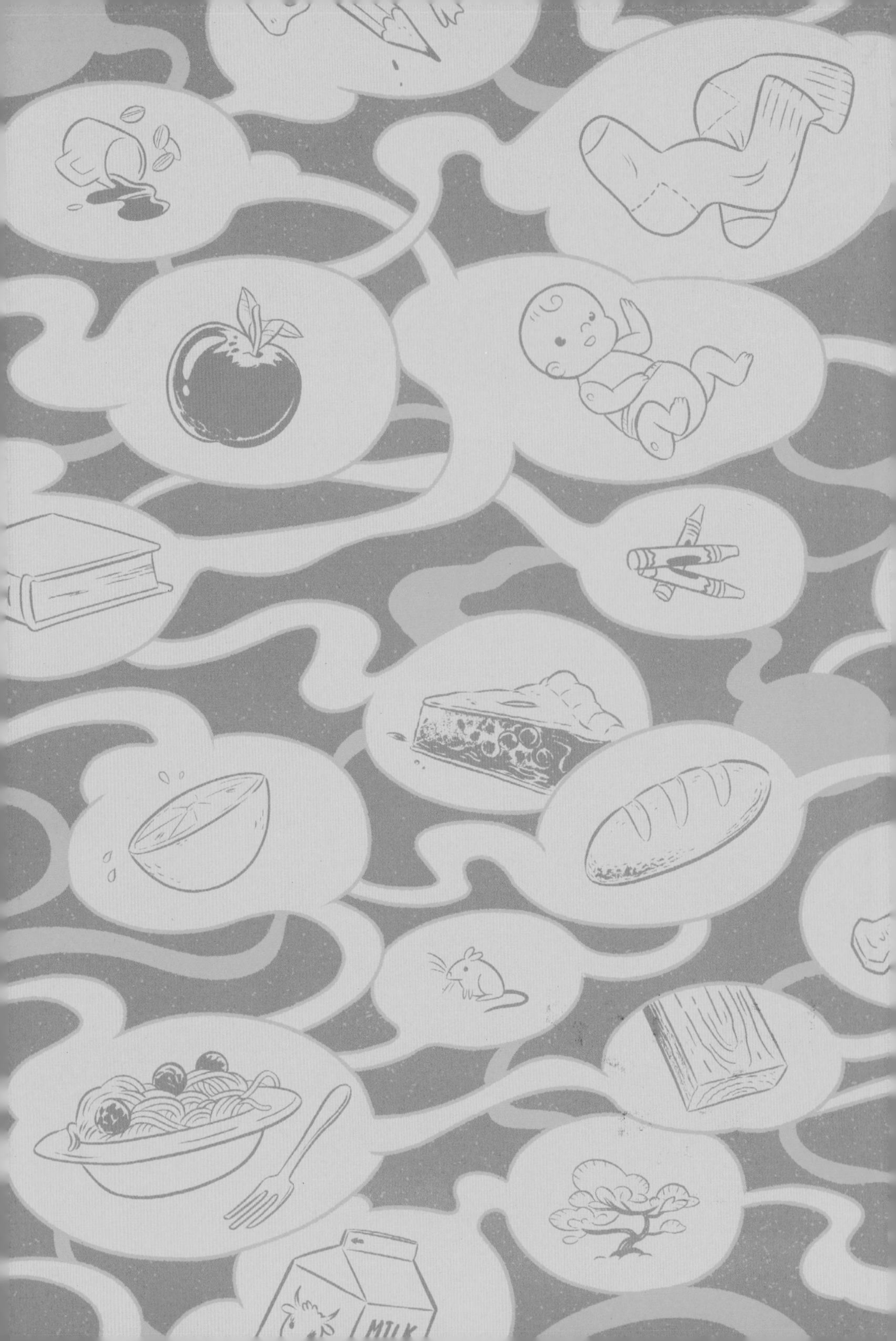
MILK